T0369424

Something About a Woman

by Bomani Shuru

Order this book online at www.trafford.com
or email orders@trafford.com

Most Trafford titles are also available at major online book retailers.

© Copyright 2006 Lloyd Plummer.
All rights reserved. No part of this publication may be reproduced, stored in a retrieval
system, or transmitted, in any form or by any means, electronic, mechanical, photocopying,
recording, or otherwise, without the written prior permission of the author.

Print information available on the last page.

ISBN: 978-1-4120-6104-9 (sc)

Because of the dynamic nature of the Internet, any web addresses or links contained in
this book may have changed since publication and may no longer be valid. The views
expressed in this work are solely those of the author and do not necessarily reflect the
views of the publisher, and the publisher hereby disclaims any responsibility for them.

Any people depicted in stock imagery provided by Getty Images are models,
and such images are being used for illustrative purposes only.
Certain stock imagery © Getty Images.

Trafford rev. 11/23/2018

 www.trafford.com
North America & international
toll-free: 1 888 232 4444 (USA & Canada)
fax: 812 355 4082

FOREWARD

I've made TOO MANY mistakes and have done a lot of growing up within the last 3 years-maturing into manhood. Life isn't easy-but NOTHING is! In fact life is a BITCH and its IMPOSSIBLE for a good man to get along with a bitch! So I had to develop into that 'Good Man' in order to be worthy, to be capable, of identifying and walking away from that bitch.

Well...I just couldn't do it! So God made it possible wherein the situation which I ERRONEOUSLY labled a 'BITCH' eventually grew the Hell up-and walked away from ME!

Now I am left behind-A FOOL holding a vaporous memory in his hands. But a memory can't talk! It can't be touched nor hold your hand and respond back to you when one whispers "I Love You!" DAMN...I WAN'T MY 'BITCH' BACK! This book is dedicated to Gemini, 6-1-70! The one stopping in my dreams both night and day-haunting a memory I should've let die a long time ago. Her soothing passion finds me-staggering across the street from our yesteryear beckoning me to return to it-To The One That Got Away! And it won't let me rest! Label me the fool who invests his waning time and energy in something that he knows he can't have. Heaven help me!

Acknowledgements

Special thanks to:

The Creator: The Architect of my struggle who made all
Things possible.

Big J: Who stood up and would not sell out! Thank
you for believing in me when no one else
found me worthy.

Elecia: Who invested in me her lifeline and tolerated
My suffering.

Cynthia: Who rescued me from yesterday and allowed
Me to salvage my dreams.

Freda: My most blessed friend who had faith in me,
lent me her trust and MADE IT HAPPEN!

PROLOGUE

HONEY I'M HOME

The bastard kept smiling! Like my rage was somehow amusing to him. So I SMASHED and I DASHED and I CRACKED my right hand over that STUPID fucking grin on his face-hurling knuckle-bone against iron dome AND MAKING IT STICK!

But he shrugged it off! No matter-I'd grab the metal tool that drives steel nails into concrete walls to articulate to his ass what my fists labored to pronounce! I HIT the raving bastard at least 7 times-emptying my combination-clip upside his grill! The flurried asteroid-belt ran over his facial anatomy at warp-speed sending the cursor of my temper across ALL 4 CORNERS of the UGLY head that TIME FORGOT!

"Oh, you think you BAD BITCH? UNGH!"

SMACK, CRASH-BANG, BLAM!

"OOWH!" The motherfucker threw me into my OWN T.V! He pushed me OFF him-before I could sink the hammer DEEP into the DRY desert BETWEEN HIS EARS! There were NO signs of life in this GORILLA'S head. I could hear birds singing! But that vast thoughtless wilderness of infertile soil and mental foliage brought with it an equally green Hulkish stooge who ZAPPED the hammer from my grasp, SWATTED me in my FUCKING forehead and sent my Welter-weight anatomy flying into Mr. High-Tech 3 G Sony plasma 40 inch Color T.V! A lesser bitch, A WEAKER bitch, WOULDA GATHERED UP HER DEAD, BANDAGED HER HEAD AND CALLED IT A NIGHT! But my daddy trained me BETTER THAN THAT! I don't know HOW to fear and I'd RIP A GAPING HOLE THROUGH SATAN'S MOMMA'S ASS before I DIED and the Simone Singleton's lost soul's Cook-out could EVER get underway! To Hell with THE OPPOSITION-this, God's child and the Devil's daughter, WOULD FIGHT! And as long as oxygen occupied these lungs and my heart pumped blood, my fists would stay clenched AND I'D BE ON THAT ASS! I got right back up at crackhead speed, shook the swirling dust clouds out of my eyes and put back up my dukes-SMILING AT THE SON-OF-A-BITCH who'd JUST TRIED to murder me!

"O.K. BABOON-you got that PUNK SHIT OFF! FUCK YOU-I AIN'T DEAD-BITCH! And DRY UP nigger-YOUR game is weak! (HAH-and my NECK WAS CRACKED!) Just look at you! 'Canei!' It's a fuckin shame! No wonder you're wittle mommy named you after a bottle of booze-the shoe fit," said the woozy warrior bitch with aluminum T.V. fragments embedded in her weave and RAZOR-SHARP glass shards up her ass! My SKIN was badly lacerated and a slight trickling part of me seeped out. My Jumper was shredded and the 40 inch T.V. WAS DEAD! So much for durable Japanese Technology!

"Oh, so you wanna kick, huh? O.K. you punk bitch! Uh-huh! Yeah," said the loser in my life who couldn't seem to remain faithful-and sober! I hoisted my left foot and tried to kick my heal right through his fucking rib cage. Canei was drunk! Normally he'd have the focal wherewithal to block or catch my feet. But I knew that 'Absolute' was messing with his head.

"WHAT, Bitch? Why you movin? KEEP STILL! SAY I WON'T SLAP THE SHIT OUT YOU! YO-I SAY I WANT SOME PUSSY THEN I WANT SOME GOD-DAMN PUSSY! You CAN'T tell me NO! You must be out yo RABID-ASS MIND!"

That turned me on! I grabbed the hammer he'd dropped and attempted to implant it in his thick-assed skull with the shady left hand.

"CRASH!"

"FUCK!"

It hit the fish tank! Flippity flapping fish everywhere. I wanted to crush his cranium but all I'd achieved was the untimely violent deaths of my daughters guppies. And from the looks of their desperate struggle they must've seen the Grim Reaper coming. A steel hammer and bad aim spelled Sea-food night in Hell's Kitchen for the poor misfortunate bastards! Lucifer would be pleased. But I was not! I cursed my aim-and kept on swinging!

"Why you duckin Motherfucker? Huh? You BAD! Man up Nigga!"

"Suck my dick-BITCH, I SAID GIMME MY MOTHAFUCKIN KEYS," he ranted!

"Uh-uh, YOU DIRTY...PARASITE! You gotta earn THIS! I ain't yo baby's momma and you ain't running nothing here!" I kept moving because I knew I could not afford to get grabbed. Canei was a lot stronger than me so I had to bob and weave-float like a butterfly. Until I could Tyson him into a stupor!

"Don't move Bitch! Keep STILL!"

"Yo MOMMA, ape-man!"

"You ain't say that when I shot some a THIS in you!" (He grabbed his penis) "BITCH YOU PARANOID! AN I TOLD YOU YOU HAVIN MY SON!"

"That's why I sucked your Homeboy Rod's DICK that time you spent the night out! Remember? You came to my house and you thought I wasn't home? You was OUTSIDE knockin on the door while your man was INSIDE these skins knockin the boots! OH, my bad! You really thought I wasn't home? 'PSYCH!' You DUMB Jack-ass!"

I was tired! This scenario was getting old and I was nauseas as a dope Fiend. I hadn't seen my period for two months and everybody SWORE I was pregnant. Well if I was, it's biological father wouldn't live to see it! If he DID survive he'd have to send a telegram-from the ICU cuz he was NOT getting back the keys to THIS motherfuckin house and he wouldn't be leaving here alive!

Canei faked a quick jab-as though he were attempting to swat a fly. I thought I had measured the bastard but before I knew it, the nigga Football tackled me down below the knees. Damn! I hate Football! I squirmed but his three-hundred pound frame fell like dead weight on top of me. The LYING DRUNK sat on my chest and I knew this scuffle was over. He rammed his right hand against my forehead. (filthy liar KNEW that made me horny) Then with one swift, solid swipe-my weave went flying across the room into the ceiling fan! THIS BITCH-ASS NIGGA pulled the tracks outta my BRAND NEW weave!

"Yeah Bitch-WHAT? Look at choo NOW! "

"Whatever, you Faggot! You cum too fast anyway! How come you can't stay HARD? Better leave that shit ALONE boo!"

"Shut the Hell up!" He drooled on my bottom lip. Sweat was pouring off his head and I could smell the Absolute taking rulership of his inebriated lost soul. He just couldn't stop drinking! It was like Liquor was his medicine and his life depended on it. I hated him for his blatant perpetual intoxication-the mood swings! I hated the Tuesday disappearances and the Friday night Smack-downs. Dogs and cats can take but a few hundred bar-fights before they get sick of each other and inevitably decide to choose a more constructive hobby.

I loathed Canei-yet I needed him! At least I thought I did. And I hated the fact that I needed him. My broken heart despised the psychological rollercoaster ride our relationship thrived on. What's a woman to do when she can't stand to kiss the deceptive lips of the monster she's copulating with? She fights with him each night of his perpetual indiscretions. He wanted to see other people. Well I had a problem with that! And I also had A MAJOR PROBLEM with the fact that my weave was now doing the Harlem Shake-being sifted and pureed on the rotating blades of my ceiling fan. Another $150 down the tubes!

"I can't HEAR you! You wanna be a man? Well I killed your FUCKED-UP weave! Go NAPPY BITCH! Now you can LOOK like a man! Didn't I tell you don't run up on me like that? DIDN'T I? DAMNIT, SIMONE! I SAID AIN'T NOTHIN HAPPENIN! But um TELLIN you-one day you gonna get FUCKED UP IN HEAR! GIMME MY KEYS! GIMME BACK MY GOD-DAMN KEYS!"

I felt him squirming. For a split second I wondered what the Hell for. But then it hit me! THIS nigger wanted some PUSSY! The delusion of Mr. Hennessy had told him he needed ME to ferry him through Paradise-the ecstasy born of a REAL woman! But his fidelity had staggered onto the WRONG platform before he'd made it home to me. AND HIS FREE MEAL-TICKET HAD EXPIRED! I had almost forgotten that before the throw down he was beggin to get on top of me and feel a far more pleasurable Heaven than the Absolute had promised-but once more failed to deliver. Furthermore Mr. Playa man had lipstick on his collar, scratches on his fuckin neck and he smelled like a BITCH!

5

So I asked him! "Yo Playa whose lipstick is that?" It was some DARK Vampirella frozen dead color! I don't wear DARK brown lipstick! "What kinda woman YOU fuckin with? Is the Bitch dead? That's the shit they use in the morgue! At least you coulda cheated with a LIVE bitch! Who wants a dead piece of ASS? You FUCK!!!" He offered no response.

"O.K. We'll move on to question number two: Where the scratches come from?" HE says he had a fight!

"A fuckin fight? Who you been fightin then? Rupaul-or Richard Simmons? Oh no! Let me guess-you an Tinker-Bell was dukin it out in the parking lot?"

"Motherfucker, you lie too much! Ain't no nigger gonna scratch another nigger like that. Now if you had an eye-jammie, I'd understand! I could SEE that...cuz niggas punch other niggas in the face. But that 'another motherfucker SCRATCHED the livin Hell outta me stuff' ain't flyin this way-YOU LYING BASTARD!"

"Now that brings us down to the third and final strike. Hey nigga-you are a nigga right?"

"Yeah, of course I'm a nigga! What?"

"You a thug right, you know-real tough?"

"Yo, of course I'm a thug. What the fuck you asking me that for?"

"Well, if you're a thug-an you tough an all that, what in the world you doin comin home...smellin like a BITCH? You a faggot? No, I don't think so! So if you ain't a faggot, you should not be walkin in my house smellin like no Bitch-unless you cheatin on me. YOU CHEATIN ON ME PLAYA?"

Then the jackal had the nerve to say 'none of my fuckin business!'

"None of MY fuckin business? Is that your FINAL JEOPARDY Answer? It better not be Playa cuz where I come from 'none of your fuckin business' is an admission of guilt! You might as well have said, "Yeah I did it! I'm guilty-so take me in!" And he got the nerve to try to stick his FINGER up my ass and get some PUSSY too? Who the fuck does he think he Is? And who the fuck does he think I am? To take that shit-then lay down and give him a piece? "Do I look stupid OR SOMETHING? "THAT'S why I tried to crack your FUCKIN skull with the hammer! And if you would've kept yo monkey ass still long enough I would've still been swinging my hammer-trying to murder you some more!!!"

Canei was breathing hard-tryin to reach for his zipper-And when that Steel hammer sprung out I could smell the basket of onions. That foul scent runnin for it's odious life peaking out from his underwear! His underarms were kickin too! Wagin war against the potpourri fragrance of my livingroom carpet. And I THOUGHT I detected some old pussy fumes around the vicinity of his goatie.

"You ate her ASS out again? You weak 'can't stay hard' chump!" I KNEW that predictable loser made a pit stop before his tired ass got here! I flew into a RAGE. And

THIS bastard kept tryin harder-thinking he could slip his nasty dick inside me! I'd rather fucking die!

"Yo, BE still!"

"Don't even TRY it…you gorilla! You SMELL!" Ned the wino was spittin again.

"God-Damn Canei! What's wrong with you? Why does a sister have to swallow two ounces of SPIT every time you open your big funky mouth?"

I wasn't giving up ANYTHING! He wanted to creep with Ronda, so fine! He should call the rotten bitch up. Tell her he was sorry I found out about them-that he was still sleepin her. She was supposed to be just his baby's momma but every time he went over there to see his daughter I knew he'd wind up boning her over the sink! DOGS DO THAT! Another thing-that little girl did not look a thing like him. I knew he was getting played cuz you know how bitches are. Well it served him right! He deserved to be played cuz you know how cheatin NIGGERS are TOO! "So you gonna cheat on me? O.K. motherfucker, good! Cheat! That's why you payin five hundred a month in child support for a child belonging to that nigger whose now in jail. Locked up on a Drug charge! So cheat-on DADDY!"

And when the nigga comes outta jail and claims his child-AND his bitch back, you'll get a hardy handshake and that ass'll be out the door. So go back to the bitch. Tell her I know what fuckin time it is and beg for another chance and a new home-CUZ YOU AIN'T STAYIN HERE!"

"Wait till I get in that ASS!"

"THE HELL YOU WON'T! Dummy…that's why Kalil wasn't really your son, bitch! Why don't you get out-so I can invite his REAL daddy over to get some more of this!"

He hated when I said that. THAT'S why I swore to keep repeatin it till the day either I died-or he died! Kalil was the unborn son he wanted to father. We had been together for two years. Canei had stuck it inside me and came in my mouth over a zillion times. Never waste a drop was our motto! And believe me-not a condom was used-and not an ounce of semen-was wasted! I got pregnant and miscarried at three months.

What's a woman's favorite line when she don't wanna be the baby's momma of the nigga she's screwing? "DON'T CUM IN ME!" Ladies you know there's a lotta niggers you fuck that ain't worthy to walk down the aisle with. Let's be for real! And every man hates that phrase. It's a death sentence-allowing a man to ride you but HE can't reach that height. The climax! That pleasure that embodies the only reason he's fuckin you in the first place. And when the executions about to begin he ain't tryin to hear you make him pull the snake out-before it's finished crushin it's prey. That's what snakes do-THEY BITE! They tear shit up! But the bite ain't over till the venom is injected! And he NEEDS to ejaculate!

Yes bitch! You getting it cuz you turn him on! Your body is bangin and he wants to cum inside it. That's it! Oh, you thought you was getting the pipe cuz you was special?

7

OH HELL NO! So when he's finished Frisbee fuckin you-he wants to cum. He gotta cum! Just like everybody else. Just like YOU just did five times from the rock-hard sensations of his thickness!

But no! You tell the nigga not to! With this, you are nullifying the needs of the one whose pleasing you. Simply put-biting the hand that feeds you! Why you wanna do that? So some other bitch can 'Smoke' him in your place? What's YOUR fucking problem? Keep it up stupid bitch! mess around and you'll be single-and lonely. Wondering what went wrong! Then you won't have to tell him "don't cum" cuz he'll be cuming inside somebody else.

Think about it! Oh, so YOU can cum yourself-but HE CAN'T! He's just supposed to ooze on the carpet-or the bedsheets. "FUCK THAT! I DON'T THINK SO BITCH! SKEET!...SKEET! Wait a minute-one more time...Ooh! OOoh! "SKEET!"

Well Canei could've poured twenty-five gallons of semen inside me every day for the rest of his alcoholic life. As long as he met his quota of five pounds of dick rammed up my spine in the process. My slogan was "go for it!" While you're doin you, you're also doin me. So work baby! WORK!

I snatched the phone and banged the nigger across the face with it as hard as I could!

"BLAM!"

"OAAGH!" He was screamin like his face was on fire! I ran into the kitchen for my 'you know what.' I THINK you know what. He damn sure did and snapped out of the pain invoked trance just in time to see my juicy ass cheeks streakin outta the room and sharp turning the corner.

But it wasn't there! Now WHO swiped my OX? The meat cleaver was kept lodged in the second cabinet behind the Pork-n-beans! I kept it there for two years just for moments like this when the drunken bastard was trying to take my head off. And for the times when I would have decapitated HIM and left the body for dead if it had not been for hisThug-alicious penetration!

Did I love Canei? I don't know! That was a question for the elders of the universe to debate on in times of ethereal boredom! Yet even they realized how much in love I was with his sexuality. CANEI WAS MY PACIFIER! His penis was! At least two times a week we'd argue and each time I SWORE it was over! I'd threaten to throw his drunk cheatin ass outta my life! BUT THEN WE'D HAVE SEX-and I'd forget why I wanted to get rid of THE STUPID NIGGER in the first place. I guess that's what dumb bitches do!

When a baby cries in the quiet stillness of the night its up to the mother to figure out the nature of baby's discomfort. Sometimes its for food, or maybe a pamper change or at times it just needs COMFORT! It is also the responsibility of the male partner to decipher and stimulate the needs of his woman. And not unlike a baby, when SHE cries for something he must stifle the yearning and put her desires to sleep! Sometimes she's horny. At times she might be lonely or discouraged or bored or simply needs the reassurance that her life and love are not being wasted on something that might not last any longer than she had initially anticipated.

A REAL man can hone in on the cause of these silent moanings and give her what she needs so that she can regain her emotional footing and continue on in this fruitful and fulfilling relationship! But like I said EVERY WOMAN NEEDS A PACIFIER! And just as mommy must fiddle through the blanketing of baby's crib for the pacifier to stop it from crying, so must a woman's man reach for and provide all that Wifey needs to stop her inner tears! If she can't FIND the pacifier she's SHIT OUTTA LUCK! If HOMEBOY goes through the same thing and can't find that MAGICAL KEY, which button to press, soon HE will be watching THE NEXT MAN strolling down Eastern Parkway with the big-butt sensual creature that USED TO BE HIS GIRL!

So Canei's sexuality was my pacifier! That fleshy black dick and balls-set that he KEPT twirling inside me in order to SHUT ME UP! And no matter how violently I'd bitch and moan about his suspected indiscretions that pacifier gave me temporarily whatever I could not receive from him on a permanent basis! A whole lotta sisters keep a pacifier around-a nigger they'd PREFER to do without till the real Mccoy comes around and rescues them from the habitual stupidity prevalent in meaningless intimate relationships. We do this because EVERY CHILD NEEDS A TOY! He was my BOY-TOY! But in everyone's life after all the BULLSHIT they've swallowed, they one day decide that they don't want to live the remainder of their lives on the juvenile level of being a mentally deficient child! It was January 17, 2005 and on this day of all days I had come to a fork in the road of my social development and it SUDDENLY occurred to me that I WAS GROWN! I HAD LOST MY TASTE FOR PACIFIERS AND DIDN'T WANNA PLAY WITH TOYS NO MORE!

I zoomed into the bathroom like a feminine black lightning bolt cuz paybacks a bitch, Michael Meyers was slowly peelin himself offa the canvas and I didn't wanna die! Dazed, shaken and wondering why the severe blow to the head did not stop his heart, I slowly turned out the lights. Then sat on the toilet and decided to just lean back-I would talk some shit and wait!

"I want my motherfucking keys! And some head you crazy bitch! I told you Mone, I TOLD YOU-I ain't fuckin nobody!"

"Suck your OWN dick playa! Steam-clean it first!" I could hear him trying to Jimmy the lock but I kept talking and pretended not to notice.

"Ahh come on Mone-you KNOW I need that shit! Um fiendin!"

"Fiend your ass over to Ronda's house Bitch! Maybe she'll scrub those nuts."

Then the DEVIL GRABBED me by my mental throat!

"Oh, by the way, were you looking for these?"

Oh NO-I knew it! But how? I watched that slick con artist from the moment he got in the house. I never seen him go anywhere NEAR the kitchen. But somehow that nigga had grabbed my Ox-AND my car keys! I had to get my shit back-but how? I conjured up

Bomani Shuru

fifty-five concurrent remedies for retrieving my shit while he slipped the Ox-AND the keys back and forth under the door. Teasing me!

"Baby…"I whispered-in a desperately subdued voice. The kind of purring he liked to hear dangling behind his ears. "I need some!"

In an instant the door slammed open and when I wrapped my left leg around his back it was ON! Canei had his power-drill in his hands and before I knew it he had hoisted me up against the sink while forcefully pulling back my undid hair from my face!

"You fucking Ho-why you smack' daddy with the phone? You like it rough don't you? SPEAK TO ME!"

I came on myself and on my own pink porcelain sink at the deep baritone foreplay of his voice.

"Oh yes, daddy!"

"Now tell daddy where you want it!" He grabbed my nipples and started to squeeze. I thought Heaven had left the skies! Or God Himself had come down to nest inside my bubbling senses-bringing a little Paradise along with him. I leaned forward and hoisted my ass cheeks so close I was suddenly almost behind him. THIS was what we liked to do! This was what we HAD to do cuz those steamy interludes were the only oxygen this asphyxiated romance could FIND!

"Where do you want it bitch?"

"Ooh!" I couldn't breath for the sheer force of my orgasm! The sink was cold and damp and I thought my cum was cascading down onto the floor that man felt so good!

"Stick it in my ass daddy! Oh God, please! SHOVE IT UP MY ASS!"

Suddenly SATAN HIMSELF grabbed hold of my head and rammed it down between Canei's legs! Oh, I don't know! Maybe it was ME who stooped-whatever! Whoever prompted the 'Deep throat' in my brain, the only thing that mattered was that I wanted to suck his dick till his dead ancestors woke up in their graves!

The onions were back and I grabbed them up!! He put his hands around my neck then pulled my hair-snatching my mouth away from him.

"Oooh baby-NO, PLEASE!"

"TAKE THIS DICK BITCH! YOU KNOW WHAT I NEED!" I knew what that meant cuz we had rehearsed it umpteen times before. I turned around and bent over the sink-whimpering and moaning like I hadn't been rocked for decades (He had just beat it up the night before) then I slowly leaned back onto him.

I could feel his dick penetrating the lower lumbar regions of where I sit. I could feel the fiery sensations of myself opening up the floodgates. I could hear him calling me every bitch in the world! I could smell foul musty sweat and the garlic balls and the smoke from my rectum-begging a racing heart to stop beating to relieve itself with instant death from that pain! And I could smell the stray little kitty unveiling the concealed rancor of where he had been tonight-And I loved him for it!

"Oh yeah baby! Mm-hm, HURT ME!"

10

"You LIKE that don't you bitch," he roared in a jungle-like strong pronouncement that put me on my submissive feline knees to beg for MORE inches!

"Harder baby-hurt me daddy! Oooh!" I wanted him to bust me open-satisfy the heartbreak and insecurity's hurt with the pain that a potent male stamina gives toward the many victims of his daily indiscretions. And I would not stop driving myself madly against him until the violence of the act made me bleed out every plasmic tear my soul could render. Until my mind's mania could go to sleep-and forget!

He was slapping my behind like a dumb hulking over-zealous Hillbilly beating the shit out of an errant disobedient steer! "SMACK!" "Say you love me!" "SMACK!" "Say you love me!" "SMACK!" "SAY YOU LOVE ME!"

"Oohh!...YES!...WHOOAH!" I literally couldn't keep my voice from shaking or cracking under the three-hundred pounds of Chocolate BLACK Motherfuckin MAN driving a ten inch spear inside me!

"Ooh...DON'T stop, baby! I'm CUMIN...ooh! Don't-don't stop! AAahh-AAH!"

I went Soprano! My intestines cursed the anal preferences of my obsessions! My sex-drive died two times on his operating table-AND NO ANESTHESIA COULD BE FOUND! After my writhing disappeared into the foamy love of two porcelain shadows caught up in deep musky sighs, my brain eloped with my heart on a rampant carpet ride to his big dark room in loves mansion! From that moment on my heart was back in his corner-and WITH him again!!

Nobody had ever touched me the way that drunken black bastard did! NOBODY-not even CHRIST could think to come close.

The bathroom stunk of two sweaty paramours sunken in the Nile of mutual sodomy! When he came I sucked it for him! YEAH! That's right-A real bitch DOES that for her nigger! Funky, sweaty dick-stained with the caramel harmony of where he ripped me-an FUCK ANYBODY who ain't feelin what I did! YOU didn't get stroked by BLACK JESUS-I DID! And I tasted my own PAIN on the tip of his erection! MY MAN NEEDED SOME HEAD! And after he damaged me right, I FACED the sour funk of a thousand DEATHS-nostrils savoring the slow unbearable stroll around the garbage bin of those boxers! YEAH-I said the nigger stank like the City-Dump-but the way he fucked THIS...it was worth it! And I would cuss out GOD HIMSELF-if he begged me not to do it again!!!

The next day Canei bought me a brand new 'BIGGER' T.V!

-1-

GENESIS

Hello! Can we TALK? My name is Simone Singleton and I'm hooked on weed! YEAH, YEAH-sometimes I add a few special effects in my blunt but it's basically "JUST" the weed! I PROMISE! I'm rated X! Sometimes I do things that a normal woman would be ashamed of-and I like it! I don't know if its because I'm high or my unquenchable desire to be pleased. But I'm NO virgin! I get mine whenever I want it from niggas I've never seen before. My friends warn me all the time. "Girl-you BETTA be careful! You oughta STOP before its too late!" But I don't plan to do a God-damn thing about it! By the way, If my language and my lifestyle offends you-WELL I'M SORRY!! I JUST can't help myself! LOOK-either you WORK with me or put down this book and pick up a fuckin Bible-and remember me in your prayers!

I guess I should have introduced myself first before revealing to millions how truly maniacal I can get over a good piece of man. Besides, a woman's bedroom embodies one of the most sensual and deeply personal contours of her feminity. The satin sheets and velvet pillowcases are mirrors of herself. They herald and portray the delicate passiveness of what she was born to be-and do. And passion, either inhibited or personified in the dry fuck of a Reggae dancehall grind, summarily defines our collective beings.

Our minds are the perfumed sponges eroticism and yearnings feed upon-something that the male testosterone could never understand!!

A woman is like a flower! If you feed it, nurture it and offer your rose a strong foundation it will stay with you. It will survive (emotionally) and remain beautiful in your embrace because you wisely took the time to care for it! But not unlike many flowers it too has thorns that will draw your domestic blood when it's mishandled. When a man mistreats or tears its soft petals his rose will no longer be HIS to torment. If you violate the central core of its heart, its inner being, what was once your lovely prize will fall apart in or leave your errant hand because you FAILED to continue to nurture it. What USED to be the love of your life will wilt and distintigrate between clumsy abrasive fingers. THAT is why all men NEED gentle tendencies. They MUST know how to delicately stroke the volatile emotions of their women. I didn't say 'GAY' tendencies! I SAID DELICATE TENDENCIES! The softness required in satisfying that which is also equally soft. At times feminity shuns a rough crude surface in her desire for a tender, fond and affectionate touch that MUST be available from her strong male partner.

I believe one-hundred percent that I am a creature of sheer spontaneity and was born to perform any and everything that my heightened sexual impulses demand! And I NEED TO BE TURNED ON! I LIVE AND BREATHE FOR IT! Now SOME brothers are fools! They just hop on top and wiggle their bony asses and think that's what a real woman needs! Nigger PLEASE! Don't they know it takes more than a dick and a vagina to create an orgasm? Don't they know that the love-making begins at the first glance? Brother-you on top of me but you ain't TOUCHIN ME!

I got 2 big hungry titties with hard nipples on them that NEED to be sucked-and licked! Professionally! I got another crevice down there-DYING FOR A LITTLE Equal Opportunity! An Ego-that MUST be stroked. A female mind that needs to be turned on and YOU ain't got the key! Take your old-school chauvinistic technique back home and get your KEYS! I GOT A NECK THAT NEEDS TO BE KISSED-GENTLY! A back that craves the light touches of finger stimulation. I even got LIPS-that need to feel you in them!

I got ALL this ridin on a 175 pound frame draped with MILLIONS of tiny sensory cells sprinkled across the mansion of my golden skin. OH YOU DON'T GET IT DO YOU STUPID? This shits too COMPLEX for a caveman to grasp! Hey ASSHOLE-you're stickin little Jimmy inside of a WOMAN, NOT a mannequin! And the love-making is not 'THE' nut! The nut is merely an extension OF the love-making. It's the culmination!

But a whole lotta stuff has gotta happen. If he goes in there all wrong there will be nothing but a whole lotta pumpin, sweatin and killin of the clock with no REAL results. He'll have a poor sister on the bottom sufferin and can't wait till the DRILLINGS over so she can rush over to the E.R. for some reconstructive surgery-THEN it's a trip to the Ammo store to re-up and load her 45! Guess whose ass she'll be LOOKIN for?

While sister-girl is deciding his fate beneath her (Wondering which Caliber to blast him with and what body-part goes bye-bye first-his puny nuts or that PEA-HEAD) he will bench-press your sex-drive till death do him part! Leaping up and down atop your mutilated corpse like the gorilla in the commercials. His last preponderance of JUST WHAT it takes to make that vital little crevice ooze with glee will meet him on the other side and be answered moments too late! The ape-man thought it took SHEER BRUTE FORCE! But he was wrong and on the way to the morgue he'll understand that penetration alone can't cut it! That's no way to treat a Lady!

Sister-girl will take a trip as well! She will fall into the discomfort-zone-FRUSTRATED, AGONIZED UNSATISFIED AND AT WAR WITH THE MALE SPECIES! This is FUCKED UP but I will revisit THIS pathetic phenomena more thoroughly at its appointed time!

My mother named me after her Grandmother 'Simone Singleton.' She was a fighter! Warlike. Known for her mouth-and her fists. I am both a creature of habit AND MYSTERY! I guess it was my hostile Crown Heights Brooklyn upbringing in a tightly knit Pentecostal home which has molded me into the arrogant spiritually wavering warrior bitch that more than a few haters envy and plentiful niggers are willing to kill-or die for!

In my thirty-three years of this impractical joke called 'life' my oldest memory took form when I was about two. I recall, as effortlessly as breathing, myself as a toddler

13

stricken with an illness that my then finite mind could not comprehend. I would shake-violently and intermittently and I could not make myself stop. I tried but to no avail. What is an infant to do when its body constantly goes off into vigorous sporadic tangents? And during each episode there is an unimaginable pain in the head, dizziness and blurred vision.

I am no doctor now and I certainly was not then-thus I was thoroughly powerless at defending myself from this brutal insipient intruder stalking and paralyzing my body and disrupting my peace. Whether asleep, at play or nursing a bottle, my entire thirty-some odd pound frame would jolt vigorously at the enigmatic command of this invisible force darkening my infancy.

I can remember nursing a bottle of some of the most fantastic shit I've tasted both then and now. It was called 'PABULUM' I think, I don't know! But whatever the shit was called, it was more dear to me than Gold-spawning an inherent chemical dependency resembling that of a Crackheads euphoria from his very first hit!

The cereal from the Garden of Eden had a picture of a tan bunny on it dressed in some Southern get up that the Old Lady in the Shoe would probably throw on while home baking gingerbread cookies and watching Oprah. I don't know exactly WHAT the shit consisted of-maybe God sponsored a going out of business sale at the local bakery just beyond the 'Pearly Gates' and decided to grant those ill-fated loathsome Sons-of-Bitches he'd created a taste of His 'Celestial Seasonings.' Who knows-but I discovered an intense organic predisposition even then for that shit shoveled down my throat from a pastel pink spoon!

Later I would find that it was not the ravaging effects from the 'Cereal from Heaven' that made me tick. My gross magnetism to the blissful sensations I felt had absolutely nothing to do with enriched oats in apple-butter at all. It went deeper than that and I could have fell out when I finally found out just seven years ago that because of my biological mother's predisposition to illicit narcotics, I Simone Singleton, was born labeled as what they call 'a crack baby.'

No, it wasn't crack! It was quite essentially the opposite. Mom-duke didn't touch the stuff that keeps a motherfucker up all week long in a zombie-like hyper-mode. Daddy later told me that she actually detested it. Instead she chose a less imbibing toxin to stiff the adolescent woes of drug addiction. My mamma, the beloved young woman who gave birth to me by a father she new a total of about three hours, chose and lived for "THE MONKEY!"

That busy little primate evolved into an enormous violent Gorilla by the time of my conception-six months into the binge. It stole and pilfered from her empty purse to borrow from any pockets bulging with the stuff to buy what she longed for. And when those limited resources were not available, she would avail her beautiful unblemished youth to satisfy this grimacing monster daily siphoning her questionable innocence.

Dope fiends don't last long and their mortality rates hover between one-half and one-fifth the longevity of their entranced counterparts-the Damned race of Crackheads! Till this day I still don't know if my mother, hooked on drugs at sixteen, was able to survive her addiction-or her tormented adolescence!

The tremors (they were medically diagnosed seizures) were my body's way of protesting the lack of chemical stimulus. I was told that just one hour without that 'Wonder-drug' would send my then pregnant mother into Earth-shattering fits of rage. The effect it had on my unborn metabolism was however far more lethal. The Physician explained it to my adoptive parents Lorraine and Wallace Singleton like this:

An unborn child is basically a creature (I am NOT a creature) composed of the genetic characteristics of both parents. Thus as it's mother is-so is the fetus. It is nurtured within a soft tissued sack called the placenta and receives its daily nourishment from whatever nutrients a hopefully drug abstinent 'mommy' may ingest.

There are various types of indulgences written off as maternal taboo that mother has been advised to distance herself from especially during the first trimester. This is a crucial gestational period characterized by multiple elements which can be fatal to the fetus' chances of survival. Plainly this cooperative mass of tissues will never become a bouncing bundle of joy if it does not make it safely out of this perilous phase.

When these 'toxins' enter the bloodstream of the mother via either forty ounces of beer, a four ounce glass of wine, just one loose cigarette, the most faint inhalations of Marijuana (Cannabis) or the neurotically damaging havoc caused by mainlining liquefied Heroine, the results are the same. And they will invariably liken themselves to and spell the beginning of the end for baby's diminutive Central Nervous System.

Once the child is hooked on what mommy abuses countless times a week, it too becomes strung-out on the syringed venom and will begin to die. If the fetus is fortunate enough to survive inevitable kidney, liver, brain and cardiac damage it will ultimately succumb to the ethereal decay of chemical dependency.

This vicious cycle embodies the Domino effect of an organic need for a fix-twenty times more powerful than mommy's craving. When SHE doesn't get it-dependent baby doesn't get it! And unlike mommy, due to its adaptive physiological ordinances, without it-baby will die!

So now, baby's lungs and other vital organs rely desperately upon the toxins which are essentially killing it! Baby can't make verbal demands or solicit therapeutic solutions to its addictions the way SHE can. When mommy does seek help and goes 'Cold-Turkey' it places baby in a grave predicament. A biological firing squad! The lack of chemical stimulus traumatizes its system. How can abruptly weaned baby die in peace without the soothing detriment of the addictive toxins that are gradually taking its life?

Slowly its body's vital signs will begin to wane. It's Circulatory, Excretory and immune systems will collapse. The blood-pressure and heart-rate will fall dramatically causing its five pound soul to go into shock. The joyful bliss of post-embryonic pokes and kicks against a detoxing belly will cease to remind her of babies tortured existence. And in approximately ten to fifteen days, dependent poison starved baby-will die!

Enter a second, less lethal drug called Methadone. It was designed decades ago to offset the terminal velocity of that little monkey which grew up to become an ape. Baby now feeds on the Methadone, forming a bond even more pronounced and intense than the heroine it was designed to replace. It circumvents the fatalities of the monkey from the perspective of having bartered between the lesser of two evils. Chemically absolved parent and her struggling fetus have carefully chosen their poison.

Now momma ain't married to the monkey anymore. She has a new domestic partner. A comprehensive regimented suitor for whom her love has multiplied but the pangs of chemical divorcement are much more amicable for both parties involved. Hence, both mother and baby are at peace. I WAS THAT BABY! And that MONKEY...was my Grandfather! And I despise every drug-induced stigma he dangled before the eyes and injected into the womb of my mother!

I later found that the quest-the hunger for the Pabulum had actually nothing to do with hot cereal at all. The monkey had fooled my infantile system into believing that it needed Gerber products when in fact I was actually ripe for a quick fix from a visit to the drug man!

An unlearned inexperienced newborn cannot distinguish between the pleasure it gets from feeding and the incessant little tree-climbing Bastard rattling siphoned Heroine into its system-thereby creating emotional, physical and chemical euphoria-and dependency! Hence-the tremors, the shakes, the perpetual inability to focus a single thought during the early formative years of my life!

It was not until I was four years old that the deleterious effects of my biological mothers dependency began to ebb into normalcy-and belated peace!

Daddy tells me I look like her. "You got the same honey-brown skin as your mother...and that pear-shaped ASS! OH MY LORD, THAT ASS!" Daddy spoke like he had been to the mountain-top and 'SEEEEN' the Promised-Land! 'Spanking' my estranged mommy's purity once or twice! I STILL wonder!

Wallace Singleton always had a way with words and very seldom found a concrete reason in his head to simply shut the fuck up! But I loved him more than life itself! The day he fessed up the expected truth that I was adopted wreaked Holy Hell on all the traditional norms in which I had once believed.

He described to me mommy's troubled up-bringing. How she got knocked-up, probably by a John! (one named 'Wallace') Daddy chose his words carefully, perhaps not wanting to be the idiot who delivered that three kilogram piece of straw upon unsteady mental madness and inevitably break my tranquil camels back! Daddy oft-times began to explain my prodigy-my stained childhood but he frequently hesitated when the sordid details got too thick. His eyes moistened and his head would drop. I don't know if he simply chose to forget those trying times, or preferred to withhold them from his once

16

addicted daughter. Maybe through masked guilt he had been truly sorry for what I deemed HIS secret sexual rendezvous with a desperate teenaged junkie (like mommy) behind the back of his Darling wife-my step-mom, Lorraine.

All men have if not an entire skeleton at least a few dozen bones rattling around in the distance from their busy little penises through their emotionally detached hearts and up into the dim shanty-towns of the collective manic male mind. For all intents and purposes my daddy, not just a step-father, was no exception.

But he was a good man. Hard-working-redefining what it meant to be a solid provider. Oh yes, he used to be a Hell-raiser and made countless mistakes (like marrying my stepmother) but nobody on Earth's radiating scale of lunacy, is perfect! He worked so hard for The Department of Sanitation for 38 years and made a home for us in Farmingdale Long Island. And I would die-happily ten times over, just to make him smile!

Daddy always felt especially close to me and never shared the sadistic pleasure my mother lived for while beating or chastising me! It literally hurt him more than it did me. And so when he raised the leather belt of justice and obedience at the bloodthirsty command of my mother, he would cry invisible tears for me on the inside, while I screamed like God had stuck his gigantic foot through my chest! Snotting and snorting like a slaughtered spoiled piglet-on the outside!

There are numerous significant facets of my youth that I've brought with me into life's daily struggles. Whenever I'm hanging out in the club and Nature CALLS me I am always reminded of the day in Elementary School when I was jumped by the entire third-grade class! Well, most of them! The nine year olds from HELL who had been let lose from the classroom for bathroom time. Too bad they forsook their essential bowel movements for some illegal covert gang activity.

In school I was always the ugly duckling-WITH A TWIST! Unlike the storied foul who had it rough from all his little playmates who despised him due to an 'Ugmo' appearance, MY delinquent peers thought it best not just to harass, but to KICK the SHIT outta me!

I never knew sadism could come in such small packages! Besides, we were just 9 years old! They didn't just scorn and ridicule me-they felt compelled to slay the horrific repugnant beast waddling around in their midst. Every day of my ninth year on this Earth I was used as target practice for untrained Juvenile fists and kicks. The little bastards surrounded me-pounced on me! They THREW shit at me each and every time our Teacher Ms. King stuck her head out the Classroom door. I was frightened to death-and DARE not fight back! Till this day I avoid public restrooms-and the small of my back will never be the same!

As I sat dismally anxious (who wants to die at 9?) I prayed that she dare not leave me alone with those monsters! Not for a moment! Not to call home to see if her OWN kids were still alive! Not to retrieve the old discarded Rexo-sheets (the ones that smelled like they'd been dipped in alcohol in keeping with student intoxication) from down the hall. And NOT for the mandatory Annual shit common in problematic middle-aged bowels. That decrepit old lady could not exit that classroom for nothing-not for a fucking second! And if she DID she'd be sporting a body-bag! MY punk ass would go Jet Li on her and see to it!

"Please Ms. King, take me with you! I'll hold the toilet paper you need to wipe your flabby ass-I PROMISE! Oh don't worry about my well-being! It's safer in HERE with your funky anal fumes-away from those predatory losers who've decided to take up a life of crime! So I'll smell your shit TO STAY ALIVE! The odor can't be THAT bad! And if it is-OH WELL! It's still not as damaging as Jungle Johnny Keeler's knuckle sandwiches-I've eaten too many of those lately! If you don't let me tag along on your bathroom breaks there won't be enough of me left to scrape off the floor by the time you get back!"

They used to hit me with their lunch-boxes in the line as we walked in size order with our partners to the Lunchroom or the Gym. Each time Ms. King turned her head- "CLANG" went the Snoopy lunch-box against my head! Baffled at the flagrant sound effects, she turned to see the origin of the clamor but even then, at that age, the budding convicts didn't give up the perp or make a sound! "BONG!" They GOT me, AGAIN! This time it was a Captain Kangaroo! I've learned to hate HIM and HIS tupee ever since cuz that heavy metal Son-of-a Bitch was wielded by that 'Doofus' Jimmy Frazier-The future Line-backer for the 'Chicago Bears!' This BEHEMOTH was the biggest kid in the fucking Third Grade! And in keeping with the invariable tenets of voracity and greed HIS Lunch-Bucket, (the shit HAD to be a Bucket cuz boxes don't come in that size) was always the fullest-the heaviest, and the MOST PAINFUL!

One day after school I had a pounding headache during Homework time downstairs in the Den! I couldn't explain to mommy that her outcast daughter, the one whose life she made miserable every opportunity she got, was the class Scapegoat! The walking Pinnata! Poor mom might get too overjoyed and have a heart attack! God forbid!

My classmates took turns using me to vent their childhood rage. (I guess gangsters and Criminals have their own Democratic laws of fair-play) When times were bad THEY'D BEAT MY ASS! I'd get jacked up for a slew of reasons! Missed allowances, missed meals, missed favorite cartoons-chicken-pox! Anything! Why they'd even attack me out of sheer boredom! Baby Niggers NEEDED no excuse! Just as long as the Sun came up, Armageddon hadn't happened yet and they caught the casual vibe! 'BONG!' IT WAS ON!! My place in the line was toward the front. That meant that most anybody could take their turn and crown me! I was small. I was a punk-I was the ugly duckling!

As I got older-and fine, the niggers changed their tunes! They went from "Kick her Ass on site," to fuck her if she'll let bygones be bygones and open up her legs! But they can't HAVE this now! I tell em all the time to treat me now like you treated me back then!

18

"But Monie, you so fine! I just wanna…!"

"I know playa-AIN'T that a BITCH?" I'm 5'8", honey-brown and my body is bangin! Weighing in at about 175 pounds there ain't one ounce of nuthin outta place-and niggers know it! Nostalgic limbs get HARD-but fragile egos go limp! Defecating on themselves as they cringe, screaming "GOD-DAMN!! What have I done? Christ-I should've fucked her when she was just an ugly duckling!" Then AFTER the verbal assault, and bitter rejection, they just OOZE away-lusting after the Ghetto Surburban Divinity they preyed upon when young! Sad niggers are ON IT-and they can't have me!

A whole lotta issues have followed me into my thirties! Like I mentioned before about an innate-I mean 'Learned' fear of bathrooms. How the Hell could a person fear the room that houses the dreaded toilet seat? Ask my injured spine! It's shattered! It still hurts at the very thought of that wicked little Bobby Sanchez and his well-rehearsed Atomic flying Elbow-Drop! Damn! The reckless fucker got me Good! Right in my spine!

And then there was that little crippled bitch-Nikki Farnsworth! I remember she resembled a Muppet the way her two feet dragged behind Her.The hostile non-walking bitch! I'll never forget it! Those motherfuckers! After they got finished whipping my Ass, they 'empowered' the crippled warmonger. As though ALL five of them needed help busting up my forty-five pound frame. The rascals brought HER into it!

Now Nikki walked with the aid of crutches-but that didn't stop her! Oh no! Little Miss Muppet did one Hell of a job on me. They lifted her up (those cruel bastards) so she could get her belated quadriplegic piece of my ass! Just like everybody else did! Talk about equal opportunity employment!

She must've hit me in my head with that cushion handled crutch at least twenty times! You'd think that ELMO from Sesame Street had gone ballistic! BAM! BAM! BAM!...BAM!...BAM! I'm STILL dizzy from that Shit! And I'm still justifiably paranoid of abrasive midgets in dark quiet Ladies Rooms! If you're taking a dump don't Fucking spring up out of the toilet stall too rapidly! I'll fuck you up and leave you laying there for the next bitch in line to trip over!

I'm not fucking kidding-don't run up on me like that! If you do, you won't be leaving there the same way you came in! So if you don't plan on bleedin to death after engaging in that sweet pleasant tinkle-walk in slow-motion bitches! You have Nikki Farnsworth to thank for that!

After the damage was done our teacher Miss King dragged her lazy ASS onto the crime-scene, stopped the bludgeoning-the Stomp-fest and saved my life! I thought my skull was fractured! Crutches hurt! Matter of fact when in the wrong hands, they can do more harm than good!

I thank God for Miss King. I'm sure she reeled from the shock of entering the girls bathroom to encounter one of her favorite students getting the grits smacked out of her by a cripple with an attitude! I remember it all like yesterday and I loathe the sum of my childhood! It bore nothing but confusion, emptiness, disappointment, betrayal and pain!

SPEAKING OF PAIN there are too many women walkin around with broken hearts! Devastated by their previous relationships. Who did this to them? Who fucked their heads up like that? It was YOU motherfuckers! The Brothers! Quite honestly, I've got a problem with you men! I've SEEN some of the things you've done to my sisters and I don't like how you get down! I'm callin you out BASTARDS! Be wary because God's avenging Angel might be standing in the Night-Club right beside you-lurking in the dark shadows-STALKING! Waiting to TAKE your social life and make this world a better place!

And I would like to serve notice to any and all of you heartless Womanizers out there in the dating-world. Wallace and Lorraine Singleton did the 'Hokey-Pokey' BUT THE SHIT DIDN'T WORK! So they strolled down to the Orphanage and adopted the 'Devils Child!" Damien SIX for you worthless uers to try an figure out! Mess with me IF YOU WANT! But I don't think you'd want to! You seen 'Chucky? Or the Exorcist-with the bitch cussing everybody out, spittin out lime-green slime and grabbin a Priest BY THE NUTS! Well what you SEE is what you GET! I am insatiable-that means you better 'CUM' right or keep that shriveled up dick quiet! I am indomitable-cuz YOU CAN'T and you WON'T beat ME-IN NOTHING! My Daddy, Satan, saw to that in Demon-training School!

Wherever you go Playas-remember, I'm out there! Plotting, Scheming like the Universal pay back Bitch that has been dispatched out among you! Dying to RIP your stupid fuckin head off! And then celebrate! Chalk up yet another gender triumph for the 'Sisters' as we kick your symbolic severed heads around the Schoolyard and then revel in the pleasurable experiences that life has to offer. Watch out PLAYA's! Oh yeah! Don't sleep! This bitch is beautiful, perceptive vulnerable and on a mission to put trifling ass niggers like you out of your misery!

If you wanna step to THIS be a man about it! I am the real deal! Exquisite, wonderful, excitable and fascinating. I am compassionate, belligerent and invincible-having my origin In Heaven and the provocative nebulous ghetto War-zone of Hell! If an angel and a depraved demon copulated and brought forth a child, that seed would be me! The ill-begotten catalyst sent from Eternity to put you BACK IN CHECK!

So step up BROTHER! Don't forget to bring your brain! Don't forget to pack the Hooked On Phonics Survivals Manual-well equipped with a slew of homonyms, superlatives, prepositional phrases and predicates to quell your ignorance! Be sure to utilize them in proper context. Unlike you've done in the past. Acute retardation is a shame! After you go scurry into the frightening forest of philology and have gathered yourself a basketful of fruits and nuts and verbs and pronouns-then get back to me! If you think you're ready-'Man-up' Rico Suave! I want to teach you that all bitches ain't stupid and contrary to popular belief-YOU CAN'T WIN EM ALL!

I CHALLENGE you to a battle of the sexes-think you'll win? Can't happen 'Joe-joe' if you're walkin around with the I.Q. of a Pit-bull! And since DOGS are not as smart as cats I've peeped your innate gender disadvantage. Well I'll be nice and take it SLOW! YOU READY? THIS ONES FOR ALL THE MEN OUT THERE!

Before you become the fool who rushes in where Angels fear to tread and jump HEAD first (you know which head I'm talking about) outta the plane without a parachute, let me show you what time it is! Now SIT yo PUNK ASS down and let me tell you my story! If you pay attention-you might learn something!

Last but not least this is an appeal to ALL WOMEN! Ostensibly DUMB bitches NEED APPLY! A WARNING that I have gone through great lengths to explain in order to appeal to your higher senses-your better judgement. This is NOT a sex-story-it's a song of redemption! Remember that! So take a page from my tragic downfall and learn from it. Because there are some predatory WOLVES out there! I mean DOG MOTHERFUCKERS and YOU-the SISTERS are getting PLAYED!

-2-

THE BEARDED LADY

Hattie was a male me-alive, witty, intelligent and born a SLAVE to her variable erotic desires. I often surmise that if I had turned myself inside out, extracting a parallel negative of my being in the outer realm, she would easily be me and I would be her-minus the small waning penis, above average height and facial hair characteristic of her innate male anatomy. Oh, and she had a heavy baritone voice that would send Barry White's ego back-packing into self-imposed exile!

Hattie was a transsexual! A transvestite...uh-A FAG! Whatever, she liked dick more than I did and didn't give a damn who knew it! "HOLLEEERR!" In her pink spiral notepad of life-all were welcome! Big, tall, short, rich or poor men-the more-the merrier!

As far as looks go, she was a cross between Blackbeard...and Rupaul! With a dash of Prince, the Wolf Man and Rick James! So you gather she was not exactly the prettiest Homo on the block! Get me? Hattie was more like a "Baby, can you turn out the lights? And tell the Moon not to shine until you put back on your clothes and get the FUCK outta my house," kind of ugly. But the silicone was bangin-the $8,000 surgical procedure was worth every dime and her steady diet of female hormone injections made the bitch feel, smell and act like a real woman-SO WHAT MORE COULD A FAG HOPE FOR? And her vivacious personality carried with it the brightness of the sun. Who NEEDS good looks when you're hanging with a bitch real as that. I certainly wasn't fucking her so she could be as ugly as she pleased-AND SHE WAS! I could see her masculinity crawling out from under her make-up. And Maybeline was losing major battles to the deep manly emissions of her larynx. With Hattie, Max-factor took MAD ASS whippings in front of her brand new five-foot wide mirrored vanity set because testosterone is a motherfucker to conceal!

But she didn't care! Fuck that! Five-Oclock shadow, phantom mustache and razor-stubble protruding through layers of lip-gloss-none of that shit mattered to her! Just hit her up right with some Long Island Iced Tea, a bright Cherry Red dress and some new Nine-West kicks and she could conquer the world! Oh-and DON'T forget the Fendi bag!

My girl had a mouth that could verbally slay every male or female on the planet-simultaneously! The bitch was a genius! And her self-confidence and raw candor reminded me of some of the best linguistic acrobatics I'd ever found in my own talkative self.

But that mouth had a flip-side. Remember, she was a faggot! Uh-HE! It-HATTIE! My girl also possessed another rare talent. All through the underworld circuit of 'Hood' society she had attained the label of dispenser of the best 'Head' from either sex! "Head-master" is what they called her.

Mad niggers would stare cautiously-on the down-low when she and I walked by through Nite-Clubs all over town. The bitch was NOTORIOUS! You'd be surprised how many of these niggas, from thug-life to the cutie-pies, like to either take it in the ASS or enjoy a little peanut butter or head-bobbing from somebody with a dick and two balls like them!

Bob-and-weave is what I called her. She hated that because she was a beautician and would 'dis' the shit out of her customers who sat in her chair with less-than-perfect hairdo's! "Bitch, didn't you see this shit comin? Why you wait till your shit is totally fucked up before you see me? Now what the fuck am I supposed to do-yo shit is dead? Next time catch this disaster before it happens! You get a cold you don't wait till you die of Pneumonia to call the fuckin Doctor. You call his ass the moment you get sick! Dumb bitch! I'm a Cosmetologist-not a miracle worker," she'd say.

Now back to the subject of the day-Hattie's special skills! Cock-sucking is a gift most women want but few possess or are willing to train for. She was the best at what she did-sucking a dick-and alot of niggas and females either loved or hated her for it. A 'Lady' has got to be on guard. Especially when you know you hold the Title-the belt, and hordes of jealous green bitches would love nothing more than to usurp the throne of Sodomy Queen. Imagine the props she'd get! The societal perks-knowing that she gives the best blow-job this side of the Mississippi. To these vain bitches with reprobate minds and swollen egos that would surpass the honors bestowed upon Miss America or even Miss Universe!

Now ladies-you know that a good chunk of oral-sex makes the world go-round! Can you imagine the heightened sense of pride you'd feel if you could suck a dick better than anyone else? ANYONE else! porn-stars included! Why you would float around town like your shit don't stink! I didn't say walk-I SAID FLOAT! You'd be too fly to let those dainty felatio-feet touch the ground! "Yeah, bitch! Look at MY flow!"

"Huh, BITCH? EXCUSE ME? Oh, my bad, I thought you were talking to ME! Yeah, that's right little bitch! Take your punk ass on! HO! Fuck around and I'll take your man-and you KNOW I can ho. Cuz the way these grimy motherfuckers are all I gotta do is SUCK HIS DICK right and believe me-he won't remember your fuckin NAME!! I can hear him now! 'Say what? Who is this? Seqouia? Seqouia who? Bitch HOW you get this number? OH no! NO, no, no no,no-NO Bitch! I can't talk now Samoa-or whatever the fuck your name is! Look, I'm kinda with my lady right now! You know-the best blow-job in town-YOU KNOW! FELATIO-FEET! Yeah, uh-huh. Right, so do us both a favor and don't call here no more! O.K? Thank you!...No-YOU have a nice day!'

There will be literal HELL to pay when a woman knows that she has been out-done by another bitch! What amplifies that pain five-hundred times worse is when a woman knows that despite all her God-given talents of pleasing a man-she realizes that she has been infinitely out-done in that department, by another man-dressed up like a woman! That shit hurts!

23

Check the scenario! Little Miss Wifey leaves Home Sweet-Home for the necessary nine-to-five knowing that she gave it all and ALMOST gave up the Ghost in terms of the Heaven-beams of carnal ecstasy she just got finished blessing her mate with.

Her lover, husband and confidant is now sleeping soundly as Wifey goes out to earn her daily bread. The lights are out-or on! Depending on which way you fuck! Wifey has showered off the semenal vestiges of one of the biggest nuts 'hubby' has ever extracted in her face! Her eyes still sting from the millions of Sperm drops he plastered upon her vision as they seek desperately to fertilize an egg not present in the aqueous proximity of her dilated retina.

Wifey's tired transfused lips have dutifully bloodletted every ounce of desire his body could produce and emit into her mouth! Scum tastes funny. Like a cross between raw egg-whites and unsweetened salt water with a dash of okra (flavors differ depending on the ethnicity of the sperm-donor-trust me! I know-and older guys taste the best!)

The tight little ASS wifey climbed into the bedroom (AKA-Rectal Execution-site) with has been gnarled and deformed into the puffy pink and brown flesh mound that she moistens and dabs constantly with A&D Ointment-to ease the epidermal sting! It looks like an erupting ring-worm nestled precariously atop her 'slap-bruised' butt-cheeks! A circular whelp for her 'Man' to habitually ooze into when he grows bored of the Missionary routine of her putrified vagina. Not all Assholes were made for sloppy dicks-however large or small!

Lastly, wifey's pussy, oh wifey's pussy, is a hesitating cough dying to happen! Sick and tired of neglectful drive-bys her lover's speedy cock teases her with. If she's lucky he might spend a total of ten uneventful minutes a week inside that seemingly unlawful entry. She prays to distant Gods of Matrimonial sanctity and splendor to find the strength to squeeze some genital phlegm-to prompt a cough from the coochie that sings the blues every second it strives 'waiting to exhale.'

Wifey's body is a refurbished and discarded sexual experiment. A posthumous Autopsy Report that her other half no longer wishes to invest the time and energy in reading. She has done all! Given body and soul and as she drives out onto the Expressway enroute to another more gratuitous world-a world excited over the scandal of her deprecating form, she knows that by the time her lunch hour creeps around that sick motherfucker will wake up!

His throbbing livelihood will invite perverse thoughts to the dinner party of some latent sexual needs he keeps hidden in the dark awaiting scarce moments of solitude. After the mighty ejaculation he needs a few hours of convalescent time before he gets the sexual strength to dig into that 'Closet' and get them!

You see, by now Wifey's purpose is served and if it were up to him she could roll over and drop dead right then and there (just be sure to iron my shirt and pack a hearty lunch before you die!) After you're finished turning him on his minds eye blares out the love song of 'I don't care about your needs!' And the minute your key locks the front door and your tattered rectum rides the bottom of your back in a flabby coat-tail of sagging meat that gravity has deflated, that BASTARD will wake the fuck up! He will press 'Contact' on his Nextel, call 'Freddy-the-fag' and press rewind on his liscentious itinerary of wayward 'dreams!'

He's gonna proposition the homosexual! Although you half-way killed yourself trying to please HIS STUPID ASS freddy the fag does it better! He engages in with ease what you've worked all your life to perfect! To Master! Or at least attempt. While your out eating a Caesars Salad in the Executive Lounge with the girls bragging about how GOOD you were to your husband last night, he's at home 'peanut-butter fucking' Freddy and tossing HIS Salad! Five minutes later Hubby's screaming at the top of his lungs-dick harder than you ever made it, swearing that this gay motherfucker's hairy asshole is the BEST thing ever to happen since the birth of Christ!

NOW THIS IS BULLSHIT! And women KNOW it! So keep your eyes open sisters-don't do them unless they do you! And THIS is the sort of mindset-the kinda hostility that these women brought to the table each and every second Hattie walked into a room full of their violent, bitter envy!

I'll go one step further. NO bitch can stand being cheated on or made a fool of! (Niggas even hate that shit) How you think a motherfucker feels knowing some other nigga with a bigger dick and a longer 'stride' is somewhere hammering inside his girl? What you think he wants to do to that bitch-an that nigga the moment he gets lucky enough to find that niggas crib or what Motel he's sticking her at?

Well how you think a woman feels-to lose her man to some other chic? Whose ass ain't so flat. Whose titties still stand up! Who can make her man cum harder and more times than she ever could? Now THAT'S some HURT!

Then how you think she feels after fucking the daylights out of your tired Rogain takin-Viagra needin sexuality for the last seven years! She opened her legs whether she was bleedin or not (well most of you niggers don't run red-lights an won't touch a sister burdened with a little blood under the clit) but that bitch did flips for your sorry ass! She let you fuck her in ways nobody else would let you touch them! And three minutes later when your puny dick died the swift death of premature ejaculation and you rolled your weak punk ass over and went straight to sleep, she had mercy on your pathetic soul! She SHOULD'VE cussed you out-that's what any other bitch would have done! She shoulda threatened to kill you if you didn't get little Jimmy hard again but then she didn't want a dead man on her hands!

She should've insulted your feeble not quite ready for prime-time manhood! That's what any other bitch would've done-but she loved your trifling ass and did not want to see you hurt! Wifey gave ten-thousand percent. Whenever you wanted it-just to please the ungrateful parasite she thought fell in love with her. And all that you can think of is fuckin another bitch or fulfilling your reprobate yearnings to cum inside another man dressed like a woman!

25

You know, now I can see why Lucifer was cast outta Heaven. He was that kinda fool and God could not stand beholding the foul aura of evil incarnate! Well this is how a woman feels when her man wants to sleep with anybody but her. She feels sickened! And betrayed! She doesn't know who to stab the shit out of first! Hubby the pervert-or the home-wrecking Fag! And that's what poor Hattie had to go through-jealous housewives who looked at her knowing that their cheating husbands had had their grimy dicks sucked by 'Head-Master' once or twice! She was notorious-and she was every woman's nightmare!

Well I promised way back then when we first started hanging out to ride or die with my girl. Hattie was a slender muscular nigger who looked like she could kick a whole lotta ass-male or females if she had to! I remember those days. Mad bitches whisperin in the dark, carrying blades and who knows what, tried us-an lost. It ain't easy or safe walkin the streets or through a club filled with people who know you slept with their mates-their spouses! Almost everyone in the room hates you and wants you dead. Even some of the 'men' look the other way-embarrassed by the very sight of Hattie. A tall unattractive homo whom they wish they could murder and erase the bitter memory of. These closet freaks slide away because they can't figure out why they let that ugly man dressed as a woman caress their penises in her big manly hands-AND SUCK IT!

Most did it out of sheer curiosity. Others, to disprove her 'Rep' for true pleasure. They walk around in their Baggy Jeans and Tims like ordinary heterosexual men. Hard-core Do-or-die Gangsters-ducking away from the sight-the painful memory of the repulsive black fag who they couldn't wait to sleep with!

Well where she was number one, I was number two on the Low-low! I could perform-couldn't hold it down like the Champ. But I still had a trail of about sixty niggas (all straight I hope) who gave my lips high acclaim as being the 'Greatest' real woman to ever touch a dick!

Me and Hattie were the one-two punch that Shaq and Kobe or Mike and Scottie Pippen aspired to be. We've been through throw-downs, getting jumped in the ladies room. All that! And NOBODY could ever run up on my girl-just as long as I was breathing!

CHURCH OF THE POISON MIND

The Pastor had wanted desperately to scratch his nuts! Somewhere between the books of Genesis and Revelations, acute jock-itch must've set in and all the fervent prayers and harmonious rantings of Trinity Baptist Churchs' Chief Disciple could not expunge nor exorcise the belligerent fungal Demon attempting to ruin today's Sermon!

He had a grave solemn look about him-like Belial the 'Lord of Flies.' minus his weekly shower in a lilly-pond. But THIS virtuous toad was infested with crab-lice-his incessant scratching testified of that! And although he tried desperately to cover up this desperate yearning to tug at his Amphibious balls, the teeming crowd suspected the Good Reverend's Sacred ablutive delinquency!

His left hand periodically attacked the grossly infected site with routine pulls and tugs designed to dislodge the microscopic huddle of Bacteria adjoined to his groin. He would jerk-then shout and wave his hand in spiritual fervor only to return it subsequently atop the root of his problem! SCRATCH, SCRATCH, SCRATCH! SCRATCH, SCRATCH, SCRATCH! SCRATCH,...SHOUT,...SCRATCH!

Such, I take it, are the occupational hazards of a Man of God in polyester trousers who sits 'Still' too long-and bathes too 'rare!' I thought that it was a given that the devout were not susceptible to the physical idiosyncrasies sustained by mere mortals. You know-just one wave of their Holy hand and the Spirit of the Lord would 'Shout-It-Out!' Dispeling any infirmity from Pnuemonia to 'Crotch-rot!'

But the Rev must've missed a few pre-requisite classes on Divine Healing! Maybe during those long-winded lectures he was engrossed in the filial Arts and Crafts of Little Rubber-Duckie and Rub-a-dub-dub! In retrospect, those lectures actually had merit after all and deferring them might have cost him his hygienic life-and led to this!

How can a man preach the Gospel with his nuts on fire? Good question! Yet he continued on-cranking out the persperous message of a Deliverance he had yet to achieve. He stomped and strolled. Strutting across the Pulpit like a man 'Dispossessed!' His right leg played a bountiful game of 'Freeze Tag' with the unoffending air-kicking at it to punctuate an otherwise lackluster oratory performance!

The Congregation cosigned his testicular dilemma-some shouting the proverbial 'Halelujah!' Some imbibed in a Praise dance they must've seen on M.T.V. There was one rotund woman (probably Sister Bertha) who seemed to feel every iota of Rev's inspired kicks because her 'Big Momma' posture appeared to wince and twitch each and every time the Good Minister lifted his leg and made a point!

Finally and toward the end of the Sermon, I don't know-perhaps the Good Shepherd could not take it anymore, but it happened! The sting of ten million Crab-bites can be one Helluva problem when your breathe is short and your trousers are tight!

27

Nonetheless, the Cosmic forces of Celestial discretion could no longer bind the private tampering that this poor soul longed for. He grabbed his nuts in Bobby Brown fashion! Like Micheal Jackson had grown dark-green and over-weight and joined the Ministry! (Eee-hee-HEEH!) I could see the overt relief prescribed by a Divinely gifted hand no longer inhibited-reaching out to scratch his inflamed genitals!!

I think Sister Peterson noticed it too! Although silent throughout the Sermon, after the vulgar display she expelled a hard and welcomed 'My Lord, MY LORD!' It is said that Christians can feel the pain and bear the psychological burdens of their Religious peers or Brethren in the faith. Well if God chose to ignore the ardent supplication of his devoted child in the Pulpit, begging spiritual coffers of mercy for scrotal desensitization or a scrub brush (whichever came first) Sister Peterson could relate! And she too could hear the 'Joy Bells' ringing as her spiritual leader entered the gates of Paradise-and soothed his lofty balls!

Sister Johnson looked like an addict who'd just left Detox without the benefit of a Certificate of Completion! Her grim face and trembling extremeties told it all! My first thought was to condemn the closet Crackhead who dared to set unworthy feet into the House of God! But then after careful consideration I repented of my judgement of her and concluded that what better place could an addict seek refuge than at the Altar?

Evangelist Perry was a ball a fire! He couldn't sit still long enough to pay attention to what the fuck Reverend Frog was talking about! His soul seemed wrestless-high-strung. I gathered him to be the Church Athlete-a religious track star who leaped and sprinted his scrawny ass all over the pews! I was right! That motherfucker could RUN! He ran like Hell was chasing and Heaven was too far away to stop now! Like O.J. Simpson at the Airport-before the murder trial! Jessie Owens would've thrown his hands up in the air and said "Fuck it-that Niggers too fast!"

Every time somebody finished crooning a soul stirring song his limber behind was up and running! It was off to the the races. People like that could be skillfully used to motivate a dull crowd into a fervent frenzy. Its contagious! You see when you're a Shepherd and you want to feed the sheep with just enough Bullshit to keep them coming back, you get some young sleek high-energy moron to tune up the comatose crowd. He will run! In place or do laps-it's up to you which effect you require! He can do the Holy Dance-like the spirit of God just rammed a slice of flaming fire and Brimstone down his throat and the cool breeze blowing outta his flaming ass is designed to quench the roaring fire burning down his aero-dynamic anatomy.

Oh my GOD! I had come out here, me and Bre, to try and instill some human decency in the form of religious worship into our embittered lives. YOU KNOW-TRY AND KEEP THE FAITH? But what I saw was to my soul what fire and brimstone would have been to a person's flesh!

But BACK to the future! The staged madness and idiocy running rampant in what was called the 'House of God!' Yeah, Johnny Blaze gets in high gear-and the crowd goes

28

wild. He is their Champion and they believe in him. He even motivates the old and decrepit to want to do what he does! His energy is their drug-their plentifully available euphoria to rid old bones of calcification and rheumatism. Even the Church cripple gets involved as their sprinting Saviour steers them toward redemption and peace!

And since they believe in him they believe in his God-the one that energizes this Crackhead into leaps and bounds of spiritual fervor. And since they believe in his God, they believe in his Pastor! The spiritual God-father of Johnny Blaze can't be all bad cuz Johnny must've learned every thing he knows from the aged Pastor-thus they transfer their Spiritual and financial devotion to the Good Shepherd-the Good Reverend Frog! HE is the Chief adviser and mentor of this gregarious athlete! He gets the glory-and it's a cinch-that he gets the Gold...the money!

That's why offering plates are passed around all the time with the psychological ramrod of an exhilarating Gospel song to soothe their monetary burden. They're partners! Offering...and song. Offering...and song! Inseperable! Like Starsky and Hutch! Bonnie and Clyde! Abbot and Costello! Porgy and Bess! Oprah and Dr. Phil! Whenever you see one you see the other. The psychological advantage of this is that the Preacher wants to make you smile-make you happy while you're giving him all your money! Fuck the rent and to Hell with your life savings! If you sing this happy Gospel song right-you'll smile that gullible smile all the way to the Bowery! Ecstatic, bombastic-a true Christian, complacent-in poverty!

Well Johnny Blaze certainly did his job today! And guess what transpired after his performance? After the Holy dance-after all the singing and foaming at the mouth-just as soon as the crowd was primed and ripe for the picking the Deacons passed the offering plate! And after the last Dollar was sucked from a desperately deluded congregation, Evangelist Perry bolted out of his seat and ran out the front door as though the FEDS were after him!

I've never quite trusted a House of Worship that takes offering more times than it prays. Now you figure during each service the Children of God usually lift up their supplications about two or three times. What with the opening prayer, the Altar call and maybe some indiscriminant cries for Jesus to deliver Sister Sue from her wheelchair or Brother Ferguson from Prison! But O.K. There must STILL be a proper balance between asking the Lord for healing and begging the financially strapped members for more money than they gave you fifteen minutes ago!

GREAT-SCOTT! A nigger could go broke! It would be cheaper to just hang out in a Club. Go to a Yankee game-shit, maybe even the Disney World! Since when does it cost so much money to be righteous?

They got a building fund for the purchase of a new Church that's been promised since your Grandmother's generation! Well, she must've paid for at least two or three of them buildings a long time ago! Yet the facility still ain't been bought yet! Where did all

29

the money go? Why does it take over thirty years for a Church of one-hundred members to buy one fucking building?

Look at the Math. Once a week at least fifty members give about five dollars each to the fund. Probably much more than that but lets be nice in respect for spiritual economic democracy! There are fifty-two weeks in a year so fifty members times five dollars equals two-hundred and fifty dollars per week that the Pastor rakes in.

O.K. then! Two-hundred and fifty times fifty-two weeks in a year. What is that? Around twelve-thousand five-hundred dollars per year! Now, the building they want is a Church building so although it must be larger than the first one, it is still relatively small! So you mean to tell me you can't put a down payment on a new Church in one year with close to thirteen G.s? SHIT! Some Houses go for less of a down-payment!

O.K! We'll give the benefit of the doubt to any asinine skeptic whose still confused! Lets get outrageous and pretend that it took the Good Pastor five years of the members hard earned money (S.S.I. Checks included) to get Twelve-thousand five-hundred which amounts to sixty-two thousand five-hundred! Now you gonna tell me that after five years they STILL can't afford a new Church building? BULLSHIT! Somebody's getting PAID! The Rev. still can't afford the 'building!' But he just purchased a 2005 Beamer! In CASH!

Churches are Non-profit Organizations and have excellent lines of credit. Moreover they get tax breaks up the Kazoo. How come sixty G.s can't cut it? There's just one reason. When they refer to 'The Building Fund' that's exactly what it is. This is in fact a building fund-It is the fund that is building the revenue generated for the Pastor's Bank Accounts at the expense of his Chosen, misled, blind, deaf and dumb flock!.

Churches are segregated! Divided into a preeminent caste system! The Leader or Pastor is known as the Shepherd! The one ordained by a Higher Power to protect the sheep or the flock. It is his sole duty to provide that which benefits his followers so that they may flourish and grow.

The Members are called the Sheep or the flock. Do you know how truly fucking dumb sheep are!

After the Sermon came the Altar-call. Rev. Frog, now free of the micro-parasites that caged his soul moments before, raised both his hands in a noble posture. It was something that Jesus, Moses or Buddha would do. He lifted his sweaty head and closed his eyes. Chin tilted and mouth agape-like he was awaiting the return of some much needed oxygen he'd expelled during the long boring Sermon. He floated his fat funky anatomy into the aisles past the gazing teary-eyed flock! They all looked up at him in obeisance-as though Christ himself had just walked on water amidst their humble masses!

When Kermit passed by me I could smell the aftermath of a sweltering little man who had just preached his anti-perspirant into submission! It was no longer working! Ineffective. The Arid, the Mitchum, the Brute by Faberge or the Mr. Clean-whatever the fuck he used was null and void and I SWEAR I could NOT have been the only one to notice it!

How can a 'man' preach himself into odious bliss? I mean what the fuck? And the females in the pews were fanning him as he passed by. Reaching out to him! As though they felt sorry for this poor righteous soul who paid the ultimate price of bad hygiene just to bless them with the Word that he swore God told him to say!

I'd have sworn Jehovah Himself was walking amongst us if not for the stench. He smelled more like a Demon! You ever smell a Demon-doin 'Da Hustle?' They shouted, they waved, they snotted and cried and HE, perhaps delighting in their support, began to strut jauntily up and down the aisles like an eclectic Bat out of Hell!

Soon his hands were awave and he bade the audience to calm the fuck down. I surmised another speech was pending. Perhaps something imparted upon him that he forgot to mention. His large beady eyes darted left to right continuously like a toad! Like a fucking frog seeking his evening meal!! His large round belly could not be convinced that it did not fit snugly into his improperly measured attire. The gut protruded like a Buddha-doll in deep respiration about to recall something he'd forgotten to say.

The forgotten Mantra evolved with the typical Baptist Prologue heard throughout the entire spectrum of Ghetto-Christendom. "WELL…" I made my brain collapse shut for the profanity I wanted to spew at this amphibious slithering human animal who resembled a frog! The Frog who'd just finished imparting to the marshy swamp creatures some ancient wisdom of 'How I Got Over!' Like he was dropping some shit on us that only he-and the Creator of the Universe were aware of!

From his red-carpeted lilly-pad now perched three feet away from me I could see the true Frog-like nature of this hopping creature in a miniature nightgown and a cheap undersized suit boldly attempting to disclose the sacred mystery of the Gospel of Jesus Christ!

Just after the 'WELL' two women began to holler and at that moment I didn't know whether to summon an ambulance or call the Police! I thought those bitches went crazy! Bugged the fuck out! The Rev. got quite outwardly pleased at the emotional outburst he felt responsible for. It is morbidly true that some preachers will do anything for a hardy and welcomed divine pat on the back. Like "Good job Rev. You really got em goin now!" An inflated Ego is the LAST to go when expunging the soul of sin-right behind debauchery and an adulterous sex-drive!

One of the two chics reminded me of the Whore of Babylon! I could just as easily picture her sucking somebody's dick as testifying about the Goodness of the Lord! Stevie Wonder could see what kind of past THIS Bitch had come from! She was probably some professional Vanessa Del Rio wanna-be who had gotten sick of the bitter salty taste of sperm for meager pay and decided to take a ride on the spiritual wild-side.

It is said that a 'Ho' could get rich in Church because every male in there is backed-up, hard-up and dying for some fresh new pussy! He's been with wifey, ole greasy fat-assed wifey, who wouldn't suck a dick if her hum-drum life depended on it cuz 'It ain't in the Bible so The Lawd don't approve of it!' And every time he waves his desperate yearning penis across her face, she bolts out of their undefiled bedroom branding him a demon, speaking in tongues and threatening to call the COPS-or tell PASTOR! Her sexual bag of tricks is outdated, prehistoric and mundane. Moreover the Gospel according to her dictates clearly that takin it in the ASS is just for fags and Prostitutes-an abominable sin-PUNISHABLE BY DEATH! Imagine THAT! You won't make it into Heaven if you slurp hubby's cock or let him shove little mickey inside your poop-chute!

Well guess what Miss blind Church bitch-your hubby WANTS a whore! A slut! A cocksucking prostitute! In facts he prays every night for your violent untimely death so he can go out on the Boulevard and pick him up a sexual MANIAC! One who will do for his sex-drive what YOU won't cuz he NEEDS that sanctified dick sucked! He's somewhat reluctant to fuck the fag but when that prostitute-that Linda Lovelace deep-throat bitch finally comes around your tired saggy Missionary ass is history! A bad memory-soon forgotten within the interplanetary and domestic scheme of things!

So this 'Ho' for Jesus is dancing. Like she's in Roseland or at the Fucking Shadow night Club or something! I think somewhere down the spiritual line she musta caught one too many Beyonce videos cuz the bitch is 'Doin It' and 'Doin It' and 'Doin It Well!'

The men in the Congregation are clapping and shouting louder than their female counterparts-perversely elated at this legal porn the Lord has blessed them with!

"We gotta put THIS bitch on DVD!" Even Rev. Frog is feelin this big bubble-assed 'Ho's' performance! Like that scrumptious fly his roving eyes were looking for just buzzed it's way past his sweaty green forehead! He thanks God and blesses her Sweet Holy Ass in the name of the Father, the Son and the Holy Ghost-insisting she join the Church.

Rev. Frog smiles and the crowd is ablaze! And the Whore of Babylon swings her tits in the air and thanks God for the positive income flow this jive-ass Church is about to donate to her. Trust me these niggers in the pews got king-sized erections! I could see it from where I was sitting and they can't wait to get a sanctified proposal from this trollop whose 'shakin what her momma gave her!'

I'll call the 'Ho' Sister Thompson. Now Sister Thompson has a dance partner. Oh-no, this ain't no solo-it's a duet and there's ANOTHER sister out there whose feelin the rhythm as much as she is! But there is something different about THIS particular disciple. She's reserved. She's refrained. Oh yes she's feelin the Power but her tears appear to have a rare unblemished sincerity never before seen in this doomed congregation!

As she jaunts her body in spiritual fashion her sweet psyche seems to be lodged in two courses of action. One part of her seems to be communing in the most pure way she knows how with a deity that she worships in truth of heart. She looks above her at what I deem as the majesty of a God that these other members have yet to be introduced to.

I look at the sister and I say, DAMN, what in the world is she doing here? Why did she opt to keep company with the Anti-Christ? In a church where devils and hypocrites and bitches and pimps and ho's thrive in a Satanic mockery of all that is good.

I perceive that THIS sister can see right through the Bullshit! That she knows. Maybe she's lost! Maybe she has no other place to worship. Maybe this Evil horde of imps and provocatuers needs the virtue of her piety much more than her absence.

This beautiful sister looks like Eve from the Garden of Eden. A bonafide Child of God! An African swan amidst a thousand reprehensible ducks profiling and showcasing. Her secondary ideal appears to be her raw disgust at the bitch dancing alongside her. Perhaps this is how an angel would feel in the company of the Devil and his cronies. Her graceful movements seem to herald a solemn voice asking itself why her devout being decided to surround itself by demons in a house of worship. She is appalled and her pure wondrous grace only succeeds in accentuating the despicable liscentous bitch sliding down the symbolic pole beside her. She asks God to cleanse her. She asks God to have mercy and save this damned Congregation all the way from the whore to the frog! She asks God to steady his aim of belated heat-seeking lightening bolts that lay in wait for Motherfuckers just like this who practice to deceive! She asks herself why she chose to dance so closely to evil incarnate. Surely even I ask God to let his wrath hit the target of the ranting whore gyrating madly in the Church of the Poison Mind!

If all went well after the smoke cleared and Heaven re-shut it's automatic trap-door, Jezebel would be annihilated deep within the smoldering crater of her grave-site. Only then could 'The Good Sister' dance by herself-praising God in virtual purity instead of sharing the stage with the disgraceful presence of the devil's daughter!

And what righteous God would require the perverse half-naked Reggae-winds and foaming at the mouth of his adherents to prove their loyalty? It was such a vulgar display of hypocrisy that I grabbed my child up from her seat before the official dismissal and ran the fuck out of there-NEVER TO RETURN AGAIN!

MINI-ME

"Breanna, did you see my brush?" I knew she took the damn thing because I had left it on the dresser before I got in the shower. But I was playin dumb to see if she would lie-hoping my only daughter would not be trifling enough to get knocked the fuck out over a hair-brush. I HATE petty thieves!

It was 6:43 A.M. I had to drop her off at the bus stop in time for school! I was due at work in seventeen minutes and my 'Time Machine' had run out of gas! And to make matters worse my wig looked like a dead wet possum hanging off of my head that it would take at least an hour to resuscitate! Something TOLD me to put the wig brush under my bed sheets so that Mini-me wouldn't see it!

I thought I was bad spending around fifteen minutes in the mirror every morning. Breanna needed at least twenty-five! Maybe those adolescent arms lacked the keen skills in brush stroke technique that I had taken years of adulthood to perfect. I DON'T KNOW! But she would just stand there-looking in the mirror and BRUSH and BRUSH and BRUSH!

As I wondered if that was what I looked like as an unlearned juvenile Prim-prim, it suddenly occurred to me that my fourteen year old daughter-the sharp mouthed miniature clone of myself primping in the bathroom with an attitude, was 'igging' me!

"Breanna! I don't FUCKING play that! You hear me," I shouted sprinting to her well secured vanity haven and banging on its shut door like 'The Police!' "You know you hear me! Open this God-Damned door!" She was stalling! Pretending not to hear to garner time enough to comb her stupid little teenaged head!

"Huh? What? I didn't HEAR you! Did you say something?" After all these years of perpetual chastisement, Breanna STILL couldn't lie right! She always peered down at the floor or looked away-not wanting me to notice the oozing wad of verbal mistruths seeping from her lips!

"Oh, you can't hear nothing now! But that time I was talking to daddy about you on the phone, you heard every damn word from your room with the door closed! Those ears hear what they want to hear Breanna! Did you take my brush?"

"Oh yeah, God! Why you always yellin? Stop TALKING so loud!"

She was SMELLIN herself-trying to be cute! And I wasn't havin it!

"Don't TELL me how the fuck to talk! Whose the fucking parent-you or me? I know what the Hell I'm doin! Nobody's stupid Breanna!"

"Whatever!"

I wanted to pick the bitch up by her left nipple but time was of the essence and A.C.S. was just a phone call away! God forgive me for calling my fucking daughter a bitch in my mind. But she made me so freakin mad, I could've took that brush and stabbed her with it!

"You don't say 'whatever,' I shouted-my lips two millimeters from her forehead. I was spittin as I spoke but I couldn't care less! She was lucky she got a few droplets of spit instead of that Nine West boot heel I was contemplating having to surgically remove from the triffling stringbean!

"If you think you're grown and big enough to take care of yourself, you can go stay with your father! SHIT, I'll put you on the first thing smoking back to Philadelphia! You'll like it there! See how good HE takes care of you-an don't call me in the middle of the night when you're starving to death! Remember that time Breanna? Three O-clock in the morning! 'Mommy, Daddy didn't give me any dinner-an I'M HUNGRY!' You can't survive too long on Lucky Charms and a bag of Skittles!"

"Uh-Boy...I wont starve-an I'll go MYSELF!"

"How you gonna get there Dummy-FLY?"

"Don't worry about me-I'll walk! At least I'll be away from..."

SNATCH-UP! I grabbed that little Bitch like she was a two ounce slug and pointed my finger right in her defiant little fucking face!

"Go ahead! Say it an see if I don't Smack you in the fuckin mouth! I was holding her half-way in the air. (she only weighed 110 pounds-SKINNY-BITCH!) Her beige Tims trying desperately to find a peaceful spot to be planted firmly on the bathroom tile floor.

She hung in the air like an Elementary-school victim-enduring a menacing glare and damaging breathe-about to give up the coveted proceeds of that prized 'Power-Ranger' lunch-box! She LOOKED like Raggedy-Ann! A ghetto version with a sarcastic smirk-a fresh weave and perpetual behavior problems! Breanna reminded me of me. Hence, I called her 'Mini-me!' Willing to walk through the gates of Hell and withstand ANYTHING, just to get her point across! And she always had to have the LAST WORD!

Her eyes were closed and I think she knew I meant business. I often wondered how well she could take a head-shot! I mean a real sucker-punch-targeted and landed at that Tweety-Bird Mega Dome-piece after some fly shit she might say out the side of her mouth one day! I knew that day would come when she'd come at me wrong and catch a blow to the jaw! The punch to quell the growing enraged juvenile delinquent trying to take over my will and my house with intimidation, selfishness and belligerence!

I might have to squash the rebellion-the slave revolt and cap her to remind her of the official domestic hierarchy sovereign around here! No, don't get me wrong, the 'Coup De Gras', the death-blow would come in self-defense of course. You know I am never the aggressor. I only break necks and fly heads when attacked! At least that's what I would tell the D.A. when those Bureaucrats come and get my abusive ass for child brutality. Yeah, so what my offspring is sitting in the E.R. with a seething hot-comb protruding from her crushed eye-socket. But the multiple gun-shot wounds to the chest were NOT my doing!

Whenever we would clash (7 days a week) I would try my best to keep the noise down. The Landlord lives directly above me and when she is not upstairs neglecting her own fucked up kids she's keenly listening in as I vigorously chastise mine! You can hear anything from my bathroom. If they fart too loud up there I can smell it! Alternately, if I deem it necessary to smash my offspring's head up against the hard marble sink just to get my point across, they'll probably hear that too!

I hoped in my bones that when my daughter and I DO clash that it don't get ugly. When she challenges me physically wanting to establish herself as a young woman-a bonafide adult and wanting to take back any lost respect squandered during her troubled adolescence. I promised myself back when she was born never to strike my child. She was my life and the basis of my happiness.

But that ideal has been drowned gradually within the Municipal logistics of Court appearances and adolescent probationary periods. Those Pill-pushers deemed her a juvenile delinquent due to gross behavior problems and a genetic social defect stemming from an over-developed knack for aggression! They prescribed a slew of sedatives to stave off the symptoms but I don't really have much confidence in their Medical diagnosis.

Breanna was a natural born fighter-as was I. Sometimes I thought that she was often acting out latent hostilities of missing her father-the no good bastard who Fucked me, married me and left her when she was one! Well I too lacked a parent and during my childhood I internalized alotta emotional anxieties that were never truly addressed nor dispelled until I grew up.

On the day I turned 21, all fucking pent up Hell broke lose! I became a bitch! An animal driven by the pains of youthful trauma and every iota of repressed rage hidden during my tragic childhood exploded onto the face of my combative personality! I wasn't fucking HAVIN it-and would just as soon kill a fool as look at him!!

It appears that Breanna was not in the business of putting off tomorrow what she could do today. She had no problem venting now what is bothering her-NOW! I shoulda been that way! Maybe I wouldn't be as messed up as I am because I KNOW my shit is neurotic! Children should be allowed to express themselves fully in order to guarantee psychological health and stability. And I am now the ME that I'd never wish her to be!

Breanna would have kicked my ass if she came across me at the same age she is now. She would've eaten me alive-like a fresh box of Crunch-n-Munch! I was a timid, diffident and fearful kid-with no esteem! Breanna is a pit-bull who won't take no for an answer and perhaps somehow in her third-eye has decided not to wind up as emotionally scarred as her mother. If I had been more like her-self-expressive to a more limited degree, my personality would not be so extreme!

Anyway, the thing behind our child vs. parent clashes is that I truly have a problem beating my child! I know that! Oh I talk a good one but I just can't do it! SHE don't know that cuz I'm a raging bull in HER mind-ready and eager to stomp the Rice Crispies outta her high-yellow body! But in reality it would literally KILL me to beat Bre! I never have and don't think I'm actually capable of such drastic measures. Maybe that's why she's so out of control-so rebellious. She needs a FOOT up her ass! You ever see a child 'Acting out?' Beggin for the belt? Then when that hard slashing leather hits flesh-the little bastard falls right asleep! He is ultimately pleased that you beat him! No more whinning! Furthermore, spanking is an organic peacemaker-a neutralizer between belligerent child and the long-anticipated tranquility of the parent.

Like I said, she fears me-and consistently fights dormant struggles in a quest to usurp the unholy controlling reins of my household! She wages Psychological wars between her own hostile personality and the errant belief that mommy don't play. 'She will kill me and leave my crumpled body sprawled out on the carpet and then go eat a Nacho-Bell Grande Burrito from Taco Bell without missing a single bite!' She BELIEVES this shit! It haunts her terrified little brain! Torments her every moment within the fiery painful wakefulness of its own presumed reality! She MUST believe it because if she didn't-if she thought she could do anything she wanted to do without being brutally murdered, SHE would be wearing the pants in this motherfucker! Cracking my old feeble symbolic head! Beating MY subordinate behind! And I, the parent, would be her SLAVE!

Some kids are inherently evil-by NATURE! They seek to usurp rulership as soon as they're big enough to hold their own in houses owned by passive disenfranchised parents! They conquer and subdue the wills of their grief stricken mommies and daddies who have lost their parental edge. The pre-teen gangsters establish their dominance! And they'll control every single aspect of the domestic ballistics-in YOUR FUCKING HOME!

You seen them little bad-assed white kids-terrorizing their mothers in the aisles of the Supermarket! Little Johnny wants a box of Creepy Clown Cereal or a new Spiderman action figure and his punk-assed mother offers a tiny speck of resistance to his unsavory and impractical demands.

"No Johnny, you can't have that!"

So Johnny bugs the fuck out cuz he KNOWS the bitch will CAVE-he got her to change her mind the LAST time! He goes off!

"What the FUCK mom?!? Fuck, Shit, Piss, Ass, Hell! God-Damn! You're an Asshole-a Pussy! Your Pussy STINKS bitch, gimme my Spiderman or I'll fuckin piss all over the God-Damned FLOOR!"

Little Johnny knows more four letter words than sweet mommy has strength to define. He begins to shout-and rave, and pulls his sour little pink dick out of a 7 year-olds baggy Sean John Jeans! The irrepressible delinquent pops out 'Paulie the Penis' and begins to hammer the cereal aisle with a steady stream of liquid toddler excrement! The little Devil pisses, and pisses, and pisses and mommy simply replies, "Jonathan Fikleflap, you stop that this instance! You're not supposed to pee-pee in the store dear! Do it again and you'll get a 'Time-Out!'"

The repulsive shit-kicker accentuates his putrid bowel movement with loud obscenities aimed at his maternal maker and fellow shoppers begin to take notice! It is an atrocity scene! They whisper and chuckle-hissing in loathsome disgust and utterly appalled at the nonchalance of Johnny's mother sucking up such verbal abuse!

Shakima Johnson and her 9 year old son Jamal stand and watch from a safe vantage point ten feet away. Ms. Johnson does not want to be peed on and wonders why that dumb bitch don't stomp a mud-hole in Lil Johnny's ass. What's she waitin for-him to SHIT all over the cereal aisle too before she finally decides to raise her voice and take off her belt? FUCK ACS! Right here right now she should give him what he needs-not what he's asking for-but what he NEEDS: A good old-fashioned ass whipping, a Priest-and some holy water!!!

"Look at that shit, Jamal! You BETTER look! Now if you EVER try some fucked up shit like that-BOY, I WILL DIE and go to HELL by the time I finish beatin your black ass! You hear me you little Motherfucker? Mess around and TRY ME if you want to!

"Yes mommy," Jamal answers in humble obedience and with the deep respect of one communing with the Creator of the Universe! He knows she's telling the truth because he can vividly recall the agony with which she peppered his ass after he was captured, tried and convicted of the 'Cookie Caper!" Seems his co-defendant little Bobby Meyers turned States Evidence and earned poor Jamal the beating of his life! He learned two lessons from that foiled larceny: Capital Punishment ain't worth 6 stale Chocolate Chip Cookies, AND choose your partners in crime more carefully!

Jamal has three major thoughts lingering in his troubled mind! Number One: Why is that little white boy making shit hard for me? I don't deserve to get threatened for the stuff some other delinquent bastard did!

His second notion is the hope that mommy will leave him alone long enough for him to put his sized 9 FUBU boot RIGHT THROUGH that little white boy's snaggled-teeth! Jamal isn't worried about the weak bitch he calls mommy-the one letting Bart Simpson urinate pubically all over the Cheerios! Shit, the bitch ain't got no heart! She ain't LIKE my momma! Hell, I could fuck him up and she'd probably just stand there an beg me to stop! And after sizing up the mini-devil Jamal deduces that it would be an easy victory. A dust off or 90 second Tyson-vs-Spinks showdown and he'd be back in his mother's arms in the time it would take for her to say "Child Abuse!" Meanwhile, the belligerent white boy is leaning on the ropes-PICKIN UP HIS TEETH!

Jamal's final preponderance is the memory of how HARD HIS mommy hits! Granted she's a bit over-weight-by 30-50 pounds to be exact! And don't piss her off during the Soaps, in front of company or while she's eating cuz she might snatch you up and beat you to death with the brand new toaster-oven she got from Grandma!! So he wants NO PART of some of the brutal shit she's offerin! He won't be bad no more! He won't ACT UP! He won't piss her off and he'll NEVER be anything like that 7 year old brat responsible for the drastic physical exchange mommy's got layin for him-JUST IN CASE!

No, let this be a learning experience! Jamal WANTS his favorite Cereal! He WANTS his Spiderman action figure! And most of all he WANTS to continue walking these Supermarket aisles-IN PEACE!!!

Well Like I said: I'm not Ms. Shamika Johnson! But at the same time I'm not that listless white bitch either! But God knows...I can't hit my baby!

I let Breanna's shirt go, slammed the bathroom door and went into my bedroom! "Get the fuck away from me-before I KILL you!" I wasn't serious. I grabbed my shit, turned out the lights and stormed out of the house with my hair still in complete disarray!

Shit! No sense sticking around! I might do something!

"Meet me in the car, 'Bre!' You got 5 minutes!" I sat in the Navy Blue 'Denali' looking in the rear-view mirror combing my disgruntled weave with my fingers. Fuck a brush! And fuck anybody who don't like it-DON'T LOOK!

Ms. High-class ass came outside in three minutes and I sped off enroute to Farmingdale ostensibly happy that she still had all her teeth! You know how these teen-aged girls are. The minute they start sproutin some titties and a few strands of pubic hair they very naively think they wrote the book on womanhood! Shit, if they only knew! It takes far more than budding 'hind-pots' and a one year membership to the 'Usher' Fan Club to run a fucking household!

JEPEDDO

I was driving along Union Avenue on the way to work trying to delete my 15 minute late transgression. When you work for the State, directly after recruitment you are injected with a probationary dose of duality which will last for the rest of your indentured servitude.

Number one you realize head on that they don't give a damn about you or anyone! If they were to behold a bleeding dying Christ, crucified and begging eternal mercies, they would boldly interrupt his martyred Crusade to ask what the HELL he was doing on a cross when he had much more pressing obligations to meet. Humanity would be better served if he would just bring his lazy ass to work! To Hell with the sacrificial lamb escapade. Save that self-impugning shit for the next gullible dummy to dare to walk the bloodsoaked streets of self-negation!

The State was the Darkside! An Evil Empire! And Lord Vader was reeling on his Imperial throne waiting for this babbling suicidal motherfucker to get his nail-scarred ass back with the Program! To put down the Bible long enough to die in peace! 'Keep still stupid-we're trying to murder you! Don't forget to take off the Crown of Thorns either 'Homey' (you ain't no King and ain't in charge of SHIT) and punch in on time and all would be well!'

Secondly you realize that you're grossly expendable! They will replace you in a heartbeat if you're foolish enough to forsake everything in a hopeless juvenile quest to appease them! THAT critical exponent NEEDS no interpretation!

Well, a bitch was late, so I concluded that the State could wait!! As I made a left turn onto Wheeler Avenue I saw something that prompted tears and laughter. Did you see Peter Pan? O.K! Do you remember the other character in tights who hung out with Pete? Oh! Uh-I think it might have been Pinocchio! I'm not sure, I was up last night with a blunt and a 'Forty' and had to take a penile sedative in order to sleep! Don't ask whose penis it was! Some things are better kept secret-and forgotten! But what I saw essentially was the lobsided travesty of a bum gettin his ASS 'Whupped!!'

There was a vagrant huddle with a group of about 6 hobos circling 2 irate aspiring combatants in what was probably to them the sporting event of the year. There ain't no Cable T.V. in a junkyard and homelessness can be bad news if you're the type who likes to keep up with the Sopranos!

They must've been fightin over a choice piece of discarded Quarter-pounder with Cheese and I'd bet my life there was a Super-sized order of fries in the mix as well, from the way they was goin at it! Poverty and hunger can turn an old lady into the Incredible Hulk-then back again when the 'Po-po' arrive and it's time to re-don that peaceful innocent persona to stave off a well-deserved Manslaughter charge! Nobody wants to take the rap for something they felt compelled to do-be it save your chicken-wing from another more voracious attacker or kick the shit out of the culprit who keeps tapping on your cardboard box tenement tee-pee all night! A famine-victims gotta sleep! It's essential-especially when you live on the curb!

So these two Golden-glovers were goin at it! Toe-to-toe in tip-top shape, except for the unseen battle with Tuberculosis which both combatants were probably losing. Homelessness is a BITCH on the lungs! However this spectacle equaled and surpassed any lackluster bout that the Producers of 'Rocky' could ever invent!

The big clean-cut mauler-I'll call him 'Rocko,' due to that left-hook and ape-like demeanor, was pummeling his smaller not quite ready for prime-time opponent with some moves I never seen before! Something out of the derelicts pamphlet on how to knock the FUCK out of a little motherfucker who don't act right! I could feel the jab! Sticking! 'BOW'...'BOW'...'BOW'... 'BOW'... 'BOW'... 'BOW-BOW,' when he doubled up! This nigger should've been a boxer! Leon Spinks would've ran like Hell before getting in the ring with THIS brawler! A set of teeth is a terrible thing to waste! Fuck a mind! Dental costs are sky-rocketing and life without dentures can only add to that unwanted 'Gumbie' effect! So it would be cheaper to win the fight and preserve your fronts!

So big man is doin work! Lefts, rights, upper-cuts, over-hands, cross-overs and in-betweens! Shit, the smelly motherfucker was NICE! I can imagine the odious aftermath that musta accompanied each an every blow. You know-my stink, coming directly behind my jab. To add insult to injury! He was a bruiser and the 5 foot tall human speed-bag he was bruising should've either took the night off or never dropped outta high-school in his noble quest to become a bum!

The little hairy warrior was squalors complimentary depiction of Raggedy-Andy! A scrawny rodent-like scurrying cave-man with quick moves, a bright yellow raincoat and a glass jaw! Each time the jabs fired at him in rapid-fire succession his unkept head would bob-seconds too late! AFTER the shockwaves instead of before! With each punch the bright yellow raincoat would be sent hurling to the canvass-or in THIS case, to the pissy alley floor! You could see THIS ASS whipping from Mars-from a distance! And for little man's sake-hopefully FROM HEAVEN!

So Jepeddo is takin a beat down! Of Biblical proportions! If David the Shepherd boy had witnessed the plight of a rookie prize-fighter who challenges a Philistine giant (Goliath) without the benefit of divine intervention, he would've thrown in the towel and called off the fight. But in THIS scenario Goliath turned the trick and reversed the Cosmic order of things because unlike the Biblical story-Goliath was kickin a whole lotta Ass! And David-well poor David was in his Elementary School play acting as the human mop a rampant Goliath used to clean up the Royal Palace floors!

Now I call the little guy Jepeddo cuz his wardrobe was something outta a King James, Sir Lancelot medieval play. Shakespearean. To be frank the curb-dweller was

41

wearin a too-too! A ghetto too-too with green leotards. A real Richard Simmons outfit! What a wardrobe to chose to have the life stomped out of you in! I'm sure it doesn't do much for the male combative psyche either! I mean, how aggressive can you be dressed like THAT! Too-too, green leotards and a bright yellow raincoat? The intimidation factor is crucial in boxing. But a nigger couldn't scare away Gary Coleman if he comes jogging into the ring in emerald spandex!

Mr. Puny-verse also had on some brown combat boots that didn't do a God-damned thing for the fashion allure of the too-too! Thus whenever he embarked upon the futile attempt to bob and weave-to duck a blow, the oversized work boots compounded the efforts of his own inability to slip a punch and ultimately save his life!

Now I understand that a vagrant can't be picky during the daily rummage sale that homelessness yields and you use whatever you got! No sense foolin yourself or wastin time searchin for some name brand shit in a garbage bin! The raw profundity of desperation has inbred guidelines that'll teach the most pompous aristocrat that when you ain't got shit you put on whatever you find! Whether it be some oversized tattered denim jeans or an old lady's yellow-chiffon night gown. It's either take it and be grateful or go naked in the wild winds of January-AND DIE!

Well nobody wants to die! To freeze to death and apparently Jepeddo didn't want to either. So he chose to don his poverty appointed attire with grace and dignity! Too bad the uninformed pitiful bastard must not have done much reading! He obviously missed the Old Testament story of David's triumph over a 9 and a half foot raging Goliath. (height doesn't always matter) And he probably also misplaced or neglected to purchase this months copy of 'The Boxers Handbook' highlighting the art of fighting for your indigent life in an alley pitted against a giant and surrounded by a bloodthirsty group of hobos who want to see SOMEBODY get that ASS kicked in! It don't really matter who-as long as the punches fly and the E.R. is notified after the homicidal ordeal!

So Jepeddo can't fight! He's losing the bout on all the panhandling Judges score-cards. He must not be too intelligent cuz if he was, a shred of common-sense would inform him that a good old-fashioned donnybrook is not the best way to spend his days off. Why BLEED if you don't really have to? In fact the loss of blood is a crime against self that could and should be avoided at all costs! Even at the expense of being labeled a coward by ones peers! It is in fact better to be a healthy, undamaged, unbroken and frolicking coward-one without the gaping puncture wounds of Rocko's teeth marks in his ass, than to be the noble intrepid post-mortem amateur fighter nestled neatly in the casket after this, his first-and last professional bout! Choose your poison! This one's a no-brainer!

But he keeps trying! And every time that hulking motherfucker knocks him down, he persistently gets up, shakes lose the bone-fragments imbedded in his brain-AND KEEPS COMING! It's a crying shame that daddy neglectfully squandered the golden opportunity to teach his hapless son a skill (like self-defense) because the way he's hittin the deck is drawing out sighs of sympathy amidst a torrent of spectator cheers and laughs!

But Jepeddo keeps on keeping on! "Damn you, you little hard-headed Fuck! Why don't you just stay down and call it a day! I gotta get to work an have better things to do than watch you get murdered! But I can't turn the channel till this bout is over! So will you please just LAY your punk-ass on the sidewalk so I can get to work before I get fired! If I do, you won't ever have to worry about Rocko again cuz it'll be ME out here beatin the daylights outta you for costing me my livelihood! Stay down Bitch! The Quarter-pounder with Cheese probably ain't worth the beat-down anyway! Just let Rocko have it an I'll BUY you a 'Happy-Meal!' Fuck it, I'll even throw in a Bud Lite to help you get over your ill-advised and unhappily ended boxing career!"

Karate-school or a good Jet Li movie could've changed this scenario to the tune of a boxing upset! Perhaps one of the biggest upsets in pugilistic history when the little guy takes Rocko's head off and stuns the world! But the V.H.S. tape must've popped or got stuck and unraveled in the V.C.R. (imagine the odds) cuz Jepeddo can't draw SHIT! Not an iota of inspiration from any well-choreographed Martial Arts Epic to save his ungifted anatomy and his gauged-out eye-socket from this-Rocko's left-hook!

I stopped my vehicle, defying unforgiving time restrictions and the Job late-comers traffic jam for this ringside seat of Jeppedo's last stand! General Custard, in HIS last stand, had it made when compared with Jepeddo as he feigned and absorbed PUNCH after ego-crushing punch! Blow by blow punishment from the Heavyweight Champ of the slum named 'Rocko the Right-handed!'

I could tell that there were other motorists stopping to witness the crucifixion unfolding to their left driver's-side because the honking of horns grew slowly silent. Everybody likes a good fight and roadside atrocities are placed highly in the ranking of what turns a motherfucker on! Eventually EVERYONE was more than willing to witness the slaughter from their vehicles and job-security, once the primal order of the day, ebbed relatively meaningless! (I guess motorists have nothing better to do in the grinding absence of road-rage! They prefer losing their jobs to view Civic bloodbaths that don't concern them.) But not a single soul got out of their car to halt or prevent the crucifixion of Christ! The last stand of JEPEDDO!

Soon the traffic was teeming and horns blared from other pleasure seekers totally unaware of what we were looking at and stopping the necessary flow of traffic for! The cars way in back began to start some noise of their own. Darn! I was in the absolute front. And if I moved then the rest of those sorry impunctual bastards could move on with their lives-and get to work! Why is everybody so eager to get cussed out by their bosses anyway? Why now? You weren't in a hurry at 6:00 A.M. when the alarm went off! So why in Heaven's name you wanna have a change of heart and interrupt my virtual reality Cable hook-up NOW? DAMN!

Well impunctuality is a pet-peeve! An ass chewing is embarrassing! Jepeddo's last stand was definitely a good source of entertainment-food for thought. But blaring Police sirens and the inevitable $100 moving violation they would engender was quite another!

After a quick glance at the outraged sons-of-bitches threatening my economic sanctity and swarming in my rearview mirror, I turned once more to evaluate the atrocity scene. JUST IN TIME! Thank God that I did cuz when I looked left I saw what amounted to the answer of many unspoken supplications! I know Jepeddo musta been supplicatin the SHIT outta Heaven while Rocko was beatin the Hell outta him! Well, prayers are good. Boxing lessons are even better and a glass-jaw is far worse. But my day was made as I put the gear in 'Drive' while witnessing the Greatest comeback in Sports History!

H.B.O, Cinemax and Don King would've ALL paid a billion for the Exclusive Footage of what was to come! Jepeddo, perhaps sick and tired of the rough slimy surface of the canvass, had decided to solicit assistance of yet another kind! The filth-ridden audience roared and gave him a Standing Ovation when he picked up a metal trash-can lid and smashed Rocko across his grimy protruding forehead with it! I saw Rocko immediately grab his head as though it were about to explode or he was being lifted from the ground-OFF HIS FEET by it! Within the defiled crowd soiled hands clapped, rank arms waved and odorous gaping jaws blared out their desolate life's rare satisfaction!

Jepeddo, perhaps sensing victory and the diminishing threat of Rocko's lefts and rights, threw down the metal garbage-can lid with a loud clang and all anyone could hear was the reverbatory "Oooowh," of the stunned crowd! It was like when somebody got punched in the face with some fly shit at a 3 O-clock School Yard Showdown!

Then my view was marred by the passing of my vehicle into some of lifes other, less hostile absurdities-like a 9-5! I was late for my daily ass-chewing. I was glad for Jepeddo and entertained the thought of going back to see what happened to him-to Rocko! Well, I guess the Paramedics could determine that mystery. Like 'Cause of Death?" A metal Garbage can lid to the head!! I would've given Jeppedo $20! Easily- without batting an eye for this grueling sadistic entertainment he had provided at the expense of his own diminishing health. Although he had not left the impromptu Boxing Ring unscathed he had still beaten the odds, dethroned the Champ, stunned the crowd and took the Title Belt! That was nothing the Gods of economic squalor would not let him into the gates of Hobo-Heaven for!

I was Jepeddo in life's complex arena-minus the brutal ass-whippings. But you know, ass-whippings come in various shapes and sizes and formats. You can be beaten physically, politically economically and socially. I've taken quite a few social ones-more than my share! But anyone can defy the odds-and like I said, 'size doesn't matter!' But I've got some belated advice for the Jepeddos of this vast unstable universe. Stay in school and learn a Trade. Embellish in Literature, Science, the Arts or whatever! But if you DON'T, before you're excommunicated from the world into the Junk-Yards of street poverty, read the story of 'David And Goliath,' pick up a copy of 'The Boxers Handbook' and learn to fight!

Leotards and a too-too are perfect attire for the Theatre and I thank God for Shakespeare's corny ass! But nothing can get a big grimy vagabond off your back like a lightning swift left jab-and NEVER wear a bright yellow raincoat to a street-fight!!

-6-

ROCKY SIX

It was cold as Hell! January is the first month yet it wastes no time declaring war on mankind! Like some divine cyclic enemy trying to take you out before the inclimate year ends. Pneumonia can be a fatality. And I don't see why God would inflict some shit like that on any of his children!

Twenty-four hours had passed since my last piece of dick but my shit was still drippin! Jesus Christ! This delayed-reactive drooling has GOT to stop! Don't my vagina know the fuckfest is over? When I got to work I could STILL feel Canei's sperm leaking through the panty-liner I stashed inside my thong! Methinks the nigger cums too much! I was aggravated and I felt that everybody could smell him on me! So I began to bark out the old faithful 'Not So-Fresh' bitches prayer-all ya'll know it:

'Oh great and mighty Goddess of blessed female hygiene...Please send a gentle breeze, fresh from your holy nostrils and purify my humming ass of ALL future and present impurities. And if at all possible-let this SMELL pass from me. Do not forsake thy child in need. And yea though I walk through the valley of vaginal insecurity, let not the whiff of a foul-fish emit from my lower anatomy! In Jesus name, Buddha-bless-Amen!'

A bitch NEEDS to know if the patients can smell through Down Syndromed nasal cavities the million drops of white 'goo' dripping down her legs! You know it's funny, every day I change the patients shitty diapers but it appeared to me that the time had come for someone to change mine!

By 9:00 A.M. I'd decided that tonight would be much better spent getting drunk at Honey's. My Supervisor, Ms. Barkley had red-lined me 45 minutes for being half an hour late. Old fat Bitch! Where do they get them people they carelessly hurl into Managerial positions? It should take more than a G.E.D. diploma and a bright red dress to qualify. There are times when a sister legitimately can't get to work on time! So for those instances a Superior with patience, diplomacy and understanding should take charge. A little bit of pity can't hurt either! Not when a bitch is recuperating from a five day revival meeting sponsored by Lord Satan and his unholy Congregation. And the smack down with Breanna this morning and loss of my hairbrush didn't enhance my punctuality much!

The title of my daily suffering is Developmental Assistant for the Handicapped-or D.A.H. I work with persons severely mentally retarded. When I had finished feeding the patients we began transporting them out to their Program Center in Scarsdale. That's where dozens of mentally challenged human beings undertake a daily dose of modified Hooked on Phonics. (for dummies) I don't mean DUMB dummies. Essentially the majority of the clients in the program have either severe Down Syndrome, Mongoloidism

46

or some other structural brain deformity resulting in mental retardatation. Some can't speak, walk, see or even control their bowel movement so you can imagine the type of shit I'm forced to deal with!

My heart breaks 8 days a week in the face of those poor souls suffering in silence. And I offer to them much more tolerance and respect than I do to many of the so-called normal assholes who supervise me on a daily basis! The Scarsdale Program Center is a daily exercise in futility. From Monday though Friday we attempt to teach minds that virtually cannot be taught! Various learning mechanisms are utilized such as coloring books, building blocks and numbered pegs. Three staff-members and one teacher are assigned to each classroom to oversee 9 'Clients' in their pursuit of menial learning.

This is nonsense! Time consuming BULLSHIT! But the State utilizes such foolishness as an unending pipeline to siphon inordinate modes of Federal Funding into their already bulging Bureaucratic coffers. You see, countless mega-bucks are allotted to the Program annually for each client. And the Program is sanctioned to accommodate three phases of the their Welfare: His or her Mental and physical Health, education and housing. They live in dorm-like settings in Scarsdale-each adorned with the basic amenities provided exclusively for their comfort.

They are provided with Cable T.V. although most of them can't understand what in the world is going on! The other half are entertained by cartoons in an enchanting way that only 8 year olds can relate to. Well Praise the Lord for a cunning manipulated N.Y. State implemented Program designed to provide an 'Education' for the mentally impaired and a paycheck for the 'Off The Book' dummies who care for them. You know, I'd bet my life that if there were a Nationwide I.Q. test between 2 teams: The officially mentally challenged patients and the 'Off The Book' dummies, those mongoloids would beat OUR score by a Landslide!

I've seen some virtual morons working as Grade-Nines in the persons of my co-workers. I mean Dummies! Now a 'Moron' is defined as an adult with an I.Q. of less than 60. And our patients are practically all defined as such. But if you were a stranger who errantly strayed into one of our Scarsdale Classrooms and witnessed the unbridled chaos unveiling before your eyes you probably couldn't figure out who the fuck was sick and who was sane!

You would see a bunch of people sitting at children's desks trying desperately to fit square blocks into round holes. They would bang and probe and manipulate the blocks wondering what in the Heaven's is preventing these square blocks from fitting their allotted round holes.

In fits of rage and frustration they would overturn the entire fucking kiddie-desks and hurl an oversized chunk of spit on top the mess they made. Grunting and screaming and barking out prayers and curses to their Omnipotent Gods at the circumstances that persecute their eruptive souls!

Also in the classrooms would be the uncouth chatter of a few ghetto figures sitting adjacent to the ones holding the square blocks. These characters are screaming unabashedly on cell-phones at their baby's daddies inquiring about the lack of essential funds she is forced to raise their 'Love Child' with!

"When was the last time you came to see your son? Motherfucker, don't yell at me! ...I'm saying though...Fuck that! Yeah, that's right! Kareem I'm taking your ASS to COURT! WHAT nigga? Oh no this retarded motherfucker DIDN'T turn over the fucking desk! Hey-STUPID! SIT yo retarded ass down! Don't get fucked-up in here! I ain't havin it today! Nah nigga, I ain't talking to YOU! I'm TALKIN to this retarded misfit whose about to catch a bad one!"

Now I know by now you're wondering: 'What the Hell is this? Retards retreat...or the Jerry Springer Show? You got some FOOL on one side, hostile like a son-of-a-bitch trying to fit a square block into a round hole! Then you got GHETTO-ASS LATISHA hookin off on her baby's daddy over the phone! She's broke as Hell and wants to 'con' the convict into giving her some loot to get her hair 'did!' So you ask the inevitable question. 'Uh-O.K. So which one of these irate imbeciles is supposed to be retarded?'

Well guess what? The truth is none of em are! These are the sane ones-the clowns put in charge to supervise the OTHER Mentally deficient! Their title is State-workers. AKA Developmental Assistants for the Handicapped.

The missing culprit-The 'Legal' retard is the subdued little inmate sitting on the floor beside these 2 'Off the Book' dummies defecating on himself and wondering how the fuck he wound up in this God-forsaken program with these psycho assholes screaming on cell-phones and throwing Square blocks and wooden desks around the room! This 'legal' retard can't understand the ability of so-called 'normal people' to be so fucking stupid! He is aware of his own bowel impairments. The retard also knows that the Square block can't fit into the round hole. It belongs in a square hole. He has also figured out that Latisha's scheme is to revive that dust mop sitting on top her ignorant head and more importantly that Kareem will never pay Child Support and is speedily on his way to prison as soon as his P.O. receives the results of the latest drug-test which he failed miserably!

But Mr. retard just sits there! He accepts the fact that his mental deficiencies won't allow him the same degree of normalcy that these 2 stark-raving mad lunatics take for granted! He is not smart or in rectal control enough to halt his bowel movements and the stench of his shitty diapers is embarrassing to him! But he IS intelligent enough to have realized that the cell-phone bickering and violent outburst of the OTHER 'dummy' throwing desks has afforded him a golden opportunity to escape and get the fuck outta 'Dodge!'

All he needs to do is inch his way past the blood-shot eyes of these pathetic staff-members toward the open classroom door, across the hall and down the stairs where the Harriet Tubman of the mentally disabled can catapult his weary soul to long awaited freedom! Oh yes, there IS an Underground Railroad for the mentally challenged as well! The Divine Courts of Affirmative Action have seen to that! Getting past the inefficient defenses of State-Workers unnoticed should not be too difficult because the third co-worker in the classroom is fast asleep in a corner in the back! Knocked the fuck out! So much for good Supervision! He had one 'Blunt' too many last night and won't be awake again till around dinner time! Like I said, this is a SHAME! A DISPLACED allotment of Government Funds that would be better spent ANYWHERE but here! But I need the money and if they shut it down I'd be thrown out of my apartment, starving to death in the cold City streets (like Jeppedo) and taking turns with my 14 year old daughter turning tricks for our daily bread! And you know the rules: 'AGE BEFORE BEAUTY!'

I do think however that the Developmental Center should be condemned and re-structured and the multitudes of 'Off The Book' dummies should be dispatched into mental institutions of their own! Let me and the 'Retards' work THEM for a change! Just hand us the keys, some Thorazine and plenty of Bandages! We'll call it 'The Simone Singleton 'HOME OF THE HAMMER!' I guarantee-Asses would be kicked, lessons would be learned and NIGGERS would act right!

Well I had seen and heard enough and decided to get my own ticket onto that Underground Railroad to freedom. Fuck it-I'd hang out with the 'retards' as long as it was NOT in that Hell-hole called the Scarsdale Developmental Center!

On the bus enroute to my appointed slaughterhouse I got on the horn and tried to call my girls-to plan my escape for the weekend! Kecia was down for anything-just to get that bastard of a boyfriend 'Marvin' off her mind! I had told the 'Crashdummy' to leave his ass alone the FIRST time he dogged her. You know its over when THREE different baby's momma's been callin your house looking for your man to come back over their cribs to finish what he started the day before yesterday.

The day before YESTURDAY? That nigga slept with somebody as recently as the day before yesterday? You know, the night he swore he was working a double and 'wouldn't be home!' And you still let THIS nigga back below your waistline to 'FUCK' you some more? Well, Kecia was livid! Too bad the crashdummy would be back in Marvin's car in less than a week suckin on him again! Reachin for the same penis he just pulled outta some other ghetto chickenhead! Oh-HE had a SUPER dick according to her. In fact the biggest dick in the world (I beg to differ) and wielded it like Conan the Barbarian after a few hits of Henney and a blunt!

Uh, right-giant tree-cock or not, I wouldn't have that shit! Tricks are for kids, an I'm all grown up now so take your lame-game over to a STUPID bitches house cuz I've earned my Masters in Mastering the Arts of dispelling illusions and taking out old stinky garbage! Hattie wasn't comin as long as Kim would be there. She had a prior engagement involving some hyperactive oral sex-giving some fag-head to an International Banker who had lived his alternate life in the closet!

But Kim cancelled cuz of some shit I couldn't understand. So Hattie reinvited herself. I still don't understand why those 2 didn't get along-something about the same Puerto Rican they were both doin at the same time! Or one month apart-at least that's what he told both of THEM! They had it out in the parking lot and the rest was history. I don't know why some women fight over a man-shit ain't that serious! Just sleep with him on alternate weekends and everybody is happy!

Mikki granted me a definite maybe. I didn't give a damn! I was still going if none of my girls showed up! If the sky fell and the world ended in one gigantic cosmic bang of desperate Assholes screaming futile unheard prayers, Doomsday and Armageddon both would find Simone Singleton defiantly clinging to a bar-stool with a drink in her hand at Honey's, waitin for a fine nigger to walk through the door and grant that one last wish! Heaven and Hell don't mean SHIT if there ain't no men over there! And if I hear there ain't, I'll KILL me a virile candidate and bring my own piece back WITH me!

Seventy-two hours later, on Saturday night-WE WENT WILD! Honey's was a place-THE PLACE in Wyandanch, Long Island where horny bitches gathered to flirt and fuck the night away! It was a singles bar for women disguised as a cocktail lounge. I felt at home an EVERYBODY knew why everybody else was there! They'd talk smug and sophisticated to one another using proper enunciation. High-class conversations where 'Ebonics' were not allowed! We had style and reserche. Exuding all the etiquette of white folk with high class and cultured elegance-right before the grinding promiscuous orgy of ripped panties, tossed semen, dripping sweat and howling orgasms! THIS IS WHAT HORNY BITCHES DO! And they ACT that way to soothe their tainted egos because EVERYBODY in the Universe knows that they brought those soggy thongs out there for the sole purpose of being sexually stabbed by the first male primate that walks into the crowded room!

On the way we got blasted in Kecia's S.U.V. Mikki never showed up so Hattie and I talked shit smoking weed in the back seat while she drained a fifth of Southern Comfort in the driver's seat! I told the drunk bitch to slow down. Comfy was MY drink and the 'ho' finished off my portion while I was in the back goofing off with Hattie!

"Bitch I told you to slow down!"

"I'm only doin 45, Monie!"

"I'm not talking about the speed bitch! You finished my drink! Now what the Hell am I gonna drink, huh?" I hate a lush! I despise a crashdummy! But a drunk crashdummy?"

Hattie interjected. "Don't worry, I got you girl! Pull over Kecia, I gotta take a piss. Monie-open up your mouth an hold still!"

"Yeah Simone…just drink some of what Hattie got-we can't stop!"

Me an Hattie looked at each other-STUNNED at what that dumb bitch just said! Here Hattie was offerin me a sumptuous hot glass of pee, and the crashdummy cosigned it!

"I don't drink piss Kecia!" She looked at me, then at Hattie-dazed and confused. There was an inbred lengthy synapse between the neurons in her brain which caused a fatal short-circuit within the vast network of her reality and reason. That's why I labeled her a crashdummy! She was STUPID! Too fuckin stupid for my patience to swallow, so I just sat quietly for the rest of the ride with my eyes closed wishing that she were dead!

The place was packed and Kecia was too toasted to fucking walk! I told Hattie to look out for her because for some strange reason, tonight I just couldn't take the brain-dead bitch. I mean I knew she was an idiot an I was used to it but THIS time I wanted to strap her crashdummy ass to a wooden chair and beat her to death! Problem solved! A good crashdummy is a DEAD Crashdummy! Furthermore babysitting was NOT my occupation so it was every man for himself and God for us all!

In less than ten minutes my eyes caught sight of a fine nigger at the Bar who looked like he had what it took! I went over to him and introduced myself but Hattie ran up on me with the 'Bitches Alarm' sirens blaring!

"No girl! Don't go out like that-he AIN'T the one!"

"Why not Hattie-YOU want him?" I asked. "Girl don't hate! You ain't cock-blockin...Hattie grabbed me by the collar like momma would yank the shit outta lil Becky when she's bout to catch a bad one-not wanting to finish the conversation in front of the nigger. As my two feet skidded across the polished wooden lounge floor he just stood there perplexed! Wondering what was up with US!

"Girl, I DID that last month, He ain't got no DICK! You know...two!"

"Huh! What the...? I was so intoxicated I couldn't understand what was normally obvious to me.

"Two...two...TWO BITCH, TWO!" Was Hattie throwing me the peace sign? Hattie made the hand sign of a wee-wee dick with her left thumb and pointer gesturing how small this nigger's manhood was!

"He got two inches girl! A rice-dick! You got your whole life ahead of you. Trust me-don't go out like that!"

It finally HIT me! "Two?"

"TWO," she whispered-then rolled her eyes.

"Girl you gotta be fucking kidding!"

Hattie stared at me with her hands on her hips shaking her head 'no.' YOU know how flagrant fags do when they want to make a point! Then she pointed to her genitals and made the 'cut-throat' symbol-easing her finger across her neck like a throat being sliced! That bitch is funny! I cracked up loud and hysterical and we hugged one another while everybody looked on, wondering what a fine bitch like me was doing hugging a 6 foot tall Rupaul looking homo like she was my mommy!

"OOooh girl you saved my LIFE! I would've been TIGHT!"

We laughed while the embarrassed hood slinked away cursing to himself cuz he had just been put on blast! She told me about how disappointed SHE was to find out about his penile deficiency on a very disappointing Thursday night at the Ingram Inn! About how frustrating it was trying to suck and ride a 'baby' dick that couldn't stay hard- and refused to grow! A DWARF-dick! With no talent!

"Girl, I had to 'do' MYSELF that night! After he got through I used a cucumber and it was BETTER than him! HONEEEY you ever ride a hot cucumber on a pillow? Just put that firm green veggie in the microwave. Three minutes is ALL you need cuz you don't want the shit goin LIMP on you! Over-cookin takes the backbone out of it. Then all you got is a bumpy green chunk of gel! But if you cook little smokey for THREE minutes-you got yourself a fake dick that cums hot pickle juice! Hey, a BITCH gotta be creative! Look what the fuck I had to WORK with! Mr. BABY DICK! I mounted that pillow and wedged that hot seething python between my legs and rode it for forty-five minutes-RIGHT IN FRONT OF MR. BABY DICK! The bastard must've thought I was crazy or gotten jealous cuz he dressed an ran out the God-damn door two minutes into the ride! Girl-the cucumber was BIGGER than HIM!"

"That's right you little dick motherfucker," I shouted behind him! "Look what the fuck you made me do! An take your STINK ass an your baby dick with you-you little FUCK! You sexual 'Premie!' God-damned BABY-DICK wanna be a man nigga! GROW UP BITCH! Grow A DICK!" He was probably down the block in a fuckin bar by then- thinkin about the fatal ramifications of those one-night stands-WITH BITCHES LIKE ME! The fag from Hell who TOLD him about hisself! Then he probably got on his adolescent little knees an prayed for some instant growth hormones, a liter of Viagra and a larger penis!"

"I never left the Hotel that night! Yeah, after pee-wee stormed outta there I rode that fake cucumber penis into the pickle-zone! Screamin like God HISSELF was fuckin me-an bustin nuts left an right! Vegetarian Nuts!"

Hattie had me in stiches! I could've died from some of the stuff that bitch talked about! The scenarios she created-but I was too drunk and horny to digest another fag story so I left her by the bar and got onto the dance floor!

In the Reggae room I was dancing with this thug nigger in a black fur coat. It was real! The shit cost money-I could see that even with mad drinks inside me. He had on burgundy 'Tims' and black jeans. He reminded me of my daddy in some strange way-Oh Lord, I know I must be sick if I'm in the Reggae room grinding with a thug who looks like my own father! Do I have some latent desire to sleep with my own pops! Some 'Electra' Complex hangover? (That's an Oedipus Complex in reverse relating to the story of a young boy's sexual attraction to his own biological mother studied intensely in Child Psychology) Oh my God! Grab the Rolodex and call my 'Shrink!' I think I might be having a paranormal episode! Well if THIS thug reminded me of daddy then dear old dad must have been a criminal cuz it was obvious to me that brother-man had done some time! He had that captive leer about him! That jailed-look!

And from the size of those arms it must've been around 10 years of HARD time! He resembled a pair of steel dumb-bells transformed into a man with a cute boyish grin on his face! His goatee was trimmed to the max. I complimented his barber and his mommy for those dark and sexy brown eyes and my insides was beggin me to find out what his DADDY had endowed him with! You know twitching vaginal walls won't take "NO" for an answer! So I invited Don Juan into the 'Ladies Room!'

He was down and in less than 3 minutes of pushing our way through the crowd-I WAS DOWN! On my knees (I TOLD you I was a whore) in front of yours truly trying to suck his nuts down my throat while doubly tantalized by his strong massive hands guiding the sexual paths of my head. His fingers pressed down into my hair-weave like they was related! Old friends! Like they were an erotic extension of one another. My scalp felt tingly sensations from his touch and I came on myself twice before he could bust his first nut!

I KNOW I am a horny bitch an when I'm drunk it's increased two-fold! I've been known to do a lot of sexual damage to my body when I'm 'on!' I'll do ANYTHING and with some strong alcohol tickling my clit I need more than just one! And my only regret was that I couldn't feel this nigger's strength between my legs!!!

He was takin too fuckin long! Somebody might come (before he did) an bust me in the stall on my knees! That shit wasn't happening-so I turned up the pressure! The big motherfucker had survived 'cruise-control' so I shifted gears on that ass! Now MOST niggers ejaculate off 'cruise-control!' They can't take the shit and cum all over the fuckin place off of that slow soft and warm circular motion of my mouth carefully stroking and teasing their penises! NOT those hard-headed niggers with them stubborn desensitized 'cocaine cocks!' Like they're numb or even paralyzed! Well I've seen their type too! An I got a special remedy for THAT KIND! So I put it on his CONVICT ass-Ain't no marathon in THIS Motherfucker!

"Cum you diesel bastard! CUM!"

Don Juan came! And I thought his SPLEEN had ruptured-IN MY MOUTH!! Thick gooey semen-all in my lungs and shit! His vise-like grip held my head in place an I was forced to either swallow-OR DIE! CHOKE to death over the white volcano that looked like it had traveled the long journey all the way from his dually incarcerated soul! I hoped in my inebriated head that he hadn't recently finished butt-fucking 'Twahn, the Prison fag' and just got out yesterday-wouldn't want to be suckin off the GRIMY proceeds of THAT shower-stall transaction! I know eatin outta a homo's ASS gotta be a filthy job and carries with it the sordid benefits of sexually transmitted diseases and anal parasites!

Well when the flood was finally over I attempted to spit out on the floor what I was lucky enough not to have swallowed! Damn! That black man had some JUICE in him! Some stale uninhibited shit that he shoulda gotten off his chest a long time before he met ME! Perhaps this was his FIRST piece of head! Good head! Or maybe a nigga acts like this when he touches a REAL bitch after 15 years of squirting inside some faggots! Oh-well, I perished the thought. I had came and it was time to wrap it up and brush my teeth!

Thug-life finally let go and my head snapped back-overjoyed to be released from the intense grasp of his fingers. I don't know! Either that jungle-like Terminator style grip or the lunging ramrod of his jammie sliding in and out of my mouth! I know it was one or two of those complimentary methods that made me cum! One of them would have to be repeated in the not so distant future cuz that was the best I ever came in the absence of an erection inside my body!

Thinking that our spontaneous bathroom antics were over, I smiled and decided in my mind to give hommie my home number! Forget a celly, THIS nigger could call the CRIB! And I wanted HIS number. I was feelin him. I guess drunkenness is a sin cuz baby I've seen better! Thug-life grabbed me by the neck and spun me around!

"What the fuck? Ain't you finished Playa?"

He bent me over in the bathroom stall-my head in the direct vicinity of the toilet.

"Hmm, uhh-I don't know playa! I ain't FEELIN this one!" The toilet was un-flushed and it stank.

"Yo, hold up!" I started to protest but he put his hand on my mouth and started to pull down my pants. Thank God for denim jeans. This nigger's STILL hard! Oh shit, I thought! And the door is locked!

I yelled at his dumb ass!

"Nah motherfucker-THAT'S IT!"

"SHUT THE FUCK UP," he shouted!

Maybe he thought I was uttering a "NO" that really meant "YES!" Like the shit that happens when a bitch tells her 'boo' to stop with her lips while her legs are wrapped around him in a "Nigger you BETTA not STOP if you know what's GOOD for you," kinda fashion! He thinks his sexual partner has turned into a five-foot tall Boa Constrictor with a BIG bubble-ass and a pony-tail whose sole purpose in life is to crush every drop of oxygen outta his lungs! And the mutating bitch STILL has the nerve to say "No-Stop!" That's one HELL of a 'Stop Sign' but THIS WASN'T that kinda party-I already got mine! And I was finished!!

So the nigger was cute-what the fuck, an I was horny! I was just gonna suck his dick till his gonads popped an call it a day! That satisfaction has never failed to arouse me. My orgasms are not restricted to the taste of a penis protruding from my lower quadrant and oral sex-giving or receiving has been known to take a bitch places where the Devil himself has never been! So I figured Thug-life would just play it cool! Relax, let me suck on it an cum on myself and we'd just call it EVEN! I was on my period and didn't intend to walk outta this bathroom looking like a 'Jason' stabbing victim! I STILL GOT SOME DANCING TO DO!

But NO! Some niggas are never satisfied! THAT'S why we call em 'NIGGERS!' And Mr. MAN thought he was getting a double-portion of some casual sex that was NOT

Something About A Woman

about to happen! Now JUST when a bitch thinks she's finished. That she'd get the proverbial pat on the head for another job well done-and a napkin, THIS BEAST grabs me and throws me up against the wall, my ASS in the air and his dick in his hand tryin to penetrate "the gooey!"

SHIT! It ain't MY PROBLEM your dick is still hard! Should've cum harder-concentrated, to make that shit go down! IT AIN'T MY FAULT! An NO you ain't getting no ASS cuz you don't know how the fuck to act!! Oh brother, now a bitch gotta fight! Sisters it's hard to fight the nigger who just came down your throat! Hard to put up your dukes for the lack of gravity and seriousness involved in the bathroom perversion you just partook of! Damn boo, I just SUCKED your dick! Why I gotta beat your Ass? Well I hoped I'd have time to wipe my mouth before I threw the first punch cuz a bitch wasn't getting RAPED!

Imagine the headlines: "HORNY GHETTO BITCH VOLUNTEERS TO SUCK THE DICK OF A STRANGER FOR FREE AND NO STRINGS ATTACHED (except my Tampon) AND GETS RAPED IN THE PROCESS!" How thought provoking-AND incriminating! Knowing them Media leeches, they'll throw some shit in the game! Make me Drug-Related!: "BLOODY CRACKHEAD ROBBED AND BUTT-FUCKED IN DRUG DEAL GONE BAD! DETAILS AT ELEVEN!" Well I got some NEWS for Geraldo! It ain't goin down like that!

I don't LIKE pain! So I put up my mental dukes and wiped that confused smile off my face! I knew the punches was comin and it's hard to bob and weave while your hands are pinned facing away and held up against the wall by thug-life an his ragin hormones! I didn't want to beat on this nigger but he was pissin me off! And you know, although he had me bent over a barrel, I knew with my boxing skills I had the upper hand!

Number one, he HAD to be a little weak from cuming. Blow-jobs have that effect on a man-ask all the niggas I've sucked the very LIFE from! Secondly he had no idea that this was NO ordinary 'you can kick my ass anytime you feel like it,' bitch! I hadn't lost one since 8 months ago. That consisted of 12 prize-fights-toe-to-toe with big Sasquach motherfuckers twice HIS size! And a bitches winning streak was not about to end-just ask Don King-and my LEFT-JAB!

Number three, the nigga was drunk! Too much Henney is a blip when you're tryin to maintain the middle-weight title! Will somebody PLEASE teach these thug-life cuties not to start fights when they can barely stand on their feet! And last but not least I could tell that this fool was nowhere near as strong as Canei-an I made Canei BLEED!

I pretended to convalesce to his demand for some ass and started to moan and groan like all of a sudden I needed that dick inside me real bad. I whispered to the uncompromising jailbird.

"You want me to suck it some more? You still hard? Let me do you again baby!" Stupid went for it and dropped his guard-and his head! He let me turn around and I decided to put my foot as far up his ass as I could! Then I played 'Pac-man!' I bit him on

55

the wrist with some slick shit Canei showed me. When a man got you down an he's much stronger than you, you twist your body just right an get the proper leverage so you can use his own weight against him! It worked like a charm! In seconds he was yellin like a bitch as my canines punctured his flesh and before he knew it I proceeded to kick the shit out of the back of his head! Prada boots-I love you!

I looked around for some paraphernalia to bang him over the head. 'Nada!' So I kept bashing his head in! Poundin my fuckin fist behind the back of his left ear-that shit makes a nigga dizzy! Mix it with some alcohol and he's fucked! I knew it wouldn't be long now. I said 12 and 0! With 10 Knock-outs-Sugar Ray, Kiss My Ass!!

Just as I was about to gloat to the highest degree of my femininity and talk some "yeah nigga-what now" shit, I heard Hattie screamin an knockin on the door. She had known where I was-who I was with and what was SUPPOSED to be happenin! Not me getting my ass-whippin on but she musta sensed trouble! A woman has 7 senses! And a fag-injected with enough female hormones to grow tits and a rippin derrier is close enough to that flavorful pie of womanhood to take a piece and qualify for the 7th Sense special!

So my girl knew! I turned around to go open the door. Figurin that either Hattie could help me finish beatin on him or rob the hostile bastard! But when I turned just for a split second, I SLIPPED! Damn! Fuck YOU Prada! I take back my compliment-I'll never wear these shoes in the ring again! Maybe it was some old piss on the floor or some sperm drops that might've leaked outta my mouth after the Free head and the "quiet storm!" But I was off balance and reelin. The nigger leaped to his feet with Spiderman tendencies-like he NEVER got his ass cracked by the boot heel! (You can never trust a 'CON' cuz you'll never know when he's fakin-playin possum!)

Thug-life football tackled me OFF my God-damned feet, THROUGH the pissy bathroom stall and up against and out of a door leading to an alleyway! 'Smash' went two bodies careening onto the hard unforgiving ground and 'Crack' went my back! And I KNEW my ASS was kicked! First of all, why in the world is there another door leading from the 'Ladies Room' to an alleyway? Who constructed that shit 'Pervs-R-Us?' So much for breaches of security! A bitch can't squat and take a dump without the local alleyway derelict clan sniffin the fumes! I revere my defecation fumes and choose to keep them to myself. So what the Hell is THIS about? Plus if I knew there was an alternate Exit, a secret entrance, a bitch could've saved thousands of dollars over the past 8 years in inordinate cover-charges! Well a bloody nose, a fractured spine and a lumped up scalp descended upon THAT fleeting inquiry all too fast! And suddenly Thug-life, this ungrateful fool whose dick I had just sucked, got up an started stompin me with his Tims and punching me like I was a man! I couldn't fight back-an for the first time in my life I panicked-and was terrified!

Now I ain't no PUSSY! I'll give UP some but don't chose to wear the passively docile mask of subservience commonly inherent in the female package! But this nigga was beatin my ASS! The punches was comin from everywhere and I couldn't keep up with the brutal frenzied sum of them. I tried to block some of the blows but I couldn't! My jaw felt like the white-boy in the movie who keeps getting punched in the face by Cagney but can't do a Damn thing about it! Like a crashdummy, before the slip I thought I was the SHIT! Beatin him in the head at will-but you know what they say, "Paybacks a bitch!"

I had fucked-up! I had had sex with a stranger that I'd just met-and now he wanted to RAPE ME! All of a sudden things weren't so funny! My nerves sneaked out foreshadowed lamentations of my daughter-left behind and attending the Funeral Service for a mother she thought would be back home to help her with her homework. I had JUST kissed her good-bye hours ago and realized I neglected to tell her that I love her.

I could not live in Peace! I could not die in peace-rest, knowing that I had left behind my little girl-the only thing that genuinely meant anything in this world to me. Bitterness and fear dispelled itself into the loathsome hate for this psycho bastard who was trying to overpower me! I had given myself to a criminal-minded Neanderthal in a fur coat! And when he could not have the total package he thought it best to begin trading punches with the opposite sex! Trying to dominate-to bully a woman who had done NOTHING to him! Who had done nothing wrong. That's what sadistic men do! He felt obliged to violate me-to take from me that which I did not feel he should have! And when I didn't give in he would leave my bloody demeaned and beaten body for dead on the pissy Ladies Bathroom floor! Robbing me of life-and separating me from the one who needs me!

The pain of his blows fell upon me as moistened terrified eyes cascaded tears down a face burning to be rescued from this beast motherfucker. Outraged cuz his hapless dinner was 'unready!' I couldn't fight him! Trapped on the floor between his legs I could slowly feel my strength, my consciousness slipping away from grasp like the gradual trickling of one holding sand pebbles as they willfully drop through the fingers toward an inevitably better place. I could no longer hear the banging on the door. Hattie, my best friend, had tried to get in and save me but the pounding thuds of her desperation were replaced by the swollen numbness of a woman being beaten by a monster who just moments ago might have been her other-half!

But God takes care of babies and fools! He protects the elderly-the handicapped-and frightened bloody bitches TOO! Before I knew it I saw Hattie comin up behind me. She couldn't get in the door and so had ran around the entire Club to get into the dark alleyway where I was! She KNEW about the back door! Why didn't the bitch tell me. (can't trust them fags!) That's my girl! Right on time-like the Lone Ranger!

"Is there a problem? Cuz I got you girl! Ah...OH! O.K! I see how THIS shit is going," she said as she pulled off her earrings! Thug-life was standin right over me as I lay on the floor-my hand on my bruised head! My girl was here now-I got cocky!

"Yo Hattie, I GOT this! This nigga ain't nothing," I exclaimed as I pulled myself off the floor while looking for what missing teeth I could find! I didn't 'have' SHIT! My nose was busted and my weave was lose. But this was only the ninth round! And I STILL had a shot!

"Bitch you bleedin-so be QUIET," Hattie demanded! "I'll KILL this bastard! COME ON!"

So what I took an 8 count! The bell hadn't rang and Michael Buffer had not yet got on the 'Mic.' Oh well, so much for a bitches overconfidence. Besides-all great fighters hit the canvass at least once in their careers. Cassius Clay, Sugar Ray, Whitney Houston, Tina Turner, FUCK-Rocky Balboa LIVED on the ropes! And Tommy 'The Hitman' Hearns slapped the SPIT outta Ray Leonard's mouth and nearly detached his retina until that fateful round when Sugar caught the wiry assassin, caved in his chest and jumped double-dutch on his grossly malnourished frame! From that moment on Tommy looked like a soft-boiled egg, a chicken-chested murder victim, an epileptic rubber-band that had been POPPED long ago stumbling through the ropes and trying to protect his nullified Afrocentric dome-piece from the zillion flurries of the man whom he'd JUST tried to kill! So who the Hell was I to upset the tainted image of over-the-hill Champs?

The drunk thug with an erection and a pretty good over-hand right threw his hulking hands up in the air shoutin! On some real Gangsta-shit!

"Yo! So wha's up, son? You fucking faggot! You gonna get a fucking faggot to fight for you? I'll fuck you UP son!"

Oh my Gosh-WHAT LANGUAGE!! Hattie just flung down her purse and ran at Thug-life like Marvelous Marvin Hagler on a rampage. The bitch was NICE! She was a natural! One, two! One, Two! Then she KICKED him in the stomach-BOW! Hattie beat the living dog shit outta him!

"That's right girl! You go Iron Mike! I told him not to COME at me like that! I was a far better Cheerleader than a Heavyweight contender.

I've never seen nothing like it before in my life! The bitch was ON! Transforming from Jet LI to Bruce Lee-to Muhammed Ali! Oh SHIT my Bitch was NICE! Have you ever seen a VICIOUS thug-being chased down an alley by a tall lanky be-weaved cross-dresser with a banging left-hook? 'Inside Edition' would've made a fucking killing! Thug-life ran so fast he lost his left burgundy Tim boot somewhere between the opening bell and the 100 yard dash to the dumpster!

"Hey grimy-shoulda chose a weaker bitch to harrass-you fuckin RAPIST! Call me TOMORROW boo-when the SWELLING goes down-CHUMP!"

I know God was on my side that night-and HE along with a good dentist and some make-up would make it all right! I treated Hattie to anything she wanted for the rest of the night! She worked hard-fought like TYSON, and deserved it. My strepid clutch-hitter passed the fuck out in some niggers lap after the 9th Long Island Iced Tea! And I took her home. It was like the good old days-but THIS time I was almost RAPED, and Hattie was there for me! And there was NOTHING I wouldn't do for her!

I'M LOCKED UP...!

I've always been very arrogant! I've often thought about death!! That if I had gotten into a physical confrontation with a man and lost I'd be too defiant and aloof to realize it. So there I'd lay-beaten to death, despite the fact that I wasn't breathing, and oblivious to the knowledge that my heart was no longer beating, I'd be still swinging away! Going for the throat! Trying to save my life-the life I had already lost 10 minutes ago! The Gate-Keepers of Heaven would have to drag me outta the ring, kicking and screaming. "Lay down bitch! YOU DEAD!! DUH? Haven't you noticed?"

"Oops-MY BAD!! OH MY FREAKIN GOD!! Ain't THAT a BITCH!! No That motherfucker DIDN'T kill me! That's it, it's ON now! Please buddy, just let me finish this round before I go!" I'd be so irate I wouldn't have noticed that I'd been Flat-lined!!

Life went on and I vowed to MURDER that criminal ON SITE! Nobody beats my ass and gets away with it! I don't make for good locker-room chatter! I wasn't designed like that! You will NOT be laughing and bragging to your BOYS about how you beat THIS bitch!

"Yo son, I had to SLAP that 'Ho' son! Know what um sayin?" And if you utter my name it will be through BLOODY gumbs and missing teeth that you inaudibly manage to gurgle out "Simone!" Or perhaps if it really got ugly you get to sit quietly and spell out the fatal sum of your foul ways. Retelling the gory tale about how this big assed Long Island bitch from 'THE BROOK' you THOUGHT was A 'Herb' sliced your nuts off an fed em to you-RIGHT before she stabbed you in the heart and left you for dead! Tell the story right playboy! No since lying during your testimony in the Appellate Courts of the DEAD! Yeah-tell your side of the beef to the Grim Reaper and see if he'll change his mind and bring you back from the grave!

So Thug-life would be dead-if he dared to show his incarcerable face at Honey's again! Both Canei AND the bouncers would SEE to it cuz I put the word out on that ASS! They would break that bitches back! Snap his spine and bend him up like a pretzel! Then force him to suck his OWN penis! 'Hope you're a contortionist playa! Oh you want some head THAT bad? SUCK YOUR OWN DICK!' Thug-life would be easy to identify. He'd be the one hunched over in a forward position like Quazimodo! With his own musty nuts and PENIS in his mouth! Well I too learned a valuable lesson: No more bathroom Butt-fucks, Monie! Cuz depraved bitches like HIM sent me into early retirement! I'm GROWN so I shoulda known better! I just wish I could take back my Blowjob!

The next night I decided to 'sit this one out!' Stay outta the Club and let the swelling of my whelped-up forehead go down. Mikki, Kecia, Canei and myself got together for a 'Feast of Buddha' and a Spade game. We all met at my house and it was my turn to 'Cop' the weed. I hate coppin-especially in Long Island cuz it's 'Mighty

Whitey' land and plain Clothes Detectives are just as common as roaches. Just when you think it's safe to turn off the lights-THEY COME OUT! Sirens blaring and niggas baffled and confused trying to discard the unlawful bag of contraband they just bought from a rookie undercover with insatiable Executive aspirations and an itchy trigger finger!

"Oh Lord-they got me! I never smelled 'Po-po' on this unknown local drug-dealer but I shoulda known cuz it's too quiet around the area where he's hustling-plus nobody's buyin." Cops are STUPID! They very naively created a tranquil scenario with Hobo props an all to lure prospective buyers into a false sense of serenity. You find yourself engaged in an illicit weed deal in an environment similar to the Garden of Eden. If you are fooled into looking around and seeing nothing and gullibly believing that the coast is clear-THEY GOT YOU!

"Oh hum-de-hum-hum!" Little Ms. Ghetto bitch drives up to a secluded area. Fresh out the Long Island projects trying to cop some weed.You know, the stuff to amplify the orgasm after she finishes suckin her boyfriend's pecker and decides to 'hop on' after he cums. The spot is vacant. Empty! Nobody's around-not even the mice. (They've already been tipped off and have wisely chosen to go buy their drugs elsewhere) So Mr. Joe Peddler is on the prowl-on the case. And he's green as a snot-rag! He's the clean-cut mulatto, with a College Education but still needs 'Hooked On Phonics' in the ghetto street skills of deceptive blending into a crowd. And he sticks out like a pig-IN A BLANKET.

So Joe-Peddler is hustling. Dealing! And there is a local bum-an alleged derelict standing-by, with a two-way Police Radio under his long smelly gray tattered overcoat that he thinks no one will notice, Now just as soon as Ms. Ghetto checks the menu, puts in her order and brandishes the loot-it's curtains! There will be no fucking TONIGHT! Boyfriend's dick won't be sucked-at LEAST not by her. He'll have to settle for a 'Jump-off!' Ms. Ghetto has probably seen her last orgasm for a while! There will be time-served in jail. Joe Peddler will most likely earn that shiny Gold Badge that has eluded him for years and 'The Fat Lady' is singing-LIKE KELLY PRICE!

Well it was my turn at bat and I had to make sure not to become Ms. Ghetto. I had to remain for all intents and purposes calm, high and out of Jail. I never 'Cop' at unknown spots cuz there's a Science to the streets. And I was always good at 'Logic,' 'Chemistry' and 'Ballistics!'

Canei drove me to my boy Pappo's spot in Brentwood. He worked out of the back of a Dry Cleaners and made more money than the owners. There's more profits in getting high than cleanin lipstick from Executive collars. Mikki waited in the front seat with Canei-nervous as a Pedophile in a kiddie pool for boys. She was arguing with him from the time they got in the car when they picked me up. I couldn't figure out what the fuck was up with those two cuz they bickered like Martin and Pam from the Martin Lawrence Show! They're ALWAYS goin at it! Constantly! He's forever trying to 'diss' her and she's always telling me to leave his ass alone.

There are times when ones mutual friends don't get along. It's like some anti-magnetic opposition keeps them sparring like cats and dogs through the obligatory neutral stance of your conjoined domestic life! Well I had a fucking headache and my 'habit' was bangin from the need of some fresh potent seedless cannabis to stave off the recurrent anguish of my fucked up day to day life.

"A bitch needs a hit so will you two SHUT UP? Hey Lucy and Ricky, I'm talking to you," I scowled from the back seat! They just ignored me-Mikki sticking her opinionated judgemental finger in Canei's face and Canei in return offering some pragmatic four letter word inferences about her sexuality. JESUS, I felt like the dazed 6 year old in the midst of their parent's daily verbal joust. The child is innocent, afraid, neglected, ignored and caught in the middle. The only way for him or her to wrestle one single fragment of their divided attention would be to slip into a COMA, have a massive stroke or go into cardiac arrest. Ultimately the rank scent of Junior's howling undies would reach out towards the front seat as the life begins to ebb from his unripe body!

"MOM, DAD, LOOK AT ME NOW! I'VE DIED AND WENT TO HEAVEN!"

"That's NICE dear-now keep quiet! YOUR FATHER AND I ARE TALKING!"

Pappo was a Dominican with a slender narrow head-like he was born with his head trapped in a vice or wore some undersized ultra strength titanium earmuffs every day of his drug dealin life. I think that one day God, mortified and embarrassed by the grand design that he fucked up and repulsed at this horrific clone of himself, raised up his wrath and decided to pop Pappo's head like a pimple!

He lifted two gargantuan hands and squeezed from ear to ear crushing the living shit out of the objectionable Dominican skull. Brain strained and cranium burst, the traumatized Latino expelled the dark gray matter residue of himself! Then God, satisfied with the cruelty of his deeds, spun around his hulking Celestial frame and trod away leaving Pappo, the repugnant mortal laying in a pile of his own meningial excrement.

Well narrow head or NOT, Pappo was on the money! And 'Legit!' I got outta the car amidst the counterproductive babbling from 'The Odd Couple' and rushed into the cleaners so that Pappo the 'Slender-headed' could help me get my lungs dirty. He was waitin inside and approached me with a hardy hug. He was consistent-always the same and I liked him for that. Armed with gut-wrenching halitosis (like he'd just drank the water in a fish Tank) and an eye-boogey in the corner-pocket! He gladly took the 30 bucks, sharply about-faced AND WAS GONE! I was outta there in three minutes flat and we sped off like Batman in pursuit of the Joker-on the day that Gotham City mysteriously burned down!

"I got 6 bags," I sighed proudly!

"Shit, we only NEED three," said Mikki!

"Fuck you," I exclaimed! "The next time you wanna ration the shit, take your tired ass to the spot! Remember, you skipped last time bitch," I scolded Mikki! Somebody else had to cop on her turn cuz she was too SHOOK!

"The bitch is STUPID like that Mone! Later for her-we goin home," Canei added!

It was a good night. We smoked and drank and played Spades until God came down and took my 'Laced' spirit back home on that Sweet Chariot Swinging Low into a long blissful comatose sleep! I dreamt of Canei and Mik. Probably because of their front seat cock-fight. In the dream Mikki had cut off his fucking head and dropped it off at my job saying, "Look bitch, I did it for you! Check out his tired ass now-I did that shit for you!"

What in the world was THAT about? I guess Henney and weed do that to the human mind. You know-concocting some 'Friday The 13th' Jason scenario to free itself from the dire stress you yourself are not capable of being delivered from. At about 5:15 A.M. I woke up-looking for signs of life in the house besides me. Had they murdered each other? And if so, what did Crashdummy do about it? At least she could've woke me up-before the atrocity scene! Bloodbaths are illegal and should be reported promptly to the local authorities. So since Crashdummies are not mentally equipped to make 911 calls, it behove me to be conscious to do it!

I went into the Kitchen and the Livingroom figuring the spattered drops of blood would lead me to my late boyfriends severed head. I thought Canei would look GOOD decapitated! But I'd still have to avenge him. Take Mikki's life to pay homage to all that good dick she would've cost me. Nobody fucks like Canei Williams! Nobody! So if that bitch decapitated him and Crashdummy just stood by, shocked and stupid, then they were both complicit-and had to DIE! My slashing Ox and love-starvation would see to it that justice, however brutal, was served!

I found Canei and Mik both laying on the sofa-bed out cold! Mikki was wrapped in a sheet and Canei had his boxers on. Now just look at these two! Much as they argue they STILL find some quiet time to sleep together. I laughed to myself-amused that the cat and mouse duo took one moment of their combative lives to rest in peace! I bet if Canei knew he was sleep down the foot from the bitch from Hell he'd throw up! And if Mikki opened her bloodshot eyes and saw HIM she would chicken-scratch a suicide note and hang herself in the bathroom! Dying and going to Hell to beg forgiveness for a crime she didn't commit!

When they woke up neither of them could remember what happened the night before. Mikki asked about Kecia's whereabouts but I told her that only God knows! "Perhaps she's enroute to the Annual Intergalactic Crashdummy Convention in order to renew her vows and her quest toward 100% Crashdummyhood! Dumb Bitch!"

After breakfast I made Canei drive Mikki home to Hempstead. He protested at first but I promised him a 'Scooby-Snack' (butt-fuck) at his speedy return so he acquiesced. That day I spent 6 hours of pure Heaven on Earth! Watching videos, drinking and fucking my man! At around 8:00 P.M. I called Bre and told her I'd get her the next day from my parent's house. Besides, it was my day off and I wanted to enjoy it.To put aside the 'mommy' role-something I rarely do! We agreed on Chinese and Canei stopped off by

Pappo's to get some more of what we started last night! Weed makes some GOOD 'Brain' feel even better! And when Canei placed his lips between my legs, my heart stopped-and the New Years Eve Ball dropped! From 10 to 1-the count-down to my cum heightened itself with each puff-clinging onto the heated throbbing spasms of my vaginal third-eye!!

AT 7:00 P.M. World War III started-between me and the yellow bitch from Hell who called herself tryin to 'get fly' at the Golden Wok Chinese Restaurant!

"NO, I said Shrimp Egg Foo-young and Chicken fried rice-NOT Chicken Egg Foo…Oh 'Lord-o-mercy' Canei! The bitch got it backwards!!"

"No, YOU TELL IT ME! YOU TELL IT ME," said the Chinese Junior High-school drop out chick behind the counter! Canei started to shout like he ain't had no sense. (just like he always does) He reminded me of Fred Flintstone-the 2005 'hood' version! And his 'YABBA-DABBA-DOO' was in full effect! Minus the High-School Diploma! You ever see an ignorant thug who can't express himself-so he screams thinking the loud crashing volume of his big mouth will make up for his lack of a decent vocabulary? Anyhow I pulled out my own 'tongue-gun' and emptied both barrels!

"LOOK you God-damn rice-eatin Chinese piece of SHIT! I TOLD your Atom-Bomb fleeing Vietcong ASS…"

"NO! You lookie! You MOTHER!"

Every righteous Psalm ever told me ran for cover-then abandoned my once peaceful state of mind in an instantaneous fit of hate!

"No that bitch DIDN'T say "MY MOTHER?"

I was livid! The dumb bitch behind the Chinese counter had said the WRONG thing! And I blanked the fuck out! If she had told me to suck her Oriental Dick, I would have understood, and been less offended. But the 'MOTHER' shit was something I had never truly learned to deal with. Especially due to my adoptive circumstances. Therefore she must've liked the taste of her toes cuz she definitely put her foot in her mouth! And I felt destined and compelled to put MY FOOT RIGHT between her slanty eyes!

I ran outside for a bottle, having a loud and obscene conversation with myself!

"Oh know she didn't! Bitch don't you know-I will HURT you? Just stay your FLAT YELLOW ASS right there!" I grabbed two cuz there was no way I was leavin outta there without wrapping the chinky-eyed bitches large intestines around her skeletal throat or beatin her to death with it! I NEEDED to feel her blood in my hand! You see, there was a pressurized twinge exerting itself right in the back of my skull! I could FEEL it-like a God-damned nest of maggots gnawing on my brain! Corroding my lost calm. Swearing never to stop until I killed this Chinese whore who had just spoken ill of my biological mother! HOW DARE THOSE FUCKERS TRAVELS 5000 MILES FROM NO-MAN'S LAND TO COME OVER HERE AND LOOK DOWN ON US?

"Yo Canei, how the fuck this bitch gonna talk about my mother? She don't even KNOW my moms!" (Christ! I didn't even know the woman either-but that was besides the point) There I was, disobeying the Cardinal rule of 'Gangsta anonymity!' I was callin out Canei's name for any wannabe investigative witness with a perked ear who could 'Go tell it on the Mountain' as to what me an Canei was about to get into. And WHO we were! That's why they never 'bring da DAMES with dem on Bank robberies or bloody shootouts!' Chics talk too much and will have you serving triple-life sentences all cuz of them loose-lips! You never hear Bogie or Cagney shouting each other out on a first name basis-spillin incriminating info like name, address and occupation while brandishing their respective Gatlin-guns at the bi-weekly First National Bank heist!

"Hey Cagney, smile for the camera whilst I empty the sacred vaults!"

"O.K. Bogie, just be sure to count the loot out properly this time. Cuz on the last caper you shorted me about Fifty-Grand, 'YOU DIRTY WAT!!'"

"Canei," (there I went again) "somebody's gonna DIE tonight," I shouted, lunging toward a barricaded bulletproof plexi-glass marble counter! It was like a desperate punified native with a grudge, attacking the Great White evil Sherman Tank that bombarded his village with European bullets of imperialism! The little scurrying rascal does not want to be crushed to death but he halts those fears in vindicative fervor-JUST to get a chance to hurl the single rock of liberation against the impenetrable breastplated steel mechanism careening towards him!

Well FUCK that! I've always been taught to root for the underdog! Canei ran toward me to stop the 'broken-bottle bitch' from ruining tonight's meal! I SAW the stupid nigger coming and dodged him the fuck out! He fell forward grabbing a major chunk of the wall and knocking down a huge glass picture! You know, the tranquil Oriental Buddha pond scene common in restaurants? Well poor pudgy Buddha musta thought it was Pearl Harbor-or 'D-day' all over again!

'SMASH!' Oops! "GOOD for em! That one musta cost a bundle-nice job, Canei! You murdered a glass picture," I shouted as the other more composed patrons looked on in horror-expelling the proverbial "OH SHIT!" often uttered by the dumbfounded!

I took broken bottle number one and SMASHED it up against the counter-perhaps hoping a vigorous burst of Godly power would overcome and guide my faulty aim and smash through the barrier forceful and accurate enough to take off that gremlins head!

'KAPLOWIE,' went the millions of glass beads in all directions towards the scattering customers.

Oops again! "SORRY FOLKS! Just move out the way!" Canei, half plastered into the wall, attempted one last desperate swipe at me but I 'shook him outta his shoes' the way Michael Jordan built a career on doin to John Starks! When HE 'Bobbed,' ME 'Weaved' and I threw the other bottle! Like a fuckin GHETTO Shotputter!

That didn't work! The yellow bitch STILL lived! She wouldn't die! I felt as though she were a tiny Sapphire-tinted Asian hobgoblin! A slanty-eyed demon! Mocking me! Leering and snickering at my bad aim. And I would KILL-annihilate the bitch for making fun of my struggling! But the unbreachable wall stood firm, resistant and unfazed. And behind it was my cackling enemy-cursing my black ass out in Cantonese! Damn! I decided I needed more artillery! Some heavier equipment to herald the long awaited moment that I would decapitate Ms.Chin, stuff her disgusting head into a plastic shopping bag and beat it up against the traffic light outside! Then I'd grab Canei's dumb ass and speed off before the authorities arrived!

The second time around when the last hurled bottle hit there was an elderly man still standing adjacent to the counter. Before I knew it the motherfucker was grabbin his head. Oh shit! I TOLD his stupid ASS to move! The yellow bitch (that's what I'll call her for now on) was running toward the back of the kitchen screaming!

There was a mournful ceremony of public sentiment for 'Pops, the beaned wonder' Who must've tasted and swallowed a solid blast of ricocheting glass flakes from my last barrage!

"You stupid old SHIT," I shouted! "I TOLD your wrinkled ass to move!" Pops never said a word-probably didn't even hear me! He just stood there holding his bleeding scalp! Never bring an old-timer to a broken-bottle fight! Another younger man jumped up outta nowhere. He scared the SHIT outta me cuz I never saw him coming! The phantom-like dwarf 'mushed' me in the face with his fingers and started shoutin at me like I was HIS son!

The adolescent looked...I don't know-FOURTEEN!

"Yo bitch, I outta break yo fuckin ASS! You fuckin hurt my Grandfather!"

Oh boy! Who told Dennis the Menace he could fight? Break MY ass? He couldn't break WIND! But I could see his point. And a tiny portion of my rage empathized with the poor traumatized adolescent. Too bad empathy is not the primal order of the day in a War-Zone! Suddenly my brain switched into auto-pilot and I smacked the GRITS outta the Gingerbread boy!

"POW!" It was a Home run-NO, a Grand Slam! Bases empty and the fastball STILL soaring past the bleachers and outta the park! But before I could rejoice and begin my victorious trot around the bases THE JUVENILE BASTARD WAS ON ME! When I had smacked him he'd just stood there-unfazed! Mighty Joe young didn't even FLINCH!

As we tussled, while the baby-faced-killer from the Projects was headlocking my weave outta my head, a flashing news report popped into my head! It was a blatant public scolding! In essence, it read:

'Hey-DUMMY, whenever you decide to 'Snuff' somebody you never haul off with a slap-an open palm tactic!' That weak maneuver don't even work on BITCHES these days cuz if your fightin a female who can scrap an you come out with that punk shit she will rip your fuckin head off, shit down your neck and use your face to wipe her ass when she's done shittin! And you'll deserve it! Especially these women today! No you gotta come good-throw your best punch from jump-street! And when that haymaker hits home, the rest of the war is yours! THAT'S when you can try all that fly experimental boxing-cuz she's already too fucked up to move! OR retaliate!'

Well kiss my ASS-why couldn't I get that news flash 5 seconds ago before Junior Mafia wrapped his mighty pythons around my collapsed windpipe! Damn! Now I Know I shoulda PUNCHED the juvenile bastard first!

He had me for a minute there but as I gasped for air Canei came outta nowhere (probably from the other side of the wall) and grabbed that little Buckwheat like he was Spanky from the Little Rascals!

"Yo motherfucker...!" 'Swoop!' That's all I heard. Next thing you know Spanky was jerked outta the picture! Canei kicked him out of the restaurant and proceeded to beatin him! Like a SLAVE-like a disobedient slave who had just made the fatal mistake of sassing 'Massuh!' In front of COMPANY!

"Oh naw Massuh! I ain't FEELS like pickin no cotton taday! It's SUNDAY Massuh! An my back is 'Huttin!" Niggers in chains don't talk shit when surrounded by a league of white Supremacists at the Southern Segregations Annual Thanksgiving Day Ball! Not when they wanna live to see Sun-up!

Well 'Massuh' had some SHIT for 'Kunta Kente's little work-stoppage campaign-it was time to stomp the rebellion at once-and restore ethnic servitude-and bountiful peace! 'Massuh,' Aka Canei, tried to transform the radical peons head into a stuffed wall-ornament! You know-like the dead petrified Stag-head or Bear-rug you might find on them white Good-Ole-Boys Plantations? A hunter's pride-Canei's pride! Vulgarly displayed for all the little wannabe thugs whose expectations out-weighed there limited potentials!

SOMETHING! I don't know what, told me to turn around. I'm glad I did cuz it was instinct. Natural! There was no sound-no warning! Just a vibe! When I turned I ducked away just in time to avoid the bone-crushing swing of a bat.

"SWOOSH!" OH MY GOD! IT WAS ON!

There were FOUR pint-sized Ninjas trying to take my head off! Two went after Canei from behind. I knew he could not see them for the necessary concentration required in stomping on his underaged victim! The other 2 lunged at me. Oh boy-who the Hell invited Bruce Lee? I know I can't 'whup' Bruce! Steven Segal maybe. But Bruce-No fuckin way! He's the one that made minced-meat outta Kareem Abdul Jabbar in that movie 'Game Of Death!' So if a bitch couldn't even hold her own with Jabbar, how in the world is she gonna be able to defend herself against Jabbar's Executioner?

They surrounded me an I got scared cuz I wasn't ready for all those flyin kicks an shit! Shootin joints is one thing-but when a yellow ninja nigga is tryin to surgically implant all 10 of his toes up your ass-in fast motion...well that's another animal quite all together! I could smell the eminent stinky odor of defeat.

One little guy had two sharp looking metal weapons in his hand-swingin them in 'Slow mo!' Didn't I see this scenario before in a kung-fu flick cuz if I DID, I remember the black bitch dies! The other guy, his irate partner, was singin the 'Hai-yah' song and kept faking headshots at me with the bat!

67

It's an incredible feeling to get pummeled with a Loiisville Slugger! Pulverized! Massacred! Beaten beyond recognition! Especially by Jet Li's 2 son's-Chin and Lin! Reality began to crawl back into the picture! I knew I had brought this on myself. This was supposed to be Egg-Drop Soup and Butt-fuck night-with a side of Chicken wings and a forty! Instead I had lost my fucking mind and attacked the DREADED MING DYNASTY! As if THAT weren't enough I had menaced and recklessly injured the Senior Citizen of the year and the God's of Rheumatism and Loss bowel control were pissed off! THIS was what I got for beaning Grandpa and it served me right! What did I decide to do, when tensions ran high-and friends were few? Of course! I got down on my spiritual penitent knees-AND BEGGED FORGIVENESS!

"Uh-it looks like I fucked-up! Again! Third time this week! Look Lord, I never planned to launch a crime-spree against poor Fred Sanford!! Um…sorry God! Didn't mean to hurt the old geezer-you know that! A sister just wanted a little peace and quiet! AND Egg-foo yong! Um…will you spare me? I know I don't deserve it-Hell nobody's perfect! Er…I SAID SORRY! An besides, Grandpa ain't dead-YET! I mean SHIT! It was just a few dozen razor sharp pieces of glass! That's nuthin he can't handle. A good First Aid Kit and some Hail Mary's and he'll be good as gold! So please don't let these Ninja Mutant Turtles do me in! Er, uh…in Jesus name-Amen!"

Moments before death I glanced outside and saw my man Canei handling his business. How come the UNARMED Chinese assassins went after HIM and the ones with weapons came for me? The 2 assholes were trying to wrestle him down! Uh, maybe it's me, but WHY would you try to Sumo-wrestle with the Incredible Hulk? The nigger is over 300 pounds! Duh! Do they MAKE Chinese people THAT stupid? Well, I had no time to contemplate the logistics of Asiatic bafoonery! I had my own problems. So if they wanted to try and bear-hug a black brother who weighed more than both of them combined then THAT was on them!

I reached into my purse-like I had something! Something small and metallic but had a big bang-all I had was 20 dollars, a couple of Tampons and some stolen gauze pads Hattie gave me for my wounds from the LAST bout! Then I went into Acting School!

"Oh, you want some? I'll shoot you in your fucking head! Jump motherfucker! What? WHAT?" I stood screaming and bluffing! It sounded real! I even made MYSELF nervous and started to believe I really HAD a gun! Everybody in the restaurant musta believed it too cuz the minute I reached, the whole spot cleared out! They were initially entertained. Enthused to see the Chinese vs. Nigger race war-filled with machetes and thugs and stupid bitches that start fights they can't win! But as soon as old 'Roscoe' threatens to pop his stainless-steel head out, the curtains close and it's time for bed! Why die during a virtual reality ghetto street-fight!

Even 'Pappa bean' ran his aged ass for cover! The bitch behind the counter started to scream. Uh-Oh! Who she gonna call NOW? The bluff went well. But there was a small problem. I don't think my two assailants spoke a lick of English cuz although the place emptied out in a hot second, they didn't get it. They must've missed 'Boy's In The Hood!' They just kept comin! Kept tauntin me! Well the yellow bitch surely got it cuz just then she shouted something in her bullshit language-somethin about the contents of my purse!

I didn't know what to do. I was real real scared! Who wants to die on the bloodsoaked steps of 'Golden Wok Chinese Restaurant?' Talk about 'Take-out' orders! Shit! I decided to try an rush one of em. Might as well go out with a bang. Never give up your life-make em TAKE IT! That's what daddy taught me. So I'd try an fight my way outta there! It was cramped up! I was alone with these two bastards and there wasn't much room to elude two machetes AND A BAT! So I had to decrease the odds by utilizing the process of elimination. ONE of these assholes was about to GET GOT! Uh-well maybe the one with the machetes! Then again if I missed-they both got me. One hits a Homerun and the OTHER dices and serves me to the customers!

I didn't have the luxury of time to chose my poison. So I football charged the guy with the bat! HE was closest to the door. To my safety-so it was HIS ass that was grass! To Hell with 'Eeny-Meeny-Miney and Moe!' And if I MISSED-then I MISSED!

But he never expected it! And when I HIT the 90 pound cheese doodle, he lost his 'Hi-yah' and started screamin louder than me! In seconds he and I were squirming like two Amateur Wrestlers outside the establishment. I WAS OUTSIDE! This LUCKY and stupid shrimp Egg-foo yong bitch had actually made it outside! ALIVE! The good-guys don't always win but I'm HAPPY to say that Bruce Lee was a CHUMP! Straight outta Punk-City! Some back-up unit HE turned out to be! I had taken his temperature and he came up COLD! The so-called Mongolian Warlord with a cast-iron baseball bat and a cotton heart continued screamin like a little girl-like his beloved inexpendible Oriental ass was at stake-and on FIRE! Baseball bat in hand! (I guess he wasn't ready to take that fatal trip to Lord Buddha's house atop the heavenly gigantic Lotus-flower in the sky) Ghengis Khan would've turned over in his grave or leaped out from it at the chance to hurl a well-placed flaming poisonous arrow into the cheap heart of this shameless disgrace to Mongolian pride!

Expectant of a good old-fashioned lynching, my opponent was stunned! Betrayed by that fleeting dream of the attack of the Huns!! He hadn't calculated the retaliation of the nigger Bitch! So HE bitched up! Who said that a cowardly swordsman could take out a nigga with an attitude? An his BOY, the invincible machete man, ran like HELL when he saw his 'Homie' hit the deck with project-girl on top of him-swingin like Babe Ruth! What a CREW! The Buddhist Temple will shit blood when they hear about THESE guys! GOOD! LET EM SHIT! Meanwhile I can plan my escape-and STAY ALIVE! The plan was simple: regain my footing, grab Canei and drive the Hell away!

Rocky Junior was STILL on the floor-Canei had knocked him out COLD! Perhaps 'Webster' shoulda minded his own God-damned business and let Papa fight his OWN prehistoric battles! All of a sudden we all heard a familiar sound. It was the blaring noise that reoccurs whenever some nigger-shit gets outta hand.

"Don't MOVE! DON'T FUCKING MOVE! Put your hands up!"

Uh-oh! The yellow bitch musta called 'PO-PO!' They dragged our asses into 2 Squad-cars-Mutant Ninja Turtles, myself and Canei! EVERYBODY went-but the yellow bitch! She flew back inside on the phone-perhaps trying to recruit a new Ginsu-man and a short-order-cook! Sirens blared and off to Grandma's house WE WENT!

All that for some Egg-foo yong! AND I STILL DIDN'T EAT! They treated us with scorn! Menaces to society! Sporting the pessimistic attitude of the stereotypical bigot! 'You better make room Billy-bob. Get 2 sturdy non-ventillated cells ready-the NIGGERS been at it again!' I mean these Cops was on some REAL 911 heightened security type 'Anti-terrorist' shit! You'd think I was Public Enemy Number one! 'Bin Laden!' And my co-defendant Saddam Hussein and I had just planted C-4 and some 'Weapons of Mass Destruction' up President Bush's Texas ASS!

Why would a Cop, WITH A GUN, find it necessary to keep close guard on a bitch in leg-irons and handcuffed to a metal bench? BEHIND BARS? Where the fuck can I go? I ain't Houdini! I can't even scratch MY ASS right! How could I pose a threat? They gave Canei the same treatment. Well he was a male-a 300 pound male and looked like he had just KILLED somebody! He was silent, enraged and immovable. And that mean-as Hell LOOK! You'd think if you cut open his stomach you'd find the bones of about 100 white folks who died bloody horrible deaths during the Nat Turner slave rebellion! HACK HACK, CHOP CHOP went the Axe of the disgruntled Black man who woke up one day and decided to kill WHITEY! Prepaid extermination can reek havoc on the collective white psyche you know!

We were fingerprinted and then placed into a holding cell to await arraignment. Arraignment is when a baggy old white man with eye-boogies and a pronounced nasal problem dons the Black Robe of Justice. He has been awakened at 3:00 A.M. cuz of YOUR criminal ass and is expected to render a fair and unbiased Verdict as to the gravity of your crimes. Now how objective can a magistrate be when you've pissed him off from jump-street committing crimes he's gotta roll offa Wifey and come down to the station at this hour to answer to? You KNOW what you got comin! The MAX! Next time you feelin froggish-fuck up in the day time! When the Sun is up!

Judge Sweeney was his name. The desk Sergeant called him 6 times to get him down to proceed with the nigger lynching. Maybe he had chewed enough dark meat in his hey-day cuz he never answered-and he didn't come! Perhaps he reappraised the true consequences of a real lynching as the ample time errant 'coloreds' spend in the 'Pokie' after committing pre-dawn larceny. I think if given the choice I would've chosen the swift and painless tree-limb lynching to the slow agonizing time a desperate nigger spends pondering his fate in the local back-of-the-woods Ku Klux Klan jailhouse! So Sweeney's clever plan worked like a charm! When somebody wakes you up in the 'wee' hours of the morning to decide the fate of some rambunctious niggers, don't pick up the phone! Answering it would warrant the unnecessary trek down to the station-save THAT punk shit for the rookies. For the untenured idiots with no time on the job. But as for HIM, his 25 years on the 'GRILL' had earned him the right to 'live and let die!' The dumb niggers could HANG for all he cared! He knew he was large and in charge-an he had me an Canei BOTH BY THE BALLS!

Since there was no Judge available we were apprised that we would be spending another 48 hours in the 'Slammer!' Till Monday-the next business day for Criminal Court proceedings! I got paranoid! Petrified! Thinking it was a set-up to force a sister to do some more time. Like they threw some shit in the game hoping these 2 stupid Negroes were too dumb to know the difference.

"Oh know I AIN'T stayin locked down for 2 days! What um gonna eat-an how um gonna wash my ASS?" The Ebonics was flowin! They do that often in desperate moments before pain and death!

"Yo Officer, what ever happened to Night Court? They got that in the City!"

"This ain't Bed Stuy genius! We do it different up here. Ain't no convicts gonna manipulate the system in these parts. The good citizens and Judges of Nassau County won't tolerate it. Why should WE suffer-make things easy for some savages so they can just walk outta here after committing felonies in OUR homes. An you know the procedure 'Little Lady,' NO Arraignment-NO bail-GENIUS!"

Who was he callin Genius? He probably bought the answers to the Police test and STILL failed the first five times! I pulled out my lines from 'Law and Order' and N.Y.P.D. BLUE to begin rehearsals. THEN I attempted that lame "I Know My Rights" jargon. (I didn't know Jack-Shit about the Law and Mr. White Supremacy sensed it)

"Hey, where's my phone call? Don't I get a phone call?"

The smug bastard handed me the phone an said, "Here-call Johnny Cochran!"

Oh Lord! I was IN IT now! I refused to call my parents cuz they would worry.

"Uh, oh shit! Never mind the call. Gimme some time-maybe later!" They said my sentence was worse cuz I had a weapon. Yeah, we were both locked up but I would be there longer cuz the degrees of the crime were exascerbated by the weapon.

"EXASCERBATED? I can't even SPELL that shit! Gee, it wasn't a fucking 45! I grabbed 2 bottles. Two innocent bottles-an I never hit nobody." If they gave ME some more time for the bottles, I wondered what kinda sentence 'Batman' and the machete motherfucker got!

Despite bread and water an Brillo pad bird-baths, I decided I had to 'Ride or Die!' My parents would not be involved. I figured I'd need bail money after the arraignment but for the time being my war-like ego was on ice! I would HAVE to make these 48 hours swift, non-combative and uneventful. Unfortunately there is no such thing as 'uneventful' IN PRISON!

Bomani Shuru

Prison was the decadent state of limbo and anticipation that only a small segment of the population actually knew about. Or chose NOT to know! It entailed a loom of time where human nature is utterly transformed into animal behavior. A competitive Caste System thriving in a vacuum resemblant of ancient Roman Gladitorial times. Where only the strong survive. And sheer brute strength, whether numeric or anatomical, is the only answered prayer that can guarantee it's captives a good nights sleep! Quiet as it's kept alot of men lose something that not a single one would speak of. Let's put it THIS way: In a dark ferocious jungle it's better to be a wolf-THAN A RABBIT!

Three bitches were scheming on me in the cell an one of em had a shenck! I knew what time it was. They all looked like men stuck in women's bodies. Horny Dykes talk too loud prior to wild-animal attacks. You'd think I was a piece of sirloin steak the way those bitches was starin! I was the steak an they were meat-eaters-hadn't tasted a single vegetable in their lust filled predatory lives! It's not normal havin another female droolin over you. Niggers, yes cuz they're the closest evolutionary link to dogs-but when a bitch wants to make love to you-you know shit is getting hectic!

They smelled! Like shit sandwiches and tuna! And SOMEBODY'S armpits smelled as though they needed to be left alone! You would have thought that an aroused dyke would know to wash her ass before each attempted forced molestation! Gang-rape and same sex brutality can create one Helluva stir! Titties sweat, throbbing vagina's reek and halitosis reigns supreme somewhere between the first punch and the final orgasm! Furthermore, not that one has a choice, but few rape victims enjoy the sour scent of fried onions emitting from the raunchy crotch of her 'Fem' superior dripping like a slave while on top of her! Trying with ALL her might to THRUST that diminutive clitoris, that wished it were a DICK, inside her wimpering subjugated victim!

Nonetheless, they was comin! An I was on my own! I started to do some Viveca Fox "Kill Bill" technique! But you know what happened to her. The bitch NEVER made it outta the kitchen alive!

"Yo, what kinda shoes is those," asked the larger one? She had arms like George Foreman. And hopefully a glass jaw. I'd prefer to fork over a pair of Tims instead of some OTHER treasures they coulda held me down for. Just in case I lose the fight my sacred maidenhood would be salvaged. Unless they decided on dessert. You give these Ho's an inch of your shit an they'll take the rest too. Tims, jeans, hair weave, pussy, ass-not to mention my Debit Cards. (Do they have A.T.M.s in jail?) Oh my God! This was my second beef today. And honestly this fist-a-cuff-madness was getting tired. BUT... WELL FUCK IT! I WOULD DRAG ONE OF THESE GORILLAS WITH ME INTO HELL! LET SATAN BREAK IT UP! And one, two, three-it made no difference to me. War is war. An if you wanna protect your neck-you gotta fight for it!

I CAN THROW DOWN! Probably ten times better than most women out there. And I have yet to meet the bitch who can kick my ass! Handily! Just ask that bitch from that club in the Bronx I dropped last month! The one whose most likely STILL in the

72

E.R. screamin out for help while the Trauma-Team tries to remove my knuckle-print from the profound embedded crevice I implanted right between her eyes! And the list goes on cuz there's an array of mutilated bodies I've left behind in my sadistic wake. I only had my ass kicked once. THAT BITCH! WHEW! Well even that one coulda went either way. And TRUST me, a sister ain't tryin to have a rematch cuz human beings should not be pitted to fight against ANIMALS! It ain't fair! So if you got flees, fangs and a tail-Simone Singleton won't be runnin up on you NO TIME soon!

Now don't get me wrong! I'm not runnin around looking for fights. Trying to fill in the hollow spaces in my life with unprovoked street violence. Like a retired boxer who can't wait to get back in the ring-just to get his ass kicked some more! But when someone fucks with me I make it my business to make them wish they had never taken up the sport of unnecessary warfare! Bullying is a sin to me-punishable by death!

My daddy used to train me to fight 3 days outta the week when I was young. This started the first day after that infamous smackdown with the 3rd Graders. After they jumped me, after they attacked his sweet innocent little girl, he vowed to impart as much pugilistic wisdom and predatory know how as he could cram into my 9 year old body! It was ON! He could hardly wait till the wounds healed from the day I was beat up to play that 'Mik' from Rocky role and save my twisted life!

Mik was the old bastard that Coached Rocky toward the title of Heavyweight Champ in the movie. It was played by Burgess Meredith. The tough Irish Sportsman who could take an Italian meatball and transform it into an Italian Stallion. I must've caught 20,000 head-shots from dear old dad. It wasn't abuse or nothing and the punches weren't designed to kill me-just stun me into being the type of opponent who absolutely refused to get hit! I learned to duck. To fake-bob and weave like the men do. And after he had gotten me into fighting shape I was 'unleashed' on those 6 little miscreants who thought that Simone Singleton was just a bad memory! A peon whom they had stomped into a lifetime of cowardice! SURPRISE you rotten little imps!

It was PAYDAY! Or pay-week! And payday is the happiest and most gratifying time of everyone's work-week. So in proper keeping with the ideals of payday, that next week in Third Grade, I WENT TO WORK! Children were turnin up missing! Beat down and abducted by some invisible silent warrior for justice. Each and every day one of my past assailants turned up missing! Snatched the FUCK up! They just disappeared. Vanished-from the Schoolyard; from the Lunch-line; from the kiddie circle at recess long enough to get back what they had given me! And when questioned by the 'Sesame Street' Authorities, the 'Lost-and-found Hellion Committee;' I caught instant amnesia! They didn't see SHIT when their precious little darlings were setting up a juvenile lynch mob! Oh NO, ya'll couldn't see them beatin MY ASS? Well you shouldn't see THIS! I KNOW WHAT YOU DID LAST SUMMER-ASSHOLE!

I'll tell you each and every one of those nefarious rascals who were more than willing, in fact found it FITTING to jump on a poor defenseless little girl in a team effort of sadism and larceny, was picked the FUCK off!! I didn't play! From that point on if you beat me to death on Friday, Saturday and Sunday were training days bitch! Bruce Lee Boot camp! Don't COME to school on Monday! And if you do, you better bring along BOTH parents, your Crew and a Shotgun! I won't tell you what I did to that little Muppet Bitch Nikki Farnsworth! Well lets just say that SHE'S STILL NOT WALKIN! They say her neurological skills are out of whack-something to do with a severe blow to the head! And she was convalescing so well too! So much for alternatives to violence-for midgets!

There were about 12 of us in the cell and I knew that this three on one was about to Jump off. I had little hope that they would narrow the odds down to one on one just for MY sake. You know, let me an Goliath go at it-Toe-to-toe. So I had to think fast. Since it was the BIG bitch who asked me that stupid ass question about my shoe, I decided that it would be HER head that went flying over the Sing Sing Wall!

"Oh, you want my shoes? Well here, fuck it! I don't need em no more anyway!" I took off my left boot. I did the left in case they jumped bad. I'd still have the safety of balance on my favorite right foot. Hah! Fighting's not just a sport-it's a way of life! The 3 dummies let me take off my boot! BIG mistake! NOW I had a weapon! Some criminals are not too bright! You can SEE how they got caught. They woulda been better off going right from the crime scene down to the Police Station and turning themselves in. Why waste time when you KNOW you're not intelligent enough to stay outta jail ANYWAY? A boot in the hand is like a homemade sledge-hammer! Trust me on that one! This is what I said and did next:

"Oh, here baby-let me get that for you! Don't worry. I got you girl." I began to untie that bitches left shoe. "You know these boots are warm and they last. My husband is a Banker at Smith Barney's and just last week I used his Credit Card to charge up 14 pairs of these." (The sound of money never fails to captivate numb lethargic hulking behemoths who begin salivating over potential cash while they're supposed to be robbing the SHIT outta you!)

"So what I did was I said you know what? No since coming back for another pair cuz you know how the lines are at Bloomingdale's check-out. So I got em all! HONEEY! Well at first 'Man-man flipped! But then I gave him a little 'Head' an we just called it even! Now you KNOW a bitch can't wear 14 pairs of Tims without having some jeans an some fly jump-suits to go along with it. So I walked my little ass over to my home-girl Charlene's crib! THAT bitch LOVES to shop! I think she was fucking BORN in a department store! So what we did was we started out at 8:00 A.M-it was on a Wednesday I think."

One shoe was off! An the dazed bitch was voluntarily helping me get off number 2. Holdin up her big an stupid country leg! It must've been a size 10. No socks to be found! (Like Tyson) Just a dusty pair of Tennis shoes. (no-name) Probably Rite-Aid

Sporting Section-And 10 large bunionized toes-crackling with the pungent savor of 'NACHO!' OH-MY-GOD!

I dodged the smell, reswallowed some bile-an kept on talking.

"Me and Charlene spent 16 Gs in Saks Fifth Avenue buying up everything in sight!" I was impassioned! Dramatic! And the 3 beast bitches were still transfixed-latching onto every fucking word that I said! Even a lot of the other inmates was paying attention. Hangin out to see what the rest of my story would entail. It's like when you in the jungle-an you're the wildebeest whose chest-cavity that hungry tiger is chewing on. The other animals in the periphery HAVE to focus on this carnivorous transaction. Cuz from the moment 'Tony the Tiger' gets full and walks away, it's feedin time at the zoo-ROUND TWO! And those OTHER voracious predators attack, drag and mutilate the REST of your post-mortem carcass! And BELIEVE ME-them animals, them BITCHES, had NO problem with 'Sloppy Seconds!'

I felt like an ancient philosophical griot! A Storyteller-imparting my prudent indespensible wisdom to the local village thuggery! But there was one catch-I was part-time Griot-an part-time Prize-fighter!

"So when we got to the cashier I told that white bitch we was payin in cash cuz my husband Marty had just closed the Aldrich deal. You know...the multi-million dollar Enterprise? Aldrich! Yeah, that's the one! So we was rollin in the money! I think $60,000-I still got MOST of it! Uh, when do you get outta here-cuz I'm about to post bail in a minute?"

When I said that EVERYBODY opened up their ears and began to take notice! A bitch cackling about lavish garments an shopping sprees is one thing. But when you speak of bail money and undue philanthropy, IN ANY FORM, trust me-the convicted felons gotta listen!

"So I counted out every fuckin dollar for that bitch cuz girl, you KNOW how they are. Whitey be clockin a nigger from the moment you walk in the store till the time you bout to leave! And I had to prove to whitey that I had more money than she got. You know what I'm sayin?" Everybody in the jail cell was shakin their heads. Even the white folks! Tryin their best to act like they was down with me! Five minutes ago every bitch IN there wanted to kill me! JUST because I was the New-kid on the block! Now, after the tall-tales of spending-sprees and bail money, I'm loved by millions of criminals doin time all over the world!

Zulu girls shoes were off! My right shoe was tied and secure. But I had high hopes and alternate plans for the left. My heart raced back into a combative world all too familiar to me-and DOOMSDAY WAS HERE! I eased myself up toward her mid-section and face, ran my hand up her pants leg along her naval and up to those big hillbilly titties of hers. She didn't stop me cuz dykes love that sort of thing and I KNEW she was queer! So she just stood there-motionless. Looking down at me like I was her long lost gay lover.

Countries nipples were hard and we all know what THAT means. I was in complete control of the situation. But there was no time for paused silence. I had to keep talking. Sensing she had a dykes hard-on by now and swore she would get the virgin pussy-AND the Tims, I played Delilah on the 6 foot tall felonious Sampson starin at me like I was his lunch!

"Now how long do you think it would take for you to spend 25 Gs?"

'KACHING' WENT THE BIG AND BURLY BITCHES INTERNAL COMPUTATIONAL MECHANISMS. But brutes don't COUNT too fast!

"Uh…" She looked up in the air-perhaps seeking a mathematical answer from the prison Gods of 'Clink! Clink!"

"Oh, just bend down a minute baby-let me get this shoe on you! Yeah, that's it!" She kept looking up-while bending down. I guess the Gods were a tad belated with their Heavenly calculations. (Study long…and you study wrong!)

"Yo, hold up," said the other Loch Ness monster standing to my right!

"Uh…," muttered Sasquach, standing barefoot on the concrete jail floor-nipples erect, stinky as sweat and mind adrift!

"KACHING!" BAM! BAM! BAM! Went my Tim boot heal! Too late BITCH! You can answer THAT question on the other side! I wailed that fucking Tim boot upside that giants head like it BELONGED there! Like it was DESTINIED, I said DESTINIED, to gravitate it's way into her ugly fucking skull!

The dumb bitch had taken her final bow. An while she was leaning over intoxicated in her tranquilizing lust for some new 'Fish' and a fly pair of kicks, she forgot This was a robbery! You don't talk during a robbery! You don't try an fuck your 'vick' during a robbery! You don't just stand there 'zombiefied' and mesmerized with Saks Stories of spending sprees. An no matter what the fuck the victim has to say during the larceny to prevent it or otherwise, YOU DON'T LISTEN! Stupid fucking country dyke Bitch!

SMACK! SMACK! SMACK! The bitch was on the ground bleedin! Bleedin REAL good! An I was ON her! An the 2 apes along for the ride was ON me! One was tryin to pull me off an the other oversized dummy was kickin the SHIT outta BOTH of us! Me AN her tag-team partner! I mean Damn, these chics were inaccurate. They were confused! They were rookies-AN THEY WERE LOSING! Getting fucked up! Either by me or one another. Thank God for small favors an even tinier lesbian brains!

"BITCH, you kickin ME" said her misfortune Home-girl-her 'Road-dog' who had just caught a size 12 in the chest!

"Ooof!"

I bit the kick victim in the breast! Fuck AIDS! I'd worry about that later! I had a more pressing issue! A more immediate threat than to worry that 15 years later I'd die from HIV! Shit, if I didn't play my cards right, I would never make it to see THAT death! I would die right here-today! In fucking prison-my final 3 on 1! I remembered one of these gargantuan crossovers had a blade-but in the heat and confusion of the moment, I didn't remember which one!

No matter! I would beat the blade outta all 3 of em! I bit down 'Pit-Bull' style! I felt no more resistance from the one I'd seduced and Tim booted to the skull! Six boot-shots put her down for the count! She was well into La La land by now-barefooted! Maybe she'll get some pussy and some new shoes there!

"BITE, BITE, BITE," went my gnashing teeth. Road-dog's left titty was my target. All my bite victim could do was bear-hug me an scream!

"Uuagh, Aaagh, huaagh, ha-hah! Bugsy-get the Bitch OFF me! Get the bitch OFF me! GET THE BITCH OFF ME," howled the mangled dog!

"BAM, BAM BAYAM" Went Bugsy's shoe heel offa the back of my head! She musta thought she was 'Pele the Great' the way she soccer kicked my head across the prison cell like that! AN I WAS A BELIEVER TOO! I felt every ounce of her extraordinary Soccer-ball kicking abilities and I thought the bitch had knocked my right ear onto the pavement! I could feel that side of my head bleeding-saying "No-No more! Please, give up the Tims and throw in a good piece of ass too! Anything! Just stop this ape from pulverizing me-or I swear I'll tell your brain to shut you down. You'll see then! You'll be out like a light in 2 minutes."

"Oh DAMN, head! Why you gonna do me like that! Just when we're winning the fight."

"You ain't winning bitch! I don't know about YOU, but I'm getting stomped! Just look at me-blood everywhere! You call that winnin?"

"But the primate on the floor is bleedin too! We got a good shot! Just hold out!"

"Uh, hey dummy, I said no more 'KICK!' One more 'Smash' to the head an you shuttin DOWN! And by the way ASSHOLE, word on the street is blood pressure is up-about 240 over 120. And heart beats risin fast-maybe 160 Beats-per-minute by now. Uh, bitch, you on your way to havin a stroke! So as a matter of fact I think you better say good night NOW," said my head!

"NO! Wait, O.K!"

There I was-BLEEDIN! Biting a dykes titty off in the decompressive bear-hug of doom and arguing with the right side of my OWN BRAIN as to whether or not to continue! This was not working! I felt the nausea tip-toeing it's way directly across the street from my semi-consciousness. My arms were two wilted led pipes begging for some divinely transfused youthful vigor to re-animate the beaten warrior who had set this shit off in the first place. But the vitality of round one was nowhere to be found here in the twelveth-I had to act-or I would not make it! I summoned and utilized every ounce of my waning strength to lift that big bear-hug bitch offa the ground. (Thank God-and Daddy for those 500 push-ups he made me do on weekdays 5 days a week for 5 years of my life) But the bitch was too heavy-I couldn't hold her no more!

"KA-PLOWIE!" We both fell over onto some members of our captive audience. I had flesh, blood and polyester prison fatigues in my mouth! But teeth undaunted-remained clenched! Pit-bulls never let go-not even after death!

If I was dying and goin to Hell, bear-hug bitch's left titty was comin with me! I'd be the one you saw on fire with someone else's breast in my mouth! When we fell the "THUD" was Earth shattering! I tried with all my might but with the terrific pain of her shoe-heel lodged into my skull, I had to let go! 'Pele' pulled the dyke with the gnarled titty away from me and drug her into a new safe-haven. Somewhere, ANYWHERE away from the pit-bull with the fast mouth and the bloody head!

I ranted and raved and cussed those bitches out! Out loud just so help could hear me hollerin an come back to save me-JUST IN CASE THEY DECIDED TO GATHER SOME MORE TROOPS AN INITIATE A SECOND WAVE OF ATTACKS! To avenge their swollen Kingpin! I wouldn't last another 5 minutes! I knew that! And so to prevent that horrid possibility I began screamin louder-this time at the top of my lungs! Fuck, if the authorities didn't hear it-God would! And I needed help from anywhere I could get it! Psychological AND Medical attention-an the more Hell I raised, the quicker and more profusely I bled! This, in prison was what is called a 'Punk out!' It's like callin the Cops an telling em whose blade it was they found lodged in your throat! And the inmates look down on this type of behaviour as cowardly! And inexcusable!

I had heard of numerous war stories of prisoners with gaping stab-wounds who refused to report such fatal injuries to the C.O.'s. After losing a secret one-on-one with somebody who'd kicked their asses in, the dumb bastards would simply go on with their lives. Intestines hanging out, shuffling their mortally wounded carcasses to the messhall or the yard-looking for a safe and quiet place to die. All THIS just to follow and obey the prison code of silence! Well silence is golden but it ain't THAT golden! Perhaps the fools didn't know they were actually gonna die! Maybe they psychologically second-guessed the grave impact of that home-made spear sticking outta their lungs (hard to breathe ain't it fool) or that razor-sharp metal shenk protruding from their fractured skull!

Well I ain't dying for nothing or nobody! An if you kill me, believe me somebody's gonna know about it cuz I'm dropping a major dime on your homicidal ASS! Kill ME an get away with it? Oh-no fool! I don't THINK so! My Daddy didn't raise kids THAT dumb! So FUCK you AN your BULLSHIT prison Code of silence! Now if I whip YOUR ass-maybe THEN I won't tell! But otherwise-IF YOU FUCK ME UP...I'm a 'Go Tell It On The Mountain!'

So a bitch KEPT on screamin-an the C.O.s came a runnin! I PROBABLY interrupted the daily donut-fest cuz EVERYBODY knows those hypocrites are crooked as a three-dollar bill! Just like the Cops! When help arrived it was on! You know how much shit cowards talk when there's somebody there you KNOW will break up the fight! Well I was that coward-an my verbal spiel fell right in line!

The C.O.s broke up the fight AFTER THE FACT! And I went off!

78

"You STILL wanna go shoppin bitch? I rocked your punk-ass to SLEEP! And your feet stink! Nah, let her GO so I can whip her behind somemore! Wash your dirty feet Ho! Yeah, WHAT? WHAT? I THOUGHT so! 'G-U-NIT!' The force works on weak minds!"

The C.O.s grabbed me-delirious and scrambling on the floor and literally dragged me to safety! I new by then the last gorilla coulda killed me easily if she wanted to. All of those trash-talkin charades would've been quelled with one swift Karate-chop to the windpipe an I'd hit the canvass with a big bang an a cloud of dust! But resuscitatin her fallen comrade-her wounded lover, was tops on her list of priorities. Thank God for 'Homo-love' and devotion!

I woke up the next morning in the infirmary to the sound of music! Ominous music. The kinda song a convicted felon don't wanna here while behind bars! I caught another charge! A social worker was standing over me and informed me that ALL 3 of those bitches had signed sworn affidavits that I had tried to kill them! That I had attacked THEM and stolen the big ones shoes!

Oh! WELL AIN'T THAT A BITCH! No them rabid-ass bitches DIDN'T! They was trained killers when they attacked me-now they're punks! Singing like stool pigeons in protective custody!

"Look at me bitch!" I was callin the Social Worker whom I'd never seen before and with whom I'd had no beef, the 'B' word! Acute blood loss from the side of ones head can have adverse affects on the human psyche! I guess the chunks of soiled flesh, polyester and gnawed on bits of left titty don't help much either!

They hit me up with a needle. Musta had morphine in it for pain cuz I slept through the head-wound and through my only phone call. My rest extended miles past the memory of the ordeal and even the 48 hour minimum they held over my head. I'd earned a new stigma. A second charge-2 counts of Assault and Battery. And Aggravated (with a weapon) Grand Larceny while in custody of a Correctional Detention Facility. I was SCARED! Canei would definitely be home before me unless some gorilla shit took place in HIS spot.

I could NOT call my parents so they were holdin me for 2 days. After the beat down and the infirmary nobody fucked with me or said a single word to the crazy Saks 5th Avenue bitch who could swing a Tim Boot like The Mighty Thor!! FUCK THEM! It was worth it. I woke up the next day and was informed that I had a visit! I felt like Sean Penn in the movie 'Bad Boys' tryin to fight his way outta the clutches of his enemy Esai Morales. I still didn't know what them dykes had in store. They might send a hit-man! Someone I didn't recognize to stab the shit outta me in the shower!

To Hell with dying! I was nervous and decided to stay in my cell. PUNK STYLE! And the only time I came out was during the visit from Hattie, Kecia and Mik!

"What happened to your head?" Mikki inquired.

"You KNOW what happened! The bitch caught a BAD one," Hattie retorted!

Bomani Shuru

"Yo, these bitches is tryin to KILL me," I added in my own defense...

-8-

DO AS I SAY-NOT AS I DO

I was bleeding like an open bullet wound! Like a sightless Matador who'd miscalculated the carnivorous stampede in front of him-and caught a bad one. Unfortunately for HIM, El Toro had calculated correctly and with pinpoint accuracy! The ace-bandage and gauze pads they carelessly wrapped around my unsightly skull were on their way out-down towards my swollen jaw-line! And I looked like a Saturn Bitch! With white shit draped around her head who had JUST lost a 12 round decision to a Rotwiler! Hattie wanted to bust out laughing at me but didn't wanna hurt my feelings! I could see it in her eyes. Little did she know that hurt feelings could not equal the pain welling up inside the multiple fractures on the left side of my brain! Fuck humiliation! I was too wounded to expend my meager strength in entertaining something as pointlessly futile as embarrassment! I just needed a raw steak for my gaping speed-knot and a nice cozy cot-bed to lay my head down in! I couldn't care less. My public could ridicule my performance to scorn all they wanted to. I'd address that denigration in the morning! You know-one painstaking defeat at a time!

Kecia just stood there-zombified! As though she had no clue as to why the Hell she was sitting there in front of me in the first place. Will somebody tell that dumb bitch to just STOP wasting her time BREATHING and call it a day! Mik tried to calm things over by adding a slight pinch of humor-to salt my bloody wounds.

There was an extra-large inmate on a visit sitting beside us who kept sparking my attention. He looked like the Incredible Hulk-the Bed Stuy version! His only visitor was his 18 year old son and during the entire visit he spent every moment trying to prevent what must have seemed to him an inevitability. The eventual straying, incarceration and social ruin of his offspring. I pretended to listen to the bullshit my girls were telling me but actually honed in on the more profound and significant father to son conversation unfolding dramatically to my left. In essence, it went like this:

"..No! I had to watch my ASS in here! I had to protect what I got. But I'll get to that in a minute. Let me put you down on some real shit bout prison lil man! Daddies don't survive 10 mothafuckin minutes in the joint! Dey don't make it behind bars an you wanna know why? Cuz if you get so wrapped up in the pain of missing your son, your daughter, your momma an the woman you promised to take care of for the rest of your life…if you get caught up in THAT shit-you can kiss your sorry ass GOOD-NIGHT!"

"No, you got to separate the bars from what you were-what you HAD on the outside! I seen a multitude of niggers-hard-ass 'do-or-DIE mothafuckers wilt down in their cell weeping like a bitch cuz they couldn't separate that shit! These hard mothafuckers-NOBODY could fuck with! Walked around here like caged fuckin killers! Would fuck a nigga up in a heartbeat without battin an eye! They had no emotion cuz they had to retrain their minds not to have none-or they would wind up dead! Forget all that soggy eyes Bullshit you see in the Pennitentiary on T.V! SHIT! They would NEVER let the 'Fam' come up here to show some love! Cuz love...an crying, an emotions is PUSSY when you in lock-down! An a pussy don't last in jail. It gets fucked! It dies-an it can't last! So a man's gotta jump outta that psychologically damaging humanity shit an go buck-wild!"

"Son, when you come in here you gotta put all that husband, Daddy shit in the ground an become a man! Or yo ass won't make it pass the chow-line! Yeah! I fucked up! I did some things but boy people make mistakes AND THEY CHANGE! But the only way I could guarantee myself that I'd be comin back home in one piece to correct what I've done was to transform my mind into a nigger that don't care-in order to survive!"

"Now you know what it's like to see a hundred niggas with their dicks hard as diamonds dying for just 5 minutes alone with your pretty green ass? You are a BITCH when you come in-new meat! Fresh fish unless you prove otherwise! No matter how mothafuckin hard you THINK your ass was before you got in here, from the moment you come in they bring your ass down! Virgin! That's what they call you! A new-jack Virgin-Mary! Even though you got 2 balls an a dick just like them!"

Mikki was babbling some shit about some new hair-spray and a Rap Concert but I tuned her ass out an perked my eardrums to listen more closer-Navajo Indian Style.

"Shut the fuck up bitch! I'm ease-droppin! Getting the 411 on prison-life from this burnt out motherfucker tryin like Hell to school his stubborn son!" Well fuck Junior! If he wasn't listenin I sure as Hell was! Long as mighty-mouthed Mikki would just keep quiet an let me absorb this Soap Opera shit with my good unbandaged ear!

"Ever have another nigga kiss at you? Whistle at you-stare at your ass naked in the shower like you was the main-course at the Last Supper? You ever have to fight off 2 or3 rapists that was trying to grease you up an hold you down-an make a meal for 3 outta your tight ass?"

Go head Ving Rhames-testify brother! I got you boo cuz the same shit happened to me just yesterday! That's how I got this gauze wrap-around. This wise convict was dropping it an I could relate! I was mesmerized-bloody head-band, speed-knot an all! Fuck those cackling bitches! The hysterical fag, the Crashdummy AND the Unknown Comic! As long as Black Aristotle was lecturing there was no way in the Fucking UNIVERSE I could listen to what they had to say! I eased closer-fuck detection, school was in-an I had to learn something! The errant teenager looked confused-but the captive philosopher kept on expoundin:

"You ever have a mothafucker say he love you an he'll take care of you cuz you need protection from time to time? You an him is standin there soakin wet butt-ass naked in the shower an he likes the way the soap look on your shiny virgin skin! An while he's proposing-offerin cigarettes, Candy bars and peaceful nights there's OTHER motha fuckers whose scared of him circling around-hopin you'll tell him no so they can jump on you too! He got a 'Rep' an they all scared of him-that one mothafucka! An they'll back off your frightened ass if he gives the word not to fuck with you! An if you buy-that peace of mind…will cost you your manhood! Is it better to be sodomized by one than to be raped by many? Soon he'll be stickin his dick inside your torn out asshole whenever he wants it! You'll be washin his socks, doing his chores! Suckin off his nasty dick at the drop of a dime cuz this is what you bargained for! You needed peace-protection from the other wolves so you must satisfy THIS wolf whom you belong to! If you piss him off or he gets sick of your ass he'll either trick you to the other cons or pawn you off to another pimp! Then HE will be your Daddy an the cycle just repeats itself again! With you trickin, and prostituting-and having your weak compromised ass kicked when the fuck ever any of those deviate mothafuckers feel like it!"

"But at the same time if you haul off an smack the SPIT outta his mouth they's STILL waitin to jump yo ass an make a woman outta you! There's nobody to help you boy! C.O.s can't SEE what they're paid off NOT to see! An ain't nobody around! Just you-an these 5 horny faggots-an the silent darkness!"

"Well I've been there! I've backed off hard thug-ass killers! I had to fight-an only a man can fight! Daddy can't fight-he's too distracted, too weak! I've been in some shit that only God could pull my ass out of! Scared to death-but I'm STILL a man! An the only way to maintain what I had-my manhood, was to forget YOU an yo momma. And everything I love in the world-JUST TO MAKE IT HOME! I had to neglect and ignore you-wouldn't let you see me. That's right lil nigga! Not even a Christmas Card cuz that would've evolved from a pin-hole to a gaping wound that might've taken me out! No, I had to be a man cuz fathers don't make it in prison! Only the strong survive and Daddy is part of a weaker breed that will wind up some niggers piece of pussy between the moment he walks in the door till when the lights go out!"

I thought to remind myself to punch Mikki in the mouth for allowing her stupid tongue to lop up and down in a tiresome effort to spit out some words which in essence didn't mean a fucking thing! And then there's that rattling dry-rotted mind-conjuring up ideas and notions to steer her irritating mass of utterances headlong through life like a nonconsequential zit-waiting to pop! Fuck, I couldn't hear the rest of my well-spoken Sermon for her and Hattie's cursed interruptive conjoined mouthpieces. It was like a Jackass duet! And THEY were the stars of the show besmirching the jewels of wisdom I felt destined to absorb! Why do bitches talk too much? They could've just dropped the $5,000 bail money off and went on their merry ways for all I cared! But the LAST thing I needed from them was a lengthy speech-without the complement of purpose to go along with it! My bionic ear was engrossed-peeping and detaching itself from the rest of my head in order to catch the climactic finale of Aristotle monologue!

"Hmm, you know it's funny-the sacrifices we make. With all my heart I believe God's a comedian and got a big sense of humor-forcing a man to make a choice between the true love an support of his family and the continuance of his manhood! Fatherhood-or manhood?"

"You know I've gone into some foul nefarious places an fought! An literally felt the breathe of life leaving the niggas body! He had a hard-on an it cost him his life! Something ran through his libido that night which talked him into runnin up on me an it Killed him!"

He LOOKED like he had killed quite a few people in the past. And ATE the rest-why would anybody in their right mind try to RAPE HIM! He looked like a God-damn Gladiator-Hulk Hogan! Shit-a would-be rapist would have a better shot at greasing up King Kong! Get past the mug an the monkey breathe an you might be able to manage a better erection! But to sexually attack THIS BEAST? This Super-nigga, chiseled and bred for war? You must be outta your rabid-ass mind! He continued:

"A few times-on several occasions after the 12th round, I was the only one left standin! Sometimes it didn't even last THAT long! Niggas will fight for what they sought all their existences to preserve. Their lives, their asses-while some other mothafucka thinks he can wrest it from him-an still make it back to his cell just in time for lock-in! They all knew! Mothafuckers knew what time it was. When 2 niggas go in an only 1 comes out! An they don't tell either! Nah, they respect you an you get a name. A rep cuz you fought for yours! Held it down. An your rep is like Gold in prison-get a good one-or die! Well next week um comin home-an it was all worthwhile. But I gotta tell you one thing son-don't follow behind me-don't come in here!"

Whoah! That was some powerful SHIT! Like something out of 'Penitentiary II. I didn't know visiting rooms could have such an electrifying, exuberant and remorseful character. That man was destitute. Overwhelmed by what prisons do to those bold enough to survive. If and when you DO make a choice the decision is costly because it involves emotional forfeiture or detachment from the memory of the inmates loved ones. Those languishing on the other side! The prisoner must do this in order to bring proper focus toward defeating the worldwind of circumstances that daily threaten his very survival.

A tender empathetic prisoner is a dead man at the hands of ostracization and the warlike hostilities that personify the prison. If he loves-he is destined to fail, and drown in his own misspent endearments. Yet if he wants to survive he must instead divert innate feelings and transform himself into a thoughtless concrete beast. One who is avaricious, callous and defunct of the humanity that he entered captivity with.

Only this new beast can endure what bondage does to you because only a creature devoid of compassion can stave off isolation. The human man was not destined to perservere in such an animalistic environment. But this new cold-blooded beast can. He can live, maintain and even thrive on the criminal antagonistic elements in his midst cuz those are the very carnivorous factors swirling deep beyond the core of his maniacal being.

If prison bars could talk they'd sing out some painful shit to society that horror movies are made of. Some sacred untelevised human butchery that the rest of civilization has no knowledge of, could never understand and spends billions annually to protect itself against. "Triple reinforce the titanium gates Bob-don't let them fuckin animals outta there!" This is a parallel Universe-with parents and sons and mistakes transformed into Jail-bids and desperation.

And so THIS inmate, way beyond the brief violence of his prison stay wants to tell his boy how much he loves him! He wants to share the perpetual Hells that have turned him into a concrete monster that does not know how to cry! He has lived through the bid but lost his higher self-his better half in the process. And although he has conquered this present battle he has undeniably lost the all pervading war of true fatherhood! The inmate wants the best for his boy-on a headlong collision course with his own tragic destiny. So he tries to propel his offspring elsewhere. ANYWHERE but towards the miserable Mansion that for 14 years has been his home. A marked and darkened gravesite!

What if that was me an Bre came up to witness the failure I had become? How could I tell her that? How could I say I'm sorry an beg forgiveness for my inabilities to live up to the standards I'd rigidly set for her? A custodial parent barks out hollow words when he or she has delivered a speech and written inflexible Commandments which are impossible to adhere to.

Kids these days scoff at that and rightfully so. They need not obey a fool with more regulations than self discipline. And they'll kick you straight up your hypocritical ass if you dare to fix your crooked mouth to preach an empty doctrine of 'Do as I say-not as I do!' No one expects them to respect the loud clamour of THAT blank verse! So a criminally disposed locked-down me cannot be heard by juvenile ears untouched by the system and careening toward a life of self-fulfillment at all costs! They do as they please. YOU DID AS YOU PLEASED! Now your dumb ass is locked up! So why you player-hatin? No, don't tell em shit! Yeah-we know about all your personal experiences and ugly shit awaitin a young innocent proselyte. An aspiring delinquent heading straight for the grave you dug for yourself. But don't preach to me mom, cuz I got me a Bank to rob! Got me? DON'T SAY A FUCKING WORD-YOU JAILED HYPOCRITE! You've lost that right-save the scolding of your beloved daughter for the prison guards! Do your time and pray to God they don't go astray an meet you in the Big-House! An if they do stray, then pray to WHOMEVER that one of us will make it outta there ALIVE!

I felt like poor old Honest Abe Lincoln at Fordes Theatre. After the curtain-call-AND THE BULLET! And I didn't wanna think about nor remember what I saw and heard ever again! Big man had gotten his point across in a major way. It seemed to me that truth sprung from his lips, zoomed right past his desperately ignorant offspring and gathered itself to rest within the stunted and shattered remnants of my heart! For real! Hattie and Mikki Posted my bail an I was outta there! Tired, irrational and vowing never to make the same mistake twice-and at the same time genuinely glad to have amassed so much wisdom despite the pains of that malevolent 72 hours of my life!

-9-

THE NAKED AND THE DEAD

"Canei! Canei...CANEI! Why is there a naked dead bitch in my bed? HELLO? Nigga YOU HERE ME! Talk in the PHONE motherfucker! Boy if you hang up on…!'"

What in the world? The phone cut of. I was astonished! I had just been locked the fuck up-FOR 3 DAY'S! Almost got my ass whipped by the local prison 'Gay Lesbian Advocacy Committee!' Three Wolfen bitches trying to spread me wide. Break me in-THEN steal my shoes. My privacy and dignity had been invaded when the C.O.s took a good hard look up my ass to make sure I wasn't smuggling any more broken glass bottles or Hand-Grenades into prison. Picture THAT! A Grenade up the old Shit-chute-and I'm IN! They told me to squat and cough! Rigid ass-stretched and sweaty! Then after my third-eye was allowed to close and I was given the far-fetched privilege of standing up, like the rest of my fellow primates do, I turned around in time to see those members of the 'Peep' squad yucking it up like cackling misfits!

What the Hell were THEY doing there in the female inmates frisk area? They were assigned to the 'Nuts and Butts male sector. So why the Hell had they defected into the 'Cracks and Backs' Ladies corner?

My entire weekend was buried in a God-damned mudslide for all intents and purposes! I got home. Tired, stinky (I don't shower with dykes) and emotionally burnt the fuck out! So I figure-my bed is a nice place to be after 3 days of incarceration. Let me dig in an tell the rest of the world to go fuck itself!

So I pulled into the driveway-and what do I see? Canei's jeep! I get out of my Denali and touch-checked his muffler. Hmm, baby's cold like a ski-dog's ass. Guess he got home before me. Way before! Like a day or so I surmised cuz I know my charges were exascerbated with the Jailhouse beef I had against 'Thugalina' and her crew! O.K.! So Canei's been here.

I go to walk around to the back of the house. Get inside, drop the keys on the kitchen table and look in the livingroom. What do I see? TWO glasses-one with lipstick on it. DARK lipstick! Oh, you motherfucker! No you didn't…! I'll KILL YOU! I panicked-looking around in Batman form. Then I rummaged in the trash-can and the sink You know the garbage-can is the BEST place to look for paraphernalia. Contraband! O.K, trash-can turns up empty. Nothing! But what do I see in the sink? Another fucking glasss-more lipstick. This time with a lighter shade!

Oh you gonna die Canei! And they won't have enough meat on your body to bury you with for an open-casket funeral ceremony! Just tell the Coroner or the Mortician if they need extra flesh to paint on your skull cavity just check my Ox! You know-the one I used to flay you with! Then as a last resort they can scrape the Garbage Compactor for some bonus residue.

This no good nigger-IN MY HOUSE! With not one-but TWO bitches! I flew into a fucking rage but just before I could soar too far I heard a car ignition turn on. I ran to the window just in time to see Canei's jeep speed off. Damn, the bastard escaped! Shoulda known when I saw his ride still hear. Shoulda tipped back outside! A bitch thought to run out and chase the truck-then beat his ass with the Golf-Club I always leave by the front door. (Who said black folks don't play golf?) But he was TOO fast! Before I could even make it outside the sneaky bitch would be GONE! I was a day late and a dollar short in grabbing his ugly head and dragging it across the icy Tundra of my backyard!

"YOU GRIMY BASTARD!" I picked up a green plate from off the table. (Somebody had been eatin waffles on it) and threw it against the fucking wall! Ooh, that felt good! Look at that shit. A nigger fucking 2 bitches IN MY HOUSE an got the nerve to feed em first! With MY food! Then I grabbed the red lipstick glass from the sink and hurled it into the Oak China-cabinet! Uh, there ain't no CHINA-just Cabinet! Well Damn! That felt even better. I was a fucking WOLF-A lion! A hungry shark looking for some dumb bastard-ANY ASSHOLE foolish enough to dive in my waters.

The temper tantrum was not working because my predatory wrath was lacking the essential taste of Canei's flesh to sate my violent appetite. I needed more meat, more blood! More satisfaction! Now-we had gotten locked up together. We went down swingin-brawlin side-by-side against the bat and blade wieldin Mafia of the Golden Wok Chinese Restaurant. I vowed to 'Ride-or-die' with that nigger down to the fuckin 'Clink!' The Damn Jailhouse for 3 days! An that greedy nigga couldn't hold out for a piece of pussy! An he had TWO tricks at my house while my ass is doin time! He's through for good I thought! An if I see him-I'll kill him ON SITE!

That's when I dialed his number and he pretended not to here me-like he was losin his signal. Well Cassanova will be losin more than a fuckin signal I guarantee you! With murder on my mind I unlocked my bedroom door an guess what I found?

There was a white chic laying across MY GOD-DAMN BED naked as the day she was born! OH MY GOD! So what the fuck NOW? I go BACK to Jail again-this time for MURDER cuz the bitch was NOT leaving my Bedroom ALIVE!

"Well I wasn't here for this one Mr.Officer! I was locked the Hell up-thanks to YOU! Remember? I was the petrified looking bitch tussling with Big Bertha an the Carpet-Munchers Squad!"

There I was-lookin down on my bed. With sleepin beauty knocked the fuck out! Happiness and rapine leaped into my Cerebellum side by side and holdin hands like the sweet-an-sour twins. One part of me pulled the Executioners death lever on the dumb white bitch stupid enough to fuck my man IN MY HOUSE and fall asleep afterward! I would wake her up an beat her down simultaneously! Violence has no color-barrier. White or black-they both bleed. And DIE!

Whitey was about to take a nose-dive in speed-knot City! Another part of me thanked the Heavenly Father of Eternal graces for granting me a witness-SOME Damn

88

body to explain to me what the Hell was goin on here! Not that I didn't kinda have an idea. But a last confession would be quite helpful and comforting prior to the crucifixion!

I SNATCHED Ms. Whitey up an shook the SHIT outta her.

"Wake up BITCH! I'll let you sleep in your GRAVE!" Bitch didn't move! I slapped her two times. 'BAP! BAP!' Fuck that! Dummy should've stayed awake after the nut-I DO! STILL no response! Oh SHIT-a 'Sleep-like-a-log Bitch!' This one will be easier to KILL! But I still gotta revive her first-for questioning.

"I said GET UP you white Ho-WHAT you doin in my house?" That was a dumb question. 'DUH?' She was fucking your man-ALL NIGHT LONG! Maybe for 3 days straight! Now the bitch is tired! Too much big black dick does that to the snow-flakes! She could use a nap so she crawled into YOUR bed. Figured since you was behind bars you wouldn't mind letting Polly-pure-bread borrow your bed for a while! Might as well throw in a toothbrush to boot!

"Oh sure Cracker-lady. Don't mind me at all. In fact da HELL wit ME! So glad to oblige ya Massuh Cracka-bitch! I'ze just A SLAVE! Shucks-I ain't no good NO WAYS! So you'se kin havum WHIN EVAH YOU FEELS like it Massuh Cracka! Naw don't mine ME! Sides-bitches doin time can't keep a man anyway!"

The Bitch DID NOT MOVE! Er, she was heavy-an felt like...uh...like a mannequin. Uh-oh! An she was...purple! How the Hell could I not have noticed the bitch was purple? I caught an E.R. flashback and checked her pulse. Hmm. Sleepin bitches heart ain't beatin too often! In fact I ain't felt the first beat YET! I put my head on the brittle bitches naked left tittie! Didn't wanna get too close-just enough to check for breathes. Oh-mi-GOD-I couldn't find none. No! Oh Lord, Canei had killed the bitch!

I had been so busy sizing her up for the grave I would put her in I didn't realize she was already there! My whole body started to shake! I HATED Canei! HE had done this shit to me! I was FUCKED! What could I do? Can't dump the body-I would be suspect if somebody saw. Oops! I had already touched her. FINGERPRINTS! Twenty-five to Life for killing the purple-white bitch Canei fucked to death! AH-that didn't make any sense! If HE killed her then I'd get off. But how do I prove I never touched her! Uh-oh again-I had slapped the Ho! Not once BUT TWICE! That 'BAP! BAP!' WOULD cost ME MY FREEDOM! But Wait-would Canei admit to being the murderer! Even after I'd been accused? I DON'T FUCKIN THINK SO! Oh my God-I was in a JAM!

Confusion beat me-literally, for the next several minutes! I was the terrified victim of circumstance-trying desperately to figure out just how to save my fuckin life! An THIS time-it was NOT my fault!

Hold it-just wait! Where's the OTHER bitch? THIS stiff still had red lipstick on. But what happened to Bachelorette number two? Uh...it was this ones glass in the sink. The same glass that I smashed to Kingdom Come! Damn, there goes the evidence!

I started to wipe off my fingerprints then said "Fuck it! I was innocent! I'd just come clean an tell 'PO-PO' the truth. That I'd come home tired from a hard day, in JAIL, and found Whitey sleepin in my bed! I tried to wake her up-got pissed off and then realized she was dead! My MAN had cheated on me and fucked her into oblivion. Oh-then after detailing my incredible story, my Alibi, I would spend the rest of my natural life-IN PRISON! Hold tight Big Bertha! An get the Vaseline ready-I'LL BE BACK! An THIS times for GOOD!

Those white boys questioned me on everything from my Maiden-name to my menstrual cycle!

"So tell us Ms. Singleton-uh, in your own words of course, just how often do you BLEED?" They fine-tooth combed my account looking for holes. Grilled me! For 6 hours. They was pissed off. A rich white bitch had died in Long Island and they needed to know what the Hell I had to do with it! What the fuck was she doin dead in MY house? I TOLD the Lieutenant I hadn't a clue-but if HE found out to please give me a call! YOU tell ME Smokey!

"WE are not trying to imply anything or assign guilt to anyone Ms. Singleton. We just…"

"Hold up, Dirty Harry! Wait a minute. Why you keep saying that? Who the fuck is 'we?' Do you like have some form of Schitzophrenia-some Split-personality shit goin? cuz if you DO-why don't you get the Hell outta my FACE an send in your OTHER half to finish up the interview?" I was irate! I was not cooperating! And I would be back in for Manslaughter the moment they let me outta there!

I purposely left out some details-like Canei speeding off away from the house when I got home. I prefered to let him die at MY worthy hands then spend the next 50 years beatin the system. He had already chosen his poison-Ms. White bitch! And the other missing Ho who was also fixin to die! I didn't tell them about her glass cuz I didn't want them to trace the fingerprint. That was MY job! That and the inevitable decapitation of her upper-body-black lipstick an all!

Canei's prints were naturally still all over the house from our last few years together so they therefore could not implicate him. But he was eventually questioned. The motherfucker lied his way right through. Believe me, I was there. He shrugged off their questions with ease. Stonefaced! Cold as DEATH! With no expression! He treated those interrogators like they was a bunch of crazy paranoid neurotics annoying HIM and wasting his time when he should rightfully be back at work-grinding out a 9-5 job! A job that he didn't have!

The Sergeant was GOOD! A fiery Columbo/Guliani pit-bull! He knew ALL the right questions-all the proper responses. And the inherent defensive gesticulations exhibited by niggers predisposed to not telling the truth! Since he knew what to look for he went into that room like an aloof over-confident, investigatory mastermind. Stalking! An unfed Lion about to take apart his next unworthy opponent with the most prolific skills that Harvard Law School could produce!

When he LEFT he looked like a discloseted FAG! An overwhelmed and out-matched peon who'd just received his first and most ego-shriveling beat-down at the hands of the GREATEST FELON IN THE UNIVERSE! I mean Homeboy high-tailed it outta there as if his ASS were on fire! As if he had just gagged and swallowed his OWN nuts!

Well Harvard HADN'T prepared him for THAT! I never seen Scholarship and Academia humbled so decisively! Mr. D.A. man could've rammed that scrolled Master's Degree up his ass! Canei had him wondering why the fuck this useless line of questioning was going on-or even necessary! Pink, profuse and particularly disheveled, the once proud stock of Alpha Beta Kappa had been reduced to a diffident sniveling recluse! One-Hundred and sixty pounds of undone minced meat hardly shook the hands of his victorious detainee-his executioner, fixed his tie and walked the fuck outta the Jailhouse probably vowing to himself never to practice Law again! Maybe even to seek and destroy the fool who allowed him to Graduate-an go out after passing the Bar-exam so ill-equipped and unable to effectively defend himself! The Lion had been 'defanged' AND 'declawed!'

When Canei and I were finally exonerated and released, he drove me home and not a word was said! He'd thought he won-beat the system. But there was another sector of Jurisprudence he was YET to face! And he would NOT escape! When we pulled up I said "I hope you die tomorrow" and went inside and proceeded to rip up and throw out every piece of clothing he had left in my apartment! THAT was only the beginning!

Aint no words to justify THIS! No explanation! An I ain't no gullible white-boy Prosecutor you can intellectually bully! You might've brain-fucked HIM but you KNOW I don't play that shit! MY NAME IS SIMONE SINGLETON Asshole! Remember? The one you cheated on! WHEN SHE WAS IN JAIL! You know, the one whose throwin your monkey ass OUT! Ariva Derche CHEATER! It's payback time! And believe ME! You CAN'T out-fuck me! By the time you're working on bitch number 5 when you call yourself getting back at ME, I'll be finished screwin MALE-MODEL number 10! BASTARD! SO BOUNCE SHIT-FACE-CUZ IT'S ON!

I wanted to use Canei's head for target practice! To split his scrotum to the white-meat and feed it to my uncles pit-bull 'Louie!' Louie could surely find a good enough reason to maul and grind them into fish-food! THEN I'd feed the residue-the remains to the pigeons in Central Park! (They gotta eat too) Let's see him try an cheat on me now-with a real big giant black dick-AND NO NUTS!

But There was no time-no purpose to concern myself with him cheatin cuz he was outta there! He came back an picked up his shredded SHIT off the curb while I watched through the bedroom window on the celly with my girl. As he rummaged through the unsalvageable pile of polyester we synchronized our estrogen time-pieces as to what would go down later that night. Hattie and I had a long conversation and she couldn't believe what that evil man had done! He had been makin his rounds-BUT THE FOOL

Bomani Shuru

GOT BUSTED! We finished goin over the details about the 'Scoop of the Century,' the dead purple bitch and her escaped accomplice with dark brown lipstick. About the Jackass I'd been seeing who lied more than President Bush and couldn't keep his dick in his pants long enough for his betrayed spouse to make bail and get outta prison. After 45 minutes of high velocity male-bashing and sworn feminine vindication Hattie and I switched over to a more satisfyingly meaningful topic! That's when we three-wayed Mikki and Kecia!

"Meet me there at 12:00 A.M!" LIKE I SAID-IT WAS ON! I hung up the celly and lay down on my bi-racially contaminated bed deciding exactly how that Shit-hole would pay-after planning 'FUCK-FEST' 2005 to be held tonight at Honey's when the Clock strikes Twelve!!

I ain't stupid an I know niggers cheat. It's like second-nature to them-just as natural as breathing and I WILL NOT-I REFUSE to be the gullible bitch married to a philanderer and sittin home waitin for him to come back from yet another Business trip! Yeah RIGHT Playa-I'm stupid! In fact I'm actually faithfully blind enough to believe that you're really at work-doin a double! Well your at WORK alright-with your penis stuck in that chicken-heads mouth! And as for the double-WELL, YOU PROBABLY BONED HER TWICE!!

Who wants their lives to embody that tragic tale and familiar scene of a poor lonely married bitch at home with curlers in her hair, an old gray sweat-shirt, last-years dungarees and an ass that's been flat since the early seventies! Or around the time when Ronald Reagan was President! NOBODY wants that bitch-that corroding hag who needs Viagra for her droopy tits and some Holy Water for that despicable motherfucker who cheats on her sorry ass at least 366 days a year!

Well God ain't sleep, time will tell AND WHAT GOES AROUND COMES AROUND! And one day this dilapidated unattractive bitch is gonna wake up an smell the Hell outta that cup of coffee! And when she does-POOR MS. WIFEY will evolve from POOR MS. NICEY into something quite different! I can see it NOW!

Poor Ms. Wifey is sick of being POOR innocent Ms. Nicey-tired of all the Bullshit you put her through! And she's fixin to lay in the cut for you to come home one night. She'll seduce you. Take you to that place where you need to be every waking moment of your life. She'll grant you orgasm after climactic orgasm-sending your tired unworthy ass out to the moon and back!

After she rides you till your swollen testicles appear to have crawled 3 steps from deaths door she will sit on it again! This time harder and more vociferously than you had been fucked before. And there you lay-butt-naked and limp dick drenched with semen you never thought you had! Your tired little pecker will fall asleep-welcoming the congenial peace from 10 straight hours of euphoria. It's good! The sleep...but it's not over Playa! Not by a long-shot!

92

Your self-righteous fantasies will be abruptly invaded by an ardent tugging at that maniacal little guy that dragged you into this sexual frenzy in the first place.You open your eyes just in time to see a large familiar looking behind descending atop your flagulating penis! But what is THIS? This is a big ass I've seen before! It's like something you've begged for-you've sweated in times past amid your forbidden sexual fantasies!

Your dick wishes it were dead! Buried within an Eunuch's tranquil tomb of celibacy. But not so fast homeþoy! Don't cave in now cuz your liscentious prayers have been answered. You bat and blink your eyes in disbelief-but it's real! No, this ain't Wifey's ass-hers is smaller, less robust and not so interesting anymore! She KNOWS that you could take it or leave it. So in her desperation to please you she has brought company along! Called for sexual back-up. She knows the utter magnitude of your frequent irresponsiveness to her own tired portfolio of sexual intercourse. But she loves you more than life itself! So much that she's invited her girlfriend Shawanda with her into the bed-chamber of your desires!

Remember that Wednesday night she caught you peekin-starin at Shawanda's ASS? Well she remembers. Wifey never forgets! In fact she couldn't get it off her totured mind. It hurt her-the way the man she loves caught an instant erection for her best friend! Yeah! SHE PEEPED THAT TOO! Now Shawanda's ass is bigger, round and jucier! It pokes out much more than poor Ms. Wifey's ever could-and the woman you married just can't compete! Should she have to?

This is your night! The fat ass that you see swallowing up your greedy little cock like the Titanic sitting atop a canoe belongs to that big brown-skin bitch you've been dying to fuck since Wifey introduced you. Wifey at first had second thoughts about introducing this fat piece of ass to the only man in her life. (Uh, that would be YOU Playa) But she checked herself and gained a degree of confidence and trust in your ability to respect your relationship. She dispelled any insecure thought of suspicion or fear of your intended infidelity.

Well Christmas is here and you're thanking Santa for the thick lower part of Shawanda's anatomy. She's fuckin you! An she's FUCKIN YOU! And you want to cry out-TO SCREAM cuz the PUSSY is so GOOD! You wanna punch the big bitch in the back for making you wait so long! You're pussy-whipped and don't give a fuck who knows it! Suddenly the moans start! An exhausted back is hunched-and your lying deceitful lips pronounce "Oouh" in a way Wifey never heard it articulated from you before!

"OOops!" "FUCK!" Mayday, MAYDAY!" You just came! INSIDE Shawanda! "SHIT! I hope she don't get pregnant! O.k, o.k! I'll just say the BITCH is lying! I never touched the Ho-and the baby ain't mine! Oh-NO, what if Wifey finds out? The bitch might drop a dime outta spite-you KNOW how vindictive women are! Hey wait a minute! DUH? Wifey sanctioned the shit! She set me up-an she's standin right there!

Watchin me fuck the living HELL outta her BEST FRIEND! NO! Watching her BEST FRIEND FUCK THE LIVING HELL OUTTA ME! O.K. Playa-relax! Get your shit together!" You've gotten so much pleasure in the last 10 hours that you don't know WHAT IN HEAVEN'S NAME is goin on!

You're drained! Your dick wishes it could detach-slide around to the other side of your body and crawl up your funky ASS! It wants no part of NO MORE pussy for at least 6000 years! Shawanda has seen to that! Hey, the bitch cured me from a busy dick! Ha Ha-my dick is dead, my DICK is dead! Now I don't have to cheat on Wifey no more! You smile, then burst into laughter as Shawanda looks back at you-her big ass dismounting from the backwards straddle position that she nearly broke your waning little Bazooka Joe with. Wondering what the Hell this mass of elated confusion is laughing about!

A willing hostage of pussy submission you lay there wondering just how much more of this your heart can take. Gleaming, Shawanda lifts that luscious leg (Wifey ain't got legs like THAT) causing your gooey aftermath to take that proverbial nose-dive from her tasty womb to your bulging stomach. The semen druels outta her 'Cuppy-Cake' like last weeks New England Clam Chowder-lilly white, chunky and forbidden cuz you KNOW you wasn't supposed to fuck her! Ain't no room in them Wedding vows for screwing Wifey's best friend! So you must've forgotten to mention infidelity during the Ceremony. And to add insult to injury you started the Honeymoon without her. Compliments of the 2 fingers stuck between Shawanda's radiant boiling hips!

After her dismount you notice the thick caramel colored beauty of those calves. Her bountiful thighs and flat stomach. Her titties got more bounce-to-the-ounce than YOUR woman's saggy departures held destitute in a 24 hour bra.

Shawanda is FINE! And you think "Hmn, FUCK WIFEY! This bitch done made me cum-HARDER THAN A MOTHERFUCKER! I want Shawanda!" Wifey can KEEP the ring, the house, the car and those 3 fuckin kids you regret you ever met. SHIT! 'You Da Man' and Shawanda is your Bride!

But the fun has just begun. Although you can't wait for wifey to pack up her Hush-Puppies and leave, the 2 best friends have planned another surprise for you. At first you object but then your greedy promiscuous notions agree-wondering what could be better than THIS? You rapidly dispel the thought of kicking Wifey outta her OWN house so Shawanda can suck your dick till it gets hard again! Shit! You've already come about 9 times today so a few minutes delay can't hurt.

"The worthless bitch got FIVE minutes-then she's outta here! I got some BRAND NEW pussy to kill! SOME NEW ASS!" And her services are no longer needed in the spiraling travesty of your life.

Wifey and Shawanda both walk into the bathroom together and your imagination is ignited.

"Oh shit! Let me find out that these bitches is on some gay lesbian shit! Yo son! THAT'S why they so tight! Hangin out together-always talking on the phone and thick as thieves. THESE bitches is fuckin!" Then it hits you. "OH SHIT!" They wanna tag-team a nigga! I might get a threesome outta this. Wait...now she let the big butt bitch fuck me-an I'm her man. But she just stood there-AND WATCHED! God-Damn! Wifey is a FREAK! 'WHOO-WEEH!' I'm the MOTHAFUCKIN MAN! I'm gonna hit TWO bitches TONIGHT! At the same TIME!"

You're livid-enamored by the many possible positions you can concoct in the sexual symphony composed of Shawanda and Wifey. I'll hit Shawanda from the back! Probably stick it in her ASS. Then let wifey suck my dick. Uh, maybe clean it off an I might bust off in her mouth! No, fuck that bitch! I'm sick of her tired ass. She can just suck my dick till I get hard again. Then I'm hittin Shawanda again!

I'm gonna blow that bitches back out. "POW, POW, POW!" You begin to imagine the sexual acrobatics you are about engage in with your body and your mind.

"Your bath is ready baby. Come on," a seductive voice says from behind the door.

"Oh shit, Wifey and Shawanda wanna do me in the bath tub! Oooh shit!"

"An don't turn on the lights honey."

You laugh. Them some fuckin freaks. You wanna call your boy! You can't believe this shit! Fuckin your woman, well ex-woman, AND another bitch on the same day. In the same room. DAMN! I think I've died and went to Heaven. So you figure-call your man Joe over cuz that nigger won't believe this shit if he didn't see it with his own eyes!

"Yo, he can HAVE Wifey! You don't give a DAMN. And you'll hit Shawanda. "I'll show that nigga-these bitches is fiendin for the kid!"

"Come on baby, we're ready," says that voice.

"Ah ha, ha, ha-hah," goes your ego! Your dumb ass jumps off the bed not realizing you forgot to take off your pants. You realize this as you almost trip an crack your egotistical skull trying to walk with your pants around your ankles. You wanna get to your cell phone to call your boy Joe. Put your Homey down on this shit but you remember you hid the phone in the dashboard of the Jeep. You can't bring that shit in Wifey's house cuz the bitch has been known for those Search-and-Destroy missions-goin in a niggers pockets! And there's too many other females numbers in there to mess around! That's what she did the LAST time! Went buck-wild-delete-happy!

"Oh...who is THIS? Uh, O.K! You say you never heard of her? Somebody ELSE put the bitches home number in YOUR phone? Alright Playa-of course I believe you. Well let me clear this shit up for you-make some room! SHE'S OUTTA THERE! "DELETE!" "CHOCOLATE?" An you wont be needin that one either! An Tabitha? Tell Tabitha Bye-bye! Who the Hell is 'Luscious?' Oh-no Nigger-FUCK HER! "DELETE!"

"Now THAT'S that BULLSHIT! That's why I'm leavin that bitch-there's just too much you gotta put up with! Oh I can't go out now? I can't have friends? A nigger can't have no privacy? So now I ain't got my celly-tryin to safeguard it from psycho bitch!

And that means I can't call my man to keep this nosy bitch occupied while I bone Shawanda! Well that's O.K. you hatin cock-blocker cuz after tonight I'm out! That's right, I'm out! Me an Shawanda's got plans. An you can keep the house! I don't want the shit!" You forgot it's HER house that you're volunteering to let her keep.

"You shoulda minded your own Damn business you nosy Playa-hatin tramp! It's ON now! Matter of fact if that bitch wants some dick she's gonna have to take it in the ASS! HURT THAT BITCH! Oh-she don't know huh? I'm the MOTHERFUCKIN man!"

"Then again I might put Wifey's ass on rations! Starve the bitch! Don't give her no dick at all! Make her suffer-beg for my shit while I fuck the shit outta her best friend! Oh yeah son-it's ON, 'I said! Nah Ho, you fucked up. Dog house for that ass! HEAL, boy! SIT-now BEG! I SAID SIT YO PUNK-ASS DOWN! Oh, you want some of THIS dick? THIS GOOD DICK? Well fuck that-I'm not in the mood! No! No, you just sit there an watch!"

You're determined to hurt Wifey in ways that cut deep into the female psyche! Her only crime-her eternal love and devotion to a man who is deviant and means her no good! Your goal is to humiliate your kind and loving wife! To fuck Shawanda! "Blow her motherfuckin back out," an make poor Ms. Nicey just sit there, horny, pussy drippin heart broken from your shattered bottle of betrayal-and mad as Hell!

Then you think to yourself "Well I don't know! The bitch HAS been down with me for awhile. She's faithful. Kinda loyal! I don't know-I MIGHT fuck her! I DON'T KNOW-it depends on how I FEEL!" Your traitorously nefarious heart has actually summoned a single belated shred of futile empathy that not even GOD knew you were capable of! And yet you expel that morsel of pity as though you were doing poor Wifey an unmerited favor.

You look at your watch and hop to the bathroom door not wanting the two women to change their minds about gratifying you in the bath tub! Hippity-hop hop-and your there!

The bathroom is sensually lit. And after your final intrepid hop you hear somebody close the bathroom door behind you.

"Come on baby-we're in here. The water's nice and hot-and we've been waitin for you boo!"

Your dick gets diamond-hard immediately. All that tired punk shit is out the fuckin window along with any shred of common sense and decency anybody ever thought you had. You see, when a hungry wolf is about to take the first bite 'itty-bitty brain' goes to sleep. Along with thoughts of consequences and fatal ramifications. And voracious unfettered appetite takes charge!

When you look down at your dick you got one of those teenaged erections! The ones that STAY HARD-AND NEVER DIE! They won't go down-an 'Fast Freddy' ain't budging! You whisper "Oh shit! I think I've discovered the Fountain of Youth! Thanks to Shawanda.' An Slim-jim is harder than a rock! "BOING!"

As you stand transfixed, proud of the hard-on Wifey could never extract from your unreasonable ass before, you feel a gentle hand! A warm carress and a hot steamy set of lips touching you. Turning you on even more as you stand there butt-assed naked, in a dark bathroom with your pants down around your ankles. In your house-slippers with 2 nude bitches that both wanna fuck the shit outta you! What more could a black man ever need or want! I AM THE KING! ME LORD TARZAN! THE MIGHTY DICK-SWORDSMAN AND THESE 2 WOMEN ARE MY SEX-SLAVES! UH-UAUAH-UAUAUAAHH," shouts the Soveriegn Ape-man!

And then it happens! 'WHOAAARGH!" Wifey cuts your balls off and sticks them up your momma's ASS so that YOU CAN'T PROCREATE-and NO bitch can ever give birth to ANY child as SICK, arrogant, demented and perversely ungrateful as YOU-HIS FUCKED-UP WOULD BE DADDY!

Needless to say, THIS fairy-tale has an even happier ending cuz cheatin-ass Canei is that emasculated Playa-an "I IS POE-MISS WIFEY!" Say good-night 'Gracie!"

GORILLA'S CAN'T TAKE HEAD SHOTS

I would've slept with ANYBODY or anything that night! Hattie and Kecia both tried to tell me to calm down but you know the scenario: "Wisdom is like poison to the ears of the young!" Well-actually, I just made that shit up. But I also made up in my mind that payback is a bitch. And revenge is sweet! Especially when that revenge involves PLEASURE! It's the best formula known to woman prescribed to stave off the pain in a lonely sex-organ on those dark and quiet nights when it remembers how vigorously and strong it got fucked!

Well Canei screwed me in that way and this bitch decided to screw him back! If he'd had a Homeboy, I'd have STRADDLED HIM and sent the video tape-the grueling footage to his job! Woulda made that "Video Vixen" bitch look like Little bo peep-THE Virgin Mary! Too bad the stupid bastard had run out of Homeboys and HAD NO JOB! But imagine-that would be some real interesting locker-room talk for that ASS!

"Yo Canei, that was some real shit yo! Did you see how your Homey spanked that ASS? BOW, BOW, BOW! RIP! "OOPS! Sorry Ms. Jackson-but I am for REAL!" BOW, BOW! And that bitch loved it too! But tell me-the way they fucked all night long like that was so natural! It looked so real, what with the sound effects, and the spit. And the cum and all the vaginal blood flying around the screen like that! Tell me brother-was that their first time-or has he been rakin his dick in that for years-JUST FOR PRACTICE?"

"I admire your girl playa. Um serious-the bitch got potential! Yo-here 'dog!' Give her my number. Tell the bitch to call me…alright Gee? No hard feelings. This is strictly business-an I got a fifth of 'Henney' and a bag of weed with her name on it!"

I'm fuckin serious! I was on some real 'Look at you NOW nigger' shit an my girls KNEW it! And they KNEW how I got down! By the time we pulled up to Honey's I jumped out of the car and left Hattie and Kecia there looking like two confused parents watching their beloved only child plunge headlong into an orgy! They say that fools rush in where Angels fear to tread. Oh yeah? Well I was Miss Bitch this night! So to Hell with the cowardly Angels! If they too scared to tread their dainty Celestial asses into Hell's kitchen, I would make up for their lack of spunk with some Fire and Brimstone sexually promiscuous antics of my own. As long as they'd stay the HECK outta my way while I'm enroute to bustin off into Orgasmic Heaven, they'd be alright!

Live long and prosper Assholes! Cuz the Devil's daughter is about to get her swerve on. You can play your Cherubic harps and reminisce about the good-ole-days all you want. But as for me-THE DAY OF THE NUT IS HERE!

I shouldn't have let Canei drive me to this madness-but you know the flavor: You play with fire-and you'll get burned! And I felt the inferno raging from my throbbing senses to my vindictive brain! Canei, the man I trusted, had done some foul shit that truly hurt me! My mind caught on fire-my heart was broken. And the pressure of a dead bitch on my bed he probably beast fucked smoldering from my minds rearview mirror of thought transformed into a flaming volcano of desire from a cheated woman's perspective. Damn! Shit really does roll downhill!

After 3 drinks and 9 phone numbers we sat at a booth talking about what this worlds hurt bitches usually complain about-and go to Night-clubs for. MEN! Kecia was on her celly trying to call ASSHOLE Marvin and asking ME why the trifling dog wasn't picking up.

"CRASHDUMMY! How the Hell do I know! Maybe he's licking somebody's ass and ain't got time to talk! WHATEVER, stupid-don't ask ME, ask the bitch he's creepin with!"

Hattie kept staring at 4 dudes at the bar and they eventually started starin back.

"Uh-oh bitch! It's on now! Hattie we got 4 tonight. You take Johnny Appleseed and Barry White on the left and I'll do Burt Lancaster and his sexy caramel partner the Rudolph Valentino look alike on the right. Kecia you can book the Hotel reservations and hail us a Taxi. Oh, and tell Marvin to pull his dick outta red-bones mouth-and put on a fucking condom! I don't want him comin back complaining to you when he's H.I.V. positive!"

Kecia looked at me and said, "Wait, hold on! You tell him when the voice machine comes on." She grabbed my hand like she was about to give me the phone. NO SHE DIDN'T! Crashdummy was serious. How fucking STUPID could you be? How did this bitch find her own pussy in the dark? How did she even know to wipe her ASS? I couldn't believe what was goin on. My girl was DUMB! I've seen more street-sense in the fantasmical minds of second graders who still piss on themselves from time to time while watching Power Rangers reruns all day!

The Fantastic Four made their way over to our table and Rudy Valentino did all the talking. He musta been head-nigger in charge! But he looked…not Spanish-but not black-Black! But mixed! Fuck it, I thought! Canei 'did' a white chic so a little Latino vengeance can't hurt too bad! Besides, today is the day of the Jackal! Fuck night! And the most fascinating thing about casual sex is that whatever International Language you just so happen to speak-A HUMP IS A HUMP! A fuck is a FUCK-AND ANYWHERE, FROM China to Kalamazoo we all cum in the same language: "AH-SHIT-ISH!" That being said-tonight I'll 'DO' a Puerto Rican!

"Hey Easy, get these lovely ladies a drink. Sweetheart, what will you be havin?" He was talking to me! But Hattie jumped all in the business like she was Vanna White or something!

"I'll have a Rum and Coke," went the fag that no fuckin body was even talking to!

"I'll have a Rum and Coke!" I imitated her in a Shananay voice and they all laughed. I had to whisper to the gay-wonder a focal piece of my mind. Sometimes you GOTTA check a belligerent homo.

"Bitch ain't nobody talking to YOU. Rudy's mine. Shit, you can HAVE the other 3-and just let Kecia wash out the condoms after each set! You can't be too careful you know!"

Hattie was embarrassed an I felt bad. But she KNEW this was my night! She knew ALL the stuff I had been through with the bastard and I deserved to fuckin chill-with Rudy! So if she didn't like it we could either shoot-joints or draw straws-I didn't give a fuck! Mess around with a She-lions cubs-or her King of the jungle if you want to!

My celly rang and it was Canei.

"Huh-hold on Playa! I'll get back to you in another 6000 years," I barked!

We sat there for about 20 minutes and I gathered that based on the conversation 2 of the 3 goons was feelin Kecia but she was too fuckin stupid to know it. Shit! They could've both stuck their dicks in her simultaneously-Gang-banger style and she would not have realized what the Hell had went on until after she was wheeled into the delivery room! Nine months pregnant, about to go into labor and the bitch don't know who the baby daddy is-Johnny Appleseed or Burt Lancaster! Up until 15 minutes ago she wouldn't have even known she had been trained! "Uh, Mone-whose dick is this in my mouth? I just went to sleep and when I woke up there it was!"

Barry White just sat there-emotionless! Like his mind was in a distant place and time. He kept looking at his Rolex and then out into the crowd. Like they were there initially to meet somebody and his 3 more promiscuous colleagues had forsaken their sacred mission for some down time with us ghetto tricks. I don't miss NOTHIN! Even after 5 Long Island Iced Teas.

I couldn't believe it but it seemed like Rudy just might be feelin Hattie. He kept starin at me like I was that hot morning coffee he'd waited 24 hours to drink. Yet his mannerisms and body language with Hattie seemed more relaxed-more natural. I know he knew she was a fag but oh fuckin well. I said to Hell with it! I wanted Rudy inside ME that night and I was gonna put a move on his Itralian ass to bring him back to his heterosexual senses. If shit came down to it me an the pillow-biter would duke it out like two cackling bitches in a cat fight! I'd do ANYTHING I HAD TO DO before I let him waste that handsome milk-chocolate hammer inside the 'Reckless peanut butter cup' of a tall hairy fag!

I mean Hattie was my girl and all-I would ride or die for the bitch. I even threw a couple of left-overs her way back in the days. But there's something about the penetrating ecstasy of the male anatomy that goes deeper than most feminine gendered relationships. I was mad. I was vindictive. I was obstinate-and I could feel an upper-cut coming! I wanted so bad to hook off on the bitch and she KNEW it! She was irking me-trying to laugh at all his fuckin jokes like she was so amused by his deflated sense of humor! Trust me, Rudy was no Chris Tucker!

In the space of about 15 everlasting minutes Hattie was literally eating outta his hands. And that's some self-degrading shit that I don't do. FUCK THAT! My motto is

I'll let the dick go if I gotta lower myself to the Penitentiary bitch who ain't had none in years routine. I'd give a man every part of me my momma blessed me with and I'd explore every part of his that his Daddy endowed him with. A man could reach the moon between my legs and my mouth would take him to planets he'd never seen. Both of us gliding through our passion Universe. BUT I don't kiss no ass! My daddy didn't teach me to do that. I MIGHT be a HO-but I don't suck up, I don't do tricks an I don't kiss no ASS!

So Hattie was cheatin-using cheap seductive methods foreign to me an I didn't appreciate it. But apparently Rudy did. I wanted to say, "Hey Rudy, look Playa-take a good look! This, my friend Hattie, is a faggot! How you gonna chose a FAG over me? I mean, what nigga in this place-no on this whole Continent, would rather fuck something with a shriveled up dick between his legs than me?" I dispelled the question when my celly rang again. It was my parents' number. I left the table and ran to the bathroom without sayin shit to nobody!

Hoping all was well I nervously hit redial cuz the call was lost by the time I got to the Restroom. Everyone was O.K! Daddy, by mistake had hit redial on the phone while trying to call somebody else. But who the Hell was he callin anyway at 1:30 A.M. Sometimes I wonder about that man. Here I am out here doin some illicit shit and this fool interrupts my 'Ho-flow' and sends me scurrying into the 'John!' For nothing!

I cursed the decrepit Senior Citizen out in my mind and said "I love you" with my alcohol drenched lips! But by the time I got half-way back to the table Hattie had locked down the situation and Rudy was eatin Maraschino cherries outta HER hands. Oh man! What the Hell. The bitch beat me. FAG LOVER! He musta been a perv anyway! But he was a very attractive Perv. I swallowed my sour grapes like a woman (I often do) and started toward the Bar. To Hell with them, I thought. They can launch the fag orgy of the Century for all I care! I just wish them luck tryin to persuade Kecia to get her Crashdummy head out of her ASS and leave the room PROMPTLY when the bangin starts! All of a sudden I didn't wanna see them no more-instead I figured I needed a little quiet time!

I sat next to this tall slender handsome guy and he started talking to me. He was nice, polite, funny and a real Gentleman. We must've talked for 2 hours and I couldn't remember exactly why I had went there in the first place I had been so engrossed in the conversation. He was the type of man that a woman would marry-and I liked that in a man.

While we was kicking it some bitch tried to move in on my territory. My TERRITORY! She musta been at least 6 feet, Rotwiler ugly and had shoulders like a Line-backer! She just pranced her Sponge-Bob Square-ass over to us an said "HI" like I was not even there! Now Hattie had cock-blocked me earlier an I said "O.K. cool-that's my girl and it's all good!" But I wasn't about to back down from Broom Hilda an let

Bomani Shuru

another piece of dick strut itself away from me. NO! NOT on Hell night. NOT on Fuck-fest night!

I jumped in McGilla's face and told her to back up but she just stood there. She must not have known me cuz I have a rep that anybody whose SOMEBODY knows! I heard Hattie in the background coming toward us sayin, "Yo-what's up? I got you girl! (Her famous last words) I knew my homey was down for some beef. I loved her for that. The fighter in her reminded me so much of myself.

"Who the fuck are you bitch-WHAT'S UP, Said the burly Neanderthal? No she didn't call me a bitch! Suddenly words were meaningless modes of communication no longer relevant in what was about to go down. So I put down my volatile 'vocab' for some shit I learned to use more efficiently-more destructively back in Junior High School!

"Oh, you think you some bad ass gorilla bitch!" I punched the SHIT outta the tall stocky primate an she fell dead on her ugly face like a sad sack of shit! It was ON! I started POUNDIN THE BITCH OUT 'Straight Outta Brooklyn' style! I was on top of her an she was screaming for some bitch named 'Yolanda!' "YOLANDA! YOLANDA!"

Who the fuck was Yolanda? Did the first right hand knock her into a nonsensical stupor where she transformed me from the Executioner of her soul into Yolanda? Then it HIT me! Yolanda must be her Homey-her Road-Dog! She's callin for back-up. I don't fuckin believe it. THIS ape bitch is callin for back-up!

Now when I start something I don't stop. I saw red and the ass-whippin had to commense cuz that's how I get down! Once I throw up the first one you better get outta the way cuz there's a tornado comin-a destructive force of nature! Fuck GOD if he gets in the way cuz he'll get HIS HOLY guts stomped-out too! PUMMELED! An if HE catches a bad one you know I got no respect for nobody else when that time comes. NOBODY! The Pope, the President, the Cops, the D.A, Mickey Mouse-the Judge AND the motherfucker who pulls the switch to fry my ass after the "Murder One" charge! I'll beat his ass too. And my girls knew that. (Stay outta the way bitches-unless you want a piece of what She-Ape is getting) So I figured they must be behind me or somewhere havin my back. Just in case Yolanda shows up a tad late and a 'dollah' short tryin to protest what I'm doin to her kin-folk! Monkeys stick together you know!

My shoe-heel penetrated the Gibbons face at least 5 times! "STOMP, STOMP! WOP, WOP, STOMP! She made a scowling helpless grimace each time the high-heel boot smacked down from 'the Mississippi to Ground-zero!" Oh yeah, I telegraphed the injured baboon-an I was havin my way! Her tall stocky Mr. T behind was getting beat-down by an average 5 foot 8 bitch from Long Island who'd just caught her man cheatin!

Nobody stopped it. After what seemed like 2 hours of a stampeding crowd scrambling for cover from the possibility of bullets flying along with irate nigger fists, I was finally tired of wailin on the Gorilla. You know Lord Tarzan's gotta keep them flea-ridden banana-munchers in check!

102

"Gorilla's can't take head-shots huh," I yelled then walked off leavin the bitch scrambling on the floor wondering what went wrong! She did NOT want to get up. That would mean some more of the same-justify further furious fists upside that dastardly grill genetics blessed her with. And she was not up to losing more than 5 pints of monkey-blood. Not all in one night!

"Where the fuck is Yolanda now bitch?" I spit at her and kicked her in the stomach when I said "bitch." Suddenly I heard what sounded like the voice of some white-boy who probably looked like Pee-Wee Herman.

"Somebody call Security! Throw her A-yus OUT," cried the punified larynx from the Red-hills of Geeksville!

"Huh, throw my A-YUS OUT? Who the fuck said THAT? And how the Hell do you spell 'A-YUS?" I guess you call that inept type of dialect 'Eurobonics' or 'Cracker-phonics' or something-I don't know! When I shouted out that question all was quiet on the Western front! Perhaps the spineless Mouseketeer lost his nerve. Or somewhere in his cowardly existence there was the Eternal struggle between unrealistic 'Honky-heroics' in the ghetto and the absence of desire to wind up like the floored Gorilla sprawled out betwixt my bloody Tim boots! And in keeping with the enduring tenets of forced submission, he concluded that there was no way he'd survive the pummeling for even 10 minutes before the Cops would arrive to rip my dukes off his unready fuscia-flavored ass!

By then the music had stopped, the prison spotlights glared on and the bout had begun and ended in round-one! It's not so good to get that ass beat in the dark cuz there's no way to garner proof or gather witnesses when nobody saw shit! Rudy, Hattie and the other 3 creeps came over and escorted me to my neutral corner and somebody turned the lights back off.

"Will somebody pick up this THING-black folks wanna get their dance on. Yo Moe, sweep up the Road-kill babe," Hattie jested. The bouncers ran over to my murder victim inquiring as to the nature of the beat-down but her swollen lips were in no mood for forming words.

The brother I'd been talking to at the Bar came over to where I was standin and I did my best to exhale the 'Raging Bull' still parlaying it's violent way through my adrenaline! I did my best to calm the fuck down long enough to salvage the rest of my night! His refined presence accommodated my tranquility and I began once more to enjoy myself-based on the soothing restraint of his tone.

He said he was rootin for me and even bet one of the bouncers 100 bucks that I would kick the Gorilla's ass. I KNEW the bouncers real well which is why they had more pressing issues to attend to during the melee. We sort of got an unwritten agreement not to interrupt a bitch handling her biz right away. I get 3 minutes grace period-then the S.W.A.T. Team swarms in. Too late fuckers-the damage is already done! Don't bother with summoning the Ambulance-CALL THE CORONER! They're better equipped to discard beaten corpses! The Head-bouncer-Mercury and I are MAD cool! Mercury was the man-my BOY! We talked for about half an hour and I introduced him to my new 'Friend.' His name was Floyd! The 3 of us had a drink and Floyd had to leave for work in 2 hours.

Mercury offered me another drink but 7 is my limit-besides I was starting to see double. Hattie and Kecia were still chillin with those other dudes but I was ready to go. Unauthorized Prize-fights take a lot out of a bitch an I felt the Alcohol was doin a job on me that the Gorilla couldn't. Mercury offered to take me home and I agreed cuz my knuckles were too swollen to drive. Floyd lip-kissed me Good-night and we agreed to see one another again that Weekend. I liked him. First impressions are important when you shootin joints from the first day you meet but I could see he was feelin me too. I assured him that my boxing skills were nothing compared to some other things I can do in the dark-them other skills! The ones I don't utilize on monkeys. He was the strong silent type but laughed hardily at what I'd said. Floyd then bent over and kissed me again-this time on my forehead. His lips were soft-and tender. With a force behind them that promised to touch a sister gently, to keep her warm but could also tear her out the frame if that's what she wanted. I loved that kiss cuz it presented to me a new beginning-one without the sour aftertaste of Bastard-man Canei. And I produced and rehearsed a fresh well orchestrated relationship for Floyd and I based solely on that FIRST KISS!

I said I was truly feelin the different seductive approach of being held by a man without the bitterness of 'Absolute' on his breathe and who didn't embarrass me every other second we spent together. You know a woman looks forward to that-and the pleasure of someone who remembers every step of the way that she is special. And won't let her forget it either-not for a second. Would you believe? I deferred the planned sexual ferocity of 'Fuck-night' for the combined serenity of spending a beautiful Weekend with my NEW loving Prince-Floyd! A woman can receive a dozen roses from an ogre-a beast but it won't hit home because beasts are unworthy of assuring her true happiness.

And then a woman could receive that same bouquet from a man-a real man, with the compliment of sincerity gift-wrapped around each petal and THAT token of appreciation will explode her senses into a forceful desire to be touched by him-to romanticize on his splendidness. Lastly that same Gentleman-that Shining Prince could offer some sweet endearing words with the resounding reality of genuineness-no dozen roses, no exotic Weekend Getaway and no love-songs playing in the background. But if the brother 'brings it right' she will feel him. A sister will acknowledge his passion and that single immaterial gift will do more for her, for them, than all the diamonds and pearls some greasy erect deceitful womanizing Son-of-a-bitch could ever offer. Not that we don't want that kind of thing cuz we do-but we don't thrive on it-and it won't keep us in your fucked-up corner.

A quiet cool man is a fine monotony breaker. A breathe of fresh air and I'm dog tired of the opposite. I meet too many of them. As we walked out I said Good-night to my girls. Hattie and Kecia stayed back with the fantastic four. Hattie seemed content in the arms of Rudy-his real name was Catharsis. Kecia had the audacity to ask me: "Mone, were you fightin?"

"Was I fighting?" Well where in God's name was THIS bitch during the ruckus? Good thing I wasn't getting my ass kicked cuz to depend on her for help would be an exercise in futility. God-Damn Crashdummy! How you gonna ask me THAT? After the brawl and when I'm walkin out the door?

"No bitch! I wasn't fightin. Who told you that? If you figured that out on your own your drinks too strong-your hallucinatin! The dumb ass actually looked at her drink and put it down! Shocked and disgruntled I flipped her the bird and walked out the fucking door leaving her there-ALONE with her foolish thoughts!

Mercury drove the long way. He probably wanted some pussy from a bitch he thought was sober enough to fuck somebody up but too drunk to say 'NO' to his BLACK Ass! Oh, yes LORD-THAT nigga was BLACK!

Mercury was so black you'd think God sat down to design his shunned portrait on the Cosmic blackboard of ebonic space, outlined a silhouette and forgot to color it in! Or maybe the Good Lord's flesh-color pen ran out just moments before he began filling in his racial hue. Better yet-after the Creator of the Universe finished this, HIS dismal Masterpiece, he realized that he'd fucked up so he blackened in the entire portrait with his Handy-dandy permanent magic marker.

"EGAD," said the Eternal Merciful Christ! "This human sucks!" He mournfully stared at the distasteful work of art looking around the Gates of Heaven to be sure that no displaced Angels had infiltrated his security alarm system and beheld this morbid sculpture of darkness. Suddenly he had an idea. "THIS NIGGERS TOO BLACK! Hmm...maybe I should create some WHITE ones too-just to balance things off! I KNOW, I'll send the white folks up North so they can cool out in the snow. They don't got no melanin so they couldn't survive 15 minutes in the sun. They haven't created Sun-block yet so the cold weather will do them good."

"Then, For these crispy critters, I'll just send them down South! Let em cool the fuck out under the shade. Methinks they got too much Melanin so the sun won't do a Damn thing to em. And I'll separate both tribes so the assholes won't start beefin-sayin one is better than the other or getting Superiority Complexes or Delusions of Granduer against one another. Hell, fuck around and SOMEBODY'LL get to exterminating-or purifying the races. So these vast mountains and 7 Seas should keep em apart-an keep the peace.

Next thing you know-EUREKA, one of God's creations invented a GUN-AND A BOAT! They named the Gun 'Mr. Musket' and the big boat was called 'The Good Ship Jesus.' When God woke up World Wars one, two AND three had began and he cursed the day that man was created!

"Shit!" He roared! "DAMMIT!" He fumed, A MOTHERFUCKER CAN'T GET NO SLEEP WITHOUT THESE ASSHOLES FUCKIN UP EVERYTHING IN SIGHT!"

Such was the modest beginnings of Affirmative Action, Ethnic balance and Racial Intolerance. Besides, everybody knows that when there are too many niggers around, shit kinda gets outta hand. Riotin, lootin, smoking weed (we were born in the jungle so it's natural to us) and acting up at lavish dinner parties that we can't afford and have no business at in the first place. You ever seen an irate nigger at a Spade game, after a bad call at a Football game or when the bum-ass Knicks lose? You'd think somebody siphoned all the oxygen outta the atmosphere, pussy went on strike or the 'Recto-lube' ran out at the local Gay-bar. It's pure unprovoked MADNESS! And don't let nobody die, have a funeral or his babies Momma come up pregnant-AGAIN! You'd think both his nuts were ran over by a cement truck if you intelligently tried to decipher or interpret the utter glare of befuddlement on Homeboy's hostile grill!

"Yo Ma, don't play with me! Don't NOBODY play with me!" Well while black Mercury ran on at the mouth thinking I actually gave a fuck what the Hell he had to say, I reminisced on my time spent with Floyd!

"Yeah, right! Uh-huh, you know what Um sayin Simone?"

"Yeah right nigga! Whatever! Go take a Snow-shower an get back to me." I could see his eye-balls rolling around hideously in the dark, I could here the voice, but as far as I was concerned there was a dead man driving me home!

Half-way there Mercury took a WRONG turn down a secluded block. Oh no! Lord don't make me have to beat HIS ass too.

"Merk, what's up-my house ain't this way?"

"Calm down baby, I got something to show you. Just sit tight! He pulled into a desolate lane and stopped the car. I was NOT in the mood. I mean the brother and I were cool and the Gang but right then I was NOT planning to take a trip to the dark steamy jungles of 'Mercury.' Home of the strepid and horny Night-Club bouncers. Besides, I was kinda feelin Floyd so I didn't really wanna take it there with HIM!

"Here, hold this babe! This is for you if you want it." He pulled out a wad of 50's and told me to count it.

"You havin problems countin out your drug money Merk?" I was kidding.

"How much Monie," he barked?

"It's a Grand Merk. You know how much it is. Whatsa matter, you been holdin back the Child Support checks again?"

"Nah baby. Look don't ask me no questions alright! Money don't know where it come from! You want it or what?"

"Oh boy! What I gotta do-a sister gotta be a Ho?"

"You know I laid off you when you was hookin off on that skeezer back inside. And you KNOW I don't play that shit up in my spots! You gotta act proper-like a lady or that ass is OUT! But anyway I let you live cuz you was handling yours-and I had plans for you tonight."

106

Merk was the brother smart enough to monopolize the security trade in that Community. He had 4 Clubs locked down and was getting paid lovely from each of em. He had 60 some odd dudes working for him 5 nights a week at each site collectively. So a Thou. was nothing to him! He was a slick shrewd motherfucker with an astute business mind. And apparently an itch that he wanted a sister to scratch for him in the back of his jeep! So he pulled out his DICK!

Now WHO THE FUCK wanna look at a half-cooked DICK? It looked like a semi-burnt piece of Salami. Cylindrical shaped, black on the outside and light pink on the inside!

"YO MERK, come on boo! You know you like a brother to me." (That's the magic potion women use when they don't wanna fuck a nigga but ain't so eager to dissolve the friendship either-JUST IN CASE!) "What about your baby's Momma? You KNOW she's 7 months pregnant!"

"The baby will eat," he answered like he was getting mad at me. "And she'll get hers-how the FUCK you think she got pregnant?"

"Yo Merk, don't scream on me now-remember-this is me! Now we go back, but you see what I did to the Gorilla. I ain't tryin to be in here kickin your behind-WITH YOUR DICK OUT! Shit won't look too good in the Newspapers!" I tried to make light of the fact that this big black nigger was handin me an indecent proposal. He acted like he been handin them out for years-an Chickens musta been bitin. And suckin cuz Merk was getting a little hostile-not bein used to being told "NO, nigga-NO!"

"SIMONE, my nuts is freezing-you want the money or what?"

"Yo Playa-I'm flattered and shit. I see the way you be looking at my ass-an don't think I don't appreciate you letting me tap-dance on the Gorilla. Cuz a bitch gotta protect herself. But...nah Merk! Sorry-I can't!"

"Yo, why not? You getting married or something?"

"Put that thing away an drive me home." I reached over and kissed him on the chin. "BOW! Take that Love-an a very Merry Christmas to you TOO Mr. black dick! Now get some sleep," I said to his horrifying cock standin at attention beaming at me. I patted the ugly little dick. "Yo Merk, you really need to put a scarf on that thing. Hard dicks are HARD to come by these days-and they catch cold easily."

"Bitch you crazy! Get the Hell outta my car!"

"Yo Merk, you wouldn't dare-say you playing!" Oh no that nigga WASN'T throwing me out his ride. I pulled out my celly to fake a move-like I was about to make an S.O.S. call! (My battery was dead)

"Yo baby, I'm playin. Since you so worried bout my dick catching the flu-YOU PUT IT AWAY! Otherwise I ain't drivin!"

"Yo Merk, you trippin! That's your..."

"Put me back Mone-an we even. Ain't even gotta talk about tonight again for the rest of your life. It'll be our little secret-just between me an you.."

Now why a nigga gotta act like that? I was about to explain to him that his pink an black dick was HIS problem but instead I thought 'what the Heck?' I quickly tucked his charred turnip back into it's Rocawear sanctuary-destitute, flaccid and unfulfilled!

"Maybe next time Babe. I might make it 2 G's if you gimme some of that pretty ass you sit on!" And no more Bar-fights in my spot or next time I'll TAKE that ASS! For FREE! So why you clean her clock anyway?"

"Well I was talking GROWN-folks business with that nigga Floyd and she jumped up at me like a played-out geriatric tiger! Black gums, arthritis and all. No PROBLEM! I'm a lion-tamer!"

"I got you baby! Bitch just couldn't understand jungle-Mathematics! Well if you a real Lion-or tiger or whatever you are, show me some PUSSY!"

I flipped him the bird and switched my ass into the house. He was cool-a gentle giant with a trickin problem and a mean right-hand! I've seen Merk do some shit to some nigga's that he should STILL be doin time for!

I kicked the Hell outta the cat and called her a dog for almost making me bust my ass on the steps. The house was warm and my bed was unmade but inviting. (Drunk Prize-fighters don't make beds between bouts) And then IT HIT ME! I still ain't had no DICK! There was nothing about beatin a dumb bitches ass that could compare to bustin a nut! I was horny and situated my thoughts between a hot shower (what the Hell would THAT do but make the throbbing worse) and dialing some nigger strong enough to satisfy my needs yet stupid enough to drop by at 4:30 A.M, eat my ass and get thrown the fuck back out! Uh-THAT nigga does not exist in my world! Hmm, a bitch gotta work on that. Never know when you might need the desperate fool. Little did I know that I had marched smack into that gullible fool already yet not thoroughly discovered who he was.

I took off my clothes and wrapped a towel around my waist-THEN THE BELL RANG! Uh, Mr. Right-is that you! Standing out in the cold with your 9 inch dick in your hand ready to fulfill my ever growing needs? It HAS to be cuz ain't no other woman doin that getting in here at this hour. I'd cuss her out for disappointing me. Shit, if I have to drag my exhausted and hung-over behind to the door you BETTER be a male! You better work some Black Magic or Voo-doo-grow a dick bitch or SOMETHING otherwise the jab-flurries is comin!

I went to the door. Enthused, anxious and when I opened it my lower anatomy did a split and popped in half. Oh DAMN-it was the Landlord! The Guyanese Treasure Troll always sweatin me to fuck him or his 19 year old High School son-whomever came first and he was standin in my fuckin doorway. Beady-eyed, disheveled and 'rank' as the day he was born in the dumpster!

"Yago! What the fuck you doin here playa? I'm sleepin, Rent ain't due for another 2 weeks." (I wouldn't even have it then) Maybe I shoulda sucked Mercury's dick for the G! Coulda gave him the hustler's special an called it a day in 5 minutes FLAT!

"Oh my God! Mercury, come back! There musta been a mistake-I changed my mind! I'll suck your ugly pink an black dick-JUST DON'T CUM IN MY MOUTH!"

Yago walked in like he owned the place (actually he does-him, his bow-legged wife and their 3 little dysfunctional kids-I'm just the peon they parasite off of) And from the moment he walked in I KNEW instantly what he wanted!

"Dere's a gas leak hin de Kitchen han me son say im smell hit. So me afee check hout de stove before sumpin appen ere!" Dat what Yago fe tell me!

Yeah right! A fuckin con-man from de hiland hof Guyana tryin to sell we a dream.

"Yeah, whatever Yago. Do what you gotta do an gwan from me place cuz me afee go ah work hin de marnin, Starr!" I was so far intellectually ahead of him it was like an otter tryin to outsmart a Rocket-Scientist. And I could see the shit oozing from his anal-mouth-piece, caked and perched for that long uphill journey toward his lying lips! I sat on the couch while Mr. Fraud faked some repair work behind my stove at 4:30 in the God-damned morning!

Yago was the gnome that time forgot who made my life as a female renter a living Hell! I can't count the times the furry bastard forgot he was married with children and offered me a dick-trick to make up some rent-money I was short of or waive the entire amount completely if I would simply come on over to the fanciful side-that tropical paradise of tormented young black women trapped in an unforgiving web of agony being the mistress of a stymied stinky over-the-hill rascal from the bitter slums of the West Indies. I DON'T FUCK TREASURE TROLLS! He was the lost soul-with buck-shot peas in the back of his head-who'd left home perhaps minutes before the Afro-pick could scrape his scalp.

There was a left-justified swagger that glided itself alongside that segment of his body-sway-back style! His face donning a well-placed distinction boldly on it's way toward being impressed with itself. But how could a limp and hobbling cripple in his late-fifties be so enthralled with his own limited capacity to boast an aloof grin on that smug horrid head of his? I always thought that gnomes knew their places in the greater scheme of things and obediently respected a Universal hierarchy. A natural order which exalted the beauty and utterly shunned the beast insofar as looks and comeliness are concerned! Besides, self-assurance should be an ideal virtually unknown to ANY Persona-nongrata! Maybe I was wrong. For HE certainly thought I was so he finshed the job that did not need to be done in the first place and gingerly continued on in his Narcissistic gait back into the foul crevice from which he crawled.

"Nuff respect Sistah," said the talking lizard!

"Yeah right-whatever! Let the Lysol hit you where the bath-tub MISSED you, Yago!" I deferred the shower and turned out the lights trying to dispel the rancid little beast I had just seen in my foyer at 4:30 A.M! But his estranged odor kept reminding me of the hideous grimace which was designed to charm my panties off and pry these outraged legs open. Hey Don Juan-Is it ME or is good personal hygiene optional in Guyana?

Well so much for the charming innovative crowbar! My panties remained intact and my legs locked but my stomach could not STAND it no more! I imagined a fuming Caribbean Treasure Troll perhaps on top of me clutching my ass-cheeks at the height of his sexual fervor, trying desperately to inject his sour little penis INSIDE me!

And he TOUCHED me! I ran into the bathroom at top-speed and puked out the entire Lobster Cantonese dinner I'd eaten-and then some! I would have gladly amputated my leg but for the massive bleeding it would entailed and decided a Brillo-scrub would suffice!

My kitchen smelled like soiled fur, musty island ASS and not quite ready for Prime-time Cuban-Cigars! But my bedroom didn't! I placed the covers over my head, then jerked-off and cried myself to sleep-feeling like a violated rape-victim! And the only tranquil thought I welcomed was the pleasant memory of Floyd!

-11-

MENAGE-TOIS

I think I'm in love but I'm not sure! If I'm not there's a powerfully deceptive imposter roaming the streets of Carle Place that just crawled up my ass impersonating the ideals that fairy-tale dreams are made of. Oooh-I want him! All I can think of is Floyd. Shit! I got it BAD and the only thing I wanna do is be his wife-it's not a sexual thing! But it IS-I can't quite explain it yet this feeling reminds me of the closest a woman could ever come to falling in love. In the past when I met a man it was simply and totally sexual-an erotic encounter that both should and would end up with two sweaty lust-filled sexual predators banging it out in the sack, an alleyway or in the back seat of a car. But THIS time it's different-and this thing I'm going through with Floyd is much more powerful. And 100 times more gratifying without the mere proposition of that Universal phenomena called S.E.X!

I'd better play my cards right-can't mess up THIS one cuz there's a lotta hood-rats out there who would LOVE this nigger-but I ain't losin this opportunity. I couldn't stand to walk idly by and watch another woman sink her meat hooks into this strong silent type. Like I said-it's been awhile since I met a real Gentleman. You know-the kind with the ability to compliment my femininity and make me feel like a real woman should. So this mysterious new emotion swirling around the once dismal circumference of my brain might not be the eternal genuine butterfly that some of us search our entire existence to find. But it's real enough for me to attach my innermost appreciations to. Therefore if I am not truly in love with Floyd the man at this premature stage of our development, I am however very much in love with the wonderful and alive way he makes me feel.

But I hadn't heard from him in days. He was supposed to call me the night after we met but the phone didn't ring. I checked the cord and made sure to turn up the volume for fear I might not hear it. Even kept the celly on high-tone-yet none of those immature methods women sometimes use to guarantee contact with their wayward spouses proved worthy. I was the jackass looking for rain in the Desert. I was poor Miss Nicey-and I cursed the male species that God had self indulgently concocted toward Mother Eve's demise with 25 Million silent violent obscenities.

DAMN! A bitch been had-AGAIN! Why the Hell don't I learn? Fuck men! Ain't none of em good but the dead ones-and even some of THEM don't act right! "Well for the love of Christ dear. Loosen up-why you so STIFF," say's irate Wifey to her dead husband!

O.K. So I hadn't heard from his monkey-ass in days. We met on Tuesday-Mother-fucker promised to call a sister on Wednesday. To make Reservations for Friday-when we could spend some time together and get to know one another. Well 48 hours later-AND NO CALL! Huh-I AIN'T CALLIN HIM! That's for DAMN sure-not on HIS punk-assed life. I don't kiss nobodies behind! That was my game-plan on Thursday morning. When I woke up I cussed him out in my mind and then went back to sleep to cuss his sorry ass out some more-IN MY DREAMS! Figure somewhere between the 2 vast planes of consciousness and unconsciousness he might hear the mournful cry of my life's displeasures absent from his company. Well either the Sand-Man didn't deliver the message or our wires got crossed cuz the nigger's STILL M.I.A!

By Noon that day (that's when ALL Showdowns occur-at High Noon!) I had turned the trick. Changed my mind! "Alright Asshole-I'll give you the benefit of the doubt. PERHAPS you lost my number-how convenient! You are somewhere, out there looking for me. You know I wanna sleep with you! (by now that's what I need cuz all this anticipation is making me horny-and 'Fuck-night' has already come and gone without the side-effects of me getting my SHIT off) Oh YES Playa-a bitch NEEDS the 'Force!' And you can't wait for me to call YOU so you can explain to me how you LOST MY number and are SO, SO glad I got in contact so we can proceed with MY plans!"

So I CALLED HIM! 6 times! 'Ring, ring, ring-NO ANSWER! Did he forget to mention to me that he was deaf too? Not only clumsy and careless with phone numbers but couldn't hold on to a Bar-napkin with a phone number on it? Hah! Anyway-6 times-and no response. So I began to feel cheated-like I was getting played! And like our entire time at the Club, our whole conversation, WAS BULLSHIT! Then I got vindictive and even started thinking about Canei! I wanted to reach over the sofa to grab my Inter-planetary remote-control and shut-down the entire male species with but a single well aimed radioactive beam of woman's scorn! But the batteries were running low, my hands were unsteady and the evil scurrying bastards wouldn't keep still long enough for me to annihilate them!

"Stand still you little fuckers-so I can BLAST you!" Pre-emptive Genocide is not easy from the vantage-point of a leather sofa. They ran like roaches when the lights come on! Such was the Mechanical futility of the destruction of the male species! But I decided I wasn't beat yet-if you can't wipe em out-FUCK A FEW HUNDRED OF EM!

"GREAT DAY IN THE MORNING!" The fuck-fest was ON! Passionate, illicit and deadlier than ever! Why did I abandon it in the FIRST place? I would go Game-hunting-for the biggest penis I could find! And when I spotted my prey I would gather my equipment (2 titties, hungry genitals and big tight round-brown ASS) cuz a woman's gotta be prepared-at all times! I would sneak up on the Nigger-grab his large pulsating manhood! Wrestle it to the ground-put it my mouth AND BLOW TILL HIS MOMMA FEELS IT! And if that don't kill him, if the sucker's still breathin, I'll pull that rock-hard ramrod outta my mouth-AND SIT ON IT! One of 2 things will happen! Either he'll go into cardiac arrest or I'll bust the BEST nut I ever had. Either way-I'm happy-THEN I'll fuck his best friend!

On Friday morning the phone rang-it was Mikki.

"Yo girl turn on the News-Channel 24. Somebody at Honey's got shot in the head last night! Right after closing time while they was sittin in the front seat of their car. Cops said it was a Hit! THE NIGGA WAS JUST SITTIN IN HIS CAR!"

"Big fucking deal! He shoulda took a Bus! Bitch we goin back to…uh, nah never mind!" I didn't wanna tell her. I was gonna set something up for that night but wisely decided to do THIS one on my own! Some things a woman's gotta do by herself-too many motherfuckers in the kitchen spoil the soup-or some shit like that. I hung up after a few useless words spewed outta her mouth about a Mafia hit that took out the Co-owner of the Club and the scattered reports about the local authorities not havin a clue as to who-done-it. So what else is knew? They never know a Damn thing. And why do they call themselves the authorities-they ain't authorities on nothing but black coffee and donuts. And shootin NIGGERS!

There was no hot water! Without the luxury of a sensible plan I entertained the thought of galavanting into work without the benefit of washing my ass. But that summation died an untimely death at the bitter possibility that the patients might wake up from their catatonic stupors just in time to smell me. They may be retarded but those nasal passages still accommodate effective sensory organs which when given proper external stimuli can detect the staunch rancor of fried pussy and caked shit from beneath my raunchy Victoria Secrets! Their only dilemma would be to decipher whose funky ass was humming so emphatically-mine or their disabled counterparts!

I would not dare chance THAT blatant discovery. Who wants to be put on blast by a mongoloid in diapers? One of em might go genius on me or become eloquent enough to articulate to OTHERS who or what the Hell is smellin so bad! I wasn't goin out like THAT! Havin a foaming retard hopping up and down shouting "STINKIE, STINKIE, STINKIE" and pointing me out to my fellow peers in the Funk Detection Squad!

Breanna opted to pass on the boiling pot water ghetto steam-bath! And that was on HER. She had the right to stink as fiercely as her adolescent hormones would allow! Don't come home cryin cuz they humiliated you for smellin up the Chemistry Lab-smellin like the walking 10 million year old human petri-dish-cuz you've been warned! But as for me-I'm goin with the Tea-kettle, the wash-basin and the snot-rag! Besides, fuck-night was looming-18 hours from now an it was ON! Picture me showin up for that humming like the Tuna-lady!

Breanna emerged outta her room dressed like a thug-an askin too many questions. Didn't she know Gangsters don't like questions? They don't ask em-an they Damn sure won't answer em!

"Ma, you goin out again tonight?"

"Yeah Bre!"

"Who you goin with?"

"Uh, some friends!" I lied-couldn't tell her I was looking for a well-hung STRANGER to Beast-fuck me into Paradise!

"Friends like who?"

"Stay outta grown folks business!"

"I AM-but why you goin out all these nights in a row?"

"Breanna, sometimes mommy just needs to relax-have some fun. Now don't you have some Homework to look over before you get to School?" Damn! The little bitch was interrogatin me. Ain't that MY job-to grill her as to what the fuck is goin on in her juvenile life-and that curious head of hers? Well she obviously had more questions than Homework so I decided to try an squash the Grand Inquisition-before she started pullin off my fingernails!

I felt like a leper. A plague ridden Buccaneer about to be forced to walk the plank to prevent further infection of the rest of the crew! Now why I gotta be the Pariah? Can't a woman go out to find and conquer a hapless male victim without the Junior Whopper Committee present to condemn her every move? Besides, I was hurtin!

Didn't I deserve some 'Down-Time' for what the DEVIL had done to me? What would Wendy Williams do? Now SHE represented the strongest black woman I had ever encountered. That woman was living proof that anyone walking around with a vagina was not limited to weakness. And being a woman, being feminine, does not necessarily entail an inherent lack of strength. I remembered hearing about how she overcame addiction and low esteem to one day transforming herself into the invincible Diva of the air waves who most men can't help but feel intimidated by. YOU GO WENDY! Unfortunately at that moment I was so far behind my icon in socially accepting myself that catching up seemed an impossibility. I was crawling-slithering on my emotional knees and needed a more realistic Heroine to emulate and upon whose shoulders I could ride-but don't count me out Wendy. You beat the odds and taught me that failure is nothing but a major set-back that has been blown outta proportion-so I'll be back!

I loved my daughter to DEATH but she just didn't understand! She couldn't because adolescence doesn't permit the young mind to comprehend fully all the shit life has got planned. Perhaps someday when she falls head-over-heals for little Jamal an he cheats-and she feels her very soul being dragged from her miserable body, she'll fucking understand! When her hopelessly devoted heart snaps in two and a bowl of Captain Crunch ain't so inviting without her jilting little boyfriend to enjoy it with. THEN-she'll recall the utterly belated seriousness of now!

My tears began a long stream of betrayal-of exposure that did not go unnoticed by my adolescent tormentor!

"Why you cryin? Ew, never mind," said the young and precocious tongue and mind that new not yet the true meaning of life!

"Breanna, you love mommy?"

"Yeah why?"

"Well say you do sometimes. Mommy NEEDS to be loved! Give me a hug!" Didn't mean to get Mushy-especially with Sister Heartless. But there are times in life when pain is much more over-whelming than our waning self-confidence and pride. SO I GRABBED THE DESENTIZED little imp I'd 14 years earlier given birth to!

She felt sorry for me-I could tell but was too callous to show it! So instead, she chose to hide her embarrassment to feel any emotion other than aggression.

"Ew! Oh my God-STOP!"

I hugged her bony belligerent behind anyway! Fuck her if she wouldn't respond! I had probably the only daughter in the Western Hemisphere who was too ashamed to audibly spell out how much she loved her Mommy. And this was one of those rare times-those Golden moments, when I needed it the most! I wished to God I had my real biological mother to comfort me. You never outgrow that. If she were right here-RIGHT NOW, drug-induced paranoia, babbling and all, I would welcome her. I would still reach out and long to have her back in my life-to wipe my tears away. People really don't appreciate one another. Children appreciate even less!

Well since I had given birth to a tyrant it became clear to me that ANY attempt at garnering basic human responses from her stone-face was moot! So I fastened my seat-belt and decided to unleash the merciless mutant of delinquincy upon the hapless unsuspecting students of Sally Grady Junior High School in Farmingdale! To Hell with her souls redemption! Let the Head-shrinkers, Priests and Nunnery there exorcise this foaming beast who laughed at my tears and psychologically danced right over my broken heart!

I drove Breanna to my parent's house, puffed up my chest and set sail in an eternal quest to have a man inside me!

It was 11:43 P.M. and I had 17 minutes to get to a place in Hempstead called "The Rock!" Why they call it that? Niggers in there got rock-hard dicks? Now that would be nice! Just let me hold a couple-uh, more like SIX! A freak gets HUNGRY at night. I promise not to eat em all at once! YOU KNOW-three in-and three OUT. I got a lot of issues-an even more spaces that need to be touched. I swear to God I'll only let 3 touch me at a time-let the OTHER 3 just sit on the sidelines figurin out just how to please me an awaiting their turn! That's just a portion of how freakin IRATE Canei had me!

If I got to the spot after 12:00 A.M. I'd have to pay 15 bucks cover-charge. I didn't HAVE the 15! So I had to blaze it! I stopped at an A.T.M. As I crept up to the large well stocked electronical device 3 customers came in behind me to perhaps withdraw funds. Damn, bankruptcy IS contagious! I strutted my broke ass forward, Cat-burglar style-not wanting the other 3 beggars to know how broke I was. Even a prospective Ho got her pride!

The premise was simple-I didn't think there was a dime to be found in that tin-can. Not for ME anyway-but LIKE THEY SAY-you never know! So I put in my bid-JUST IN CASE! Who knows, maybe the monetary dispensing device had suffered a Stroke. Parkinson's Disease or Alzeheimer's! YOU KNOW-temporary memory loss. I hear old Machines get that too! Now if there WAS some extra Chump-change I could use that to get in the Rock in case I missed my deadline! You know a sister gotta make power-moves in her tortured quest for sexual-survival!

By the time I'd entered my PIN number I realized that it was me who had lost my fucking mind-MY MEMORY! The computer was fine. I selectively forgot I was broke-but the stingy metal contraption in front of me didn't! It just stood there-laughing at me. Grinning at the black vagabond without a Shiny copper penny in her pocket. With a bitches hard-on the size of Texas-and a Bank Account the size of Rhode Island! An they got the nerve to call this electronic bastard a 'NYSE' Machine!

"INSUFFICIENT FUNDS," said the only possible benefactor of my Pussy Plight-my depleted economic fate! And I swore that the 3 patrons behind me could hear the reverberatory rejection of this-my last stand! Damn you NYSE Machine-what's so nice about you? You ever solicit an A.T.M. for some funds-some monetary apples you know you ALREADY picked? Oh yeah, you picked em all right so you can shake the tree all you want BUT THERE AIN'T NO APPLES HERE BITCH! Don't you remember what you had last week? Apple Pie! So what the fuck you comin back here for? BOUNCE, YOU HARD-OF-HEARIN, NONCOUNTIN BROKE BITCH! BOUNCE!

Well from this point you might as well negotiate an anti-starvation deal with your stomach! Think of happier times-an go lay down somewhere! SHIT! I walked out the spot PISSED THE FUCK OFF! Better put the petal to the metal otherwise 'Fuck-night' is canceled-AGAIN! An I don't think my throbbin clitoris can survive another disappointment! I bet prostitutes don't have this problem. Hell-suck some dick an hoist that battered ass in the air and WHA-LAH-Sirloin Steak an potatoes are on the table and HAPPY DAYS ARE HERE AGAIN!

The "Rock" was the worst Club I've ever been in. Nothing but nerds in business suits. I didn't see even a handful of candidates I would even consider sleepin with. There was money there though-I recognized a Rolex in the dark from about a hundred yards easily! And somebody parked a 2006 Mozaretti outside-AND a 2004 Rolls Royce Phantom. It was Champagne colored-with suicide doors!

By 3:30 I had more drinks than I could count! Rich motherfuckers give it up in a heartbeat if they see a piece of ass they think they can buy! But I wasn't opening up my legs to them-Hell NO! There ain't that much booze in the world! Not even on Fuck-night! I got scared wondering if I'd be back home again-ALONE, violently jerking myself off on my bedsheets, cussing Canei to Hell and crying myself to sleep! I was smashed! So I decided not to drive home because it's not so good to go to jail drunk-remember last time! I know them bitches is still waitin. So I hailed a CAB-4 Cabs! None of em stopped! Oh my GOD! I'm stuck out here-don't know a living soul. I wasn't going out like that cuz you know how it is in unchartered territory-you can turn up missin! So I switched to plan 'Z' an hopped on the L.I.R.R. It was only about 7 stops away and I could sleep with one eye open till my station came. Then get a ride from Hattie or Mik tomorrow to pick up my Jeep!

I was defeated! The Nigger with an attitude was reduced to the poor fair-maiden who couldn't pick up a one-night-stand to save her life. I started looking at the passengers on the train. You know how a cat looks when it's in heat-she keeps elongating her sleek horny feline body till either Mr. Good-bar rolls up or death comes!

Well HELLO MR. GOOD-BAR! This fine brother in black leather pants got on the train 2 stops into the ride and sat down right next to me! He looked GOOD! Like a tall well-built goateed HAM HOCK! I had no time for Bullshit!

"Oh boy-I can't WAIT to get home," I said! To set him up for the kill!

"So where you live," he asked!

"Just a few stops away," said the desperate bitch on 'Fuck-night!'

"You live alone," asked my scrumptious prey?

"I do tonight, why? You wanna come over," asked the Bitch with the noticeably hard nipples?

"Maybe I will!" He said his name was Meth! He looked like a 6 foot tall, leather clad talking penis. Maybe somehow the alcohol had transformed his appearance. But I didn't care! YOU SNOOZE-YOU LOSE! And I wasn't fuckin sleepy! Meth and I got off the train after another couple of stops so he could pick up his S.U.V. Then we rode for 10 minutes to this real small house in the boonies where he said he lived with his room-mate 'Iggy!'

"Iggy? What kind of name is THAT?" It sounded like the type of name that someone would give their pet Tarantula! "Does he bite," I joked?

"Only if you want him to-and only in certain places."

Satan himself jumped into my imagination and unfurled before my eyes the picture of 2 niggers rocking my world! In the vision I was screamin at the top of my lungs, I came so hard. I would have done a lot with this fine brother-'Fuck-night' or not cuz somewhere between the Apple Martini's and the 'Thug Passions' Meth was looking good! The erotic encounter dispelled itself abruptly from my head with a final vision of me clutchin onto the wooden leg of a coffee-table while Meth was havin me and me getting a 12 inch pole rammed in and outta my mouth by his mysterious Homeboy-IGGY!

When we got inside the tiny one-bedroom apartment it smelled like a whole slew of niggas lived there. Perhaps a Football team. And all of em had just completed suicide drills-running around Giants Stadium in 100+degree weather. I could also smell the scent of funky armpits on the large reclining chair. Oh well, I see how you livin in here. So you might as well introduce me to your Homeboy Oscar Madison!

"Yo," Meth called out toward the dark. A large well-built light-skinned man in his late thirties emerged wearing only black nylon boxers, a wife-beater, black sneakers with no laces and no socks. He had a six-pack like Evander Holyfield and was cut-up and 'Pretty' like a black Adonis. Brother-man was SO diesel all I wanted to do was open my legs and foam at the MOUTH! THIS nigger looked like an exotic dancer he was so chiseled-like a male stripper. And immediately I dismissed the raunchy stench of nicotine and stale sweat-socks inundating their comfy-cozy rats nest with the notion of how much I could use a naked fine nigger with no clothes on!.

I don't give a fuck playa, that your crib resembles a drug-haven for Cokeheads and Monday Night Football or that the rats and roaches have probably abandoned the BOTH of you sloppy Motherfuckers for a more sanitary spot to curl their thick grey tails and lay there heads, I just wanna get rocked by you and your man so violently that the very sight of this junk-heap will be no more of a catalyst in my life than the sporadic memory of the nigger who cheated and broke my heart-what was his name? I could feel the alcohol swirling around bungie-jumping from my guts to that soaking wet part of the female anatomy that wolfs down a male sex-drive in the dark. I imagined that these two losers had NO clean bed-sheets-just a soil-spotted war-torn mattress and an old green Army blanket. The same one General McArthur musta slept on on nights before he went out on a rampage.

'Ten-HUT,' cried the little-ole lady downstairs-bangin on the pipes and beggin for some heat! I speculated to myself that Iggy had done some time! Oh NO-hope he ain't nothing like the LAST nigger I said that about-otherwise if he is gullible Ms. Simone Singleton won't be makin it outta here ALIVE! He strode outta the room and came over to greet me with his massive arms out-stretched in a firm handshake. His boxers were oversized and immediately my probing eyes could see why. There was a chunky piece of meat binded up in there-behind the nylon, that might've easily been mistaken for a baby Boa Constrictor!

"Oh my God! What the Hell is that," I wondered to myself utterly confused as to whether to fixate my gaze at the handsome aging man in front of me or that 15 pounds of meat he had stashed behind sleek and shiny BVD boxers? I chose the boxers!! My vaginal walls did a flip-caught a flashback and spasmed their way toward an inevitable handshake with that coiled snake.

Iggy looked better than Meth! Oh my GOD-I struck gold! I'ma fuck BOTH these fly niggers TONIGHT! (UP JUMPED THE Devil again in my head) Meth introduced me to Iggy an in less than 15 minutes I barked out THE QUESTION!

"I wanna suck you dick," I told Iggy! "You an your man with it or what?"

I was so horny and it had been too long so I would've fucked the Devil that night if he had come at me right! Meth thought that he needed some alcohol and some weed to get me to pull my panties down. He was wrong! He had all he needed in one package protruding outta those sexy black leather pants. Iggy leaped outta his boxers and I got on my knees. Oh that nigger had a BIG DICK! I've seen some dicks in my day but THIS motherfucker looked like he had TWO of em-JOINED TOGETHER! And I could smell the brown-skinned masculine flesh-behind the boxers! Waitin to stick itself deep inside my broken dreams! I pulled on it-to check the circumference-AND POWER. It was heavy-and felt like...like a God-Damn dead fuckin SNAKE! It was thick, hard yet soft to the touch-like he had just oiled his ramrod for the impending line-drive he'd had planned for the back of my mouth!

"Oh...baby!" I needed two hands to hold the entire deceased reptile!

"I got 14 for you baby," Iggy moaned and Meth slid up behind me grabbing my erect titties and pullin at my Blue Mini-skirt! Sounded good to ME-No use getting fucked in the Club-clothes!

"Hold up Gee-leave that shit on! We hittin THIS bitch with that shit on!"

Oh my God! It was happening-these sexy male-models was gonna bust me wide open! An I was gonna pump BACK, suck a whole lot-and let it happen! The Prison-pile-driver situated my head comfortably between his well-made thighs and guided my moaning lips back and forth with the gentle stroking of his hand. It felt GOOD!

My top and bra were off an I gobbled up as much of Iggy as I could grab. Meth had his meat out and was underneath me in a female-superior straddling position tryin to work it into my ass. He was small but at that point it could've been invisible-I didn't care cuz Iggy had enough to go around. Meth had done a line of coke before they started finger-fuckin me an I could taste some on Iggy's cock. Is THAT how your steroid dick got so big I asked myself as my tortured tonsils fought back gravity and limited circumferential barriers to squeeze a small submarine into an even smaller female oral cavity. Meth penetrated me and it felt just right. I wanted him in my ass so bad that my lips let go of the submarine so that I could ride that fine brothers little-meat till my voice cracked.

Meth had that cool deep voice and kept taunting me with it! Iggy Super-spear sucked and ate my nipples like they were black cherries while I tried to break his home-boys dick off with the siphoning power in the crack of my ass!

Then Iggy came in my mouth! I pulled back overjoyed that the Great Flood gushing from the snake had NOT penetrated the empty spaces below my waist. WHO WANTS THEIR PELVIS CRUSHED? I'd planned to used my vital organ at least once more in the not so distant future and did NOT want it to meet its brutal end at the hands of his deformity-NOT TONIGHT! I preferred to on suck it! It would've felt like somebody rammed a Nuclear Warhead inside me! His stinky feet smelled like Doritos! I could smell them all the way up here, but the flavor riding my tongue was on the money! 'COCAINE!' I came and felt like my soul had separated itself and divided into two halves. I never had this much pleasure at once and I was letting them know-lettin the world know how much I loved the way they was Gang-bangin me on the Livingroom carpet.

There are times when a woman needs to be ripped-have her walls banged out! Savagely subdued by the butchering strength of her man's hips! At that moment the Art of docile love-making was a virtue strictly for Televangelists, paraplegics and virgins. Well THAT Gospel did not apply to me! I was a cheap whore-the Nymph, givin it up for free an lovin it! I NEEDED the Thug-Passion that electrifies the female personality! That keeps her INTERESTED and makes her knees shake! I CAME there to be pleased. FUCKED! For some down and dirty intercourse that could blaze me till my heart stopped! I wanted to smell the sweat and love-juices of those two giants grinding out my senses! From the steady stream of dynamite hanging between his legs, that veiny dick slithering down my throat, Iggy was makin it happen! And Meth was layin it down ghetto style with the savage strokes he was spillin in my ass!

"UUAH-OOH, EEWH!" I was singing the freak song composed for Canei to eat his heart out to! If only he could see me now! He would have a fucking STROKE or go into caniptions from watching these two motherfuckers go to town raw-dogging his Boo! "KISS MY ASS PLAYA!" Serves you RIGHT for doing me WRONG!

Suddenly I felt the waning power of Meth's trembling hips and he groaned out some noise that sounded like 'MONKEY-CHATTER!'

"WHO-OAAHM! WHO-OAAHM!" Tarzan woulda bolted outta his coconut tree grief stricken to find out what in Tarnations happened to his darling baby baboon if he caught wind of THAT S.O.S. cry! But there was no Lord of the Jungle IN SIGHT-SO Iggy answered the call! Sensing his Homeboy was in DICK DISTRESS, knowing poor Meth was about-to-blow, Iggy pulled me up off the sagging 5 inch killer and flipped my ass into a 69 position. He got on top of me-sliding the scaly reptile directly between my eyes and licking the forbidden inches pulsating between my womb and my anus! I came again as his darting tongue was shooting in and out of my insides and I could see Meth sitting on the sidelines resting in peace while trying to get his second wind!

Iggy rolled off and hoisted my body on top of him! He started deep tongue kissing me and stuck his finger below my clitoris as he positioned my butt-cheeks up in the air in Meth's direction. I was moaning and Meth, unable to restrain himself from the gaping medley of passion gyrating in front of him, LUNGED AT ME! LIKE I WAS A DEAD FUCKING DEER his predatory penis felt OBLIGATED to pounce on-and STAB! Meth grabbed my grinding hips away from Iggy's penetration and pulled me toward his crotch and began licking and kissing the back of my neck. He pressed my head forward onto Iggy and I sucked the reptile-lopping it up and down in my mouth as Iggy's Tag-team Partner entered me from behind. THESE NIGGERS WERE GOOD! SYNCHRONIZED-THE MENAGE-TWINS! LIKE THEY DID THIS SHIT BEFORE! He glided it in and in less than 5 minutes I started to scream-and pinch his dick with the strength of my feminity. I was in fucking Heaven-in no-man's land getting pipe from some niggers who looked like fucking L.L and Tyrese and I wouldn't have left that smelly rat-infested apartment in the Long Island ghetto even if my Momma brought Jesus to drag me out!

I was grindin my ass fast as I could and Iggy stuck his tongue down my throat. I could taste the alcohol on his breath. Suddenly Canei's face popped into my mind.

"Oh-no you DON'T nigga. What the fuck you doin HERE? Messin with my flow? Well like R. Kelly said: You ain't gotta go home, but you gotta GET THE HELL OUTTA HERE! This ain't no foursome you has-been-and I got too much business to take care of to entertain a smoked-out piece of pipe I already had a long time ago!" I didn't want to think of his cheatin ass! Not now-not here! By now these two gladiators was havin there way with me and I hoped to GOD this GOOD dick would never stop! I was on all-fours with strong-as-a-bull Iggy bearing down and my head was bobbin-tryin to kill the murderous black snake I was suckin on the size of a 40 ounce bottle of 'Corona.' Meth had stuck his finger inside me and thrusted my hips down toward his cocaine imbibed dick so he could ram it through the other side of my body!

"Yeah you dirty NIGGA," I demanded! "Stick it in-STICK IT IN!" He shoved that diamond rod into my mid-section and I yelled out-while Iggy was re-entering my mouth with the SNAKE THAT WOULDN'T DIE! I squeezed Meth's dick with my pussy-lips as tight as I could hoping that the intense strangulation method would snap Canei's fuckin neck wherever he was!

I wanted Meth to cum inside me-get me pregnant. Then I'd bring the baby to Canei and say it was his. FUCK HIM! Take that fuckin 'zit' to the poor-house where the Dog niggers dwell! I had 2 men inside me! Hell-night! 'Fuck-fest-the Sequel! And if there was another motherfucker there, it would've been a foursome! Every time I dug my hips down on Meth's rock he moaned in a deep loud voice. It turned me on while I sucked the Torpedo Iggy was tryin to shove down my throat!

I came and shouted, "FUCK YOU! FUCK YOU!!!" Them niggers musta thought I was crazy. I steered around and lost my God-damn mind! I wanted Iggy's big dick inside of me. Never mind the Submarine Sandwich-I would eat the whole fucking thing with my 'OTHER lips! And if I succumbed to premature 'Death By Big Dick' then that was the way I was fuckin goin out! All of a sudden I RIPPED myself offa Meth's little ass and SAT ON THE the tree-limb! The penis GRIPPED my insides as the first several inches of Iggy lay invisible inside me. MANDINGO! Sexuality's well-endowed warrior bit his lip then threw his head back as I took him in. Enduring all the incompatibles Hell's nature could bludgeon me with-and he smiled. But there was NOT very much for me to grin about!

"OWW! Oh-My-God!" What a bitch will go through to hurt her man! Shit! I don't know how HE felt about it! He didn't even know it was goin down. But it was KILLIN ME!

Iggy's body started shakin like a cold-turkey junkie and Meth came over to skeet on my face! I hardly notices the 2 pints of thick cum splattered on my lips-DOWN INTO MY LUNGS cuz Iggy's python had ruptured my intestines and was on it's way up to crack open a bitches skull! And I loved it! Moby dick grabbed me and THRUST it in me some more-like about another 10 feet or so. He overcame my female superior-THEN JUMPED ON TOP of my rotating legs. The big beautiful predator was ON ME-deep inside and plunging frantically. Like a fuckin MANIAC! THIS WAS WHAT THE NIGGER WANTED! To hurt this pussy and give me ALL I could not bear to miss! Stretching my inhibitions and teaching them to forget all the pains I'd experienced before

THIS one! He hurted me! Canei had broken my heart, my will! And now Iggy was hurting me too in the way that I needed-forcing me to dismiss every waking moment of that former bastard who did me wrong! One man can surpass another by leaps and bounds when a woman's intentions really NEED him to!

I started whimpering. The pressure was unbearable and I wanted the blunt fuckin spear outta me-SO I COULD BREATH!

But they COULDN'T stop! I would NOT allow it! And they would have to KILL me first before I let go! FUCK THAT!

The pleasure was enticing-but NOT HEALTHY! I could feel their intense erections flickering through my insides in unison. I could feel their heartbeats adjoining to mine and overwhelming my subordinate womanhood. I could taste and smell that male breathe exhaling sensuously on my glistening skin with a soft but dominant demeanor. The kind that can make a sister cum more than one time a night! And I needed it! To ravage me and kiss away all the mounting strife I'd endured since the day I met Canei! I had about 20 inches of manly power riveted through my lonesomeness and I begged them to spit the flavor of their satisfaction from the combined projectiles of my happiness. That's it baby-ejaculate all over my face and erase Canei's memory once and for all. I came again!

Iggy started to SCREAM-like he was cumin! Good for HIM!

But my bludgeoned sexual organ felt like it was being torn apart! Iggy was steady banging-harder than before. I could NOT survive another 5 minutes of THIS! By the time he barreled his way past the 25 yard-line and safely into the end-zone a flag went up! NO PAIN NO GAIN! THAT'S BULLSHIT!

I whimpered a desperate hardy "WHU-UAAF" and ripped that savage telephone pole outta me-swearing to NEVER be a whore AGAIN! I wanted NO more of THIS! This shit is for the birds-or the vaginally profound! So it ain't for me! The giant throbbing elongated dick was removed and I laid down on Iggy's stomach. Meth came outta my mouth and glued himself all over my swirling vision but Iggy STILL wasn't finished. And when I bolted off him he shouted "NO," as the slain pussy went "PLOOP!" Air-pockets and sparks began flying outta the terrified shredded walls! ICU had itself another victim! AND I COULDN'T HOLD HIM NO MORE!

"OOPS! Sorry brother-a sister just couldn't take it no more," I gasped! When I pulled him off my legs went dead and my entire body hunched over into a fetal position. THE PAIN WAS UNBEARABLE! Iggy was mad-but I didn't give a flyin fuck-HE WASN'T KILLIN ME WITH THAT THING! Shouldn't have put COCAINE on your dick-DUMB ASS! And who the Hell you been stickin anyway? I tell you that penis could NOT belong to a human! Looked like he coulda used a baby Elephant for target-practice.

We all lay there-our love-juices adding to the foul stench of the carpet. Iggy looked like an exhausted Mandingo warrior with a gigantic black spear, perhaps his own, impaled in the chiseled crevices of his groin. I lay there with my pussy singing out fart-tunes. You ever hear a pussy tootin out the gruelin shit it's been through-AFTER IT'S BEEN FUCKED? It's something like this: "BART! BART-BART!" It relayed magical tales of how these two fallen Angels from Heaven sodomized my violated body into the lust and satisfaction of a multiple-orgasm. My vagina drooled with semen. My mouth, dry the way mouths get when you cum in them too much and my brain tryin to figure out why I waited so many years to take this blessed trip to dual-dick Paradise. And Meth, poor Meth, musta came about 10 times cuz I felt his little dick go into shockwave after shockwave of penile seizures the way he was bustin off in me.

God musta been somewhere watchin. Evaluating that horny 20 minute illicit ordeal that I waited patiently all my life for. And the Devil probably got a raise-for making me fall to temptation and leading my doomed will-power deeply into the Valley of the Shadow of Death!

I kissed Iggy on the lips, and thanked him. And apologized.

"Sorry to stop you baby!" But my soul was on fire and I'm in desperate need of vaginal surgery-it will take perhaps a dozen sutures to close the gaping wound you've embedded in my genitalia! Cause of death-your Super-sized Weapon of Mass-destruction!

It was OVER! I had finally done it and slowly my mental pains ebbed into relief. I vowed never to see these stocky losers again. Then I got up and dressed without bathing! To Hell with Iggy and his insatiable Python. I hated to CUM and RUN-but there would be NO sloppy seconds TONIGHT!

By the time I got home I felt like the Whore Of Babylon! Dirty! Disgusting-like Lucifer, fallen from the Golden Gates of Heaven into the lowest and most seething furnace Hell could produce! My body still reeled. I kept saying it to myself over and over again. I FINALLY HAD SEX WITH TWO NIGGERS AT THE SAME TIME! And it was GOOD! But I couldn't tell nobody-not even my girls. My conscience was on fire-but somewhere deep inside of me, in spite of the humiliation, I hoped to do it again someday!

Yeah right. Go out on the town, have a few drinks, get my dance on-an suck a couple of dicks! Simultaneously! Maybe NEXT weekend! I can call Floyd an tell him to go fuck himself.

"You serve no PURPOSE Playa? Why would I need YOU when I can have TWO!

When I went by my parent's house to pick up Bre that morning I tried not to look at daddy! I felt as though he could see the white gooey residue on my face and smelled the shit my violated underworld expelled onto Meth! He was small-but so was my esteem at the time-that's why I wanted him. Guilt was swallowin me up slowly as we stood on the porch talking and he noticed it.

"What's the matter with you?"

"OH nothing-just some School stuff! But I'm O.K. Dad." It was high-time for me to salvage my dignity-by paying a visit to Mr. Henney!

"I'll see you an Ma tomorrow." I ran back into the car picturing him staring at a big 14 inch penis protruding outta my ass as he watched in awe while I hobbled back to the Jeep. Did he know? I had fulfilled every father's nightmare of his sweet innocent daughter with somebody's dick in her mouth! Getting butt-fucked on the orgy train. At that moment I began to hope that God did not exist because if he DID he definitely knew what had happened and I'd be in the Spiritual Dog-house with him for at least another 400 years. I could never even fix my lips to pray any more because the Preacher's daughter had committed the unpardonable sin. She had forsaken the straight path, turned her back on the Creator and had an affair with the DEVIL HIMSELF-AND ONE OF HIS HOMMIES! In a filthy Ghetto apartment. And due to her abominable sin she has vowed never to set foot in the House of God again!

I figured the Lord had no time for Jezebels. Besides-the Universe was vast and needy and full of OTHER more virtuous members of the human race truly worthy of his Eternal graces! I didn't even KNOW those niggers. What if they decided to SMOKE my ass AFTER the threesome?

The next day at work I felt that everybody at the job had seen a video tape of the nasty shit I had done the night before! It had also began to dawn on me that there were somewhere around 60 billion Sperm Cells floatin around in my uterus trying to make more of that night than what really was. Not one but TWO Gladiator looking motherfuckers had ejaculated in me several times apiece. I mean EVEN that pre-cum stuff that people talk about that oozes outta a man's penis moments before the final tidal wave is enough to do the job. And they had BOTH stuffed themselves inside this desperate body more than once! OOPS! OH HELL NO! I was the walkin carnal sponge-a human Sperm Bank and if just one of those deposits got through my weakened defenses it's W.I.C. checks and Food Stamps for the slut who got trained in a Hell-hole!

I wasn't havin that! The way those two looked I begged Satan not to let their collective sperm be in nearly as good physical shape as their diesel bodies. I mean these mutants were BIG! BOTH of em! An they CAME in me so their over-zealous genetic warmonger semen could kick down the doors of a bitches ovaries-TERMINATOR STYLE! An plant that seed in the twinkling of an eye. "Niggas I am NOT havin YOUR babies!" I got paranoid-even thought I felt the baby growin!! So I called my girl Hattie-AND CONFESSED!

"Fairy-God-mother forgive me for I have sinned!" It was all good cuz Hattie was a true friend-the kind who wouldn't sell you out when shit got thick!

"Bitch, why you do it? You couldn't CALL me? I told you-whatever's on your mind-just call?"

"Yeah but I didn't want you to try an talk me OUT of it! I had to get that nigga BACK! YOU KNOW WHAT HE DID!"

"Oh-Canei-'YOO-HOO' Look at me sucker-I got your ass NOW! Right by the balls! Hah-I got A.I.D.S! What you gotta say for yourself now PLAYA? 'REST IN

PEACE YOU DUMB BITCH," she scowled in a sarcastic voice! The bitch was right-I was FUCKED! But Hattie had a hook-up!

Her ex-lover's sister worked in the Pharmaceutical Department of a large Medical Clinic and had access to shit it would cost an arm and a leg to get a hold of. They had stuff like Flu-shots, Antibiotics, tons of condoms and Viagra-AND the Morning After Pill! I begged her to get me a 6 pack of the shit cuz I didn't want no one-night-stand love-child babies crawling outta me 9 months from now.

I had blown it-screwed 2 drug-laced low-lives whose names I'm not sure I'll EVER remember! Breanna ran inside Hattie's house for the classified package and Hattie came out and said, "Don't worry girl-I got you!" We didn't let on as to what was in the sealed brown bag. Fourteen year olds don't need to be informed of how their horny mothers got gang-banged and now fears H.I.V. or the births of ugly little unwanted bastards spillin outta her defiled womb.

Hattie said, "when you take this shit, your prayers will be answered. An embryo or fetus CAN'T survive THIS shit! It's like an Atomic Bomb that dissolves those illigitimate snot-lickers into Never-never land!"

I KNEW the bitch didn't care too much for kids-says they use to tease her when she was a young aspiring homosexual. Hence-the repugnance. But why she gotta be so graphic-to turn ME into a Baby-killer?

I snapped BACK at her!

"Oh Great Scott Hattie," I whispered in her ear! "Thanks be to God-I won't be having a baby after all. If it weren't for the A.I.D.S. virus they pumped into my mouth and anus I'd have it MADE! You slick bitch-you got something for THAT?

-12-

FISH-NOT CAVIAR

For the next 7 days I went into hiding! No work an no play and the only time I left the house was to either take Breanna to School or to pick her up! I was a recluse and set off to purify my body and mind! I mean I was on some real Buddha shit-depriving myself of any and all pleasures of life, while waiting to exorcise my tarnished conscience of the deviant act I had committed! Guilt is by far the most formidable foe a person can engage! And self-loathing is a burden too heavy for many to bear. You see, It's not a peaceful thing when you don't love what you are-when you behold in the mirror the repugnant image of self that you wish you could abandon. Simply because you perceive that others reject you in return! That is a self-negating dilemma and I had to do my best to expunge both the circumstances of that violation AND to completely do away with the desperate mind-set which created this crisis!

I went out to eat with the girls at Red Lobster. But I didn't EAT! Just wanted fluids and some stimulating company. Kecia passed me some of her baked-chicken.

"No thank you-I won't be eating anything." I was on a fast but I couldn't tell that to a Crashdummy-it would be like speaking Chinese to a Swede! She was such a dumb-Ass! (Pardon me for cussing while I'm fasting but this spiritual reformation is a slow grinding process. It allows for very little food and even less patient tolerance for utter absurdity)

A fast is a religious proclamation where will-power and down-turned plate team up to petition God for divine or natural favors by way of hunger-strike! Number one it disciplines the adherents to deny him or herself not just food, THAT would be easy, but also any and all pleasures toward which they would normally gravitate. So when I fast, I not only abstain from ox-tails and rice and beans but also the more erotic nuances of life! For instance, "Thou shalt NOT bust nuts during the Sacrament of Fasting!" It would be not only counterproductive, but also summarily asinine!

Look at the logic behind it. How can you tell the Creator of the Universe that you're whole-heartedly willing to submit and cease from your desires by day and still indulge in some of the most illicit shit a human can engage in by night? "Oh yes, Lord! I've thrown away the ham-hocks and the collard-greens, but may I please get back to you on the Prayer-line AFTER I finish letting this Jamaican Thug eat my asshole and stick his nuts in my mouth? But NOT to worry Dear Heavenly Father, as SOON as the bed-spread dries, it's back to the Fast and the rest of my bruised ass-cheeks belongs to you!" Get my meaning?

The same goes with alcohol. Oh NO bitch-no Red Alize for that YOU during anorexic-season! No 40's or alcoholic consumption of any kind. You see, you can't truly deny yourself-unless you DENY yourself! Fire-water included! And that getting high

126

stuff is definitely out. How you gonna offer your body as a living sacrifice-pure, Holy and undefiled, while you got cocaine in your system? Angelic beings don't take too well to inebriated Jackasses soliciting unabashed prayers during drug binges. So a crack-heads prayers never go past his head. And the only ones that hear them are the other sky-high motherfuckers sitting in shit puddles near the crack-spot waitin for 'Scottie' to beam THEM up into toxic Paradise!

So you gotta be clean-to God! And the logic stands to reason. If the 'Man' won't give you a fucking job even scrubbing the piss from filthy bathroom stalls, (They don't trust crack-heads one iota. Not even with mopsticks or other cleaning utensils.) what makes your ignorant ass think the righteous Creator Jesus Himself would look the other way and let you slide up front in his symbolic line of gracious gift-giving?

There's a whole lotta well-meaning faithful devotees out there who deserve some of this good shit on the spiritual bread-line more than you! So why would Jesus let YOUR reckless soul skip them for some Manna from Heaven. Shit! You BELONG in the back of the line. And if Divine Jurisprudence were based on selfless merit then you would not have been permitted on the line from Jump-Street! Thank God for small favors and a little bit of Mercy!

Now the second tenet in fasting behind complete self-denial is the Divine principal of showing God that you want to please him. That you believe in him without compromise or condition and you KNOW that HE is the Almighty. The Eternal One. The Lord and Master and KEEPER of your errant soul! This is an unspoken profession of faith characterized by a humble spirit toward the magnificence of his or her Maker.

This ordinance is equivalent to the Muslim 'Shahada' or recital of faith but differs from it in that the adherent acts on his or her beliefs in deeds-rather than words! It is one thing to say "Yeah, I believe in God!" But it is yet another to put said statement in practice and allow your actions to sanctify and seal those beliefs.

Lastly, the fast is performed essentially to petition the Heavens for a specific blessing! The physical cleansing has removed toxins from the body invariably resultant from unhealthful food intake. Now you must show God that you mean business and have decided not to eat until either your prayers are answered or you DIE from starvation. But ultimately the purpose, the main objective of the fast, is to prove that you WANT this and am disciplined, dedicated and willing to undertake the doctrinal prescription HE has established in his Holy Book in order to get it! And you KNOW that he is able to provide it for you!

Now that's some heavy shit! When God sees this he is caught in his Celestial tracks because he knows your heart and realizes this Do-Or-Die nigger means business! He means what he says! And if I don't give the poor desperate bastard what he wants he will kill himself trying!

"Look Mommy-over here. Notice me! Playing in traffic on the Major Deegan Expressway during morning rush-hour!" Now what wise loving parent would sit back

127

and watch little Johnny's perilous plight-his eager and eminent demise without offering the juvenile fool a hand and a road-map on 'How To Walk On Cars' like Jesus walked on water, to defray a tragic vehicular Manslaughter?

A GOOD parent-A compassionate father and Creator would not allow that catastrophe to commense. He KNOWS how pitifully stupid you are. He realizes that you have already rehearsed and taken to heart the pre-ordained prescription he laid out for you in that King James Bible. He has detected the remote seedlings of unadulterated defiance your psychologically imbalanced brain was nurtured upon. He loves the fuck outta you. (gullible mind and all) And knowing that you took him at his Word when you read the passage: "Anything you want-ask God for it!" So what the Hell? Hell can't HAVE this, his treasured Child. "So I'll just bless him and send him on his foolish way!"

If he doesn't bless you he will have to make Funeral arrangements and provide an extra bed in Heaven for the niave Jackass who starved himself to death amidst solemn prayers and a fatal fast! He doesn't want to lose you-but doesn't want to win your unready emaciated ASS up in Paradise just yet either! You've got so much growing-developing to do. And besides, if he just stood back and let you die what will the neighbors say? What a tragedy! The poor faultering idiot-savant tried to beg God's bread and commited suicide in the process! People might talk! And if word got out a whole lotta otherwise religious congregants might become disillusioned from the blessed Universal Campaign and Earth's Christian population would be replaced by Sin-City. A backslidden social order that lost it's nerve moments after witnessing the departure of a slaughtered lamb-50 pounds underweight and maltreated.

So God says "What the fuck? I got plenty of the shit that this child wants in stock so I'll ship some down to Strong Island via UPS and shut her up!" Well with all of this in mind I felt more justified in my dietary sacrifice and concluded that it was worth the temporary nauseousness, the stomach cramps and the incessant passing of gas in order to capture the attention-to catch hold of the wing of an Angel from the Cosmic throes of Creation!

A barbeque buffalo-wing or ice-cold 7-up can't hardly compare, so praise the Lord and pass the mylanta! God have mercy on my soul at 3:00 A.M. when this pitiful little proselyte goes up against the Goliath of ALL temptations armed with a sling-shot and a dream to stifle my desire to bust a nut! Sex climbs higher and digs deeper than Goliath and even David, the Shepherd-boy, had his off-days!

"FUCK! I'm getting horny! To hell with the dinner and Dessert! I can feel the violent vibrations of a woman's periodic needs-that 9 foot tall black penis trampling my way! Anybody seen my SLING-SHOT?"

The next day I began to catch a faint whiff of blessed assurance each time I sat down or opened my legs. My period was coming and I didn't feel like being bothered. The bloating was here and the cramps were howling within earshot right around the cyclic corner. I was so fucking glad I wasn't pregnant-Hattie's shit had worked! And the combined sperm of those 2 assholes had not reached their mark and I was not gonna rear a one-night stand baby! There IS a GOD! I could see the tinted red lights embarking upon my panty-liners in the not-so-distant future.

I had waited for this day like a 20 year Jailbird longs for his release date! The day those stupid pencil-pushing geeks at the Parole Board set the reformed convict free to go back into the corrupting city streets among innocent law-abiding citizen to fuck up shop all over again!

Why do women bloat? Swell up before death? Like a sacrificial lamb placed on the altar of smoldering hormones and female anatomy about to bleed out-from ovaries to vaginal discharges!

I guess sheep, as dumb as they are, also go through physiological metamorphasis prompting their doomed bodies to swell inevitably as they walk through death's door! Am I a FUCKING SHEEP? Do living organisms inflate themselves to accommodate the slaughter about to beckon their premature demises? Now a short-lived Sheeps life can't hold much weight in the butcher-to-plate scheme of things! But a bitches body, knowing it will lose vital fluids through a monthly excretory phenomena, must first double-up in size. Increase her mass maybe 4 or 5 pounds so that the 5-7 day 'period' of menstruation will not render a sister dehydrated.

If I was a pig or a turkey or a lamb with it's head on the chopping-block about to meet it's Maker in a blinding array of stainless-steel, I would NOT puff-up! THAT would give my executioner more of a fleshy target. Why would I want to do that? Would my logic be that swelling would repel the slicing blade from puncturing my feathery frame? God forbid-that's absurd! So why does the body make itself more available to a Yom Kippur or Thanksgiving Day bloodbath! The sensible thing for nature to do would be to 'thin-out!' To decrease the size of the Bullseye in order to entertain the unrealistic attempt to dodge the blow and prolong one's life!

In keeping with this physiological paradox, this problematic stratagem chosen by nature, I was BLOATIN. By the minute! To the uncomfortable tune of a few ounces a day and all I wanted to do was lay in bed and watch "Two Can Play That Game" and "Deliver Us From Eva" re-runs! Perhaps THAT would bring the swelling down! "By The GODS!" There would be plenty of 'Pamprin' and 'Aleve' purchased in the next 48 hours! And I vowed to KILL, TO FUCKING ANNIHILATE, any creature stupid enough to agitate my suffering!

Will somebody help me with something? A concept I've wrestled with way back when. Ever since the primal droplet of pubiscent bleeding! Why does pussy smell like…something floating in the Hudson? You know…like FISH?

Now don't get me wrong! I wasn't smitten with naivety. I can comprehend the phsysiological ordinances of a woman's anatomy-what with the divinely comical sense of order in the mind of God to make sweaty feet smell like cheese, a person's stinky arm-pits smell like onion and garlic Potato Chips. Why does Ass smells like ASS and morning breathe emit the sour fumes of nausea? Why do premenstrual fumes reek like cinnamon? Pussy is pussy! Whether she be a deep dark-chocolate momma with a bone in her nose from the steamy jungles of wild Africa or the salmon-skinned blonde hair and blue-eyed snow-flake from Icelandic Switzerland. Why the HELL did God make the delicate essence of a woman's vagina smell like the odorous proceeds of a stale fish-sandwich? Smoked mackerels; blood-soaked tuna! Christ, I don't even EAT fish! So why is it that every 4 weeks or so, like Clockwork, I have to SMELL like one?

It was Sunday night and I asked Mikki to come with me to the Poconos with Floyd for the following Weekend. We had finally hooked-up and he offered me 3 days and 2 nights in a Pennsylvannia Cottage! Shit, my period would be over by then. But Mik was being a bitch! Talking about "I don't know! I'm not sure which jump-off I should bring!"

I said "Bitch-bring your fuckin FATHER, Al Sharpton-the Milk-man! I don't give a FUCK! Just hook a sister up! I need back-up-JUST IN CASE! Cuz you know these men act up! They's STUPID these days!" THEN she had the nerve to say to me "I don't know Mik! I'm on my period!"

"Well WHO AIN'T ON THE RAG? Bitch I'm bleedin like Jesus! So fuckin WHAT? And although SHE might have been hemorrhaging like a beaten slave, MY CLITORIS WAS THREATENIN ME WITH SUICIDE if it did NOT get 'ROCKED' ASAP! You ever see a dead-clit before? The shits horrendous-like a wilted dead body recently sent flying through the windshield. AT CRASH TIME! Besides, another 5 days or so an I'D be done! So if she chose to bleed more than 5 days THAT was on HER!

I had already arranged a babysitter for Breanna. Mommy promised to let her stay in Farmingdale for the price of a Bucket of KFC! Greedy bitch! She's just too easily bribed. We gotta talk about that cuz she would sell some ass for a CANDY BAR! And she's diabetic too. Well, all was going according to plan an I looked forward to a good time with this new Romeo who I'd forgiven for losin my phone number scrawled on a Bar-napkin. The same sweet gentle creature who got turned on watchin me beat up on a Gorilla!

-13-

NECROPHOBIA

Men are like Tropical Storms! There's a time and a place for em. You can see em comin a mile away. They fuck up everything in their paths. They ruin peoples lives and homes and they always leave you drippin and MAD AS HELL!

Did you ever hear about Hurricane Floyd? The weathermen were shakin in their boots-fully aware of the destructive force it represented. When it came everybody's ass was grass and an ominous forecast of the most prolific storm to hit in years came to fruition. It was the real McCoy-and it was devastating! But I got a Floyd too. Mine also promised unmerciful blinding winds that KICKED down walls and blew the doors off shit! But my carbon copy couldn't bust a grape! It left me wondering!

He hit it and hit it-thrashing violently into my body like a human cattle-prod. But the cattle-prod had a short in it of sorts. Oh yes the raw power was there-but lost was the seething Atomic bomb that blasts a women into trembling fits of shocking delirium when she's about to lose her fuckin mind-that MAN-DOG BITE that zaps her control-button; that sends her longings into the carnal world of doggie-style to fetch for a pleasure that makes her damn and cuss the man plunging himself inside the pit that CAN'T be filled-bending her onto her seductive knees and puting her fast asleep at night! The sisters know what I'm talking about!

A GOOD man will make you the BAD BITCH who frowns when he's stickin it in, clutch the bedsheets and close her eyes-seeing through blindfolds the vision of his sexual profile rammed 200 miles into her body, into her drooling fantasies! THAT SHIT JUST WASN'T THERE! My mating call could not be heard-AND IT WASN'T ALL THAT! This is an obligatory factor in the lost valley, the undiscovered and seldom patrolled chasm of female sexuality that must and will be explored more thoroughly in the proceeding pages!

The weekend was 'O.K' yet left room for improvement! A whole lotta room and I was slightly disappointed. I literally KIDNAPPED Floyd for 48 hours in what could be described as a sexual abduction-AND TORTURE! Well a bitch was backed-up! I needed a whole lotta lovin for as long as I could get it! Why did I then rape the poor unsuspecting new man in my life like a prison escapee? HE WAS THERE! He was the only game in town! He was not allowed to exit our cabin from the time we arrived to the second we left-except to eat. Let me tell youI I was on top of Floyd for literally 6 hours a day-FOR BOTH DAYS OF HIS CAPTIVITY! He didn't smoke or drink (Said he had a minor heart condition-good for HIM) but that didn't stop ME! I drank-and I drank! AND I DRANK! And the more I drank the hornier I got! It was like my voracious sexual appetite had forgotten all about the previous nut I busted (about 18 total for the entire 2 days) and it was back to WORK for the Cardiac-patient! I burnt his ass out! Goood! That'll slow him down-teach him not to duck me for days without a single phone call!

Many of the hopeful romantic feelings I had garnered for him during the initial stages were marred by his inability to contact me for those lonely days. I was desperate and felt jilted-that was what drove me to the Mena ge tois! It did not HAVE to happen-and it should NOT have! If Floyd had just called me sometime during that time of agony I I KNOW I WOULD NOT HAVE BANGED THOSE 2 LOSERS! I WOULD HAVE UNDERSTOOD THE CIRCUMSTANCES-AND WAITED! I WOULD HAVE HAD SOMETHING SOLID TO GRAVITATE TOWARD AND PSYCHOLOGICALLY CLING TO! AND ALL WOULD HAVE BEEN GOOD! Even right now I would have trusted in him and not been forced to create a defensive barrier around my feelings to protect my broken heart. To protect my PEACE!

But it didn't go down like that! The bastard did not call! And my integrity careened downward into a spiraling Hell-hole of looseness and destitution! So I BLAME HIM FOR MY MORAL LAPSE-AND MY LANGUISHING FEELINGS OF ROMANCE! You know, a woman needs to be loved-cared for. And when those virtues are absent from her life she sometimes does things that she is NOT proud of. Things that she will live to regret! Not that the entire travesty was his fault-but I assigned to his neglect a degree of the blame. I HATED HIM for his part in it-And I'll never forget!

Floyd was a very handsome and sexy man. BUT as I turned him into a willing and confused rape-victim, I learned something! Around the third or fourth time we did it, I was letting him fuck me in my ASS near the dark blanketed fire-place. I was giving it to him so good (I loved it) but I was NOT sure he felt the same passion. There was a long fat chunk of ecstasy tearing into my insides as I rocked my body back and forth on top to accommodate the tremendous size. I came! REAL HARD! TWICE! Screaming out loud enough to wake up the ancestors! But I felt UNFULFILLED. Because I felt that he was! I did him AGAIN, this time with my mouth and the results were the same! Still no affect! Well I was absolutely crestfallen but took it on the chin figuring after all that humping a man can't be expected to do everything a nymphomaniac might greedily demand. Two days of 6 hour sex might have been a bit much for his sexuality! Besides-first time intercourse often don't turn out good as it does when someone has time to learn their partners body-and what it needs.

So I put my egotistical tail between my legs and continued on our weekend of heightened sexual acrobatics-at least on MY part. Yet I still retained the desensitized stigma I'd gotten from him which tainted my female ego. Floyd's silence in bed made me feel bad about myself-unsure! By the time we left we were both exhausted and took a few days off from work-AND SEX, for some mandatory down-time. To recover from our vacation!

Necrophobia is a mental condition described by psychologists as an irrational fear of death! On the other hand, "Necrophalia" is the unnatural sexual predisposition a neurotic person might possess toward dead bodies. Well, nobody's perfect and I never claimed to be a Saint-Heaven knows, Im not exactly the "Freak of the week" either. I mean I've heard of some real low down shit before. Like some perverts paying a Bitch to cock her funky big ass up over his head and squeeze intestinal muscles like Mother Goose in an effort to produce the largest most prolific chunk of human excrement she can muster-and hurl it down onto his perverted yearnings just for kicks! That shit don't just happen in Hollywood and smutville! As a matter of fact, I'd bet my life that the Good Lord is somewhere right now, about to throw up his sanctified guts on the diamond studded staircases of Heaven, repulsed by some Political Candidate with a limp wrist and a receding hairline-ordering his sixteen year old gay lover to Shit in his face! Fuck that poor sobbing bitch that the Priest labeled his "Wife" whose at home waiting patiently for him to return from this most recent "Business Trip." His sick demented heart belongs to the pangs of reprobate intercourse and that underaged aspiring sexual deviant who grants any and every salacious whim, his masked homosexual tendencies could ever crave for.

So with all that shit goin on everywhere, from the White House to the Hood, my sexuality should never be questioned. But I gotta make a confession that will probably shock anybody who truly knows me in the same way that it ultimately shocked me! So I'm just gonna just say it: You know that "Necrophalia" thing? Well, you know I think I caught some of that shit! And now, as a result of its traumatic effects, I also caught some of that other "Necrophobia" stuff to boot! You see I recently discovered an unnatural fear of dead men, mostly niggers of course, impersonating good lovers and trespassing their sexually rotting potentials into my once actively exuberant bedroom. The terminal illness started when I had met that FINE new brother named Floyd.

The last time we made love I mistook him for a corpse that must've died weeks ago! Now when I'm fucking, I need a nigger to talk back to me! But during the entire boring Procession he never said a word. You know, you can never detect a putrified asshole until after he pulls his mute limp dick out of your mouth and says good-night!

OH NO HE DIDN'T! Don't climb the your punk ass into MY bed without first rehearsing some Sweet Nothings for me to chew on!

But all THIS mute Motherfucker could do was gyrate his lanky narrow ass in a desperate attempt to put my sexual fires out! But he wouldn't make a sound!! Well I was under the impression that somewhere, somehow, somebody had done the female gender a preeminent sexual favor by symbolically stabbing the SHIT out of his tired uninspired libido! Alright then! Well if this nigger died, then why didn't somebody BURY his ASS before the Gods of Divine intervention brought him MY way?

Now Ladies, if I 'm sucking a man's dick or riding him like a bitch straight outta fifty years of Solitary Confinement, the Motherfucker should at least make a sound! I mean God Dammit, tell me you like like it! Or tell me to get the fuck off cuz my pussy game is Whack! I don't give a fuck! Anything, but Damnit-TALK to me! Now I could take a poll on how many lames got turned out after experiencing the sexy exotic pleasures dangling between my legs-the vacuum-like oral force men feel when my tonsils meet their penis!

Believe me, I KILL erections! And I'm ten times better and much more reliable than Kirby. And MAD niggers have lost their minds when they got the "Treatment." Hell, I even "created" a forty-nine year old stalker-not that I'm proud of that but THIS motherfucker would just lay there like I wasn't doin shit! THAT FUCKS WITH A SISTER'S ESTEEM! You see, that's the kinda shit that will make a bitch mad enough to go an give the cookie to somebody she knows who'll appreciate her HARD WORK and even sing for her!

So it's Wednesday morning after the Maury Povitch Show and I'm suckin Floyd's rock like my life depended on the oscillating air I caught from the back and forth motion of my head bobbing over him! Trust me, a bitch couldn't breath! When you suck a dick like you s'pose to, you have to make the often terminal choice of vital oxygen and sacrificing necessary respiration in order to acquire the title of Heavyweight Champion of the World! Cocksuckers are not merely highly trained staff-members of life's carnal society. They are CREATED! BORN! Anyway, after fifteen minutes of this self torture, lacerating my lips and mutilating my esteem into tiny specks of demoisturized semenal crud, I lapsed HEAD first into a slumped mass of exhaustion. My mouth was bitterly parched-stuck in an "O" shaped waterhose nozzle position and was beggin me for permission to redeem itself in a loud thunderous fucillade of well-deserved obscenities.

And my Pussy hurt!! I looked up at his sorry decaying ass in a wide-eyed frantic juveniles quest for it's parent's approval and all that bastard could give up was the dumb fucking gaze of a depressed zombie-punctuated by some far and few in between canine grunts and barks! This ain't no SOLO motherfucker! Consentual intercourse never is! So if I'm screaming at the top of MY lungs, how come YOU ain't singing WITH me? THAT"S when I realized that I had gone to bed with Uptown's version of the living dead!

Now who wants to make love to the living dead? Check this shit out-cuz THIS is for all you sorry bastards in the world who GET DOWN just like HIM. When you make love to me, you gotta have THREE things: At least 7 inches, I don't ask for much-I'LL WORK WITH YOU! Now it takes AT LEAST 9 when I'm drunk (a Bitch CAN'T cum when her liver is threatening suicide and billions of cerebral brain cells are well on their way toward extinction, compliments of Alcoholic genocide!) but what the Fuck?

Number two-you gotta be able to HANG out! Nobody, I mean nobody, wants a dick that's gotta be in before sundown! You know-a "Curfew dick." A one minute-man! Why you think poor Missy Elliot MADE that song? The bitch was probably speaking from experience and venting to the world some traumatic shit she'd been goin through! A dead nigger who E-Mails his application in to PUSSY-HEAVEN.COM won't get past nobody's "Bitches Beware" alarm system! You can't work a full-time, twenty-four hour female sex-drive on a part-time basis and not expect to come home early from work one sunny day, and see some big black muscle-bound nigger named Clive stabbing the living shit out of the gaping hole that YOU USED to slide your dull four-inched fragile number two pencil inside of!!

You get my meaning? THAT torment cannot be tolerated! No wonder the sisters crosses over sometimes to the other side of street when they see you tired niggers comin. Nobody knows what makes one woman tick like another woman, and sisters are fighting back! Besides, what with Viagra and other more permanent and much less invasive Medical Technology a nigger shouldn't have to put a woman through that misery. SO WHAT you got a bad heart, Boo? Handle that shit! Be a man and do what you gotta do. An if the viagra causes a massive heart attack and your impotent ass drops dead, don't sweat it! If you hit that "G" spot, an I came right, believe me-I'll be already on the other side of the grave, 'V-Gina drippin and my panties down, waitin for your sorry deceased soul to meet me there and "Hit it" some more!

Hmm, I gotta linger on prerequisite number two a little longer cuz of the blatant disregard for a woman's needs it poses due to the brevity of it's length. Do you realize that one minute, "Uno Momento," comprises of only sixty-seconds? Sixty fucking Seconds-that's it! What is that? Thirty pumps? Or maybe LESS if the nigger gets tired and stops for air! You know, THAT sixty seconds could cost a brother his life! Especially if Mr. Limp-fuck rolls over and falls asleep or doesn't at least attempt a Round Two! If he runs into the wrong bitch, he's a dead man cuz bitches have been known to bring knives into the bedroom-just in case!

So a sisters just sittin there, waitin-with the gooey proceeds of some niggers premature ejaculation drippin from the hungry mouth of her clit! Now you must agree that a bitch gotta eat! So she ponders a timely innovative idea while the trifling bastard sleeps that will hopefully save her dynamic and unfulfilled libido from utter sexual starvation! What does ANYBODY do when they're hungry and they don't like the shit Mickey D's is serving? The answer-they take their business ELSEWHERE!!!

I'm sure that everybody enjoys a good laugh from time to time and like I said-nobody's perfect! But that one minute dilemma will break up any marriage. A man who hasn't yet learned to walk his dog and keep that squatting canine beast in the bushes long enough to get his excretory shit off, is a fucking joke! "Woe there Rex, easy boy. Take your fuckin time and don't 'Cum' on the pavement, 'Go' in the grass!"

That's some Sesame Street shit! A little boy can't piss straight and rarely knows how to control the raw or logistical power of an erection and nobody has a problem with that because the little motherfucker is just a kid! But nigger, if you're in your twenties and you can't maintain an erection longer than I can hold my breath then you might as well hang up your balls, put that lazy tired half steppin dick of yours on the Bachelors shelf of shame and join the Priesthood!! I'm sure those poor little Altar boys would really appreciate the anal relief of a child molesting pedophile-gifted with the God-given occupational hazard of Premature Ejaculation.

I'll take it one step further-but we're still on step two: I'd bet that even the Virgin Mary could use a long stiff one on those quiet hot and steamy midnights in Bethlehem! At LEAST on weekends and Holidays! And believe me, when that Sister got her first piece of dick after the Immaculate Conception and the birth of Our Lord and Savior Jesus Christ, ask anybody round the way and they'll all tell you they saw those untainted feet "Creepin" out of the hut after dark, enroute to suckin some handsome Shepherds dick! She didn't know the streets of Jerusalem had eyes. And to keep it real, on the down low, she musta hit each and every one of the Twelve Apostles (just to make up for lost time) as soon as the Messiah was safely stashed away back in Heaven after the resurrection! I'd bet my next one hundred orgasms on it!

But back to my Bitches Creed! I said a woman demands three things from a Nigger in bed. Now the last thing is just as important as the first two. Brothers...if you wanna fuck me-an you DO wanna fuck me. I can see your One-eyed Jack doin push-ups with no hands behind those Sexy-ass baggy stone-washed Rocawear Jeans you got on! But listen, if you really wanna knock my boots, you GOT to know how to talk back to this kitty-kat with your body and tones. Besides, communication is the most important factor in any relationship.

Now, some brothers jump in there like Bruce Lee (don't get me wrong, I like Bruce-he's just the wrong guy for the job) and they try to "Dick Kick" the shit out of a woman's vagina! But after a few thousand humps a bitch still ain't cum! So Professor Macho just sits at the end of the bed-limp dick in hand looking down at the "Tims" his arrogant stupid ghetto Ass forgot to take off before the love making-pardon me, "Beast Fuckin," began!

The "Ignant" G.E.D. wannabe has got his chest poked out like he just whipped Superman's and the Incredible Hulks Asses simultaneously but he couldn't handle horny little 5'8" me! The Jerk fools himself into allowing his swollen ego to propose the dumbest fucking question ever asked because although severely retarded, his feeble brain had reminded him to check his wrist-watch before and after the gory rape-Scene (oh yes, I'm bleeding by now) and although he cannot tell time, he knows that when he began, the small hand was on the twelve and the big hand was on the three. Now, forty five minutes later (Homosapien time, virtually unknown to Neanderthals with criminal records) he sees the big hand has wound its way onto the twelve, so his finite sense of logical calculation commends his odorous hulking frame on the satisfactory amount of time he spent thrusting his big dick inside me. No, he Couldn't tell time to save his life but those primitive uncouth instincts have taught him that whenever he pumps his prey so brutally long that he can smell the foul stench of his own nuts then it's safe to say that the entire carnal slaughter must have taken about an hour!

"So how WAS it," asks the funky little caveman laying beside me? Through blurry eyes I can detect miniscule specks of pubic hair, lacerated skin, and vaginal droplets of blood and semen on the bed-spread directly below my pelvic area. My left nipple has been virtually gnawed off by the fanged primate! Inches away from that forensic paraphernalia I see a nuissant swarm of flies hovering around the rancid smell of the most sadistically demented sexual parasite I've ever laid eyes on! The sweaty nigger who just pulled his sloppy wet dick out of my shattered pelvic bone! And the unkept lumbering monster had the NERVE to cum inside of the carcass that he just got finished bludgeoning "In The Name of Love!" I just hope to God...and Jesus, and anybody else misfortunate enough to witness this, my dreadful violent sexual demise, that THAT bastard didn't shoot inside my womb the ugly seeds of his future ignorant offspring!

"Girl, next time you fuck 'Bigfoot' or the 'Loch Ness Monster,' make sure you MAKE that motherfucker put on a condom!"

Yes, Dumbo asks the inevitable losers question and my pussy, despite missing genital teeth, attempts a faint smirk through gaping swollen lips!

Well...a REAL nigger, you know-one who could really fuck like he's supposed to, don't HAVE to ask no STUPID shit like that! A REAL nigger sees how you lost your fucking mind when he was on top of you! He felt your pussy popping while his dick was communicating with all your feminine needs. He heard your Love Zone crying out "Thank You" with every Buck Wild stroke! The blood is still running down his muscular back from when you scratched the Hell out of it, wishing you could reverse the course of nature and thrust his entire massive body back into the isolated domiciles of your womb-just so that none of those other sleazy bitches could have him!

You wish you could drag every iota of his manly vigor back to the isolated dark caves on your island of in-disatisfaction and nonfulfillment. And he still hears, through deafened ears, the echoes of traumatized screams when you cursed him out in ways only a satisfied woman's man understands.

"That's right, you big black ugly Bitch! Fuck me you stupid Bastard! Tear this pussy up, hurt me!" Those are the sexual inferences of a woman who is being touched so good, that she can smell the scent of her trembling-and dying of happiness as the love juices of her drooling libido succumb to cardiac and pulmonary arrest!

And your ears are also ringing at the drowned sounds that he strokes your eardrums with from the manly animosity emitted from his base vocals to his ten inch hammer.

"Take that baby-give me that BIG ASS! Um gonna KILL this pussy! Gimme that shit you nasty bitch!"

When a woman is TRULY turned on she'll endure anything to keep that throbbing sensation pumping inside of her.You can speak any language from Ebonics to Chinese, she'll understand the underlying message of what your body is saying. You can shit on her, piss in her face, (Ask R.Kelly, he knows) call her Momma, her grandmomma and her four kids bitches and she'll still say "Oh yeah!" You can stick your dick in her ASS and her mouth and cum on her face and hands till the white yolk-like fluid resembles cataracts over her eyes and she still won't give a FUCK! Shit, you can slap the shit out of her, fuck her best friend and tell your ugly homeboy to pull out HIS Mr. happy-if you hit that bitch and hurt her right, she'll suck HIS dick till he cums in her mouth and makes her take inventory of and swallow every sperm cell her lustful lips can drag from his waistline. And don't get mad at her or take it personal! She's on her knees suckin off some other nigger in reverence to YOUR potent sexual dominance which forces her by the minute to pull her hair out-to obey, and to do shit her mommy warned her NOT to!

Why you niggers think your dear darling innocent little sweethearts display that pre-arranged habit of sucking on your dirty-ass fingers when she's in that "Zone?" Wake up losers! Honey is trying to tell you in the best way she knows how that she's truly feeling it! She needs oral stimulation while she's on that rare path to an orgasm and a little more dick rammed anywhere, between her sweet twitching legs and her hungry mouth, wouldn't hurt!

Get the message? When that time comes you better either call for back-up, or stick that busy dick inside a place that will hold her attention span!! Quiet as it's kept a whole lotta us bitches, myself included, would rather have two or sometimes even three dicks in them, when she cums. They don't have to be twelve inches a piece, but a little here and a little there never killed anybody!

And when you grind that pussy-YELL AT IT! Tell it what to do and let a sister know exactly what she means to you. Excitement brings ecstasy and that's what a bitch needs-a brother with balance! Who can coordinate his filthy innovative mouth with the back shattering ramrod of his beautiful black dick! Soft niggers need not apply!

Ladies, you know what I mean! When a man hits you right his body is talking to you and the best nut in the world is when you get that deep male powerful dialect telling you that you ain't shit but how much HE needs you while his organ tries desperately to embed itself permanently into the lower strata of your cranium!

I must admit, most men don't have the self-confidence, the passion, or the balls for that which we need the most. Well MY cranium was still lonely, still untouched and it wanted to be sexually shaken. Dominated! Why you think REAL women like it when a nigger grabs her by the head or pulls her hair or arrogantly smacks her on the Ass! We LOVE to be dominated! Treated like a whore or a sex slave because that brings out our true passive self-our hidden femininity that only a true man knows to search for, to control and subdue. And we MUST know that our man is stronger than us so that we may find him worthy to look to in times of need! Thus when a woman is being man-handled in the bedroom, her tender psyche pulls off the rugged facade she's forced to wear outwardly in this male dominant society and the raw aggressive persona of her lover allows her to gladly submit and be what God created her to be!

Well Floyd was my sexual nightmare-the lacadasical force that turned my necrophalic encounter into an obsessive fear of the dead...of dead niggers! Like I said, he took away my femininity because it could not ultimately find in him a genuine male figure to gravitate toward. I was scared I might meet another undercover sick fuck just like him. Necrophobia! My ever throbbing clitoris fell into a six week coma and my cranium felt as if it would suffocate from the lack of an attentive strong male hand to stifle its sexual thoughts, keep it warm like a winter hat, and guide its docile posture into the promised land. That shit was over! The son of a bitch had crucified my female ego with his humdrum weak sex-drive. A Jolly-green giant penis with a Tiny Tim Program! And when that Harlem-world half-naked zombie was finished, I climbed out of bed and realized I'd had enough! That's when I decided to give Dre a call!

-14-

THE MISSING LINK

Dre stole cars for a living! He never had a job and was scared to death of the very THOUGHT of working for a living! But he knew what to do for me sexually and I needed him to come an do what he did best. Talk me through an orgasm! And Work some magic with a 5 inch dick like NO other BIG well-endowed nigger EVER could! You see, I'm an Equal Opportunity sister and everybody has their own place in the psycho-sexual land of fulfillment. Well HORNY was NO place for ME and Dre new how to reach me-to TRULY touch me.

Not with his little ass dick! He was hung like a squirrel! A NEWBORN squirrel! But when he slid that part of himself inside and dazzled me with that voice-OH, that voice took me to places I loved to go. Places that Floyd could never IMAGINE bringing me to in a million years! Dre was only 5 foot 9-BUT WHEN HE SPOKE...! My pussy thought that a 7 foot tall Ape-man was about to tear it apart! After the attack of the 'snake that size forgot,' the pygmy python, I knew otherwise. But no matter-by then I'd came six times and didn't really quite need a number 7! Now how many bitches YOU know can brag about a man who could supply THAT many orgasms-IN ONE SESSION? You can count em on one hand-therefore Dre was SPECIAL! An Ace-in-the-hole who I could count on when times got HARD on the BOULEVARD!

Usually during our interludes, by the time I got off he would climb on top an fuck me with the 5 inch killer and I would just laugh inside and pretend the 7 foot sledge-hammer slaughter was still goin on! I got a GOOD imagination! He could hang for awhile but it's too bad he didn't have much going for him. Besides, what good is decent 'Hang-time' when the size of the penis feels like your being humped by the Easter Bunny! Big fluffy-ears, buck-toothed and a little furry dick? My 12 year old nephew's dog-dog is bigger. Just joking-I don't have a nephew. I don't even have a sibling cuz I'm an orphan-but YOU GET MY POINT! Anyway I didn't care how miniature his manhood was. As long as he did the sister right, me an him was cool-and-the-gang!

If you heard Dre tell it, he was CONVINCED-that egotistical nigger SWORE he blew my back out from the moment he injected that slingshot slider of his, till the time he pulled Pee-wee out! And it was my fault-cuz despite the overt dicklessness, Dre excited me! And I was ALWAYS blowin up his celly or the two-way pager-so he thought he was the man. If he wasn't why else would a fine female like me call? So he added 2+2 and got 6! The right calculations but the wrong answer cuz he forgot to carry the one. The ONE reason I kept callin his ass was due to the benefits of how he talked to me. Whereas his manhood was small-almost invisible-his manly voice was huge and powerful! That was the thing. He could have left his baby-dick home and brought that voice to the orgy and that would've been all good.

I dialed Dre's cell-phone but he didn't answer. He knew he had owed me money and probably thought I was callin for some of it. About 150 beans to be exact! So since I knew how he thought, knew what a hustling cheatin backbiter he really was, I left him a message that the loan was not as much of an issue as his puny penis was!

THEN he answered back-assured that I didn't pose a monetary threat! We chatted and laughed and I told him how much I needed his micro-monster inside me.

"Come on baby, I'm backed up. Just give me the when and the where!" I always talk straight up! Time is of the essence and can't be wasted on Bullshit! We agreed to meet in the Diner on Nassau Street at 2:00P.M. There was a Co-ed restroom there that would serve as a free Motel-room for about 10 minutes and believe me those workers in there NEVER check. You could get Married, have kids and send them to College in their and they'd never be the wiser. They're too busy selling illegal loose cigarettes to shady customers in expensive cars to give a fuck about our little bathroom sexual hijinks.

I waited 20 minutes and it felt more like 2 hours! I was hungry! Didn't need a full-course meal-just a snack. And time and anticipation can be something as a woman languishes to find some food to place between her teeth. I'd hoped to finish up by 2:40 so I could pick up my daughter at School. Maybe catch HER out there unexpectedly or something. I'd hate to have seen her doin what I was about to do! To see her giving it up in a Public Restroom in broad day-light like I was to a man I see only when that seething little Spice-worm crawls up my behind!

I got impatient! The Nigger better not be frontin on me! For all I knew he could be in Queens somewhere getting his hustle-on in Ritzy Communities committing larceny while silly me was sittin in a greasy-spoon haven of contraband waitin for something I was not about to get! I remember one time I radioed him for a booty-call. It was some 5 months ago and he still owed me the money! I got him into a Hotel. Cuddled an kissed his ass. Got his 5 inches athrobbing into that zone that a lot of men would live and die for. I even sucked his dick, his LITTLE dick, that would've been better served as Dental Floss! And just when he wanted to cum I pulled that under-developed Termite out of my mouth! He looked at me-STUNNED! Like he wanted to curse me the out!

"Huh he started? Then I asked him for my money!

"Yo Dre, if you want the rest of this blow-job gimme back my buck-fifty!

"Oh FUCK girl," he shouted. He pulled his 2 fingers outta my ass!

"OOW! NIGGER, SLOW THE FUCK DOWN!"

"Come on Monie, I TOLD you-I'M HURTIN!"

"That's a cryin shame Dre, cuz you know WHAT? I'm hurtin TOO! An this BLOW-JOB'S OVER! I got dressed-shaking my ASS as much as I could. I even walked close to him so he could smell what he thought he was getting! I LOVE to fuck with people who fuck with me!

When I was dressed I came over to him while he was still laying down on the bed with his pants and boxers down. I didn't know what the Hell he was waitin for cuz the

SHOW was over-maybe he just didn't get it. Cuz he was NOT getting it! CAN'T HAVE NONE BITCH-ASS! That's something MOST niggers don't get!

He musta been prayin for a second chance. NOT WITHOUT $150 you won't! Maybe he was beggin the God of men with little dicks-that meat-shortage diety runnin around on a cloud with a silver-lining horizontally challenged! So Dre SAT there-offering supplications to his non-beneficent Creator-the one who'd fucked him for life to be cursed with a toddler's penis. He begged and he begged that God to Hocus-Pocus $150 into his pockets so he could get some head and finish cumin in my MOUTH! You see the sperm had been SUMMONED-siphoned from it's home in the nuts and sent forth on that sensuous journey to Climax-City! But the 'Goo' was stuck! Tricked into the cylindrical tunnel of his urethra expectant of a serious NUT! But a bitch like me fooled the SHIT outta them! I tricked them into the point of no return and they were caught in the agonizing synapse far from their testicular beginnings, yet only about an inch and a half-2 seconds, before ejaculation!

Well the little dick God was not in! He musta been stretched-out on the Cosmic Operation Table about to solve the preordained anatomical deficiency characteristic of his creed! The Shrimp-dick God had gotten discouraged one bright and sunny day and decided that enough is enough! Eternal humiliation is a crisis not even Divinity can bear! So he grabbed up his scanty nuts in his hand and boldly strolled into the Penile Enlargement Center right across the Street from the Milky Way. A stone-throw away from the bodega between The Black Hole and Celibate Parkway!

I rubbed it in his cocky little face! I bent down and kissed his head-hugged him and patted that limp 5 inch silk-worm now laying dead across the street from his stomach! I haven't seen his ass since that day. Uh-oh, bitch! You SHOULDA known! It was 3:05 p.m. and the motherfuckers working there were startin to take me for either 'Po-po' or the fool who'd been stood up! I redialed his number and cursed him out over his voice mail VOWING to send a Hit-man with a foot-long hammer to murder HIM and FUCK that Chicken-head bitch he was in love with! It served him RIGHT! And he can watch her getting her HEAD-SPRUNG by a real man with a REAL dick before he takes that final trip to meet his Little-dicked Maker!

Hell would be a darker place armed with the knowledge that the love of your miserable life is catching the HAMMER that YOU could never give her! And she'll still be catching the MASTER-PIPE-that GOOD-DICK till the end of time! While YOU and your BABY-DICK is sittin in HELL'S kitchen WATCHIN THE SPARKS FLY OUTTA HER RUPTURED ASS! Now, that being said-THINK GOOD THOUGHTS HAPPY CAMPER! FUCK YOU AND YOUR GRANULAR WEE-WEE! Now! REST IN PEACE!

Floyd and I were not on the same page and I wanted so badly to cheat on him! The only question was WHEN-and with whom! When your lady ain't feelin you no more like she used to this early in the game a man should wake up-an cut his losses. But not floyd! He felt destined and obligated to ride this one out till the cows came home!

The only reason for my planned sexual romp-in-the-restroom was that I was SICK as Hell of Floyd and would've entertained the thought of sleeping with a God-Damned Mandrill if I could-just not to have him touch me again. I'd only known him a short time-but he made me SICK! He was boring! And it felt like years. THAT'S why I ran like Hell from the mundane tortured wife Syndrome-perhaps when I'm 90 it won't matter! I won't give a fuck! But absent from Parkinson's Disease I CAN'T STAND TO LIVE LIKE THAT! So where's my Mandrill-give him a pair of Tims and a wife beater and he got a GOOD shot at knockin the ZOMBIE outta the box! Well for the time being I had to spend some time with 'MY MAN' So we went on a family outing to pretend that all was well in BOTH of our lives! Thank God good acting skills come for free in the complex repitoire of being a woman!

We drove up to the corner of Albany Avenue in Brooklyn on the way to pick up Floyd's kids. They lived in the Projects 3 blocks away so we continued onto Fulton Street. As we approached a Stop sign we noticed a budding homosexual casually sauntering by-peering at every male that crossed his effeminate path.

Why do faggots walk around with their mouths open? Is it some type of oxygen deficiency or something? It's like they're trying to invite some straight future prospect to evaluate the depth of their oral cavities. Who wants to look at FAG teeth? Who wants to stick little 'Fast-Freddy' ANYWHERE between those tremendous hanging J.J. lips to go in search of a pink-tainted set of fag tonsils? THAT'S NASTY BOO! "You gets no head from no straight nigger pal cuz your breathe smells like the collective stench of the last 5 dicks you sucked! A DECENT man's got better things to do than slump his dick into a gaping symphony of crooked-bicuspids and cheddar-cheese!

I caught my girl Hattie doin that once. Walkin around like Leon Spinks. Teeth bangin and lips hanging! And I cursed the bitch out!

As I pulled up to the Apartment Complex Floyd's baby's Mamma was sittin on the stoop and SHE didn't look much better! Her weave looked like an electrified wombat had crawled on top of her head-frightened, woozy and waiting to die! She had PRONOUNCED upturned nostrils. Like Micheal Evans-J.J.'s father from 'Good Times!' You know-the guy who played a matured 'Kunta Kente?'

Her forehead was protrusive-Neanderthal-like! Like she had a Grand-Pa named 'Herman!' AND THOSE LIPS! OH-THE LIPS! Well lets just say they were whispering 'B-A-N-A-N-A' and singing the Baboon Tune! The Cro-magnon song! What the FUCK was on God's mind when he picked up his 'PLAY-DO-SET' and made HER?

My, what an ugly neighborhood, I wondered! Methinks me better speed off out of this grimacing territory with it's inhabitants looking like the mouthpieces for a rotting teeth commercial. Floyd got out to talk to her and she told the person ranting loudly on the other end of her Celly to hold on.

"They comin out in a minute boo!"

Who the fuck she callin 'Boo?' That's MY 'Boo!' So what I hate his guts, no ugly-bitch calls MY man 'Boo!'

"Laquanna, Aiyesha-COME DOWNSTAIRS! Daddy's HERE!"

What a GHETTO BITCH! THIS is INKA? I couldn't believe Floyd's pretty ass actually stuck his DICK in THAT! I looked at the PRIMATE-Smiling wildy with her monkey-lips and hunched demeanor. Then I looked at FLOYD! Like he had JUST impregnated a BABOON! She looked like the fucking Missing-Link-a pivotal ancestor of modern-day civilized MAN! So what do I call her? INKA? NO-INK THE MISSING-LINK!

And when she smiled her mouth leaked out a prehistoric yodel in a sad cacophony of red-lipstick and missing teeth! It looked like someone had dragged Curious George off his steamy tree-limb and took him to Duane Reade to buy some Cosmetics. The crimson-hue barely scratched the surface or found it's mark on her wide saucer-like lips and one could easily conclude that neither adult, nor child, had besmirched this creature with the lipstick. It had to be an ape-who ruggedly vandalized Inka's abundant mouthpiece with several ounces of Cherry-red lip-stick! Hence the ancient war-cry:"AAAAA-OOOOO-UUAAAGH!" Floyd was a DOG!

"Whew, Playa-YOU HIT THAT? An CAME? Well what's YOUR secret? How did you CUM? Was it Henney or Rum? It would've taken amplified Crack-Cocaine for ME cuz I don't care WHAT you say-FUCK YOU! The bitch is MAD UGLY! Like she's so ugly her DADDY'S mad about it! Now THAT'S UGLY! Not to mention her mother-it don't look like she HAD one! Looks more like 2 grotesque tree-climbers got together and had THAT cause 'Human' bitches don't make kids THAT ugly! So there goes the secret of her Homosexual bloodline! The bitch got TWO daddies! Mixed chromosones-some Mutant shit! "BANG, BANG, BUTT-FUCK!" "BANG, BANG, BUTT-FUCK!" "HENNEY-BUTT-FUCK!" "CRACK COCAINE BUTT-FUCK!" "SUCK, SUCK BUTT-FUCK!" "Don't spill a drop UGMO! AAAH-NOW! STICK IT BACK IN! I'M ABOUT TO CUM! FUCK!" And "BOING!" 9 months later-SHE POPS-OUT! Slidin down the rims of 4 sweaty ape-nuts! Now THAT'S MUTATION!

So the Missing-Link sits at the top of the stoop of Albany Projects and she has a newborn baby. And I pray to God that THAT child don't end up ugly like it's Momma! Looking like a baby Missing-Link! The daddy was probably a talking primate too cuz what else can you expect when 'INK' the Missing-Link joins together in carnal matrimony with another flea-ridden beast like her?

Now we got us a situation cuz I'm really rootin for this poor baby's well-being. It's facial health! Inka, It's mother, was for all intents and purposes a neanderthal! She truly looked like a woman caught up in a grip of evolution who'd climbed it's way up the ecological ladder and was suspended in a state between Cro-Magnon Man and Chicken-head! You ever see a Gibbon? On a stoop talking to her Homie 'Di-slexia?' On the cell phone and devouring Barbeque Pumpkin Seeds-WHOLE! I mean SHELL AND ALL! Good GOD!

"Laquanna, Aieysha-hurry up," she howled as she spit a bad seed out down toward Floyd's left Tim Boot! Now like I said, I'd seen some shit in my day. But I prayed for that blessed child cradled in the arms of it's mother-the Gorilla! The Gibbon. Inka-the Missing-Link!

I also cringed at the possible horror of beholding the 2 big…uh, 'kids' Laquanna and Aieysha. I could see them now, gorilla walking or swinging down the project steps. On all fours or strolling on their leather-like knuckles-out the door to Mommy! Strutting their Babooned-stuff-with matching pink and white 'Osh-Kosh' suits and a white 'Polo' Baseball Cap! Teeny-bopper gorillas 'DO' do Project Stoop Fashion Shows like their trifling-ass parents with the bamboo Tarzan-vines and mopped-out hair weaves!

I popped outta the Jeep and introduced myself to Floyd's ex-wife-dying to look at the baby. I had to make sure it wasn't HIS! Inka got off the celly and hugged me like she knew me! Like me an her were old friends or I was her baby daddy-fresh outta the Joint coming home on a day that essential pampers and crack-money had run out!

"Let me see the baby, Inka," I inquired! When jumbo, the ghetto-girl peeled open the top blanket covering the yellow snow-suit, I could've DIED! The child was gorgeous! Beautiful. How the fuck did she cock her legs open, lay down and make THAT? Musta been some ghetto-magic! Project Voo-doo! Like when you mix a forty, a spliff and some Food Stamps together and-HOCUS-POCUS! "PRESTO-CHANGO!" And 'POOF' The ape-bitch leaps on top of her convict-man and rides him till the shit comes to a boil! She stirs those hips frequently, tryin to gyrate them hideous genes to one side. Make them separate form the 'Good' ones. Then she gorilla-hops off and makes his illiterate ass drink the concoction. He will drink it cuz he can't even SPELL the word P.O.I.S.O.N. and wouldn't have sense enough to suspect foul-play!

When he cums, his criminally-oriented sperm cells will undergo a blatant transformation by the time he pulls 'Jimmy' outta her raunchy womb! And out comes The GOLDEN CHILD! Handsome-unlike his father. De-furred-unlike his mother. He is affable, radiant, promising and HUMAN! This is a one-shot-deal so don't try the potion no more! If you do, it'll backfire and you'll give birth to a child much more terrifying than YOU! The entire maternity ward will explode and Pa-pa convicts nuts will go flying too-right over the perilous heights of Albany Projects! So much for Chemical Reactions and second-chances! Or didn't you know-lightning don't strike twice in the Hood!

Inka and I sat and chilled while Floyd went upstairs for his 2 kids. The baby began to cry and she fiddled for the pacifier but couldn't find it. After a couple of moments of shrill infant cries she noticed the pacifier laying on the ground by the curb.

"Oh-SHIT, dere it goes," uttered the disengenius mammal!

"I got it Inka," I exclaimed!

"Nah, nah girl. Sit down," she insisted and bolted, baby in hand, dangling like a rag-doll. Then she scooped it up! "Mama got it, boo-boo, see? Yeah, here go yo Nookie!"

Ah fuck! Wait a minute! No that bitch WASN'T…I sprung into action!

"Lemme wash…" TOO LATE!

"Chill Ma, I got this! I do it all the time! Right Mama? Yeah Mama!"

The BITCH! The GIBBON! The Mother from HELL put the pacifier in her OWN stink-ass mouth! Called herself washing it off and handed it right back to her baby!

Ohh-I wanted to fuck her up-right then, right there! On site! Ass-whippin, teeth, blood, blows-infant witness and all! A fuckin Stoop-Homocide for a stupid ghetto-queen and the salvation of her helpless innocent offspring! Now don't she know she just got finished suckin John-john's dick the other night? The nasty bitch! And John-john represents her own male counterpart cuz every dirty bitch has a dirty nigger!

So here is Miss. Missing-Link, polluting her baby's pacifier with the same mouth she uses to lick some ghetto-convicts ass with, that she's seeing from time-to-time! He probably lives in the P.J.'s not that that matters completely. But he's probably some 2 bit scumbag cuz look at HER! That's how SHE is and 'Dust-Bunnies' stick together! He most likely hits anything that moves! Any ghetto-fabulous ho that oozes outta dark tenement roof-top crawlspaces every weekend of her life in a never-ending search for tranquility, a couple of bucks and some dick!

So this foul nigger is fuckin Inka! And Inka-dirty ass Inka, is caring for the baby! And diseases don't give a fuck WHO they infect! And all that corrupt bacteria and FUNK and spit and Garbage-bin Gibbon mouth smellin like John-john's ass-AND POOR LITTLE BABY GORGEOUS GOTTA SUCK IT OFFA HIS PACIFIER!!! Now that's a chain of events-a slum Domino-effect for your ASS! I looked down at the helpless life she carelessly cuddled in her errant unskilled hands-and I prayed!

Before I could punch the Gibbon in the mouth Floyd returned with 2 beautitul daughters running down the steps and hugging Queen Kong Good-bye! THEY DID NOT LOOK LIKE THEIR MOTHER! One looked like him-the big one.The little one looked like a cute humanoid version of Inka the Gibbon! Wow, I thought-there IS a God! He did his thing on these 2 cuz they looked like future Super-models. Damn, how could an ugly Leon Spinks looking ghetto hood-rat produce such lovely offspring? I mean she was 3 for 3! Perhaps the ugly gene got jealous and broke the fuck out moments before conception!

"Da-da, come outside an say Good-bye to your sisters," commanded MaGilla!

Oh Damn-WHAT THE FUCK IS A DA-DA? Perhaps HE is the Blacksheep! The ugly child-the hideous-one! I didn't wanna stick around to find out the degree of his comeliness! To see if she was 4 for 4. Or if strike 3 came in like a hungry tiger and painted itself grotesquely onto the face of 'Da-da' her oldest perhaps most repulsive offspring.

We drove off before Da-da could make his belated debut. I had seen enough-and didn't wanna barf enroute to Carle Place Long Island to pick up my own 'obnoxious' daughter!

We stopped at an all-you-can-eat Chinese joint after we picked up Breanna figuring the kids ages 5, 7 and 14 would enjoy some adolescent play-time-and some M.S.G! There was a large display of heated foods. I especially loved the Lobster Cantonese and went back for fourths. Floyd preferred the Spare Ribs. Breanna gobbled down the Beef Lo Mein and the Wonder Twins grabbed ANYTHING hot or sweet they could get their greasy monkified paws on! Oh yeah-they were wonderful, polite and mannerable children but they attacked the buffet table like the food would grow legs and run from them!

They wolfed that food down like they hadn't eaten since Easter Sunday! Like Christmas had come and old careless Saint Nick had fool-heartedly dropped a red bundle of toys-IN THE PROJECTS! You ever see Crackheads scramble for loose change on the ground? It's a crying shame! At one point Aieysha hoisted an Egg-roll to her mouth. There was NO TIME for chewing! Five-seconds FLAT between insertion and excretion! "SCOOP! GULP! BELCH!" No more Mr. Egg-roll! "Damn, boo-your punk-ass Daddy don't feed you?"

And Laquanna was even worse! Diving into the Buffet-table FANGS-FIRST! All you could see was her narrow-ass wiggling in the air and those tiny pink Payless shoes-twitching with glee! Reflecting the insurmountable joys her grinding teeth were having with the Buffalo wings!

If their mother Inka LOOKED like an animal-her 2 carnivorous offspring ATE like one! After the feeding frenzy little Laquanna had the nerve to ask for a bag of Doritos! I grabbed Floyd's head and pulled him toward me to whisper in his ear! I pulled no punches.

"Your children are embarrassing me-they EAT like fucking Pac-Man!"

The big one, Aieysha, looked timid. Affable, shy and diffident. She had Oriental eyes. The kind you see hoisting up a warrior stare and a Samurai Sword in a Bruce Lee movie. She was very slim and her features were small. But something bothered me about her. She looked like she had been agonizing on the inside. Like she was destitute and somehow perpetually reliving horrible tales of misery deep within her consciousness.

I surmised her mother-the primate was the culprit rooted in the child's anguish and cursed the unholy day that ghetto Inka was born! Aieysha was made of glass! Her intangible will drowned right in front of me whenever they came by-recanting traumatic pictures of what life was like back home. What was Inka DOING to this poor child? I wanted to cry and swallow her back into my womb. Fuck Inka! THIS was the child I should have had! Gentle, loving, unselfish and inherently amiable! Unlike Breanna.

It's not that I didn't love my daughter but she coulda took some lessons on humility from this lovable 7 year old! Aieysha reminded me of ME-as a child. Before I got fucked-up and grew up to become the bitch that I am! There was a silent everlasting comradery present that drew us together-one that neither my own daughter nor HER mother could ever match. I loved her tender delicate self from the moment I set eyes on her. Maybe I could switch the 2 and send Bre's violent abusive ghetto ass back to the banana-munching beast Inka!

The younger one, Laquanna, was totally the opposite! She was a fucking Monster-WITH ISSUES! She was Hell's version of the Virgin Mary and I wondered how in the world she could have come from the same womb, fallen from the same tree, as her older, more serene and even-minded sibling! Laquanna was stuck up-AND RUDE! She reminded me of the nasty little brat that could! The Devil's seed, who vowed to add wrinkles to my face-and subtract hairs from my head! Perhaps even years from my life. I wanted no part of this kid. And you should've seen her in the dessert section! Fucking up shit-mixing vanilla pudding into the chocolate and dropping green jello into the God-Damn raisinettes. I LIKE Raisinettes! Why the little bitch gotta come up in MY spot? My shit-an get 'Home Alone' clumsy while a sister's tryin to get her raisin on?

I exuded parently patience for the first 5 seconds-THEN I LOST IT! Can't be too patient you know-or Bebe's kids'll walk all over you! Thus when I evaluated the scenario I concluded that THIS creature came outta Inka! And Inka's sickening ghetto-prodigy would not ruin my $10 a plate meal! My patience wore thin!

"Come on baby, let me do that for you." You fuckin up the game I thought! Or at LEAST let me heap some of that green shit onto YOUR plate an get your imp ass outta my way! GROWN FOLKS GOTTA EAT! She did some Linda Blair, Exorcist shit-restating a few well-rehearsed expletives under her foul demonic breathe! If looks could kill the bitch woulda took my life-right there in the 'Chen How Duck Resturaunt!' Right between the Pu-pu Platter and the Peking Duck!

I wrestled the ladle back outta her hands and she attempted to kick at me!

"Bre, hold her down for me! An if the bitch moves-GO TO WORK!" Breanna, 9 years older and far more deeply entrenched in the tenets of evil, took the job-with pleasure!

I called for her Zombie father, over in the booth devouring Spare Ribs and chicken Egg foo-yong, and he came running. Floyd was shocked at his kind little sweetharts' vulgar display of 4-letter words and hostile 'Foot-Action!' I warned him not to let that shit happen again! Put little Dennis The Menace in check-or she sleeps in the garage. Without a HEATER! Only way to kill a juvenile delinquent Demon is to freeze him out!

"Floyd, I love your older daughter-I'd give her the world! Send her through Medical School and even adopt her. We could switch! You know-you take Breanna! But that OTHER little brat, the one spat from the Devil's own mouth, needs some fuckin beat-downs! On a daily basis! Nothing violent-just body shots! An if THAT don't work, send her Gangster-ass to a Priest-OR BACK HOME TO HER GHETTO-FABULOUS MOTHER!"

-15-

FUCKING FOR RENT MONEY

Prostitution is the oldest profession known to man and everybody does it! From the Multi-million Dollar Celebrity Athletes (Being bought and traded to different teams as long as the contract has enough zeros in it) to Corporate Firms merging together in a cesspool union blessed by the CEO'S, the Stock-holders and the Devil himself! Politicians do it for Campaign money-selling out their misinformed contributors (the good Citizenry of America) for donations that will culminate in the Election of a self-serving greedy bastard that does not have the greater-good of the general public at heart!

Women stuck in dead-end relationships do it to circumvent bankruptcy! Rent's gotta be paid! Cable's on the blink and her hair and nails have gotta be 'DID!' Hence, another meaningless perfunctory romp in the sack with the Son-of-a-bitch you can't stand! The one who called you last night for some essential cock-sucking! Thanks be to God you do THAT good! You won't let him stick it in your ass-so if it wasn't for those sweet swarming lips you would live on the CURB!

"Come on over Playa! And don't forget your wallet. Ain't no pussy free in the entire Universe! Specially MINE!" He knows you HATE HIM! You wish an ancient high and mighty oak-tree or a bi-plane with engine troubles would fall outta the sky right on top of his stink-ass and bury the foul-mouthed trick right where he stands! Now THAT would be nice!

Some sisters stay in the relationship for the kids-they think their kids cannot live without their useless fathers and will stop breathing the moment they throw him out! Truth is, YOU CANNOT LIVE WITHOUT THE CASH HE GIVES AND YOU WOULD STOP BREATHING FINANCIALLY just as soon as his belated departure chokes those hard-earned dollars of his outta your dependant lungs! TRICK! These women feel they can't afford to survive without the Prince of Darkness under their roof! And the minute they dump his worthless ass they fear life by themselves!

He just don't do it for her anymore! He's most likely cheating with some local skeezer! Where else would a man be at 3:00A.M. when he ain't in your bed? And if she catapults his tired existence back to the wilds of 'Dogville' from whence he came, then destiny could not have come at a better time! But she hangs in there-till something better comes along or perhaps H.I.V. or terminal brain or Prostate cancer zaps her 'Problem' away!

So don't look down on the neighborhood 'Ho!' Her analytical skills are lacking and her budget is tight. There IS a better way then to give it up to every Tom, Dick and Harry! But the WHORE is pure-out in the open, and much more sincere than we could ever be! Let me explain!

Prostitutes don't waste time and economize their sexuality and their minutes in a delicate web of profitable business practices! The average woman meets a guy and spends weeks to months squandering precious time! BEFORE SHE GIVES IT UP he has to pay for it tenfold in time, gifts and services! THEN he has earned the right to cum inside her!

A Ho recognizes that transaction as one lacking the fine and obligatory principle of 'Expedition!' Time is Money! So she makes the same financial gains that the other stupid bitch has made. Only 100 times more! She fucks him and gets her down payment in advance. She is not afflicted by transient emotions and hurt feelings commonplace in domestic relationships. She will easily elude the stroke or the heart attack the other sickly bitch is moving toward cuz she don't give a fuck about nobody but number one! That is an extremely healthy concept! Eventually, if she continues to play her cards right, in time she can quit the game and become wealthy enough to establish herself as a financially independent woman whose world possibilities are limitless. So what her butterfly's been stretched beyond the Twi-light Zone! If she's been 'lucky' enough to elude 'The Monster' or genital herpes riding in on the cheap torn condom perhaps or perhaps not used by the 'normal' bitch who caught a whiff of some similar communicable diseases, she's got it made. If not the 2 might meet in the forbidden zone of the Health Clinic despite their assorted and contrasting lifestyles!

Now lets take a look at old beat up and emotionally scarred Tawana (the 'normal' bitch). She ain't got shit! She never HAD shit and most likely will never get shit. Oops! That's fucked up cuz despite all her presumed virtue-she still done fucked a whole lotta niggers in the 10 odd years she's been dating! She has expended her life-force many times over and is now a spent-song waiting to be shelved in the Great Halls of antiquated music! Her pussy is dried out and her tits have called in sick and that ass has been demoted from a sonic-boom to an inaudible mutter! She still holds her head up high but no one knows why. Perhaps she should've chosen a more lucrative occupation-one with room for advancement!

Well, as Tawana fiddles with her purse looking for change to get on the Cross-town bus to visit that nigger who she's still not sure she trusts, she notices that former whore driving by in a Black Lexus! Tawana manages a smirk on her face and her mind laughs out loud.

"Damn," she muses, "I'm sure glad I didn't wind up like THAT!"

At the same time the 'Ho' peers through HER rear-view mirror at Tawana reflecting to herself and saying the same thing!

Lets look at the scenario in another way-because I am in no way encouraging someone into taking up the life of prostitution. I am however advocating female long-term self-determination-earned with at least a minimal degree of intelligence, wisdom and innovation!

WOMEN! US! WE, the female gender will force a man to wine and dine and buy us things the proper way (the way a decent woman should be treated) before he meets the criteria to have bought in time, services and assets-EXACTLY what a whore is paid for in cash from the beginning!

So you think you ain't a Ho? Good! Test yourself! Let that SAME nigger not treat your hungry self-righteous ass to a movie or even buy you a drink! Let him not wait 2 or 3 months to smell what the 'Rock is cookin!' That diamond sittin in the store window between your legs-BEGGING to be bought! Give back that 3 Karat ring-since you're not a whore and you don't sell sex for money! Let that motherfucker stand in your face-after he ain't gave up SHIT to your Mother Theresa delusions and demand some of that hoarded vagina you'd rather give away 6 weeks from now-after ALL the procedural Courting Bullshit! The civic protocol and mating pre-requisites! Let the only thing you get outta him be the demand: "YO BITCH, DROP YOUR DRAWS AND LET ME STICK IT IN! Fuck a date, you'll get that later!"

Look ON bitch, an see if you'll fuck him then! RIGHT THEN AND RIGHT THERE! Without the structured foreplay! Without the charitable donations and dainty romantic rendezvous that make you smile. That makes your financial life a bit easier and makes your cunt 'loosen up a little!' I SAID FUCK HIM RIGHT THERE-INSTANTLY! Without the expensive gratuities! I bet you'd tell that unworthy parasite he's outta his mind! He ain't getting THIS! CUZ HE DIDN'T PAY DOWN ON IT! He thinks he's gonna just run up in here-RAW? And he ain't put in on it? OH HELL NO!

Now if you DO give up the pussy, you're either a God-Damn fool or you're a REAL LIVE WOMAN! And if you won't, then you're NO better than the whore you've just condemned! No better than Lokisha-the street-walker. I know what you're thinking. "It's not that I give it up for money but I need time to get to know him. And that 'feeling out' process entails courtship-dating! And dating isn't free!"

Oh yeah, well how would you feel if you had to get to know him without the luxury of him taking your starving ass to B-B QUE'S? Without a trip to Vegas! Let him get to know you without a Broadway Play or a JAY-Z Concert! In fact what would you do if you were actually asked to get to know the motherfucker simply by talking to one another. Good conversation! Do you think the getting-to-know-you process would be as effective if it were limited to telephone discussions and livingroom chatter? What if you had to sacrifice the crab legs and the Shrimp Scampi for some good old-fashioned and wholesome heart-to-heart talk-in the comfort of a neighborhood park bench? Would you go for THAT? Cuz your not a prostitute so you don't require monetary compensation for the time you invest in garnering and nurturing your friendship!

I DON'T THINK SO! YOU WOULDN'T GO FOR THAT SHIT! And why wouldn't you? CUZ YOU'RE A WHORE-A DOWN-LOW HO! You just require high-maintenance and a whole lotta socially-acceptable propositional foreplay to get you in the

MOOD! And when you ARE in that mood you will do in 10 weeks or 10 months, what the OTHER HO accomplishes in 10 minutes!

Once more, for you hard-of-hearing and comprehensively challenged muck-minds out there who are perhaps outraged because your severely limited mental capacity has informed you that I AM TEACHIN YOU TO BE A HO-I AM NOT! I am merely recanting and illustrating to you the collective sum of your STUNTED sexual perception! To re-iterate this topic in a NUT-SHELL-No matter how much we CLAIM not to be motivated by money, the naked truth is that we are ALL 'MATERIAL GIRLS.' No matter how fancifully sophisticated we try to dress it up! Both men and women date with an alterior-motive in mind! HE WANTS PUSSY AND WILL ENDURE A LITTLE FRIENDSHIP IN ORDER TO GET IT! YOU NEED TO BE CHERISHED-AND DESIRE FRIENDSHIP! AND YOU'LL GIVE UP A LITTLE BIT OF ASS IN ORDER TO GET IT! As long as these combined motivations are respected and satisfied, there are NO losers-and everybody is happy! He gets to smell the savor of that large rotund sexy backside you lug with you every where you go and your internal desire for comfort and comradery which you misconstrue as 'true love' is essentially quenched! END OF STORY!

Well you can put away the gasoline and the book of matches and dry your soggy eyes cuz you're not the only one guilty of this insipient dilemma! You're not the only one! HO! Mind if I call you 'HO' for short? O.K! CLOSET HO!! I TOO, IS A HO! Just like the rest of us-but I was only a 'TEMP!' YES, I'LL TELL IT LIKE IT IS! I WAS A HO AND FLOYD WAS MY 24 HOUR DESIGNATED JOHN!! Oh, I serviced other Johns simultaneously-for free! But HIS ass was payin! I wasn't feelin him anymore! And if I gotta keep myself from gagging and chill with you from time-to-time-believe ME, YOU GOTTA PAY!

Spring sprung! And it brought with it the most peaceful 2 months I've experienced in my entire life. All through May and June Floyd would come over a total of about 2 times a week. That was not enough for him. It was plenty for me! He had been working over-time 4 days a week to save up enough money to put an adequate down-payment on the house. The idiot was under the impression that I would move in with his sorry ass and spend the remainder of my days-miserable, lonely and tied to him! What the HELL was HE smoking? And he also had the audacity to ask me NOT to go out unless HE was there with me.

WHAT? Hold up-you mean, you claim to be MY MAN! And since you THINK you my man (you ain't really cuz if you WERE you wouldn't have to beg me to stay home. I'd be glued to you IF I LOVED YOU and would GLADLY die for the opportunity to stay home with you) I'm supposed to stay home-ON WEEKENDS, cuz your corny ass has to work? PLAYA-IF YOU GOTTA WORK THAT'S ON YOU! THAT'S YOUR PROBLEM! I'm off-an guess what I'M doin on my days off? Let me put it this way-by the time you figure out where I'm at-I'LL BE BACK! So dumb dumb was delusional!

"No NIGGER-I ain't stayin home! An I ain't movin in-not on your CREEPY life! Save that eternal punishment for some other bitch." Since he had less time, I had more time-to play! I went out 3 nights a week. WITHOUT HIM! I was out of control! And I knew that whatever I did-or said, he could not stand the thought of losin me. So he put up with my SHIT! The brother was STRUNG OUT and lived and breathed for this fucked up one-sided relationship. And no matter how many times I shitted down his God-Damned throat I knew he would always be there-waitin till I got home so I could SHIT some more! I could NEVER have done that nonsense to Canei cuz he would've snapped my fuckin neck from jump-street! But Floyd was NOT Canei! Floyd was in love-and that was FLOYD'S problem!

I could've came home drippin with some other niggers scum hangin from my pubic hairs and canine tooth-prints on my nipples and he'd welcome me! Just the same! Hugging me, kissing me and giving me a third of his check!

I wished Floyd had a twin brother as gullible as he cuz I'd probably bang him too-on the D.L! Just to keep the happy days here again-and the Jackass' Moolah rollin in! I was 'Home Alone' from April 2nd to June 2nd and I wilded out just like the little white-kid in the movie! Bre went from shopping for her Easter Sunday dress to bunny-hopping on a trip to Disneyland for the Memorial Day Weekend! Then to stay with my parents till mid-June. It was the answer to my prayers!

All I did was get laid, and get high, an party, an get laid, and call out from work-an get drunk so I can go get laid some more. Then I'd get to work late the next morning-multiple orgasms make a bitch tired! It was Heaven! God should've wiped my skeezer-ass out cuz what I was doin, the way I was carryin on an getting down, HAD to be a sin! I knew it was!

SHIT! The niggas do it! Every man on the planet Earth will conquer a new piece of pussy every chance he gets! It's natural. So if a man can do it-why can't I? What you gonna do Lord-KILL ME! Throw me in the lake of fire for daring to be equal with those perverted motherfuckers you created before me? You don't kill THEM when they run around-do you! And if a man died every time he fucked somebody he had no business touchin, the entire male population would be wiped completely off the face of the Earth! So don't panic Lord-EASE UP! If you won't annihilate Adam for his continuous philandering, show the same restraint to Eve! If you wanna set it off on the controversial issue of fornication, START WITH THEM! An save me, the best, for LAST! Besides-I got a few thousand nuts to bust!

Oh yeah it was a summer for the history books! Having different men over to quench my loneliness! Getting it whenever and from whomever I wanted! Sometimes it was Canei-yeah I FINALLY forgave him-partially! I needed his services at times and found him to be an asset I would not completely discard! At times it was 'Black.' A

153

nigger I went to School with back in the days! He was charming and funny and I enjoyed his company. He kept me laughing-an I kept him hard! Every now and then I radioed Dre-WHEN I FELT IN THE MOOD FOR SHRIMP! And whatever time I had left was spent tolerating my part-time man-FLOYD BAXTER! The corny nigger I lent my body to (for a price) with mute and mortified bedside-manners-AND RIGHT CORONARY DISEASE!

My 'sexcapades' stemmed from a female desire to be loved! I felt empty-like my heart had been extracted from my body and replaced with an ice-aged mass of frozen dreams! I wanted to find the person that all of us have been told exists but have never been instructed in how to find. Every day of my life embodied a duality of directions that this wayward consciousness traveled to opposing poles to obtain. The little Devil in me said: "Fuck it! These niggers ain't no good-so fuck em, suck em and chuck em," Dragging me to partake of as much casual sex as I could find in the obligatory quest of the desperate to enter Paradise.

Then there was that Angel, (he didn't show his face too much) that beneficent entity, who advised me on the path away from that fallacious Paradise toward the true enlightenment and peace found only in love! Guess who won-and guess whose ass I sent scrambling outta my den of iniquity. A bitch can't have no company-no third-wheels, when she got some adultery to commit. Each day I anticipateded several thunderous yards of fornication reaching out their sensual tentacles within the barricades of my genital anatomy. I inhaled every Heavenly inch of whoever's lust-DEEP beyond the pubic cobwebs of a heartbroken woman's lost sanctity. AND MY SEXUALITY HAD NO ROOM FOR MORAL COACHING!

I couldn't stay home! I couldn't keep my panties on and my legs remained stuck in an open position. (I caught a few dozen backshots too) After enduring the bullshit at work every day it was play-time. When the sun went down-the sex-attacks, the nymphomania, went up my body from clitoris to brain-stem-and it was ON! My celly was as busy as the condoms and the box-springs. And not ONE SINGLE SOLITARY DAY-NOT ONE DAY PASSED, WHERE I DID NOT LAY DOWN WITH THE SOOTHING OF ANOTHER MAN'S PENIS INSIDE ME!

Sometimes I creeped out of the house at 3:00A.M-when the rest of the civilized and less promiscuous members of society were asleep! I would warm up the engine and speed off in the dark, in search of that night's victim of my cravings. On other occassions the pipe-line did a drive-by-boned me in my bedroom, in the shower, by the stove or over the toilet-seat! I even did Black right underneath the entertainment center with the lights out after we had come home from a Knicks game. Then I rushed him outta the house (told him my daughter was comin) and fucked Canei all night long-30 minutes after Black left. The semen hadn't dried yet-an I was already movin on with the next jump-off! Bent on revenge for my life's pain, I earnestly fulfilled every fantasy that ever found it's way into my deviant and sexually over-heated mind!

154

And Floyd-poor poor Floyd, didn't have a fucking CLUE about the foul dirty shit his 'WOMAN' was doin while he was hard at work! But he was content-just to have me! (or so he thought-EVERYBODY had me) Just as long as he got a bi-weekly piece of ass and a pocketful of 'head' to take back home with him. To hold him over for 5 days till the next time he could crawl back to my crib and borrow this pussy some more!

Oh-by the way, he had gotten down on one knee and proposed to me on a Carriage-ride in Central Park on the Wednesday before Easter. That was when we got engaged-after having had a romantic dinner. (Romantic to HIM-I was bored) We ate at an exquisite Restaurant with a glass encasement that revolved around the Manhattan Sky-line! The lounge was on the 48th floor of a reputable Midtown luxury Hotel and it was beautiful!

The rock was a 1 Karat White-Gold Princess-cut Diamond. Seven Gs' I think! I neglected to mention the Engagement to my brand new devoted fiancé because of all the God-Damn fun I'd had in the 2 months following the proposal. Creepin, cheatin and fuckin everything in sight!

My intended husband wanted us to go away to Atlantic City for the weekend but my rent was due. I needed $950 and my purse was short by about $400.

"It don't sound like a happy time in New Jersey to ME! Why go give the rest of my bread to a slot-machine with a hard-on for armed-robbery? Sorry baby, I got rent to pay! Now if YOU payin and re-stockin my purse, maybe THEN we can talk," I told him!

I got a rule! Benjamin Franklin speaks loud and clear! And Hamilton an Jefferson and the rest of them dead Presidents can get a ladies attention with the quickness too when the Cableman wants his shit back and rent arrears are steam-rolling through my desire to make ends meet!

Don't come to me with Washington or Lincoln cuz I might barf on what you're handin me! Those minimal units of currency can't keep up with the economic norms I've set for myself and won't compete with what the Jones' push back and forth to the Club on Friday night! Who wants to get out and push a Volvo when they can cruise in a Jeep? Get it? Don't be a fool! I said I don't WANT the finer things in life-I NEED THEM! So if you can't indulge me in Crystal and Dom P. on Jet-set excursions when I'm thirsty, I'll go without! NO PROBLEM! An you can keep those Budwiesers and Miller Lite cold in that ghetto ice-bucket you brought for the long lonely solo ride back to the slums of Projectsville from whence you came!

Do I look like the Atlantic City type? Everybody knows that that place is for Senior Citizens with false-teeth and canes hobbling around like ancient disgruntled muppets-not to mention younger low-lives like Floyd who had absolutely nothing else to live for! Well it was either take the trip with Floyd or have to go through yet another episode of "THE INVASION OF YAGO," beggin for some ass-OR RENT MONEY and funking up my tiny apartment! The choices a bitch has got to make in life-the zombie, or the troll? I eagerly chewed my cud and swallowed my pride while meeting The 'dead man' at the 34th street Bus Station. I was only in it for the rent money and if I could squeeze out an extra $50 for Con Ed then I'd thank the Matrilineal Goddess for kicking in a bonus! I accepted my doom-2 days with Floyd. A ho HAS to make sacrifices. And if I was lucky enough to survive-all would be well. I didn't expect much really. Perhaps a good meal and a few phone numbers-but as for actually having a meaningful orgasm or the pleasure of sex with my eyes OPEN-that was dead! I couldn't stand the sight of the man I called my fiancé-on top of me! And although I might let him screw me-I WOULD'NT LOOK!

"Damn baby, didn't you cum?"

The 5 Star Hotel was elegantly adorned in glass, oak wood and lavender drapery and the bed was on the money. If only I had brought along a REAL MAN to enjoy it with! I could see Floyd's dick attempting to bore a 6 inch diameter hole into the satin sheets as we lay on the bed inhaling combined sexual fumes in the blue dim lit room! The nigger was large-EXTRA-LARGE! And if it weren't for the rigor mortis punctuating his libido I might have actually enjoyed the gift he'd been ramming inside me! The 10 inch monster kept jumpin up and down like a smothered Jack-In-The-Box trying to free itself from celibate excommunication. He had already cum once. But you know I guess SOME motherfuckers are virtually immune to the gravitational woes of an orgasm! Most of the time he'd fall asleep with his third-leg still appearing petrified-like I had never fucked him for that hour and forty-five minutes straight!

He reached out and smacked me on the ass in a belated semblance of erotic passion. He always did that to let me know that it was time to play ring-around-the-zombie for yet another lackluster waste of meaningful hours of my life! I WASN'T HAVIN IT! Too late nigger! You had your chance! But that lazy tongue was too flat-too timid to utter a fuckin sound! So I don't give a fuck if your rock-hard dick goes into epileptic convulsions. It can bob it's circumcised head and wave good-bye at me all it wants to! It can learn to speak 7 languages at Mute Cock-University and Graduate with Sterling oratory Honors. It will STILL be a cold day in Hell before I climb THIS ass back on top of YOU!

I came out of the bathroom holding my crotch, as if someone had just used it for target practice, and rummaged through some mental notes pre-arranged for times when a woman decides she ain't givin it up to some dry-dick bastard she wishes was dead!

"Oh No boo, I'm bleedin! I think you brought down my period!"

"What," asked the sexually aroused cadaver who had just bumped-and-grinded me for what seemed a milinnea without barking out a single word?

"Baby I can't do nothing else-you know you can't stick that big thing too far up there! FUCK! DAMN-there goes my weekend!" I had to lay it on real thick cuz he had been known to display sporadic beams of intelligence at times-a sister didn't wanna get busted. My job was over and my work was done! I had TOLERATED his mummified ass for as long as I could-ONE NIGHT! Now the rest of the trip belonged to me! If he got mad-then WHATEVER! I didn't care! I couldn't be bothered! If he wanted to reneg on the rent money trick then THAT was all good too! I have been known to disappear on a nigger! And there were plenty of willing prospects out there in Jersey who would love to have a woman like me accompany him to his lonely Hotel room for the remainder of the Weekend-LIKE THAT brother on the back of the bus I saw on the way there. Fool couldn't stop eye-ballin a sister! Floyd could fuck-around if he wanted too!

The trifling sucker looked at me with an expression I've seen before. Somewhere between genuine empathy and the proud self-indulging arrogant aura a Knight wears boastfully on his chest after having slain the emerald scaly dragon threatening his beloved virgin princess. Men are so fucking stupid! They don't realize how gullible they truly are because women have hit and fooled them with the oldest trick in the book for eons! I guess Mother Eve pulled it on old Mr. Perfect Adam at least once or twice in the Garden of Eden at times when she didn't want to be bothered.

You know if a woman has to look at the same naked dick every night of her life for eternity she might understandably implement the Tampon trick every now and then. I mean DAMN-give a bitch a break! O.K, so WHAT she's the Mother of all humanity? Let a sister breath for awhile! Then-maybe tomorrow, after a good breakfast at IHOP and a few episodes of 'The Young And The Restless.' Perhaps THEN she will be in the mood to bust some nuts from the most monotonous sex-life in Creation and resume her female duties of procreating mankind! (I bet God never taught Adam to eat pussy or do it doggie-style)

Floyd pulled me gently to the bed and embraced me in a position I might liken to the demonstrative carress of a man who truly worships the shit outta the woman in his arms. He kissed my forehead and asked me if I was alright!

"Yeah DUMB-ASS! At least I WILL be after you get dressed, hand me about 1500 and get the fuck outta this Hotel room! Sure-then I'll be FINE! Don't bother washing your stinky-ass! There's plenty of soap and water back home where YOU live! I've SEEN your apartment! So why don't you go out on the Boardwalk and play catch-WITH A HATCHET!" (If ONLY he could HEAR those thoughts!)

We held each other for a couple of minutes and gradually my estrogen instincts detected an ebbing of empathy buzzing through his brown little pea-head! His head was MUCH too small for that 6 foot 3 frame!

"What are you thinking," I asked as though I truly gave a rats-ass? He could've died for all I cared. (Just not in front of me-I don't need the drama)

"I was thinking about YOU boo!"

"Boo?" Hah-such a profound word-for a ZOMBIE! When a nigger lies he often heaves a heavy sigh as though those lying words are a cumbersome fetus being forcefully extracted from his deceptive mouth! 'Tricks are for kids!' You ain't thinking about ME you dead nigger! You probably imagining how many dumb gullible sluts you can stick that big dick inside while your woman is home bleedin like she just got jumped by

'Freddy Kruger' and 'Micheal Meyers' in a dark broom-closet! Well guess what Playa? She ain't bleedin! And as soon as you finish telling this, your last lie, (I can see right through you) I'm gonna show you just how fresh and clean (Bloodless) this pussy has gotten over the last few minutes!

You know it's really funny how much attention, affection, love and support Wifey gets as long as her man can stick Mr. Happy deep into that succulent 'terd-cutter!' But the moment dearly devoted Hubby observes that pesky little white string hanging from what was once his favorite nesting spot-ALL BETS ARE OFF! The poor bitch transforms from sex-symbol and everlasting love to the 'Plague that bleeds but just won't die!'

LISTEN UP DUMMIES: Contrary to popular belief, it's when a woman is menstruating that she needs your sorry ass the MOST! Every minute of her menstrual cycle she must fight ablative battles between the raging hormonal imbalances characteristic of the feminine anatomy and the gangster-lean uterine walls that must produce and shed the ovarian aftermath of self-purification. TRUST ME-she may punch you in the mouth or drive you fucking crazy with her whimsical emotional BULLSHIT! But this is the time when fair-weather friends don't help! And if you hang in there and support her-make her feel beautiful again through these trials-you might WIN! If you take the time to love her-make her feel as though she's the only woman on the Planet that deeply concerns you, believe you me, when Wifey STOPS bleedin-IT'S PAYBACK TIME! All of that perservering tolerant hard-work in being a good and dependable man will be rewarded!

I was too tired to give this played-out scenario another valuable second of my time! It's hard to form words decent to the ears when you are caught up in the presence of some termite that doesn't mean a damn to you. I felt nauseas and wanted to take a fucking nap! Who knows-maybe if I just slept for the duration of our stay he would become disenchanted and go away! Won't hurt to TRY! I attempted to con my tormentor into goin out that night to gamble-to have fun without me!

"Baby I'm crampin. You go an chill an I'll be here when you get back," I demanded! I could tell that he didn't want to. But he wanted to please me so he reluctantly dragged his narrow co-dependent ass on!

"Free at last!" THAT wasn't too difficult. I decided to call it a night–FOR REAL and at around 9:30 P.M. I crashed. It was the best sleep I'd had in a while. In my dreams I was a married woman who had met and truly fell in love with my soul-mate. The man of my dreams. An hour and a half later I awakened hoping that it all was for REAL. Shockingly and to my regrettable dismay, after saying the Lord's prayer 5 times and counting to 10, I woke up an opened my eyes in time to witness the world as I knew it crumble before me! The Living-Dead had crept back into the suite not so very long before I drifted and snuggled himself closely beside me. I WISHED I WERE DEAD!

Then I wished He were dead! Why should I die when he could do it for me? Can't a nuisance, A MOSQUITO BITE, disappear-just for ONE NIGHT?

I WOULD GIVE HIM HELL TOMORROW! It's not easy fuckin for rent money! Trying to force yourself to sleep with a person who couldn't turn on a lightbulb! I said I would DESTROY his stubborn ass-take him to the poor-house on a shopping spree! Serves you right STUPID-GET A LIFE. I would strangle his pockets-and if that didn't kill him I'd cock-up my leg and squeeze out a flying blood-ball for his ass to choke on! But first things first! For NOW I needed him alive long enough to dish out $950 to offset the debilitating over-head of being a single mother!

-16-

CATHARSIS

I got into an argument with a fellow student and my Theology Professor as to the race and ethnicity of Christ! I attended the class every Thursday evening because I was given an extra exemption when filing my Taxes under the pretense of being a 'Student.' Not that I was a true full-timer but by the time those bastards in Albany realized I wasn't, I'd have already spent MY cash flow that they erroneously felt entitled to. You know this society is fucked up. It's corrupt, criminal and covertly genocidal. They will get at you any way they can-economically or physically. If you don't believe me ask the brother who was tied and dragged from the back of a pick-up truck by 2 hilbilly white-boy racists. They were simply carrying on the legacy of hatred taught to them by their white supremacist granddaddies!

So if a sister fights back and bucks the system for an illegal and unliscensed dirty 'Roscoe' in the closet or the gleaning of a few thousand dollars of her own money from the Govrnor of Babylon, the powers that be should not be devasted. 'The beat goes ON' chumps!' So WHAT I won't let you economically castrate me again this week-crucify me! Then kiss my poor black ass!

Anyway back to the Academics. I've always been fascinated by religion and love to do research because I don't believe EVERYTHING everyone says to me! If I have doubts those doubts must be satisfied-or dispelled. I was raised a Preacher's daughter and that in and of itself is a blessing and a curse for the investigative mind that that same preacher raised me to have. So I have no problem discoursing about religion and politics cuz I ain't no punk. Those who say 'don't talk about those controversial issues' are 100% bonafide intellectual chicken-shits. Straight up cowards!

Well that evening this student (white-boy intellectual) was trying to convince the entire class that no one truly knew the color of Jesus. The rest of those spineless morally bankrupt assholes just sat there listening to his bullshit in the vacuum of their own mental incapacities and fear of a slave rebellion doomed to be exposed-AND CRUSHED! Perhaps they needed a passing grade much more than their sense of justice would allow them to risk insofar as truth and dignity were concerned. Or maybe they were too hopelessly gullible or ignorant to challenge this mighty whitey anthropological Rocket-Scientist condemning the prodigy of the Son of God to the corrupted crock-pot of Eurocentric falsehood.

So as soon as he stood up and opened his smug and errant mouth, rank with the foul odor of racial bias, Jesus Christ was transformed from a poor nigger from Galilee to a great and mighty noble Caucasian who went down in Anglo-saxon history as the Hero who kicked a Helluva lotta Roman, Jewish and Demonic ass. Now how THAT happen? I couldn't stand to sit THAT one out-so I OPENED MY FUCKING MOUTH!

"JESUS WAS NOT A WHITE-BOY!" The classroom swarmed from a virulent rumbling to a sea of silence! I had challenged this be-pimpled-Einstein and the nature of our debating protocol was to POLITELY disagree with ones opponent-then continue in discourse until the accolade of the audience in the neutral body could decide upon the winner based solely on that applause. Well POLITE is an ideal quite foreign to me so I stumbled and fell on that aspect of my argument. But the rest of the shit this sister squeezed off between Pink-Floyd's eyes was something that even Brother Malcolm would wake up from his slumber and clap for!

I contended that if HE were a true practicioner of logic then history and biblical facts were shouting in his pink fucking Yoda ears that Jesus was black! Acne-boy noted that the Bible had no specific inference on Jesus' color and that it is difficult for us today to describe the actual color of Jesus. Moreover according to the same depraved logic he proudly announced that evidence in fact bades a logical person to believe that Jesus was white because Jesus was a Jew and present day Jews are white.

I could've puked right there in my seat and then shitted on myself! But my ass could not emit shit as foul as the defecation shooting out of this pubiscent Devil! And my lips had to be dry to formulate words to slay the repugnant beast lying in my ears and foaming at the mouth!

"Uh-Doctor, mind if I call you THAT?" He seemed comfortable with that prestigious title-his limited perception unable to detect the utter sarcasm I'd hidden behind the term. This Bastard was so used to everyone bowing down under his feet and kissing his Holy jaded-ass, he must've mistaken himself for a Demi-God! Well if HE were GOD-THEN GOD WOULD BE ASSASINATED TODAY! He Would DIE the bloodless death of humitilation!

"First off nature-boy, the Jews in Israel who have white-skin are the ones who migrated there in 1948 after the war. The United Nations set up Israel as a sovereign State and gave them all that was required for Self-Government so that they could thrive as an independent people. Those migrants were the former victims of Hitler's plans of Nazi conquest. You DO remember Hitler, don't you-he tried to kill off the Jews. Thus a large segment of those who fled Europe both before and during the War were Caucasian Jews. White Jews! But those OTHER indigenous inhabitants of Israel were called Palestinians. They were there before the European Jews who migrated in 1948. Have you looked at the Palestinians lately? They are not white-they're dark! They are also the descendants of the original Philistines with whom King David's Israel had to combat back in ancient times. Notice the similarity between the words 'PALESTINE' and 'PHILISTINE!' It was the same group of people in the same geographic location. Why is it that the original Palestinians skin was and is so dark and the Jews skin was so light? It's because the European Jews had intermarried-they had amalgamated with the white Europeans there!"

"And haven't you heard? Everybody in the EAST during Biblical times except for the Romans and the Greeks were BLACK! Professor Periwinkle stood up before us on the very first day of class and expounded that harsh reality to us. Tell me Doctor, did you miss that class-or do you have selective amnesia-DON'T ANSWER THAT DOCTOR. It's a rhetorical question! We will revisit that later."

"Now if one were to follow that same logic then what of the present population of Europe-the indigenous ones, what color are they," I inquired.

"Europeans are white! Everybody knows that!" The scheming little Devil-the historical Nutty Professor had the nerve to try an get FLY with me on that answer. He didn't know what I had in store for him. He was so accustomed to the docile homage payed to his ego by those other idiots in the room-he mistook me for THEM!

"Well it's unanimous then. Would everyone under the sound of my voice agree with the Good Doctor and myself that Europeans are primarily white people?" The question seemed asinine to the terror stricken masses-the future leaders of this fucked up society. Sitting around like crashdummies agreeing with every word that emitted from the mouths of those the cowards deemed as intellectual giants. They would agree for fear of being singled out-of being embarrassed or put on blast. I can understand their collective desire to keep their tremendous ignorance to themselves! But if THEY represented our future then our civilization was doomed and the future looked grim! I'd only hope that Jesus or Buddha-Allah or whomever would return on Judgement Day to scoop up their spiritually faithful before THESE assholes took over. Their inherent weakness made me sick-even moreso than the pompous bastard I was about to behead!

"O.K. All of you agree! Well then will somebody tell me, if Jesus was white cuz present day Jews are white, since all Europeans are white, then how come their progenitors-AN ANCIENT RACE INHABITING EUROPE KNOWN AS THE GRIMALDI'S WERE BLACK? If the Grimaldi's were black WHY THE HELL ARE WHITE-FOLKS, their descendents not black as well? Now I'm trying to follow along the same logical parameters that the good Doctor is following! WHAT HAPPENED? O.K. lets consider THAT phenomena an aberration! What of Rome? What color are the Romans? Are they not white? YES! Well then how about their ancestors-the Etruscans? Were they not a darker toned race? How about the ancestors of Japan? And Mexico? Were not their ancient divinities portrayed as dark-skinned? Dark-skinned divinities reflecting the physical countenance or appearance of their ancestors? YES!" The room was quiet-you could hear a mouse fart!

"Is there anything else," asked Lucifer?"

"As a matter of fact there is-let me go to the voice of a Eurocentric authority because white society can only accept truth when spilled from the lips of their own! So I will put my own Afrocentric ideals aside, the way Professor Periwinkle taught us to do, in the interest of objectivity." I knew the Professor enjoyed that exultation (I didn't really mean it) and I could garner a longer time period if he felt it would entail more of the same fruits of scholarly acclaim ascribed to HIS ass!

A cell phone rang! Who the Hell? It was mine! I had the Lord of the Underworld by the balls-and Nextel would NOT save him from a slow violent death! Picture a war stragetist-an intrepid Commander-in-Chief just seconds before he could press the button and win World War III!

"Oh wait," says the General. "Hold on Mr. President-we'll have to postpone Doomsday! I gotta take a call. MY MOMMY'S ON THE LINE!"

"JUNIOR, YOU FORGOT TO CLEAN YOUR ROOM!"

"FUCK YOU MA! And say good-bye. I've got Worlds to Conquer!" I bet Alexander the Great didn't have those problems!

I answered it!

"Yo Hattie, what's up bitch?"

There I was-GHETTO-GIRL! QUEEN OF THE SCHOOLYARD, on the podium fighting against the Honky-tonk Classroom bully and chattin away on my celly.

"Monie, what you doin-there's something I got to tell you. We need to TALK!"

"Can't talk now girl-I'm throwin down!"

"You fightin? Who you fightin-cuz I'll…"

"The Prince of Darkness-Gotta go!" I hung up the phone, apologized to my perplexed audience and countered with the proverbial left-cross-all in the same breathe! She sounded hurt-and desperate! I would get to THAT battle later!

"Ahem!" I dug into my prolific research on Diodorus Seclorus and Josephus, the Jewish Scholar, to blow some swiss-cheese holes in his story. But before I could articulate Professor 'Nobody' INTERUPTED! (That's what I call him cuz he's too fearful to take an uncompromising stand on ANYTHING and prides himself with being dubious. Fuck dubious! Give me some facts and your hypothesis based on those facts or SHUT THE FUCK UP!)

"Well…" he interjected to sort of quell the odious debacle which was about to ensue. At the expense of his prized student-the geekish-wonder!

"No Teacher-brainiac can't have this one. LET ME SPEAK! The JEWISH Historian Josephus described the ancient Hebrews he encountered as DARK and resemblant of the Ethiopians! What color are Ethiopians SIR? Furthermore Diodorus Seclorus was called 'The Father Of ANCIENT History.' He was a white-boy too I might add, which increases the legitimacy of his claim! RIGHT? He SAW the Motherfuckers! (Oops-I cursed) He saw the Jews-the Hebrews. And said they were DARK! Now was this white man-a prestigious National Hero and Champion intellect of your culture a LIAR? Or is THIS human sponge, (I pointed to the Geek) the greatest student to ever grace your classroom, more knowledgable than this-Europe's most renouned Historian?" Either way they answered-they could NOT save face!

"If we must go and re-write the History books-I'll alert the Media! Scholars contend that 'Jesus was dark-and simple in appearance!' King Solomon, a Jew, in the Book of 'Songs of Solomon' asked not to be looked upon because he was dark-but comely. He even said that as if being dark-and being 'comely' were two opposites. Two irreconcilable characteristics or differences which could not co-exist in the same person. You KNOW-like if you black, you can't be comely. Or if you're comely you can't be black! 'Comely means handsome' At least that's how your Scholar King James the First-the FAGGOT, had the text translated." I was stepping on toes-I could feel the crackling under my feet! CRUNCHING BENEATH ME! But I couldn't stop destroying them! Because I was BORN TO KILL!

"Solomon said the sun had smitten him and did not want to be judged based solely on his tawny color. Perhaps that ugly little gremlin known as White Supremacy was present even back then. Or maybe he was a prophet-and foretold that you white folks would have a problem today, 4 thousand years after he lived, with the non-white peoples living in your midst!"

"John, the Divine and beloved Apostle, summed it up best when describing Jesus saying 'His body was like Beryl-Jasper. His skin like brass as if it were burned in an oven. What color do you get when you're burnt? Pink or black? And Jasper is not pale-its dark! The Greek term used in the book of 'Revelations' is 'Pupermones' signifying also that which has been burnt!"

"Uh, well..." the defiant psuedo-scholar stuttered into the microphone. "The Bible is replete with allegorical terms but we..."

Just then the Bell rang and I politely instructed him to get his ALLEGORICAL ass out of my face before I dug my boot heel into his mouth! I hated him-sitting arrogantly in the front of the Classroom kissing the Professor's saggy pink ass and boot-licking all the squandered pee-pee water from between his ancient nuts! He answered all the questions right-EXCEPT THIS ONE! And I was NOT impressed!

"Take that emerald twirling beanie off your fucking head, BITCH! And grow some balls," I shouted! I was beside myself. "The ancient Hebrews were BLACK men. If Solomon was, then his PAPPY King David had to be! And so was JESUS having come from the pure bloodline of Judah! NOW YOU HAVE A BRIGHTER DAY, FUCK-FACE!"

The classroom emptied out and everybody was talking about how the intellectually inclined nigger-bitch had taken Lord Geek-hearts microscopic pink nuts and shoved them up his tight-ass! Professor Nobody cussed me out in his own snobbish, aristocratic and eloquent way and I just stood there and took it. Onion breath, spit-flakes and all-cuz I had won! But I was worried about my girl Hattie so I called Mommy and told her I'd be there late to pick up Breanna. If life is filled with giants-obstacles, then we all had our own barriers to face. Who would have ever known that Hattie's giant was of the same brutal character as those who had stoned and crucified Jesus. This giant was vicious! He was reprobate-and he would give Hattie Hell before it was over.

Hattie jumped at the chance to bone a nigger whose father was a white man. SELL-OUT bitch! I guess even fags share this errant belief that white men are better. That it's more elegant and socially acceptable to fall in love with a blonde dick than a black one! Like THEIR Caucasian genetic design yields a more powerful status symbol of opulence and genteel on the ethnic hierarchy of a fags erotic needs. Like I said-THE BITCH SOLD OUT!

But even heterosexual women like to play that mighty-whitey shit and send it hurling down the average brother's throat. We like to taunt our men with, "Look what whitey did for me Playa! Hmm...2 Karats-that's something YOUR broke-ass couldn't do for me in 25 of your miserable life-times! So handle it baby! Oh, don't be blue! You know sister girl loves you. See you later boo! I got an all white escargot affair to attend. Just keep the black-steel hard. In case I get horny before midnight and have to run back into the hot and steamy concrete-jungle! You know-the place where Mr. white-cock can't take me. Only there can I get what every woman needs." The 'Fuck-factory' where she grinds his ghetto male anatomy back onto the peaceful shores of her deep ebonic Congo up-bringing! "Aaaieeeh!" Fuck me black Tarzan! Even a high-classed ethnically imbalanced jungle-fevered bitch gotta cum!

Sisters are really doin it up these days. "My man is light-skinned. He got that GOOD hair-better than Jamal's got. It's so easy to comb-so natural! You know we're gonna get married and have his kids. All 12 of em. They'll have that good hair-like their white or half-white daddy's. So they'll come out Cauco-negro fabulous! I Can't wait to get his white Howdy-doody ass between the sheets and lay some of this sweaty black pussy on him!"

Well I guess I shouldn't talk cuz as much as I despised Hattie's selling out, I too wanted to ride her man from the first night we met! So here's to YOU bitch-FAG BITCH!

Catharsis was a fine Motherfucker. A perfect, complete and total waste of handsomeness and male vigor! Why was it a loss? Well, he was gay. He dedicated his every waking moment on a few well-organized principles! I'll save the gay preference for last to harp on a few major idiosyncrasies far more significant and far-reaching than his squandered sexuality.

Catharsis was a murderer! He killed people for a living-a Hitman! He did jobs for the Mob and oftimes performed Political Assassinations on their own colleagues as well. There are times when during the natural course of doing business, the 'Family' owned Cartel finds it in the best interest of their collective Clan to take out the garbage. To do some spring cleaning or better yet-wean out those particular shit-stains which are no longer necessary or productive to the overall plans of the group.

When this time came and the Mob-bosses finally deduced who it was who might have been guilty of being a snitch, or a plant or a stoolie-they would die! Or if someone was grossly fucking up and had to be gotten rid of or whose balls were not particularly large enough for the looming mission at hand and might bob when it's time to weave!

Well on this important meeting of Executive 'Itralian' and Sicilian minds, HEADS WOULD ROLL! In this self-purgatorial act, the 'Clan' would cleanse itself of ALL unclean human matter and thus pave the way for a new prosperous year of indiscriminant murder, extortion, racketeering and Organized Crime! Without the previous danger of an insipient cancer in their midst. A danger which could ultimately tentacle and careen out of control!

Every civilized society must have a head, a tail-and countless significant other functioneers in the middle. Catharsis was number 3 in Command and held the pre-eminent title of Supreme Garbageman. HITMAN! He did the dirty work of taking out the trash and doing that which well-manicured and socially acceptable "Made-men" wasted no time engaging in. His half-brother held the number 2 position. But Catharsis loved his work as Mafia-executioner-and repelled numerous opportunities for advancement. He supervised a Squad of over a hundred men-each to be used wherever and in whichever capacity he saw fit! Catharsis was paid handsomely for the purifying of a well coordinated Italian cell and the inherent security of well-established Mob-ties-for life! As long as he continued to fill that perpetual dead-man's dumpster with bodies the Cartel no longer needed, he was guaranteed wealth, prestige and power.

But Catharsis was a 'Club-head!' He loved to hang out. Although the bi-product of a night of reveling between his full-blooded Italian father and the desperately needy Bar-maid he propositioned in the back of an Elite Night-Club, Catharsis could not stay out of the hood! He prided himself on being around his people. Black people!

His outward appearance resembled a comely Sicilian man in his late thirties-but he was NOT! Sicilians are mixed black and Italian due to the far-flung rampage of the Carthaginian (North African) Warlord named Hannibal centuries ago. So this fine Italian nigger would galavant his expensive European-suited refinery onto flashy Mid and Uptown's party circuit. Chilin with the sisters. Hanging out with the brothers. Turning up his nose at the all-white dignitaries who stared at him with doubt, malice and envy. He was a peoples person-quiet, charming, down for any gathering a nigger could come up with. And he had an insatiable hankering for fags!

Catharsis also had a flip-side that perhaps no one would ever suspect due to the tranquil appearance of his outward demeanor. This morbidly complex man could fool ANYONE and gave absolutely no clue as to the full extent of his inner passions!

I pondered on the Satan story when I found out about his hidden persona. "Oh Lucifer, why art thou cast out into the Earth." Lucifer was the best, the greatest Creation God made. The term 'Lucifer' is the Greek translation of the words 'Luci' meaning light and 'ferous' meaning 'bearer.' It therefore means bearer of light or brightest star and

Lucifer is personified as the Son of the morning. Just as the name 'Christopher' means bearer of Christ! Like Christopher Colombus did! Anyway, He was excellent in his Heavenly personification. Handsome, intelligent. But he was banished from Heaven for his immense self-pride. Lucifer subsequently went from most exalted Angel to the titles of 'Belial' or 'Beelzebub' meaning 'Worthless one' or 'the Lord of Flies' respectively. And the most ego-deflating blow dealt him was to have been accursed by God-smitten with some ugliness to replace the matchless beauty he'd had. The magnificent beauty he had before his apostasy with which he formerly brought up the sun-hence his exalted title 'Son of the Morning!'

Lucifer was also perverted. It seems likely that after his apostasy he became a fag or susceptible to self-defaming abominable acts. He swayed from God's original divine plan for the prefered protocol of the male species. And he also swayed others from that same natural affection males have toward females to a sexually maniacal predisposition of 'same-sex relationships.' This was and is the Biblical origin of homosexuality. The deviant perversion created by Satan in defiance or disobedience to God! This was the abomination which infected the evil twin cities of Sodom and Gomorrah and their lewd practices-and Babylon-the seat of Idolatry. That's where the word Sodomy stems from. It means unnatural or deviant sex! In these cities were men who had been perverted by the Luciferian rebellion and modified their sexuality accordingly. Just as Lucifer became the lover of self, the lover of men and the lover of others-LIKE self, having garnered a reprobate mind.

So what does Heaven do when it's Arch-Angel, the one beautiful and adored, runs around fucking niggers up and having intercourse with them? Well naturally-it sics my girl Hattie on him!

Hattie and Catharsis had been dating for a couple of months and finally begun to go steady. He would take her to Classy Restaurants, Dinner parties, Executive Mob brunches and such. The nigger's pockets were deep! And cuz HIS pockets were deep-HER pockets were deep! She told me he gave her16 Grand. One night after he got finished butt-fucking the shit outta her he turned over on the Posh Hotel bed and handed her bleeding ass a Diamond bracelet and 16 G's! I MISSED OUT ON THAT?

FUCK! He coulda ripped my ASSHOLE APART-from here to Kingdom come! I wouldn't care! Sixteen G's is Sixteen G's! And I get to sport a 4 Karat white-gold Diamond bracelet to the E.R? Four Karats is a big fuckin rock! You know the Street-value on that shit! A bitch gotta fuck for about 10 years for that type of loot!

"Well fuck me IF YOU WANT TO MR. CATHARSIS, SUH! I'ze is ready! An Stick it ALL DE WAY IN-CUZ I'ZE WANTS MUH 16 G'S AN MUH ROCK MISTA BIG-DICK!"

"An Look-I'll hoist it up for ya. Want me to sucks yo big black dick furst? Yeah sure-give it heah! OH Massuh-I LOVES YOU! OH LORDY LORDY LORDY! OOH LORDY LORDY LORDY! THE BIG DICK IS IN ME LAWD! THE BIG DICK IS IN!

167

SWING LOW…! Fuck that-I WOULDN'T CARE! After the rectal reconstruction I'd be the Motherfucking DIVA! Hobbling through the projects-WITH A GAPING CANON-BALL SIZED HOLE IN MY ASS-an a bleeding problem! But for those fringe benefits-HE COULD HAVE MY ASS! And I'd even throw in MY DAUGHTER-just for added insurance to show him I'ze ain't goin NOWHERE! SORRY BRE!

But a yard and a half of Oreo-dick was not all he had to offer! Hattie would come home late sometimes and ignore the celly when he called to check up on her and he didn't play that! Catharsis possessed the same problem that many Italian and nigger men are affected by. He mistook dating and the giving of lavish gifts with ownership! Like if he's hittin a female then he OWNS her! And Hattie was one bitch that you COULD NOT OWN. Her spirit was too free for that! When she'd get home he'd be waitin-with friends-and an attitude! And that's when the beatings would start!

My girl ran to my house at about 4:00 A.M. one night-lookin like Mike Tyson, Rocky Balboa and Biggie Smalls had just stomped the blood-stains outta her! Her jaw was almost broken. One of her ribs was fractured and her windpipe had been moderately constricted because that oreo-fucker wanted a truth that Hattie was not prepared to give!

"Who were you with?" I tried to convince him it was ME but his many spies had already informed him otherwise. The bastard had people EVERYWHERE! Hattie had nowhere to hide! Nowhere to get away from his violent paranoia! And I never knew fag-fuckers had jealous feelings of insecurity too! How you gonna get possessive when you boning a homo?

There were times when Hattie begged me to let them come hang out by my place. She rented a small apartment in Riverhead from her uncle. But he hated Hattie for her sexuality, micro-managed her social life and screened ANYONE who came through her door.

"There won't be none a that SHIT in my place," said the nosy imposing bastard. "Or OUT you go!" He had promised her deceased mother to look out for Hattie-to take care of her, before she died. Was THIS the way he took care of his beloved God-son-just cuz Hattie happened to be gay? Anyway, I looked out! She wanted me to get to know Catharsis. To see his good side so both her best friend and her lover could share in a mutual friendship. I couldn't see 'good-side!' All I saw was bruised Itralian knuckles and the prison time I'd face if the son of a bitch ever REALLY hurt her. In one way I felt powerless cuz I was aware of his far-reaching connections. THE MOTHERFUCKER killed people for a living! But then there was that ignorant stubborn part of my body chemistry which taught me that I could win any fight. SOME WAY-AND SOMEHOW!

After they'd hang out I'd let her in. They returned drunk and I would just unlock the door and prepare the livingroom for them. She loved him so much. She wanted to make him happy. But at the same time-she was scared an figured if I was around-maybe he wouldn't bug the fuck out. But he was psychotic-AND SHE WAS WRONG!

I could hear them in the room-stereo blasting. First they sounded like lovers-newly weds. Kissing and cuddling like first-timers glowing with new-found passion. But eventually the kissing stopped. The cuddling and giggling blew over. And before you knew it Hattie would sound like a rape-victim! Like the victim of a God-damn murder-squad being executed! SODOMIZED! Taking it in the ASS-12 inches of lust, and cocaine and RAGE! AND HATE! He would taunt her while he hurt her shouting some "Whose ASS is it," shit or making her swear to suck no other dick but HIS-OR HE WOULD KILL HER!

The nerve of that gay sick bastard! I wanted a thousand times to run in that livingroom-ox in hand and end Hatties suffering! Do for my girl what she couldn't do for herself! Just one blow-THAT'S ALL I'D NEED "SWOOP!" That's it-NO MORE HORNY VIOLENT ITALIAN MAN!

After the sex he made Hattie suck his dick! I know cuz she told me-and I heard it! "Yeah black bitch-SUCK MY DICK! And I swear-don't you ever...!" What the fuck is this world coming to. I would stare, unnoticed of course, at him. At this pretty mulatto with an attaché case, a business suit and a charming seductive grin. And I'd say: "WELL I'LL BE DAMNED! What's the MATTER with this bastard? IS HE SICK? IS HE FUCKING SICK? Why do he do that shit to Hattie? What's he got against her? What she ever do to him but turn his PERVERTED ass on? THAT'S WHAT THE BITCH IS GUILTY OF-MAKING THAT BASTARD CUM! She keeps his dick hard-THAT'S WHAT SHE'S DOIN WRONG!

You see he was highly attracted to Hattie-but Hattie was a fag! And perhaps since he hated the fact that he was turned on by a fag, he would commense to whipping her ass. PISSED THE FUCK OFF! Mad as a motherfucker about some sexually deviant shit that he himself was guilty of! THAT'S IT! He's mad at her for being a fag. Cuz he likes fags instead of women and couldn't stand to lose her. That's why he says that shit when he's beatin her-he would die if this fag walked out on him. Or he would rather KILL her first-before she could leave! Meanwhile he's burnin up inside because he hates the fact that he desires and needs something as disgusting as a homosexual. So he beats the shit out of her-and begs her-NO, demands that she stay. I never knew Lucifer was a hypocrite!

On the mornings after their stay Hattie would rarely face me. But the bedsheets sprawled on the carpet would testify to her pain. I would see brown stains and blood. A lot of blood. And I thought Damn-what the fuck is this! Why does my girl put up with it? And was it worth it? The tremendous size of Catharsis was a lot-FOR ANYBODY! But was it worth the abuse? The physical and verbal threats? I just couldn't see how anybody could take that from anybody!

I wanted to tell! To have his sick queer-ass locked up! Forever!

"Whose ass is this? I'll KILL you if you ever give it to somebody else!" Hmmn, boy the only reason I put up with this is becase my girl begged me NOT to intervene! I'd turn up the T.V, the stereo-hope that Yago and nosy bitch didn't hear the fuck-fest from

Bomani Shuru

upstairs! I'd pray they didn't think it was ME! Then again if it wasn't me, then who the
HELL was getting beast-fucked in MY house?

Was I pimpin out some ho spots to brazen horny Johns on their property? God, I
thought! This shits got to stop! And I had to send my daughter to my parent's house
whenever they'd come. On some lame-ass excuse like I need to study or I gotta work
late! Yeah right! Mommy and Daddy had my job number so who was I kiddin?

On the evening before Memorial Day me an Hattie had a long talk while walking
through the park one night! This was the first and last time she explained to me why!
Answering the question that I had asked myself since the beatings began.

"So girl-whatcha gonna do with this nigga? You better leave him!"

"Where am I goin girl? You KNOW I love him!"

"Hattie, you better than that. That ain't no love boo! He beats your ASS! You
know I can't stand to see that! This is some burnin bed shit!"

"Mone, you heard him! What he say he gonna do if I leave him? I won't make it to
the train station he got so much eyes!"

"WE can think of something!"

And I'll be dead-while YOU'RE thinking. But you know...up till I met him I never
felt like I was alive. I want us to be together-people change!" She had a tear in her eye.
"Anyway, b-before, I would do my thing-you know. And run around an shit. But I was
never truly happy! Till I met this man Simone! At first-in the beginning he was good to
me. It's just recently...look, I know shit is fucked up now...."

"Hattie don't...!"

"No, we could go back to the way it was before! Cuz girl nobody else makes me
really happy. I don't wanna lose...!"

"Hattie, there's a million men out there who will respect you!"

"I don't NEED...look, respect means different things to different people!-I need
what he was giving me...!" She broke down and I wanted to comfort her with all that I
had inside me. Hattie was my heart-my separated heart and it was slowly dissolving itself
of true life and laughter before my eyes. You know when someone is in pain it is very
difficult to say that you empathize with what is making them miserable. It's like what a
mother feels when her baby dies. Her world, the world as she knew it, has ended. And her
life is a spiraling conduit of hapless breathes merely prolonging the peace which comes in
a better place. If she could've died for the infant she would have smiled at the Creator for
this splendid negotiation and spit in death's face for trying to take away all that she has in
this world. And her own demise would bring with it an end to the suffering present at the
tragic departure of her offspring.

Yet if the baby's life IS taken then there is no further need for hope. All hope has
died in the tiny coffin bearing her seed. And she is left but a shadow-gravitating toward
the Heavenly bliss of one day rejoining the eternal prize she lost after giving birth to it.

170

I wanted to kiss Hattie in the mouth-to resolidify that bond we had before this Devil entered our lives and separated her from me. It was not a sexual desire to kiss-but the profundity of what a mother goes through witnessing the torment of her offspring. The torment of her new, innocent and better self. Hattie was by far my better self-and she was drowning. And for all the closeness she once felt for me there was a distance which I could not wade through. A distance provoked by a fear of what Catharsis would do to her-do to us, if we ran. If she tried to believe in me again for her survival! And a fear of what he might do to me if I took up her cross, dived into certain death and tried to save her. To save the only life I had left in this world besides my own daughter. My mother was gone-a memory in the distance between my birth and the realness of now. But there was yet another valley to cross. The one separating me from my girl-filled with poisonous snakes threatenng to take our lives if we joined together in an attempt to be free! The distance which kept me from saving the drowning heart I lamented for in desparations hollow wake.

But I'd be damned if I didn't try!

"Girlfriend, I'll FIND you another man. Shit I'll buy one! One with a smaller dick!" She smiled. "We'll go shopping together. Fuck-this ain't right! You worth more than that. You don't deserve it!"

A bird flew by.

"You see that? He's free. YOU on lock-down!"

"Fly away little bird," she said looking up!

"Fuck around and you gonna be flying away too bitch!"

"No girl-I don't want THEM kinda wings! No! Not no time soon!"

"Who said you gonna be flying in THAT direction? You might be FRYING! Bad as your ass is! Shit, you better make plans. Where you'll be you won't be needin that new Sherling he bought you."

We both laughed and held each others hands. I truly loved HATTIE. More than any of my other girls. I swear I would march proudly to my grave for her-just to ease her suffering and I entertained the thought of fighting back. Beating this nigger and goin on with our lives. And if we lost-THEN WE LOST! At least it was for something good! I looked into her eyes and detected the fear she wished I hadn't seen. And we hugged like 2 sisters-identical twins separated at birth by incomparable chronology and gender.

"You know HE was the one who shot that guy in the head back then in front of Honey's They had beef and homeboy wasn't forkin over the money right. They was getting extorted-so Catharsis killed him. Good Lord-why I got to date a Hitman? I shoulda let YOU have him!"

Her voice was crackin an she kept wrenching her hands. That's what Hattie did when she was nervous! When she got scared. I grabbed them and kissed them.

"Don't worry baby. We'll do something. Just hang in there-I know some people! Just don't make me cry for you Hattie," I said trying to swallow the apple-sized intruder, the emotional pain, welling up in my throat.

"No I won't," she whispered. "Just don't ask me to give away my life! To give up my happiness!" I had known Hattie for almost 15 years-maybe more. And she was always honest. If you didn't like or agree with what she said you had to either suck it up or she would happily whip your natural ass to make you see things her way. I loved her. She was real! But at that moment I felt betrayed. Because for the first time since our early childhood, on that day in the park Hattie had lied to me. And I knew it! I knew she was lying and it cut me deeply. My girl, my best friend, had stood there in my face-attempting to reassure me of something she was not TRULY sure about! I had told her not to make me cry for her an she looked me dead in my eye like an older sibling attempting to comfort their younger sobbing sister. She answered me in the expectant tone that I wanted to hear and said "I won't!" But in her heart Hattie new that sooner or later I would cry for her. After she made that solemn promise, a promise she could not hope to keep-we walked hand in hand out of the park without another single word!

-17-

TALKING IN YOUR SLEEP

I got a call at 3:00A.M. that Floyd was in the hospital. A nurse had said something about he had a heart attack but then my cell-phone went dead. There was no number on the caller-ID so I could not check back! For the rest of the night I was kinda worried. I couldn't find out what happened or where and there is a degree of powerlessness one feels at the sudden illness of a person whom they often mistreat! I wondered if I was to blame-for my callous behavior. Did I stress him out and the Motherfucker's heart just say "Fuck it! We're outta here. The bitch ain't actin right so we'll just leave her miserable ass on Earth-among the land of the living. Alone with her fucked up male-bashing ways?"

A tear dared the steep perilous leap from my eyes and I felt like my heart too would do me in for all the shit I made him put up with. I vowed to mend my wicked ways. He was a very nice guy-just wasn't my cup of tea. So when he gets outta there I'm gonna fix him a big dinner-make up for the bullshit. And then I'll jump on that 10 inch dick an ride it-gingerly-IN ZOMBIE FASHION! Slow motion mode-just the way his sickly narrow ass likes it. Don't wanna burst any blood vessels!

I was depressed-I couldn't fuckin believe it. OVER HIM! So I decided to go out. I COULDN'T STAND THE WAITIN GAME. Waitin for a call to see if the nigger was dead or alive so a long night of debauchery would settle my stomach-until the zombie got around to callin a sister! I promised not to screw nobody else-at least until he was back home safely. Then, when I saw his health was up to par, I'd kick his bony ass and cuss him out for making the bitch from Hell fear for his sorry life! I figured he coulda called-maybe he was just trying to make me worry. It was working. Or maybe he was not conscious-I DIDN'T KNOW! Well there's a saying: Confused bitches drink! So I called Mikki and Key and we went out to Honeys. Hattie was on lock down and I was also worrying about her and PSYCHO! SO BE IT, I THOUGHT! I'll mourn for em both!

I got the call from Floyd's nurse in the Reggae room. She said that it WAS a heart attack-a minor one, but there was no need for concern. I wanted to speak to him but she apprised me that though he had been initially in the ICU, his condition had improved so drastically since admittance that they had transferred him to the Cardiac Care Unit! That was news to my ears.

"Tell him I love him, please" I told her-and hung up! Thank God-my man was NOT GONNA DIE. Now it's party time! I had 3 Apple Martini's since the phone call. Then I got my groove on.

Floyd was still in the hospital 2 days later and wasn't supposed to be out till the following Tuesday. Play time! So I told Canei to meet me after work so we could 'Get to Work' early on shedding some fat off the sex-drive that never dies! He knew about Floyd and was happy to get to spend some time with me cuz after that foul shit he did he didn't think he'd ever taste me again! But the zombie was on ice-hospitalized. And just as quick as I made the vow of celibacy, of devotion to Floyd, Canei's black ass was movin up and down in my bed, and I had forgotten it! I figured I'd let him stay overnight-make up some creative shit to tell Floyd when the nurses permitted him to call like inadequate cell-phone technology or the usual bullshit about how hard I was sleepin!

I don't know if he believed it or not and I didn't fucking care. We BOTH knew that! One time I fed him that tall-tale but I didn't hang up the phone properly when I thought I ended the call. Too bad the sneaky motherfucker stayed on the line. Now you figure you tell a nigger 'Good-night' the sorry bastard should hang up the fucking phone! AND GO ON WITH HIS MISERABLE LIFE! But NO! THIS TRIFLING low-life kept listening-and caught an earful!

So I guess I musta been talking in my sleep with home-girl Mik on some Super-natural telepathic 'girls night out' hot-line! Modern communication never ceases to amaze me! Cuz in our dreams (twins separated at birth often have conjoined dreams) we were planning on a search and destroy mission to find that fine nigger I'd met just weeks ago. Like a fool-NO, MORE LIKE A DRUNK, I LOST HIS NUMBER somewhere in the binged inebriated distance between HIM and the dark spinning Parking-lot.

Now me an my girl are talking about this and silent Harry (aka hopelessly devoted ease-dropper who needs to get a grip) is suckin up every word into his paranoid demented memory-banks. The skinny FUCK! So I'm telling Mikki about the way I tried to maneuver this OTHER niggers rock-hard dick under my skirt so that my love-starved senses could feel him! And how that dumb FAT bitch kept bumpin her sweaty ass into us against the walll in the Reggae room each time I moved my body in just the right position! Why do fat people go to Clubs? THERE AIN'T NO FOOD THERE-and they only fuck things up for the rest of us!

I came twice in 30 minutes while clutching onto his shoulder and waistline. The nigger to our left heard me moan and musta knew it was ON! I must've torn the leather part of his Barn Jacket because I STILL can't find that left pointer finger 'Press-on nail!' Maybe it's still lodged in the niggers Barn Jacket. I don't KNOW! SHIT, a bitch gets emotional when she's getting dry-fucked! That's why I CAME on myself!

Well if details and circumstantial evidence were convictive components in a criminal murder case then my ass was hangin from 'Hang-up' to 'Hung-on!' Yeah, motherfuckers should hang up the God-Damn PHONE! An I guess stupid bitches like me who talk too much should check themselves before going into serious details about how they wrapped their legs around a total stranger on the reggae floor!

So while I'd thought I hung up the home phone with Mr. delusional-I was spillin my guts to Mik-AND HIM!

You know it's funny how some desperate STALKER could be keen enough to listen an see if a bitch is cheatin-but too fuckin afraid and insecure to leave her when he finds out, plain as day, that she is! Life is filled with many mysteries and I'm forever astonished at the lengths of unconfidence and bafoonery the male human mind can manifest!

Now back to my scenario with Floyd-the love-sick zombie. He just sat there and listened to his woman boast about how badly she wanted to fuck some OTHER nigger. Well my prayers were answered. NOBODY on Earth, including Job the perfect man whose righteousness God bragged about, would go for no obvious shit like THAT! I had found the Greatest fool in the Uniiverse-besides the crashdummy. The perfect FOOL! And Floyd, sweet punk-ass Floyd, STILL found an innovative way to swallow it! To forgive and forget! To vigorously suck the symbolic dick of infidelity-Dick-head, shaft, hairy nuts and everything! And his hopelessly gullible esteem sucked evey traitorous ounce of semen he could bear WITHOUT the compliments of a condom!

With THAT past us I now pray for 2 things. Number one-his convalescence. I can enjoy him better alive-so let him die-another day! But God, don't let the stupid zombie get well too quick! That 'get well soon' stuff is DEAD in my book! It would spoil my weekend and force me to endure the drudgery of 48 hours nursing and babysitting his heart-diseased ass! So PLEASE-let him get better-SLOWLY!

Lastly, they usually save the best for last, "Lord let me run into that sexy nigger from Honeys again. You know-the one who had his finger stuck in me? The one with the deep brown eyes and the nice smile. Yeah, that's him father! Oh, and one more thing before I go…You know I've been stricken with a deadly disease that attacks dumb bitches like me while we slumber. And it's quite simple-I'm beggin you to heal me of the infirmity of TALKING IN MY SLEEP!"

-18-

EAT SHIT AND DIE

Well some things never change and Floyd was outta the Hospital and in my Damn apartment making my life miserable and making up for lost time. You'd think he'd never been sick and I entertained the cruel thought of how good a time it was for him to have yet ANOTHER heart attack. A good old-fashioned MASSIVE ONE with desperate gasping for air and raging blocked arteries screaming for death-just to alleviate the pain. I tell you the zombie was on some "I'll get back at you for almost costing me my life shit!" He was insecure-thought a bitch was out laying with everything in sight as he fought for his miserable life-breathing tubes, nitroglycerine, crash-cart and all! BY GOD-WHAT A LIVELY DEAD MAN!

And he was mistaken-I had not layed with everything in sight. In fact the only OTHER nigger to hit this pussy (3 times) during his trip to meet his Maker was Canei. So what another man had hit his horny fiancé from behind! YEAH, I LOVED EVERY MINUTE OF IT-THAT'S MY BUSINESS! The shit turns me on! Pain!! So then I made a sex-video outta it! "BIG FUCKING DEAL! I still came home to YOUR mummified ass and penciled you in for sloppy-seconds! So don't have a fucking seizure!" Was the pussy too loose for you to SQUEEZE your big hairy dick in Playa? NO! So then shut the FUCK up! Get a LIFE! And don't bother me-or I swear your next visit to the Morgue will be more permanent!"

You know the sorry low-life actually had the nerve to bring up my phone-call with Mikki? The one where I was talking in my sleep about the 2 nuts I busted that time at Honeys in the Reggae room!

"Yeah you DUMB fuck! Me an Mik was playin your creepy ass cuz we KNEW you was still on the line listenin in like a bitch! Got me? You been PLAYED! Tricked-serves you right. So don't come to me with that lame shit NOW cuz you shouldn't have been listenin. STAY OUTTA BITCHES CONVERSATIONS! Or next time It'll be worse!"

"How you know I was on the line," asked the zombie?

"I heard you FART in the background fool! An you was BREATHING too hard-calm the fuck down next time you easedrop. An if you can't TAKE IT, hang up the phone! Huh, I told Mik to turn up the pressure so you could here what you WANTED to here!"

That was that! He BELIEVED it! My day was ruined and my head was bangin-but I guess that's what a zombie does. Pluck a bitches nerves. He had messed up for real this time cuz I had been actually entertaining the thought of trying to chill-trying to make it work. cuz for some strange reason, when he got sick, it pained me! And I felt partially to blame and thought of maybe settling down with Floyd-treat him good for a change. God knows what he went through with me! But NO! Now instead I would fuck Canei harder this time-suck his grimy dick and make the zombie tongue-kiss me Good-night when I got back home! "Yo Floyd-TASTE THIS AN TRY AND FIGURE OUT WHOSE DICK I SUCKED TODAY! SAY CHEESE YOU BASTARD!"

He lay on my bed as I prepared for work and he most likely would be there when I returned-to make me miserable some more. The Doctor said he had to be cool-stay off his feet due to the Angio-plasty he had undergone! I guess that's why he felt so insecure-so powerless. Cuz when your heart stops you can't fuck your girl right! And there is NOTHING worse for a man's ego then a dead shriveled-up dick! And he was miserable-so why not make Simone Singleton miserable too? Screw up HER life! And he would stay there at my house-in my bed for at least the 3 days the Cardiologist prescribed for him to stay off his feet. Yeah, I was appointed official babysitter. On zombie-watch-but I had to go to work. And every man should know that every woman, whether married or single, has another existence outside her home. A secret clandestine lifestyle that suits her needs and keeps emotional food on the table when Hubby's not around-or when he's just 'THERE!' Occupying space-taking up oxygen but not satisfying her female needs. Think your Wifey ain't got an alter-ego? Better think again!

So Fine! I would be back-3 hours after work. Canei would be home and he lives 2 minutes away from the Scarsdale Center, so wait-on Hell-Boy! I'll be back with the wetest most juicy kiss a cheatin bitch ever layed on a zombie!

Well some things never change. All of a sudden Floyd was figurin out some shit that I had done weeks ago. What took him so long? Why the delayed reaction. As I drove to work I pondered on the possibility of admitting it and telling him that maybe I, and we, would be better off separated. Yet this strong urge kept creeping down my spine every time I saw him, to give in. To finally give in and be his wife. I was confused-who wants to say "I do" to a zombie. I swear one part of me wanted to blast his lanky-ass outta the cannon of lost-loves and send him shooting through the Milky Way drifting aimlessy till a black whole swallowed him up-or he crashed into a blazing Meteorite. What more fitting end could a zombie have! You already DEAD asshole-so ACT like it!

But another rapidly growing essence of self felt a morbid desire to be in his arms. Because he was always there-despite what I was going through he could easily dissolve for me whatever obstacles life presented. And I loved him for that. So I was an ambivalent wreck. I coulda watched him die a thousand deaths-and gobbled up buttered popcorn during the bloody ordeal. But then like I said, other sensations snuck up on me despite the hatred and assured me that whether I liked it or not, his thing I constantly rejected was actually something GOOD. Something DECENT for a change. Something I needed! Maybe somewhere deep inside I felt he was too good for me and I despised him for it-was ashamed that my own feminine virtues did not measure up. I don't know-and that was a topic I would no longer entertain. I had to go fight the powers and had no time for unnecessary philosophizing!

I settled down alone in my bed and smoked a joint. I'd had a little of the residue of the dust from the last time I got plastered and mixed it in. IT WAS HEAVEN! I TOLD you I don't 'drug' MUCH-just a little to get me away from all the shit I don't wanna handle.

All day long I thought of Floyd-the mixed emotions I had for him. I wrestled with the idea of coming clean and giving him the full version of self. And if he accepted it then so be it. But would I still accept HIM. I thought about Canei and why the Hell I was still wastin my time-an my body on the loser who caused me so much grief. There was no comparison between the 2. Floyd was more of a man in many ways. But sometimes in the confusion of life a woman will not chose the good man. She instead choses that which stimulates her. It could be the Devil himself-don't matter. She'd be down on her knees giving pleasure to the one who pleases her and loving it!

I guess that's how it was with me an Floyd-he didn't stimulate me like Canei did-yet I KNEW that he truly loved me-an Canei didn't! Chose your poison bitch! If I were forced to make a choice-to come clean when I really think about it I think Floyd would've been forgotten like the stale fragrance of yesteryear. Now I'm not an ungrateful person an I got feelings of empathy just like everybody else but why bring a guppy to a shark-fight? Or in my dear father's own words "A limp dick is a gun with no bullets!" Floyd was my limp dick-an embarrassment whose presence I could find no reason to justify!

There are certain secret passageways deep within the ambiance of a woman's psyche. Innate drivings, passions, empty spaces that need to be filled and innumerable needs that need to be met and poor catatonic Floyd just didn't measure up. There are also various times in a woman's life when although she is outwardly satisfied with her man, those vacant moments of silence confirm a relentless zeal within her to be turned on. I've noticed that there are also times when we fear that the vast intricate components of our sensuality can never be fulfilled by just one male partner. God made us a batch of erotic synchronized impulses interwoven so characteristically unpredictable that not even a Rocket-Scientist could analyze or accurately decipher them. Hence it takes 2 niggers, or one GENIUS, to equal the longitudinal profundity of one woman!

Remember the Spike Lee joint "She's Gotta Have It?" Notice how it took 3 different personalities to do for her what one couldn't? She needed in her man something she had to seek from 2 others as though one was NOT enough! And sometimes it takes 3 or 4 of you shallow creatures in order to stimulate a real sister 100%. I've been bitten by those fangs on many occasions. Friday night with Billy just can't cut it so I modify my sexual appetite on Saturday with another throw-back! Should I just SETTLE for poor inadequate Billy and put my psychological tail between my legs an call it a night. Just like some sorry hush-puppy who doesn't get what it needs and so lays down and dies! HELL NO! My estrogen levels won't ALLOW me to do no shit like that! There must be a plan 'B!'

Who knows, maybe some of us weren't born to settle for monogamy. Can you imagine being banished to having to pump on the same old dick every single solitary day of ones existence? That's a fate worse than death! Worse than all the fire Hell can muster! Why would God claim to love us so much and commit us to THAT? MONOGAMY! SUFFERING! I'd rather go to HELL! Rather choose eternal damnation than be stuck for my entire life with the same lame nigger!

I mean really-FUCK HEAVEN! If monogamy is the BEST sexual ideal God has to offer then direct my horny ass to the celestial complaint-box cuz WE GOT BEEF-AN WE GOTTA TALK! The Creator is undeniably All-Powerful! A divine Mastermind gifted with the wonderous beauty of diversity and change. Those factors are the basis of his character-and orgin. Why would a Supreme Being, one who placed a variety of billions of species of organisms from an amoeba (that is a one-celled animal for all you dummies who failed Earth Science) to his highest and most intellectually sophisticated invention 'Man,' command us to "look but don't touch?" Why would this motherfucker (EXCUSE ME LORD but you know I gets emotional) command us to partake of only one! And chew on that same shit (sexually) for the rest of our natural lives.

That shit is cruel! Monogamy might in fact promote extinction cuz a person would be too bored with the SAME OLD tired piece of meat to even be bothered. "Fuck the nut, I need some sleep-some time away from this single mate the gracious Creator cursed me with. DAMN, I already hit it 6 million times already-how much can a nigger TAKE? NO, just let me lay here. BY MYSELF, with some good weed, a 40 ounce an a porno-tape-AND MASTURBATE! Cuz LORD if I have to stick my dick in that tired piece of ass ONE MORE TIME I'll go find me an Angel, one of those motherfuckers with wings, and spit in his face! Then I'll puke out my guts AND COMMIT SUICIDE!" (CUZ I KNOW YOU GONNA KILL ME ANYWAY-FOR ASSAULTIN YOUR ANGEL!)

So he CAN'T expect monogamy to satisfy man's many errant ambitions. Not if he knows any better. And furthermore since he IS All-knowing, he should realize that as fucked-up as mankind is, monogamy won't work! God is also a Prophet. Just like He warned Noah of the impending flood cuz he saw it coming, he shoulda seen the day coming that niggers and bitches would be engaged in the biggest fuck-fest seen in 10 trillion galaxies. So calm the fuck down Lord! A good old-fashion orgy never hurt nobody.

Even MEN know the foolishness of an alleged monogamous relationship. They might actually play the game with a gullible chic for a good piece of ass. But in heart and action they'll still screw anything that moves cuz that fairy-tale romantic 'married-for-life' shit is invariably a feminine trait inherent in a vagina and a set of tits! But a nigger will play-while that dumb-dumb still holds on to 'that Old Rugged-Cross!' She is monogamous! She still believes in his deceit and every word scrawled upon the outdated ideology of the King James Vesion. (By the way, HE was a cocksucker and must've sucked much more than his royal share) She still holds onto some ancient papyrus scripts whose sacred guidelines have absolutely no relevance in today's society.

Monogamy, staying with just one person amongst Earth's 5 billion, is a literal joke! Why would a woman decide to commit to just one? What if he ain't got what it takes-does she still stay? What if she discovers in time he ain't ready? Five years later-ain't it a waste of time?

It's like if you got a steak…when you EAT IT-it's good! You'll probably enjoy it again the second time. But after a while shit gets tired. If you have to eat that steak every fucking day for the rest of your life that steak will start tasting like SHIT! But you still eat it. Now if you were to give that piece of steak to someone else they would appreciate it-and thank you for giving it up. But if you don't let it go-if you keep it you'll learn to hate the steak and forget you ever enjoyed it in the first place. LEARN TO MOVE ON! Bitches should let that steak go so it can be enjoyed by someone else! And when they do they can make room for another piece of meat they can sink their teeth into-this way everybody is happy!

Eventually, as you cling to the misery that life and that steak is giving you, you've chosen to continue to suffer-holdin onto a rotten outdated piece of meat. Think about it! How that look? You-the dummy, clutching on, tightening your grasp to secure your hold tighter onto that which makes you unhappy? If somebody offers you something else you SHOULD take it right away! They could offer you ANYTHING, if you wake up an smell the coffee-you'll take it! A rabbit, some cotton-candy, a baloney sandwich, a rubber-dick-A PIECE OF SHIT! ANYTHING! Yeah-you'll gladly accept a piece of shit just to get the bad taste of steak outta your mouth-to remove it's tiny annoying particles from between your teeth. Now that piece of shit most likely represents the NEXT sorry nigger you meet. But you don't care-you just wanna get as far away from that steak as you possibly can. So you CHOOSE a piece of SHIT instead! And that piece of shit tastes good to you at first cuz you just need something else in your mouth besides what initially made you unhappy!

Now you know things are raggedy when you'll choose a chunk of feces over a piece of steak but those are the blatant logistics of the domestic disasters we face! Your man becomes the steak-representing that which you no longer desire. And now that your tired of the steak, almost ANY replacement will do. He could look like Quasimodo, a caveman or a rhesus monkey-I SAID ANYTHING-but steak!

When I got home he was gone-OH SHIT! Mr. IV-tube was on his own. I called him at his house but he hung up on me. NO HE DIDN'T! I wasn't gonna keep on playin those fuckin games of mouse-tag with him over the phone. Floyd was callin me 20 times a minute and my patience was wearing thin.

Now nigger, if you wanna argue or you think you gotta say some shit, bring it! A woman that don't give a fuck whether you live or die can't hear a simple word your stupid ass can pronounce! So if your ego longs for some manly redemption an you wanna haul off on me with the speech of your life, SO BE IT! Just speak your peace! Don't worry that you've been tuned out and I'm either doin my nails, takin a dump or giving your best friend some head! Just tap me when your done so I can wipe up, floss, throw your monkey-ass out an go on with my day! I swear even God woke up this morning knowing that Simone Singleton didn't give a fuck!

But when you shoot your punk-ass verbal gun and only bust-off one bullet at a time, per phone-call-THAT IRKS MY NERVES! BASTARD! But I guess you know that! That's why you do it. So that psycho, 'I'll love you till the end of time' asshole kept callin me and shootin his punks-pistol, then hanging up the phone before I could retaliate.

I'm grown-33 to be exact. Who would've ever known that 'stuck on stupid' would pluck my nerves till his head got split open? Two-by-fours are plentiful in these parts and the bare sight of raw-meat never failed to excite me! You know I equate couples fueding and dissing one another in lover's quarells to dog and cat, cat and mouse relationships! Dogs chase cats! A dog can whip a cat's behind-and men are dogs. Alternately women dwell in the symbolical realm of weakened Kitty-kathood! Yes-we get our asses kicked by those niggers-by the dogs who've been raised to emulate men and visa versa! Now then, deep within the logistical sputum of the oft one-sided ass whipping cats endure, there are also infrequent semblances of hope! The same hope a woman got in defeating a man!

So Joe cat got his ASS beat! AGAIN! Savagely and for the third time this week. He limps back to his appointed position and locale of submission with the bruises that are commonplace in the internal schematics of their struggle! By now Kitty's left paw has been abandoned to that metal trash can where he took that fatal left turn prompted by fight or flight and that decision most likely cost him the upper-hand-AND THE FIGHT!

Kitty's face is lacerated and bruised. He's missing some whiskers. There is a gaping gash directly below the left ear that used to be shiny brown fur. Now there lies the moist residue of a drooling pit-bull-his usual conqueror. And small droplets of crimson blood pour out of his ruptured tail like fleas abandoning the scene of a new and more potent flea-collar. Kitty-kat is fucked-up! Just like little timid Shamika-Kitty's human counterpart. Like Tina Turner! Like Hattie! This brutality permeates all phases of life from Billionairess to Project 'Ho!' Everybody gets their turn!

But one day Kitty-kat begins to ponder on it's precarious situation "DON'T FUCK WITH DOGS!" With canines-a furry feline's and desperate woman's worst and most fierce nightmare! Kitty or Shamika is confused cuz her head has been rocked by the lethal heavy paws of their domestic partner "Rover the Boxer!" There comes a time for any creature, from caveman to Nuclear Physicist, where every aspect of our development comes to a saturation-point. And it decides that enough is enough! Everything has a beginning-and an end. It's like when you drop something from the roof of the Empire state Building. Cause and effect dictates that it must fall. When you drop it that represents the beginning or the origin. When it finally plummets Earthward and hits the deck, that natural phenomena represents the saturation point or the end! This idiom also relates to life and it's multiple attributes. Life, although blissful or malevolent, must cease. It can no longer continue to be after it's appointed time has come!

When something exists its birth is its origin. This is an INVARIABLE component to the VERY existence of things. But on the flip-side ANYTHING that has a BEGINNING must also have an acme or high-point and then meet an eventual END! That's just natural-LIKE DYING And that end comprises of DEATH! So if you LIVE-YOU MUST DIE! Sooner or later! Therefore when you are born, BIRTH is your origin and DEATH is nothing but an eventuality that ALL living organisms MUST look forward to. Furthermore the fear of death is asinine-juvenile! Its just as ignorant as hoping something will NOT hit the ground after you drop it and it plummets downward!

HELLO MOTHERFUCKER! If you drop a quarter off a skyscraper or an apple-OR A FUCKING TOYOTA, it MUST FALL DUMB-ASS! Now when you let it go (BIRTH) it WILL FALL! As it descends (LIFE) some vast and adverse shit might happen to it, either impeding or accelerating its demise. Those are circumstances inherent in life which ultimately make or break us insofar as destiny and misfortune are concerned. GOOD! BUT DESPITE ALL-IT MUST FALL! And in the end, just as sure as shit stinks, it MUST hit rock bottom! (DEATH) Gravity and it's sheer momentum will see to that! So whether you like it or not and as one tries to scramble UPWARD in a futile attempt to stave off death (don't even TRY it-take it like a MAN) inevitably the principle of here today and gone tomorrow NEVER faulters! What begins MUST ALSO END-PAIN, AGONY and PLEASURE alike!

Such is the fate, the destiny of poor little Kitty-kat. The destiny of Tina, or Shakima! The ass-whippings must stop. That's the destiny of Hattie-the beatings must stop! Just as everything has a beginning-so must it also come to an end!

Now a cat has been blessed with a few inborn defenses of their own. For instance cats carry knives! The claws of a cat are sharper than those of dogs. Somewhere within the lobsided silly-putty ideals of ecology God saw to that! And they can make minced-meat outta their enemies-IF THEY CHOOSE TO FIGHT BACK!

Cats are also elusive. You can't catch em! Jesse Owens couldn't catch one. A cat would kick the the Road-Runner right in his ass in a street-chase and they are so agile! So nimble that they've been known to take turns better than anything Ford, Lincoln or Mitsubishi could ever hope to create. "MEEP MEEP" for your ass Rover!

Lastly, a cat is cunning and cunningness is the 'Father of Rebellion' against tyranny or superior forces. When someone's got common-sense, street-smarts, some manipulative psychological stratagem coursing through their senses, the plantation, the alleyway or the battlefield becomes a much more even playing-field! Cats are much more shrewd than any dog would ever be. Brute strength ain't got nothing on an astute brain. And although they're stronger than us, a woman can do some real bad things to a man. 'Hell hath no fury like a woman's scorn!' Just like a female's got much more sense than

ANY guy. That dumb motherfucker can't figure us out to save his life. And yet we can see right through his transparent aspirations as though he were made of plastic!!

Well Shamika, Kitty-kat, Tina and Hattie-you are your own greatest and most faithful benefactors in this social Chess-game of love! But when a nigger puts his hands on you, despite his granite dome-piece, that stink-ass breathe and hulking frame, YOU GOT A KNIFE! AND IT'S BEGGIN TO BE LODGED IN THE FUNKY CREVICE RIGHT BETWEEN THOSE NUTS! I've seen some women get the dog-shit beat outta them! STOMPED OUT! CRUCIFIED! Well guess what-I DON'T DO CRUCIFIXIONS!

So I'm getting mad calls! I turned off the celly but then the home phone started ringing. I swear I wanted to pick up my 'Roscoe' and go to his job and shoot to kill! The dumb nigger infuriated me! You know how it feels when a person's letting you have it on the verbal tip and your just layin. Waitin to get your nut off as soon as the ravening monkey stops yellin. But just when that little flittering combustible impulse rears it's ugly head from the pit of your eternal feminine soul onto the profane utteral pages of a well sharpened tongue, the 'jackal' on the other end of the phone hangs up on me!

So I'm just standin there. Like yesturday's gullible fool looking beneath the strewn trash remnants of my female ego. I was never one to stutter but 'Sleepy-Floyd' caught me faultering between "look motherfucker" and the uncompromising hollowed echoes of "Click!" The dial-tone! I could've pissed blood! Could've spit in my parent's face for blessing me with an oratory genius that was ineffective in foreseeing the blaring sign of lost opportunity to speak. To imbed that 'genius' into an odious well-timed slitting of his symbolic throat!

I panicked-thought maybe he or I had clicked over to the other line by mistake despite my predominate women's intiuition screaming "Bitch, you been HAD!" Now I don't know about another woman, but I NEED to get things off my mind! To articulate-no matter what! Furthermore, I WOULD SPEAK MY PEACE TO A DEAD BODY! If I felt whatever I had to say had some relevance after I stabbed the living SHIT out of the BASTARD!

"Yes Officer-you got me! I had no choice! I just wanted to get his attention! But he wouldn't listen-wasn't hearing me! And that's why you found my crazy ass in a livingroom bloodbath communicating with the dead! Rapping about some shit I felt obligated to say. I'll bet he hears me NOW! "CAN YOU HERE ME NOW? CAN YOU HEAR ME NOW?"

Floyd wouldn't answer the phone each time I called him back and I'd be damned if I was gonna answer his call-so he could hang up on me again! So we kept on with the dog and cat game that lovers, AKA cell-mates, play in the prison game of life!

If I had a big fucking red-brick and a fast-ball like Nolan Ryan that loser would have met his Maker in a dust-cloud of pain and obscenities! Two hits-the brick hits him and he hits the floor! And I have been known to hit a Homerun or 2 back in the days! FUCK AROUND! I swear I'll levitate that emaciated skull of his onto the upper-decks of

Yankee Stadium and think nothing of it! And by the time the abulance zips by trying to save his worthless life, I'll be in the Reggae room at Honeys getting my freak on with some big handsome musclebound nigger named Joe! GLAD THAT HIS LIFE-AND THIS ROTTEN RELATIONSHIP IS OVER!

But I chose to keep the volatile sum of these thoughts to myself! Instead I re-channeled the hatred for him into an onerous night of infidelity! Canei would be FUCKED tonight-at Floyd's expense! Let him peer through the window-AND WATCH! I would ride and sing out my freedom-high off of a blunt and the beautiful contours of my UNWORTHY TRIFLING lover's cock! AFTER ALL-ALL IS FAIR IN LOVE!

When Floyd called me back that night I picked up the phone only to explain that I was too busy to talk because I had to prepare dinner!

"Oh no-it's not for my daughter Bre. She's at my parent's house for the night! It's for someone else-you know, a spirit of the moment thing! Now Floyd-I'm sorry, and I'm willing to discuss anything your tender heart wishes baby. But we'll have to do that tomorrow! But right now I 'm busy cooking love. It's you're favorite dish-baked-ziti! Oh, no boo-it's not for you. You CAN'T come over tonight!" So far so good-THEN I HIT HIM WITH IT!

"Oh Floyd, I gotta go, somebody's at the door. Don't call back cuz my company's here and you know a real man don't like to be kept waiting! Good night love-CALL ME TOMORROW! BYE!"

YEAH-WHAT NIGGER? So what he was supposed to be my man! Everybody knew, even his dumb-ass, that this shit wasn't working! And I'm too young and sensual to be handcuffed to some lame scenario that ain't goin nowhere! And besides-his SEXUALITY didn't turn me on no more!

-19-

WHERE BROOKLYN AT

On July 1ˢᵗ I died and went to Heaven! Then woke up on the other side-laying across Ice's chest. IT WAS MY BIRTHDAY! Ice was the love of my life whom I had broken up with during my reckless youth! THIS was what a real man was SUPPOSED to be! Unlike Floyd-The walking cadaver who had made my life literal HELL for the last few months! The one whom I would rather die-then let touch me! And the one who'd called and cursed me out an hour earlier-vowing to cheat on me before the sun went down. Just as soon as he could get that diseased heart of his pumping again!.

I said, "GOOD FOR YOU BLACK MAN! You shoulda did that months ago! What took you so long?" Then I warned him to take it easy on the new piece of pussy cuz it would be ashamed if he had suddenly taken ill and went into Cardiac Arrest on the first date! "The poor woman would be TRAUMATIZED-to have to give your sorry ass mouth-to-mouth resuscitation right in the middle of an orgasm! That leaves a bad taste in a bitches mouth. It's embarrassing-and I bet she'd never wanna fuck you again!"

"But move on Playa!" And I wouldn't care if he stuck his zombie dick in every female this side of the Mississippi-I wouldn't bat an eye! "So don't call me!" I didn't wanna tell Ice that Floyd was a stalker cuz this nigger could be pretty hard on the competition! So I lay there-basking in the tranquility of just seeing him-and being with him.

Ice was the MAN! Tall handsome and charismatic. He loved to speak-and I loved to listen to him. And he knew that. He would talk sometimes for hours-about life, about us and what he wanted out of life. And I sat there-mind transfixed and sexuality riveted-drinking in every intoxicating word that ebbed from his seductive lips! He could dress better than anyone I'd ever seen and he terrorized the Club-scene. The bitches all would die for a 10 minute taste of his sexy brown physique. And mad niggers would either hang up there playa-belts or pull out their green guns of envy the moment he darkened the doors of a Club to challenge them for the pussy there. It was no contest!

"Mone, Baby I miss you," said my caramel-colored God-father and sexual Saviour of my broken soul!

"How you gonna miss me-all them women you gettin? Nigger, you SMELL like pussy! You swimming in it-come here let me smell you!" I never wanted a man as bad as I wanted Ice-AND I COULD EVEN TASTE HIM IN ME! The nigger had a stockade of chics and their phone numbers-waitin in line. Yet all he could think of was ME. The slut he dumped for a life of purity-in Bachelors Paradise!

"Well how you think I feel-dying a thousand death's every time I see a Navy Blue colored Denali pull up. Knowing that in any minute I'll see some punk nigger march outta there flossing with the love of my life. I know when they get back behind closed

185

doors he'll be BLAZIN my soul-mate-THE ONLY FEMALE FLAVOR I'VE EVER FELT! Baby I loved you-but I hated your lifestyle!"

"How can you hate something you love?"

"How can a man have confidence in a relationship with a woman who has a hobby of sleeping with every OTHER nigger she meets? That's a fucked-up habit Mone-it don't make for lasting relationships!"

He was right! But I didn't wanna hear it. I had met Ice when I was only 25. And at that time I couldn't appreciate what a good man meant. When we dated Ice was my life. But selfish me still cheated! I couldn't help myself-I still can't stop it! And now, now that I could really use him in my life as a positive force amongst countless negatives, NOW HE CAN'T TRUST THE ME THAT I'VE BECOME! The me that still exists! He would be the perfect mate and MAD BITCHES have been lining up-throwing their symbolic panties in his fire. BURNING to get a piece of that fine black peaarl! But Adonis still loves ME!

"Baby I know you still have feelings for me...but you got plenty of opportunities. You get pussy...!"

"YEAH, I GET ASS," he raged! "More ASS than a toilet seat! So 9 out of 10 bitches I meet wanna lay down with me cuz their sexual curiosity tells em to! They're no longer in love with their significant others! These sisters HATE it when their husbands touch them! It makes THEM SICK! So they look to me! For someone to talk to them in words HE cannot pronounce! They just need a friend! Someone strong-yet affectionate. Someone who can DOMINATE THEM and justify their desire to abandon a hopeless doomed relationship!"

Ice was on a roll-an I knew he wouldn't stop till he finished what he had to say. So I lay there quietly-listening to just what my shining black-prince had to offer! If I could have opened up my trembling legs, mounted up on every whisper and straddled the massive vibrant masculinity of his tone, I would have done it. His words penetrated me-and he knew how much I wanted him! I was a willing slave-vulnerable through my needs and the man in my eyes could have it all. All of me. Swallow up my inner purity and conquer that small emptiness occupying every woman. The swelling pelvic heartbeat ascending toward the vigorous male sensuality!

"Every day of my life there's a bitch under me with a fat ass and a pony-tail. I wanna see that pony-tail ride-twitch from the incredible size of me. Her spine is bent the fuck over. Her legs are on my back hanging off my shoulders while I'm suckin on them! But she can't feel my lips on her tender brown calfs. I tease them and nibble-tasting the mocha sweat and perfume emanating from open pores dripping with the chills of how far she'll go!"

"But all she can feel is the virile explosion my dick sends through her stinky little underparts. Yeah, that shit is stinky-with the odor of a woman driven to sexual anticipatory madness! I can smell the sweet funk on her thong as it rips and swirls onto the size of what I've perpetrated in her guts! Her ass is envious of my extension and it wants me too. It wants me to send it to the place where her satisfaction has gone!"

"The ass-cheeks drool and suck in the rhyme-scheme my hands mold them into. She's moaning-commanding me to stick it in her! I get harder cuz I KNOW that ASS ain't ready for the kind of attack her fronts just came from! When I turn her over and lick the place where she misses my manhood, she sobs. I'm pinchin her titties and the nipples call me a sweet motherfucker through the sound of her passion. The kind of sweet motherfucker she wants to leave her weak-ass man for-and marry!"

"Before I let her have it in that tight passageway I make her suck on it. She "Oohs" and "Aahs" cuz she just came when I stuck it in her mouth. And I just squeeze that head. That pony-tail and let her deep neck-line tug at what's inside her. Something seaps out. She looks up at me, lips conspiring to keep inside what's dripping in her mouth and she smiles while her hunger slides up and down what I need her to do.

"SHE LIKES IT! The horny bitch likes the taste! The woman-MARRIED OR ENGAGED, WITH A HOME AND KIDS AND A 6 FIGURE EXECUTIVE POSITION, LIKES THE TASTE OF MY CUM AND WANTS ME TO RELEASE IT IN HER MOUTH! This is the bitch who couldn't stay away from me! Who couldn't resist the desire to call in muted voices while her man lay baside her asleep to her needs-knocked the fuck out on the bed of their woe!"

"She has earned her Master's Degree. Her Bachelors! Graduated Valedictorian and earned Scholarships! But all that shit dissipates because she is STILL a woman! And we're EVEN! Socially and sexually-when I inject my 'Poor-Nigga-from-Brooklyn' Pipe-line down her well-to-do Suburban throat!"

"But she can't HAVE it there-she's gotta take it in the back cuz I won't sleep good tonight till I make this high-class black bitch feel me in her dark fucking intestines! I pull her bobbing head away from my crotch but her eyes beg for just one more lop to retaste what she just swallowed! I turn her around. Then I pull her big ass into the air-she's changed her mind by then and wants to take it wherever I want to go! I wipe some cum onto her asshole-perked and looking at me. Dying for some brutal attention! Some ghetto affection to get crammed into that swollen aristocratic system!"

"I wanna make this bitch cum-again, so I stick my dick between her-cheeks slow and easy! At first she shuns my pelvic thrusts with her left hand but when I slow my grind it sends waves of hunger through her circular passions and at that moment she wants MORE of me! The trick needs it-needs to be pummeled HARD by a vicious dick that wants to hurt her. She feels me-banging out her insides!

"FUCK ME DADDY-HARDER," shouts the CEO of Smith Bailey Ltd-as a thug rips har marriage apart-WITH THE STRENGTH OF HIS BACK!"

"My grind is solid and not pleasant! It is the victory I craved from the first moment I saw that bounce! Like what a man feels when the feet on her legs whiz by him when he's on top. Putting it inside his woman and slammin the shit out of her. TAKING THE

BITCH and teaching her with every stroke WHY HE WAS PUT IN CONTROL! WHY HE IS CALLED MAN! From that moment I had to have it but she thought it was forbidden cuz of her social and marital status. Affluent royalty don't engage the groveling peasantry. But from the moment she felt me-she can't stop dissing her fiancé, standin him up for another 10 minutes with me. An she WON'T STOP CALLIN! So NOW I GIVE IT TO HER-IN THE QUIET FORBIDDEN PLEASURE-CHAMBER OF HER MAN'S Master-Bedroom! I'm FUCKIN his BOO! Wifey! And I'm smacking that ASS from here to kingdom cum-and she loves it!"

"The bitch can't even remember his name! Or the prediscussed time his punk-ass is supposed to get back home from work! Her entire existence reverberates around the deep slaps of the jungle-strength protruding from her."

"She begs me to go deeper! Her only memory lies in the sensual universe revolving around the weight of my backbone pumping this fire unmercifully up her spine. Her ass is ripping! The pussy is wet and she can't stand it!"

"She is now glad to be a woman and infinitely happier that she met a nigger like me. I can hear the trembling moans as I beast somebody else's pussy-like I own it! Like it's mine! I love the smell of her sweaty ass-gliding up and down as I wipe her tears away-then cause more to fall 'doggy-style.' I can smell it and it makes me want to cum. And the way I bring her to her sexual knees-the submission makes her want to disclaim and disinherit that selfish bastard that wastes her time and keeps her from me!"

"She wishes her man were here to witness what a REAL nigger could do. And I abruptly end her life of daily misery with the size of my temper as it pumps the life back into the married woman gyrating beneath me. She is crying and bursting-sucking my neck like a vampire and clutching the bedsheets. She leaves her mark on my skin to stave off the opposition-to keep the other women away from her prize. She hopes they won't want me-she MUST NOT let them have the Champion of her night-time desires!"

"I can kiss a woman's longings Good-night. I know what that look means. The one I see when she beholds the King of her Salvation. And the new way of life that she is willing to abandon everything that she has for. She will no longer aspire to or tolerate the morbid world that she once knew. She can appreciate the way I dominate the emptiness characteristic of a past filled with ungratifying intercourse. And now she is willing to forsake all! To give me the house, the car and the keys of a sacred vault. Her Bank Account-she would even sell her priceless intangible God into slavery at my command. Sell his High and Holy ass and take back every unheard prayer she has tossed his non-reciprocating way. Just to inherit the ecstasy, the comfort, of having THIS DICK inside her for the rest of her days!"

"You know I've encountered the psychologically drained and emotionally battered sisters who've said some of the most degrading shit about their not much better halves. Meanwhile they call me 'Black-God' and want me around till they meet their grave. But they CURSE the man who thinks they love him with expletives too gross for me to repeat! This is what I do Simone! Every fuckin day of my life. I make bitches CRY! AND SCREAM AND WISH THEY WERE MINE! My existence is a lonely one though! Cuz every second of each episode there is somewhere else I'd rather be. Somebody else I'd rather be touching. And all the pussy running amok in the universe can't fill up the empty void you left. The space I reserve in my heart-searching one day for a better you. A more faithful and devoted you!"

"The world has been flipped upside down-ever since you turned your back on US an fucked that nigga Canei!"

"Ice-WHY WE GOTTA GO THERE!" He coulda been a motivational speaker. In 10 minutes my panties were motivated to jump off this flaming consciousness and dive into the smothering manhood echoing in between his legs-from within the power of his voice. But a fuckin lecture is something that NEVER fails to turn a sister off!

"Nigger you ain't no better than me! Listen to you-you musta forgot the speech you just made on how to beat up some pussy-an catch the 'Monster'. So don't try an sell me on that Bullshit!" I'm good Ice-MIND YOUR FUCKIN BUSINESS!"

"Mone-don't be like that. I took that turn in life the day you walked out on us! I was FAITHFUL-when it was you and I! Remember?" But LOOK AT YOU! YOU AIN'T CHANGE YET-YOU CAN'T GROW THE HELL UP! You STILL out there since day one-check it. How many niggers you fucked so far?"

"HUH?" What the Hell was HE talking about?

"What month we in? July right-July first! How many niggers you done hit, SIMONE? COUNT EM! TELL ME I'M LYING!"

"HOW THE FUCK I KNOW? How many BITCHES YOU hit? SHIT!" What an incriminating question! Who the Hell was HE-THE PUSSY POLICE? Protector of lost and wayward vaginas? I looked at the handsome probing bastard and decided to answer the question cuz it didn't matter-an I couldn't see where this interrogation was goin!

"O.K. Asshole!" He could see I was sweatin-A BITCH DON'T KEEP TRACK! Ice should've been a Private Eye-OR A PASTOR! This was the kinda shit that broke us up in the first place. He tried to act more like my DADDY than my man. I know I did some things back in the days-BUT NOBODY TELLS ME WHO TO FUCK! So what, you my man? When a woman makes up her mind she wants to get it somewhere else, there's NOTHING a man can do BUT STAND THERE AND WATCH! PRAY THAT SHE DON'T ENJOY THE DICK-an hope it don't happen too often! But I decided to play his game. He wanted my DICK-STATS-THEN HE'D have them! Hope you ain't got a weak HEART PLAYA! Then I made my move.

"Well there's Floyd, then Canei-AND DRE!" It had been months since I'd given it to Dre-but I wasn't gonna tell HIM that! Figured I'd mess with his head for even ASKING me a question like that! That's girl talk! So if he wanted to be a BITCH for 5 minutes then he'd have to swallow some hurtful truth!

"...And that FINE nigger in the bathroom at Honeys. And Black!" I was getting heated-outraged at the self-righteous prick who was trying to call ME a 'Ho!' Internal survival mechanisms signaled an offensive. Warning me that I might as well send HIS blood-pressure up too!

"Then Clive...and Leon!" I didn't even know a Clive or Leon. Niggers should not look for something that they can't afford to FIND!

But as I tabulated, played with his mental, I suddenly realized how fucking DIRTY I really was! I was telling on myself! Puttin myself on blast. It was the month of July and already I had hit around 8 or 9 different men. Closer to 10 if you really got down to it. There were more niggers rippin at my feminintiy then there were months elapsed on the calendar! And for the absolute first time in my life, I WAS NOT PROUD OF MY TRACK-RECORD! And I Damn sure wasn't gonna mention the threesome cuz I can't even remember those niggers names! I'd never seen them before-and Ice woulda flipped! I could hear the Preacher-man now:

"SIMONE, You let TWO strange niggers hit you at the same fuckin time?"

No wonder Ice didn't wanna sleep with me! An like a DUMMY I was digging my grave deeper! Tryin to win his heart while braggin about how much of a trick I was! I stopped tryin to sell him a dream and decided to halt my carnal mud-slide at 6!

"Damn baby-you see, YOU OUT THERE! An you think you got shit locked-down? Your ass is OUT there! An you still screwing strays in the BATHROOM? When you gonna learn that life ain't ABOUT that? MONE YOU BETTER THAN THAT! Look at you-you're the finest thing alotta these creeps ever seen! Why you carry yourself like this? Why does a beautiful woman gotta act like a piece of trash in order to wipe away her pain? If a man play you, you don't LET that shit in your head. If you do what you do to stifle the hurt and get BACK at him then separate your mind from it. There's someone out there who NEEDS you-who you deserve an he deserves you! But he can't have you like that, baby! I can't have you like that. I need a real woman. One I can depend on-an trust!"

He was a hypocrite-he was just as dirty as me! But Ice's voice cracked and the tear streaming down his face that he tried to hide with that macho turning of the head vividly sold me on the dream that he meant what he said. And that he truly loved me. Ice was the answer to my prayers. I didn't know if I could be the woman he wanted. That he needed-but at that moment I wanted nothing more in the world-THAN TO TRY! To dig in-grow up, an learn to be as decent as I was born to be! Sometimes people luckily come across a diamond-stuck in the mud. Ice was the man God sent to deliver me from corrupt and reprobate self-to stop me from abusing what I was-in the justification of self-loathing-and pain! I would try-from here on-IF HE WOULD JUST GIVE ME THE CHANCE!

"Baby, Ice-couldn't we just start over. I'm gonna try. Can't we..."

"Mone, don't you gotta man?"

190

"MAN? Who FLOYD? Oh PLEASE, he's just a TOY-a bench warmer-I'll chuck him like a wet-dream!"

"Baby-HOLD TIGHT! See, you ain't ready. That's your problem-You can't do a nigger right. You can't KEEP him! As soon as you get bored-you'll flip! Then toss him aside an sleep with his grandfather!"

"NO, don't do that! It ain't like that! Floyd is just..." Ice was not playing fair. I KNEW I had a man. But that was NOT where my heart was. And I couldn't remain faithful to something I did not truly want-or need. Why should a woman hold onto a dream that died so long ago? I don't have to settle! But I DID love Ice! He was the man that could captivate my wandering soul-an I wanted him more than the air I breathed. Not for sex-an not just as a fleeting fantasy. I had loved him from the beginning! But back then I'd been infested with that sinister defiance-that waywardness that drives a woman from what is good for her. But I knew I could do right-cuz I'm a good person. I just needed help-some nurturing! And the comforting love that rescued me once in this life-time from a bitter destructive id. I begged God for this chance-begged Ice. But for all the truth that spilled from my heart-my being, the pain and hurt of yesturday's broken heart kept his crushed and sorrowful ears from hearing me!

"Baby, I told you over 10 years ago. I want you to be my wife. But I can't have you like this. Mone you gotta change. And It can't happen. Cuz if you break my heart again..."

"Ice trust me I..."

It was no use-as we lay under the twilight of unheeded sincerity and self-rejection both our souls fed on the quiet emptiness of the night! Not wanting to run away from the silent grasp that once brought us together long long ago. My senses could feel his immense breathing exhilarating the quiet consciousness a woman clings to when her eyes are empty and her body longs to have the man laying beside her. The one now running away from her unproven devotion!

I could smell the masculine sweat cologned scent that won my youth the moment I first laid eyes on Ice! I caught Hell in the genital brain a million degrees hotter than the sun at that moment. The same thrill that enslaved me at the beginning-the first time he touched me and held me from behind. His dick was hard as Kryptonite and it titillated my estrogen-ALL NIGHT LONG! Why a bitch gotta go through this? It's like when you starving an you got a hot platter of gourmet-food! An some jackass says you can TASTE it. You can even chew-but Simon says you can't swallow! Sorry Playa-RULES IS RULES!

And my tormented body would drool. Beg and cry for the forbidden touch that I was not yet worthy of! Ice was the ONLY man I KNEW WHO WOULDN'T FUCK ME UPON REQUEST! Like my body was toxic nuclear waste-but that night, as always on my Birthday when we'd meet there at his house, I was determined to use every ounce of my female sexual prowess to get that brown Stallion to have me again. I could not fail!

The way he always made me love him some more-yet go home lonely, unfulfilled and heartbroken! ONCE A YEAR FOR THE 10 SOME ODD YEARS SINCE I'D LOST HIM!

The Marathon was on! I groped and wrestled with the man I needed just to taste that memory! I moaned and I groaned. Trying everything. Utilizing the seductive cunning manipulation that ALL men have fallen to since time began. THE ASSHOLE! Adonis fought me off! I pounded and kicked! This corrupted bobbing head trying to infiltrate the forbidden-zone below his navel. A bitch was on fire-but nothing worked! I couldn't stand it. The dick was right there-I COULD SMELL IT! You ever smell a penis when you're horny? It's like a giant delectable banana-dangled before the eyes of a desperate starving little monkey!

I cried myself to sleep in his arms. Something he had told me once before reverberated in my head-mocking me!

"Simone, if I can't have you-YOU CAN'T HAVE ME!" That meant I couldn't be with him one day and then still go out an fuck somebody else tomorrow! AND LIVE TO TALK ABOUT IT! Ice was serious. He didn't waste his time with what didn't matter to him-and the man truly cared for me! Once he committed himself to a woman-he would kill ANYBODY, if he felt his eternal prize was being threatened.

When I woke up there was an envelope with 5 G's left in the place where he had slept. Every year we had this, our time, together. We promised one another from the beginning to always remain faithful to this reunion. No matter WHAT! I picked up the money and totally ignored the celly. It had been ringing all night long and there were 22 Messages on it-FROM FLOYD! Some niggers NEVER learn! There was a small note inside of the envelope-it read: "To Simone, till the end of time, ICE!"

It was still dark outside when I got downstairs and there were only a few people walking around. (Guess most normal folks don't get out much before 5:00 A.M.) I figured I'd rush home by 6:00, shower off my sexual frustration. My disappointment-maybe jerk-off once or twice-then stash the loot! As I walked down Pulaski Street I noticed about 6 low-lives standing by the 24 hour bodega up ahead. It was pitch-black and the Crack-head Squad turned to watch me as I passed by. Why did I park 2 blocks away from the house?

"Yo ma-what up," said one of them?

"Yo mama is back upstairs in the crib-worried stiff about your punk-ass- Junior!" Why did I say that?

"Oh shit. She getting fly son," said one of the group! I can't fight too good in the dark. I walked faster never looking back! (never let em see you actually give a FUCK) I gave a fuck. About ME-an my 5 G's! The black hoody one caught up-his breathe reaking and that foul mouth sayin some shit that didn't quite matter to me! The others lay behind but one of them went up ahead.

There was an elderly woman in front hobbling along like she was a champion sprinter in the Senior Citizen Special Olympics! She kept looking back-in fear of her 93 year 'ole' life!

"Don't sweat it Grandma! You ain't got much life left to lose no way. But stop looking back cuz predators take diffidence as a green-light to bite a chunk outta that depreciated carcass!"

Juvenile pulled up close! Granny kept steady looking back and there was one perp close on her tail. She looked as if she wanted to run but wrinkles and rheumatism immediately killed that noise! Besides, the train station was a block away and that's a deadly trot most antiquated limbs can't handle. Perplexed as to whose ass was grass, mine or Granny's, I tossed up a prayer for the old geezer.

"Lord, she can't take too many head-shots-so let the scuffle be swift-and painless."

Granny was STEADY looking back at me! At my juvenile stalker. I didn't have nothin but my purse and there were no broken bottles to be found! I got nervous. This old chicken-shit bitch worried me more than the punks who called themselves scheming on us! Maybe they'd robbed and beat her ass before-back in the days! If you coulda seen the look of FRIGHT on that geriatric face you woulda thought the 'A' train was about to hit her and take her EXPRESS where she was NOT yet prepared to go! I turned and stopped-starin the young Devil in the face and challenging him!

"Nigga, you tryin to rob me or what?"

Just then Granny turned around-them ancient ears musta heard the million dollar question. She opened up her mouth like she was about to shout. Like that precious Social Security Check was about to be set on fire or her dentures had slipped and fell in the toilet. And suddenly-IT HAPPENED!

"BIP, BAP! BOP-BOP-BOP! POW!" They caught me from behind! Damn, Granny-you shoulda warned a sister! I was on the floor-looking up. AS THE WORLD TURNED!

"WHACK, CRACK, SMACK-STOMP! STOMP!" All I saw was flickering black boots and a blurred fucillade of delinquent kicks and punches. I felt like the bright yellow duck in a shooting gallery. JUST like I felt back in Elementary School on the lunch-line! And that object they cracked me in the head with musta been a hammer or a crow-bar the way it was smashed across my SKULL! I couldn't focus a single retaliatory thought.

The fuckers wouldn't give me a chance! Wouldn't let me up! There were 3 of them beatin on me and all I could do was reel on all fours. Swinging my purse like an old lady, LIKE GRANNY, trying to whip my attackers to death-WITH MY PURSE!

Damn-I shoulda looked back-like SHE did. Whoops-there goes my purse. Somebody snatched it! Now that they'd stripped me of my deadly weapon I knew I was a goner! Suddenly as I staggered to my feet, Ray Charles blind and weak as a pneumonia victim-ON DIALYSIS, a lightning swift kick caught me with my bulging eyes open (I could feel the heel inside my eye-ball) and ended my hour of need-in a blur!

When I came to I heard a peaceful considerate voice.

"You alright? You shoulda gave em the purse!"

"Yeah right! An YOU shoulda screamed-or something, you old batlacks!" It was GRANNY! "Thanks a lot! Whatsa matter, cat had your tongue? Or you forgot how to call for help?" What was I goin off on HER for? She didn't whip my ass! A white man came over and asked me the question of the Century!

"Miss, you alright? I saw the whole thing from the car!"

"Oh you DID? An what did you do about it when I was getting my HEAD CRACKED?" I was FURIOUS-AND DIZZY! "You shoulda stepped on the gas an ended it! Blew the HORN or something! What's WITH you people? There I was. Beat the fuck down! Robbed, bleedin-the Suburban bitch who caught a bad one-ON PULASKI STREET!

I got to the Precinct feelin stupid. Like somebody's pig-in-the-blanket. Or the hog with a dumb look on his face as he lay on the Chistmas dinner table. Stiff as a board, honey-glazed and wondering just what went wrong! No wonder deer look both ways before crossing the Highway or taking that perilous drink from the water-cooler valley stream located in the middle of a dark forest inhabited by lions, tigers and wolves! Turkeys don't have much to be thankful for in November either! I WAS THAT TURKEY! Checking it's calendar-beak open and eyes atear regretting that fatal Holiday mankind stuck somewhere betwixt Halloween and Christmas!

But it's not long before the Wild-turkey, sickened by his pedigree, looks to his omniscient Creator questioning the precarious occupation of his temporal birthright! If he weren't so abhorrently speechless perhaps he would petition the Celestial Powers that be and seek to circumvent his starring-role at someone's delectable annual Holiday banquet! I GAURANTEE he'd prefer a much more dominant wrung on the ecological hierarchy of life!

The plumpened turkey's sole existence is squandered at early adulthood when age is ripe and maturity heralds an untimely end. If only he were a ferocious tiger stalking the sweltering jungles in search of prey! If only he could rise or slumber every day of his life without the looming technicality the muzzle from some Game-hunter's shotgun poses! If only he could rip the SHIT out of anybody bold, eager or foolish enough to hunt him down for the mere thrift of sport.

But a wild-turkey does not stand a chance because he is just-A TURKEY! He will inevitably wind up suspended over the flames of the Stevenson's family reunion sizzling skewer or be the bloody road-kill of an inescapable Mountain lion whom she slaughters and feeds her cubs as a nutritious mid-morning snack.. I WAS THAT TURKEY! Raped by the helpless violation of unprovoked assault. And submission! And if I could've taken the Game-hunter's shotgun and blasted him with it-I WOULD HAVE!

I didn't study hard in School to Graduate, grow up to become the half-eaten side-dish for some young wannabe Gangster's appetite for Grand Larceny! And THAT'S why I hate sorry niggers who rob and steal because that stick-up kid invariably becomes a menace to society. In chosing a life of crime he has inscrutably jumped the line in the societal food-chain somewhere between a hard-working job and undeserved sustenance! The indigent bastard can't feed his face for lack of fundamental literacy. His misspent ambitions hinge on and shift between a previewed episode of 'Cops' and 'Late Night Comedy Central'! His horizons are dependent upon a bottle of 'Old Gold' and his baby's Momma's monthly WIC Check. I don't give a Damn about the lazy, the slothful or the gleaming parasite who stinks up my Castro-convertible with his dingy boxers while flicking the living shit out of my remote-control. Your dick-game ain't THAT tight playboy! The remotes outta battreries and your 14 month old son needs some Similac. So go get a job and handle your business or you can remote-control your way outta my HOUSE!

The one with the gun was young! (oh yeah, they HAD A GUN) I could tell by the underdeveloped crack he tried to conceal in his voice. The other one hit so hard and ran so fast that he must've been either a part-time boxer or a pro-sprinter. I've been hit by mad niggers but that stocky little buck really hooked-off! Like how Tyson used to be before prison and Givens drained the life outta his soprano lisp!

The Cops treated me like I'd walked through the Projects alone at midnight stark-naked with a hundred dollar bill stuck in my Ass-BEGGIN da project people to rob me!

"Why were you there, Ms Singleton? Did you do anything to provoke them? What could you have done, Ms. Singleton, to PREVENT this tragedy?"

"You think I TRIED to provoke those assholes to TAKE my rent money?" He acted like a sister got it like that and don't mind giving up her shit as long as the ass-whippin don't cost her her new weave?

"I BROKE 2 NAILS PEANUT BUTTER BOY! You ever stand still an let some cock-diesel Johnny blaze career felon bust you down with some straight-an-narrow head-shots? Oh yeah-I forgot. You prefer BACK-SHOTS-MOST FAGS DO! Anyway the shit HURTS! An it's not worth the negative attention! Open your fuckin eyes you faggot! Do I look like I need some attention? YEAH! Maybe some Medical attention-this eye is bangin and getting larger than life by the minute. But I ain't YOU!"

I could see his gay ass now at a fag party on the weekend. Rolling his eyes at bitches finer than he! The bitches he desperately envied and wanted to be like. Starvin for ANY nigger horny enough to look at his scrawny black sexually deviate self! You might as well carry a picket-sign saying 'I LIKE IT IN THE ASS' cuz your peers here in the Precinct have already peeped your hole-card! I know you wish you had what I had-feminine genitals that worked so you could give that crunchy little asshole of yours a break! This pillow-biter made me SICK! He was the type of jealous arrogant fag-mad at the world and hoplessly angry at the entire female populus cuz he feared the daily one-

sided losing battle to true womanhood. He was in a competition that he NEVER expected
to win and so he couldn't stand the bare sight of ANYTHING with a pussy. A pussy he
was born not to have! THIS Boy-in-blue was an unattractive homo too-outright pissed off
cuz of what he looked like. NOT LADY-LIKE! You ever seen one of these queers-WHO
HATE YOU ON SIGHT! And spear down your womanhood, your feminity, with
multiple brazen daggers of spiteful leers and snide gestures?

THIS THING was the gay-blade from Hell! Now I truly respect ANY man who
although born male navigated his life toward homosexuality through some inordinate
desire to find a true happiness absent in unsatisfying heterosexuality-LIKE MY GIRL
HATTIE! She's a good fag-one who doesn't HATE! But when you 'dis' me every chance
you get cuz God forgot to hand you out some tits-WE GOT BEEF!

When the DECENT homosexual meets and befriends an understanding
heterosexual woman, like myself, SHE respects and brings out in him (the fag) that inner
beauty composed of a gentleness which far exceeds progesterone or ANY hormonal
ideal! She makes him the woman that he really is-abetting the transcendant gender escape
his evolving docile self has sought while stifled within this organically male body.

I'm no psychologist but I KNEW that Mr. Queer-patrol was tryin to play me! 'IT'
wanted to assassinate my esteem because 'IT' could not ascend to the heights of
womanhood that came easily natural to me! You know no matter how much perfume,
hormone treatments, and operations a cross-dresser attempts, his goals invariably fall 100
miles short of the prize.

But back to the brutality! I FELT RAPED! NAKED and I will NEVER get used to
the idea of being someone's victim! Alright then-the Teenaged Mutant Ninja Turtles got
4 Tampons and some Aleve. So by NOW their juvenile mentalities know what time it is.
BITCHES BLEED! I could hear them at the neighborhood Arcade now: "Gosh Mom! Is
that blood leaking outta your ass?"

Well little Johnny, it's something like that! Mommy HAS been known to bleed
from time to time!

My mother's picture was in the purse with the words: "To my baby." I had the
$900 Floyd had given me-something TOLD me to stash it in my bra. WITH THE 5 G'S!

As I sat in the waiting area a Samuel Jackson looking officer strip-searched my
tired anatomy with his eyes! (More freaks on 'Po-po' Street than behind bars) When he
got up and called out my name for yet another interview I could see the dumb look on his
face as he tried to dislodge his hard little dick from the crunchy wrinkles of his dark blue
polyester pants. I burst out laughing and the stunned gum-chewing lady about to take my
complaint looked at me as though I should be laying on a couch or taking a Rorschach
Test!

My house keys were a problem since my driver's liscence would reveal to the
punks where I resided and if they chose to switch from a life of Armed robbery to the

more lucrative occupation of burglary then my new $3500 50 inch Plasma color T.V. would die a thousand deaths when bartered at the local pawn-shop!

-20-

ROBOCOP

I WASN'T FEELING THE WHOLE SET-UP! There were only 2 black Officers in the entire Precinct. One of em was the Samuel Jackson guy with the annoying erection. And the other was cream-colored-but he didn't know he was black. He had a British accent and so musta probably forgot. He sounded like the personification-the NEGRO prototype, of white imperialism the way he enunciated them vowels. When a nigger sounds more white and more refined than his Caucasian boon-dock buddies HE'S STILL A NIGGER! If he forgot he was black I'll bet the overt Klansmen sittin next to him didn't! I'm telling you this NIGGER, this educated monkey, parroted the white man so much you'd have thought King George had cum in his mouth-right between those large blubbering black lips! And Winston Churchill was stickin the unsung dialect of European rape straight up his ass too! And what sickened me the most is that I could tell that he was far more proud of that British accent than he was of the Afrocentric color of his skin. You know, like his Caucasian attributes outweighed his self-degrading Negritude!

The Good-ole-boys were speaking in their usual genocidal tone.

"An with dat Dewallo fella, you know-da African. I woulda shot his monkey-ass 17 times too! FUCK INTERNAL AFFAIRS! Cuz hey, you nevah know? An Officer arrives on da scene an you never fuckin KNOW!"

They just sat there like highly trained racists-like it was a glaze-donut party and I needed my picture taken. It reminded me of NYPD Blue. And 'Detective Sipowitz' was talking some "Kill the niggers an let God sort em out," crap while my eye was growing! But something ole hillbilly-bob had said caught my attention. I KNEW I was in Dixie-land and didn't want to wind up like poor Abner Loima so I decided to keep the peace-TILL ICE ARRIVED! THEN I could launch the Revolution! Black Panther style! But still I had to get the Neo-Nazi's attention. And Daddy never taught me to hold my tongue.

"Hey Willie Lynch." I knew he wasn't smart enough to define that one. "Can a black woman get some assistance here?"

Sipowitz looked up over his black coffee. "Hey, she talking to you or what," he asked Robocop?

"Huh? Scuse me sista-but we'll be with you in a few minutes. Unless of course you wanna help me finish some of dis paperwork!" His Bensonhurst jargon was the pure embodiment of Crackerhood! A living stereotype! I knew I was in for some rigid opposition-some inter-racial butchery. WHO CARES! The ass-whippin got my female combative juices boiling! If you can't beat 3 niggers robbing you-beat the hill-billy bigot Cops in the Precinct takin your report!

"Uh, excuse me homeboy! But I need my picture taken and my 61 Complaint Report signed. The Desk Sergeant in front said one of you could help me. Sorry to interrupt the Twinkie-fest! I dropped the Complaint forms on Robo's lap and sat my black ass down on the swivel chair with my hands folded-left eye feeling blue and bottom lip slightly bleeding. I must've looked like a nigger zombie who'd died just yesterday and had escaped the confines of her coffin-bursting into their Police Station at Tea-time!

"Hey LADY," shouted Robo's compadre! (he thought I'd be intimidated by the raising of his voice-I DON'T 'INTIMIDATE')

"Look, who the HELL do you think you are? Who let you in here? Sarah...SARAH! Can you show dis sista-girl BACK to the waitin area? I got fuckin work to do here! You want you'se picture taken-FINE! BUT YOU'SE GOTTA WAIT OUTSIDE LIKE EVERYBODY ELSE! JESIS!"

I wanted to stab him in the face! But my 'Ox' was back home in the cabinet! So I chose another approach!

"Whoah there Hilbilly-bob! Sorry to disturb your 'Lynch the Negro' Stories but let me tell you something HOWDY DOWDY...!(THAT'S who the asshole looked like-HOWDY FUCKING DOWDY! And the other bastasd was ROBOCOP)

"If I was that brother Amadou Diallo's wife or poor mother I'd hunt your racist-ass down and get you BUTT-FUCKED by the niggas Uptown!"

Robocop got red and started spittin! He didn't appreciate the way this disobedient Citizen was talking to his BOY!

"How you mean to talk to us like dat? You see dis Badge (I couldn't see shit-NOT THROUGH THAT EYE) We can lock you up right NOW for disturbin the peace! And if you WAS that De-Dewallo PRICK, I'd shoot YOUR ASS down TOO! The nerve of you'se people!"

"Why can't you speak proper ENGLISH, DUMB ASS! Didn't Mama teach you that 'YOU'SE' is NOT a fuckin word? It's white boy Ebonics-SHIT-FACE!"

I needed to learn when to shut the fuck up. Here I was mouthing off at the scum-bags who'se responsibility it was to take my report-and ultimately issue me an Order of Protection. And I couldn't even get along with Robo and Howdy. Some black folks ASK for trouble! Pink Floyd got mad and started to grab me but Robo over-ruled him. I believe he felt embarrassed about my insolence and needed the satisfaction of telling this sharp-tongued nigger bitch off! White boys can't hang with the sisters-especially the ignorant ones with golden Badges. All eyes were on us and I don't think Robo wanted to squander the opportunity of saving face with a simple arrest.

"O.K. hold it, HOLD IT! Lets see if Ms-uh 'Freedom of Speech' really knows what happened up dere in the 'Bwonks' Ey, BIFF, let er go! He put his chubby little fists on his hips and got to doin some hill-billy head-bobbin. He was Center-stage and couldn't stand to lose this one! There had to be a meeting of the minds! ONLY THEN could the unsavory demise of Ms. Black mouth Almighty commense!

"You so smart huh? Well den you just tell me 2 dings! (What in the world is a DING?) Number one what proof do you got dat 'Dewallo' wasn't carryin a piece? An 2

199

what would you do if it was YOUR FATHAR out dere tryin to save YOUR neck from crooks like dem? You got 5 minutes!"

"You gonna give me FIVE minutes to talk? Without getting your feelings hurt by what I say an snatchin me up before I finish so you can lock me up? I got your word-AS A GOOD WHITE MAN? An officer?"

"Look Miss-I SAID 5 MINUTES!"

He musta mistaken me for a dummy. The type of nigger who couldn't effectively articulate his thoughts into words. YOU KIDDIN ME. I LOVE WORDS I! GOTTA ZILLION OF EM-AN THEY'RE MY BEST FRIENDS!

Now I can't remember that I've ever been asked such a ridiculous question in all my life! I looked at the JACKAL! At the pale Goblin from Hell! He'd probably failed the Police Exam. Then they squeezed him in on some moron's Affirmative Action designed to let a few mentally ill-equipped white applicants into the force-AT THE EXPENSE OF A HANDFUL OF COLLEGE GRADUATED NEGROES!

The volatile little bafoon maintained his head-bobbin swagger. And HIS hands NEVER LEFT those raunchy bow-legged cowboy hips! All was suddenly quiet in the Precinct. A morning orgy of exchanged slavemaster stories and chocolate covered confectionaries had erupted into the morbid blood-rites of the "Last Supper" for the dumb bitch who'd challenged Howdy-Dowdy and Robocop to a verbal joust! He wanted to degrade me! In Public! Dehumanize me to prove to himself and the whole world that no matter how you slice it-white is right. And niggers should stay in their appointed places!

He felt as though he could dominate a black woman in the same manner that he and his abusive constituents had practiced the Rodney King move on the black man. I wondered how many of ours were beaten senseless within these racially profiling confines. They were well versed in pinning the convictive tale on the Negro donkey chained in the back seat of the Klan-mobile! Each white bigot gazing at me appeared to be awaiting the early departure of this black and blue ghetto winch. The fool who fought the powers ALONE and must now die the death of 1000 black boots-beating the words "PASSIVE, OBEDIENCE AND SUBMISSION" into her rebellious frame!

"Now Mr. Robocop SIR, number one the man was guilty of no crime other than the sin of standing in his own fucking doorway. Minding his own business till your Gestapo Homies arrived! The alleged Perp had a gun. But Mr. Diallo had only a wallet and a set of keys! How the Hell else could he get into his own Damn apartment? Also the call over the Radio was that there was a rapist in the area-WHO WAS BLACK! Now tell me Robo. Mr. Robo, how many black men are their in the Bronx? ROUND IT OFF! Do we kill every nigger in sight till we find the actual perp! Does being black offer incontrovertible proof of his guilt?"

"Number 2-Did Mr. Diallo have his dick out? I think NOT! If he did, it would've been front page headlines in every newspaper in America. "BLACK RAPIST CAUGHT

WITH BIG DICK OUT-APPREHENDED BY NEW YORK'S FINEST!" So if his dick wasn't out who told you he was the rapist? YOUR WIFE?"

He was turning red and sweatin! And by now I could smell Robo under that dingy polyester uniform. He pulled a wedgy outta his ass and shifted his weight! And I continued!

"Now Robo if it were my 'Fathar,' whatever a 'Farthar' is, you don't talk too well do you? But if my FATHER were out there trying to save my 'neck' from crooks like 'dem' he would exercise discretion enough not to shoot an unarmed man 17 times. I think that's a bit excessive. You remember those 2 bad little words you couldn't pronounce back in the Academy? 'EXCESSIVE FORCE?' It means unnecessary restraint! Police brutality! You are only allowed to use the amount of force that is used against you. Minimal force! What type of force was being used against the 4 cops standing 10 feet away from a black man who had no weapon? Did they fear for their lives and conclude that they would have been murdered if they had not executed this poor immigrant from Africa?"

"You white folks fear us. And you don't respect us because you think that we are causing all of your problems when in fact YOU have caused ours! Your bad conscience abuses you into paranoia and violence for all the wicked deeds you've done in the past! So the only way you feel you can live in peace is to make war with us! Get that racial violent shit outta your lives OFFICERS! Then maybe you and you families can appease your consciences and sleep better at night!"

Robo had just lost his reign of terror. It was over-his sovereignty and my 5 minutes! I didn't expect none of those white folks to agree or clap cuz liars only CHOKE on the truth! But I felt proud. I had made whitey stand up and listen. Robo spun around and surveyed the audience wondering just how many of them were still on his side-and still wanted to lynch me. Something told me to run. Bolt out the door but I figured their well-trained bullets would find me 100 yards away. Shot in the back before the triggermen could make it out the door! OH LORD!

"Hey Ms," Robo shouted! "You sit down here an you don't say a fuckin word-to nobody! Leon," he shouted to some subordinate in the back!

"Listen-an you get dis straight. Search dis...LADY an take her in the back! Search her for drugs AND WEAPONS!" Oh DAMN-they were gonna plant some shit on me. Frame a sister! He continued. "An when you finished take her report an look it over. And her picture! AND GET HER SOMETHING FOR THAT EYE-FOR CHRIST SAKE!" Then he looked at me nodding.

"Ma'am!" Robo was too through! "Damn it's hot in here," he shouted and stormed the fuck out-slammin the door behind him!

Thank God the lynch was off-they musta ran outta tree-limbs! Howdy-doody was assigned to look over my report and I could see that reckless streak had abated after Robo was dethroned from his pompous cracker sanctuary! Howdy was extremely humble during the questioning. I think Robo was in charge and had instructed him to lay off the nigga lady with the black eye!

"No my stalker didn't kick my ass-somebody else did," I shouted!

"Now let me get this straight, you have a stalker but your stalker was NOT your assailant?"

The motherfucker was a genius!

"What's to get straight Matlock-I want an Order of Protection!" Finally they informed me that I couldn't be protected from a perp whose name I didn't know! "So maybe I'll ASK the little bastard the next time he stomps a mud-hole in me," I contended! Howdy condescendingly tried to persuade me that although the report had been filed nothing could be done! Just then Ice walked through the door and all the rebellion inside me just faded away! To Hell with jumpin bad. The Revolution was over and all I needed was a raw steak for that eye and 12 hours of sleep! As for my attackers-I'll see the Boys in the Hood next year. July 1st. 5:00 A.M. SHARP! We gotta date-AN THEY BETTER BRING FRIENDS!!

-21-

WHY YOU BUGGIN BOO

I woke up that morning happy to be alive! My eye no longer looked like this weeks rendition of ghetto Cyclops. Ice had drove me home and stayed with me again that night. I cried like a helpless damsel in distress trying to get him to have me but he knew how I was. Always wanting his touch while my swollen mouth begged to swallow him whole! We stayed up all night and after he left I tried to go to sleep. It was 6:30 A.M. and I lay in the bed taunting myself with the pleasurable redemption that THE NEXT TIME-I WOULD GET IT! That FIRE that he used to feed me with! Ice wanted me! I could feel his male desires growing! And his defenses were weakening! The phone rang!

"Simone, I don't know what to do!"

"What Key? What's up? Is it that nigger again?"

"NO! He can't find his rubber!"

"HIS RUBBER?" What the fuck was the Crashdummy talking about?

"It was there when he put it in me. Cuz he said he put it ON!"

"WHAT?" No this bitch didn't let a nigger lose a condom UP HER ASS! "Did you SEE him put it on?"

"No, but he said he did!"

"Kecia, the motherfucker's lying! He probably didn't use one! Go back to sleep! Niggas lie about shit like that ALL the time boo!"

"But I think he did. Cuz I still got the wrapper!"

"Uh-oh!" Maybe Crashdummy had something there. I looked at the Clock-it was 7:46 A.M. and I wondered! It's gonna be a long fucking day-a bitch can NEVER sleep till 9:00 A.M! So now we either go to Dr. Butcher (MY GYNECOLOGIST) or his first COUSIN Dr.Giggles in the Emergency Room at Plainview Hospital! DAMN-either way-the bitch is DEAD for sure!

"Kecia, go sit on the toilet an try and squeeze girl! You GOTTA try an get that shit to come down! Act like you shitting or pissing or something!" I didn't want her to get an infection cuz once the fever and chills start, THAT'S YOUR ASS!

"I did that already yesterday-it didn't work!"

"YESTURDAY? Kecia, what you mean yesterday? You mean to tell me you had a condom stuck up your ass for 24 hours? And you just now deciding to do something about it?"

"Well Marvin said don't worry cuz it'll come out on it's own after awhile-so I waited!"

"BITCH YOU CRAZY? You don't keep things like that in you! YOU DON'T LET SHIT LIKE THAT GO! You can't keep a motherfucker's condom stuck up your ass and live to tell about it!"

"No Simone, it's NOT up my ass. It's in the front!"

"I KNOW Key. Uh-MAN! Girl get dressed-I'll be right over!" I don't know why I put up with so much shit with her. The crashdummy shoulda made MARVIN'S ass go right to the E.R. an get the condom out! It's HIS 'glad-bag!' NOT MINE! I didn't fuck her. So why the Hell I gotta creep outta my bed and take her dumb ass to get the shit out?

I called his Mr. stupid on the phone and he musta known why, so he didn't answer. So I cussed him out on the voice mail.

"Why I gotta go to Plainview an help YOUR bitch get YOUR condom outta her rotten Crashdummy body? Paybacks a bitch homeboy! And next time you fuck her-DON'T USE A CONDOM CUZ I WON'T BE EXTRACTING THE NEXT ONE! And if you do, wear a tighter one. You know-the kind that can fit snug around your shrimpy little dick!" "SLAM!" I hung up the phone and grabbed my coat! By the time I got to the door it had suddenly dawned on me-I HAD FORGOTTEN TO WASH MY ASS!

"SO BE IT," I grunted! I guess there will just have to be TWO stale bitches in Triage! One smelling like she got an ancient fish-stick stuck in her and the OTHER about to give birth to a 2 day old condom!

We went to the Bayshore Clinic and sat down-waiting 4 hours to abort her unborn child. "DUREX" the lost condom! In the waiting room I was embarrassed! I felt as though everyone in there knew Kecia had a condom stuck inside her! I wanted to ease my entire body into the Magazine I held just inches from my face. Would someone notice me? And if this chic is giving birth to a scum-bag where do I fit into the picture? OH FUCK! I'm nauseas! These bitches gonna think I'm some 'Dyke' freak who strapped on a dildo and lost my 'baggie' inside the Crashdummy sitting beside me! WHO PUTS A RUBBER ON A FAKE-DICK?

I must've died 10,000 social deaths in that seat.You know, the ones where your esteem is the first to capitulate to the folly of the moment at hand. And then the rest of your anatomy sinks into a deep congested grave filled with the assholes who've proceeded you down fools path. Before I could fit my wounded self-conscious soul into the slimy crawlspace of self-nullification, a lady called Kecia's name. And as Ms. Stamford walked into that eerie room down the hall my ego began to puff up-inherently glad that the executioner of my dignity was gone!

It was over in 15 minutes and Kecia came out smiling.

"Did you preserve the evidence," I joked?

"No! She said she didn't need it any more. She just wanted to pull it out!"

Oh my God! Wrong answer bitch! "I know that Key! Who needs a leaking condom that's been stuck uptown? ANYWAY, you shoulda sent it back to Marv's baby's Momma! Let that HER figure out what kind of man she's blowin 5 nights a week-when YOU AIN'T AROUND! I was heated! I was tired. And I was outta there!

Me and Daddy had a ball munching popcorn and Jolly Ranchers and watchin the Sci-fi Channel. The old man was so much fun.

"Get his ass! GET HIS ASS! OH NO-LOOK OUT MOTHERFUCKER!" He couldn't stop dramatizing. He couldn't stop gobbling up the snacks-despite his type 2 diabetes. And I could never stop loving my dear old dad. THEN HE STARTED TO TALK! 'Troy' was on-my favorite movie!

"You know folks is always worrying bout shit that don't matter-things they can't do nuttin about!" Where he get that from? What that got to do with Troy?

"I tell em to look at the world picture-the whole universe. I read a Black Hole can swallow 10,000 suns. TEN THOUSAND SUNS! You know how big the sun is? Imagine 10,000 of em mo-fo's-POOF! GONE! So in comparison what the Hell are we-what is man? We hold high regard on our silk suits! Our houses and cars-OUR ROLEXES! What the fuck is a silk suit or a Jeep Cherokee in the vastness of the universe?

Achilles was about to beat a giant barbarian to death! And I couldn't hear the sound-effects!

"Daddy, wait-hold up. SHUSH! No talky-talky and T.V. at same time!"

"Big man took a dirt nap! 'WHHOO-OOWEEH!' You see that? Them fools was CRAZY? Ohh-LORD they was vicious! They was DEALIN! 'HACK-UP' 'HACK-UP!' 'CHOP-CHOP!' I couldn't go out like that. Fightin for your life. You trying to beat this 8 foot savage down while 2 of his boys are trying to take your head off with meat cleavers and launching arrows through your ass! 'FWOOSH, FWOOSH!" Shit-all that brawlin. I would've invented the bullet MYSELF! All that scrappin? All them punches ain't necessary!"

"If you gonna GO, why get clubbed to death? CRUCIFIED! I ain't Jesus! I'd CREATE a bullet. Outta sand, or glass-AND some SHIT! No Mongo! Don't beat me DOWN! Takes too many blows! IT HURTS! Look what I came up with! Just use one of these-take aim-and BAYA! Flat-line! Instant relic! Now go tell Atilla the Hun, your boss and the bastard who started this shit in the first place, to mass produce em! They come in multiple Calibers. I guarantee-he'll take over the world in a week!"

"Yeah, yeah daddy." Talk on-just don't eat all the Jolly Ranchers. The Motherfucker just couldn't shut up! Biological father or not-no wonder I'm so messed up!

"Onion." He called me onion. "You take the car to the shop?"

"Yeah daddy."

"You pay last month's insurance-an the car note on time? You KNOW it's in my name!"

"Uh-THIS MONTH daddy! I'll pay it with this month's payment! I was backed up-BUT I GOT IT NOW!"

"Oh GOD! DAMN worthless kids-just like I was! Whelp, there goes my Credit-Report! Guess that's what I get for cloning MYSELF! You see-niggers shouldn't HAVE kids... an kids shouldn't have cars. Shoulda bought you the BIKE!!"

"Daddy-don't worry about it! Besides, what's a little credit problem-COMPARED TO ALL THE OTHER SHIT? THE BIG SHIT IN THE UNIVERSE! Just be glad there ain't no black holes around!"

"Hey," he pointed at me-"Shut the FUCK up! You TOO Damn smart-just like yo mama! AAH-Don't you sass me!"

"Da..."

"I WILL WHUP THE FLEAS...OFF YO ASS! Say I won't!" He drew back his right fist and looked as if he were about to pull the fraternal trigger of obedience on one of 'Be-be's kids!' Then he laughed!

"Little bitch-bet I scared ya didn't I?"

"Nah, old man. Ain't nobody scared a you-fuck around! You remember you taught me how to fight-bet you didn't know you was training me to whip yo tired ole ass. You got yo insurance paid up cuz a bitch been broke...who knows, I might TAKE YOU OUT!"

"Take me out...TAKE ME OUT! Just gimme some sugar first-a little kiss." He puckered his lips and closed his eyes. "It'll get me a little time away from yo bullshit mama any way!"

THAT MOTHERFUCKER WAS A MANIAC! And people ask me why I drink! Hell, if you was raised by THAT man you would DRINK TOO! But you'd also be blessed to have had the company of the most kind and loving, supportive father Creation ever exalted kissing you and tucking you into bed at night! And my father was my peace-treaty against my hostile mother! I hugged the number one man in my life till I could feel his lungs deprived of oxygen and beggin his crazy over-zealous daughter to either STOP or make the necessary Funeral arrangements-cuz its time to get PAID!

"I'LL SQUEEZE THE fuck OUTTA YOU!"

"Oh got-damn GIRL! LEMME GO! LEMME GO AH SAY! MOTHAFUCKIN KIDS PLAY TOO GOT-DAMN MUCH! GO FIND A MAN...OR GO BEAR-HUG YO MAMA!" The old man grabbed his back and sat the fuck down!

"And DON'T fuck around an get robbed AGAIN! Had no business runnin around out there in Brooklyn NO WAY! Why you think we moved AWAY-CHICKENHEAD! Huh-huh...look heah...you shoulda bear-hugged THEM LITTLE BASTARDS when they was robbin ya! Hu-hah...SQUEEZE...SQUEEZE-AH GOD-DAMN-MY BACK!!"

"Look under the candy jar daddy, you left something!

After stealing a few more Jolly Ranchers I shot upstairs like a young pony. Oh yeah, bitches armed with 5 G's and a cloaking device to protect it don't sit still too long. I was glad those amateur Gangsta wannabees were gullibly satisfied running off with the idiosyncratic proceeds of my purse. So what you got the punk-ass $900. I bet business in Jimmy Jazz is boomin right now and the weed man can take the rest of the night off with you rookies smoking up a little piece of the pie.

Stupid Brooklyn niggers! Don't they know a real woman's deep treasures don't lay in her purse. They chill in her brazier! Her organic vault! Didn't your criminal ass daddies teach you where to search Pee-wee? I see he taught you how to swing cuz that left hook is still talking to me. But what good is the knock-out punch that can't bear no more fruit than a few hundred beans? Damn playas-YOU been robbed! Tricked outta the lump-sum thanks to my Gucci deterent purse-and my right nipple-clinging to the emerald spatter of Benjamin Franklin's mouth. I got the paper. I got the paper! Next time you rob a sister try searching her first. You know-before you start pissin on yourself and smackin a bitch around!

I gave daddy $500 off the top. Put it under his Jollies cuz if I gave it to him in his hand he'd say no. He could be bankrupt facing foreclosure and the proud fool would simply refuse. "Oh, your mother and I will be alright.Yeah, they took the house but it's comfortable in the garage-an we got better heat too!"

Mommy was another story. She HAD money-so she could only reap about a 'Hunert' and a bucket of KFC. I loved her and all but the monetary laws of economic balance dictated that she'd already had ample amounts of daddy's money to squander. To trick away on mail order over-expenditures.

"What you want from the store Ma?"

"I don't know Simone, you goin by KFC?"

"How many pieces?"

"Only 3 or 4-I can't eat too much."

"Yeah right, 3 or 4 pieces don't qualify as too much! What dietary world YOU livin in? Ma how come you never let me go away that time when I was offered a College Scholarship in Indiana?" That age-old question just POPPED into my head before I could say Original or Spicy!

"Oh Simone, you were too young. I wouldn't let no daughter of mine go off in some place nobody knows. Them people is crazy! You never KNOW-them places is dangerous! A beautiful young girl could have problems out there."

At 16 I had been offered a full 4 year Sholarship at Indiana's most prestigious University. The opportunity stemmed from the Sterling performance I'd achieved on a literary essay offered to Seniors at my School.There were over 5,000 students enrolled in the Statewide Incentive Program and my composition was ranked third in the entire nation.

My guidance counselors met with my parents and advised them that the College would take care of all my expenses. I could have BEEN SOMEBODY! Something much more than a Grade 11 Civil Servant earning just over $28,000 a year. Wages just adequate enough to keep me alive from paycheck to paycheck-livin from week to week-kept barely alive. So I wouldn't perish before I could live to see the NEXT WEEK-when I would suffer some more! Daddy was too proud to hold back the tears and started bawling right there in the Counselors Office.

But Mommy didn't see it that way! She utilized every TRICK-every scheme that green-eyed yellow-tinged stubborn head could think of not allow her only daughter to attend College and achieve greatness-absent from that "HOUSE OF WOE!" There went my writing career!

Mommy didn't answer at first but beamed into the distance bubbling in the midst of this UNWARRANTED issue. She NEVER talked to me-never really WANTED to unless she was starving to death or needed a lift somewhere. And when she DID she made me feel as though it was a major TASK for her to communicate with her adopted daughter the way she did with the rest of the world. When I came with good news she would dismiss it rapidly, change the subject, in order to bask in the opportunity to fish for and expound on my many negatives! And when I was stupid enough to mention to her that which hurt me, that which I needed solace from, she would handily bury me in the blistering cauldron of her tongue-lashing-AND MY SHAME!

Was THIS the way to love your offspring-to BREAK YOUR NECK AT THE CHANCE TO DEMEAN AND SCRUTINIZE THEIR IMPERFECTIONS? Why was she this way to me-and NO ONE ELSE? Did it have anything to do with her ill-feelings toward my biological mother? Had daddy cheated and brought me forth as athe result of an illicit carnal affair he had with the desperate young addict that bought me into this world? I DON'T KNOW! I often wondered did this woman truly love me? Did she actually feel for me what I, despite opposition, felt for her. I stared deeply into the outer crest of all the deception with which she superficially pacified my unspoken curiosities-but answers were few, suspicion was high and if I were but a mere granular particle of her focused hatred-I JUST HAD TO KNOW IT!

Why did this woman invest a majority of her hostility into me-the only one besides daddy, who faithfully cared for her-granting UNMERITED respect and devotion that she did not rightfully deserve. As I beheld the smoldering mindset of this my adored maternal question mark, I wondered about my real mother. The woman who gave birth to me. Was SHE this unkind? And in her desperate abandonment of an infant 'Crack-baby' was her treachery equal to the volatile sum of this person's raising that child in the neurotic bitterness of jealousy, self-pity and abhorrence? The raging disgust for a life which had not ASKED to be born?

There was a slow-moving tear descending from mommy's eyes-I could see it despite her fruitlessly juvenile attempt to hide! Mommy was tryin to play it off-so I wouldn't see her pain. You can't hide it from me mother dear. I don't miss shit! I could see a FLEA scratch his microscopic nuts-FROM ACROSS THE STREET!

"I'm gonna lay down now," she said-wiping away the humiliating residue of what was to me regret. The guilt felt by a living soul truly ashamed of a life-long decision made for the wrong reasons. Mommy put her hand down for a minute-the salty beaded liquid tear-drops splashing all over the light blue denim blouse she wore as she sat in the house living her life through the windows of a squandered past-time. As I came toward her I regretted-and wished I could swallow the convictive inquiry that heralded her pain!

"Ma look at me.Your little girl is proud of you. I understand what you did-an why you did it. I am a mother-I have a daughter too. And I don't hate you for your decision. Mommy, you here me?" I held her cheeks and made her look. Made her look at the child she raised. The child she held back and perpetually maltreated. I was the pariah she did not appreciate-AND ME, HER CHILD, was not at all spiteful over what she did to it. For all intents and purposes I felt as though my existence, my only purpose in her life, was to serve as the official chicken delivery-girl in the self-indulging world of the woman who reared me-THE WOMAN WHOM I WAS TAUGHT TO CALL MY MOTHER!

When I got home I made dinner for Bre. And got in bed. It had been a long fucking week-no, a long fucking couple of months since January. In fact the year was still ripe-still new and I had gotten my ass busted for what seemed an eternity. Suddenly the 5 G's didn't mean doo-doo to me! I had went to jail, almost gotten raped, then went to Brooklyn to beg for some dick I STILL CAN'T GET! Now I got jumped, robbed and beat down! It occurred to me that pleasure and pain lived in the same house. They're neighbors. Best friends. And when they clash the underlying aftermath can cause your happiness to deteriorate.

At 7:30 I called Kecia. Figured I'd chat with the poor misfortunate Crashdummy who'd just had a used condom stuck up her. Peace of mind might come in different forms and I was in no position to decide on which pleasant diversion to focus on. I needed something-ANYTHING to rescue my consciousness-my embittered confusion away from sinking self. And Key was one helluva diversion! Giving birth to an unwanted 50 miligram piece of rubber can be just as engrossing as an Epic Block-buster Video. And the NERVE of some niggers! Her so-called man Marvin trying to deny that he was the father. The proof is in the pudding. And DNA evidence don't lie Mr. Man! I know the bouncing baby 'Durex' was yours playa-spittin image of you written along the 1000 faces entombed in the elastic sack of scum aborted 2 days after conception.

There was no weed left! I thought I had my re-up but that was gone too! I rummaged through my junk-drawer! FOR MY JUNK! Nada! SHIT! DAMN! FUCK! Now what um gonna do-you ever see a crackhead WHO LOST HER CRACK? I fiddled through my purse-nothin again. Then I checked my forbidden stash-the small crack in my bedroom between the wall and the floor-board. WALLAH! A brand new nickel-bag! I rolled that shit up as though it were granular gold and smoked it in seconds flat-THE WHOLE THING! I PUFFED AN I PUFFED AS THOUGH IT WERE GONNA RUN AWAY FROM ME. Can't afford to lose THIS one. And I betta replace it cuz I always keep an extra 'nick' in the stash to ease my mind on the days when this life is unkind! After the fires went out I was blessed with the Heaven that had so often come back to nurture me. Till the next episode-when my fleeing cowardice convinced me that I couldn't take it no more.

I speed dialed her number calibrated under 'Crashdummy.' Oh yeah-that's what my Nextel called her too. As I keyed in the name I HEARD SOMETHING! It was a static sound coming from up above. I looked at the spliff! Maybe I had smoked too much-TOO FAST! Or perhaps the drug man gave me some BAD shit!

"BUZZZT!" There it go again! Couldn't be the drugs! I sat in the bed looking like the juvenile frightened bitch whose bed began to shake up and down from the floor! I looked up, not really wanting to, to place the sound-it's eerie origin. UFO? Maybe Alf or E.T. might jump down from their respective hidden crawlspaces in the tile drop ceiling and spatter their Alien life-form seedlings down into my gaping mouth.

I would become impregnated-orally. Like some transcendant artificial insemination shit from the Sci-fi channel and my body would be it's host. The cocoon for some hostile spawning embryo hatchling like the one who burst and tore it's way outta that white boy's stomach in the movie 'ALIEN!' Oh SHIT! A 5 minute gestation period and "WHOO-PEE!" THEY'RE HERE! Instant Gremlin! Oh DAMN-there go my intestines! What we bitches have to go through? Now I know what Key felt like. A terrestrial Crashdummy giving birth to an extra-terrestrial violent oozing green little motherfucker! The one who just tried to rip her insides to shreds. I think I'd better call Canei-or Floyd. See how a zombie or an alcolic womanizer can get along with a baby humanoid! Or let them die the deaths E.T's got planned for me!

I was not so in the mood to be cocooned! Not on my day off with $5000 in my purse! I bolted outta the bed and decided to launch a more thorough investigation. NO STONES UNTURNED!

"BRE, Come out here boo!" SHIT! Why not call my beloved offspring? That's what slaves are for! They're bred to do the horrific shit their cowardly parents are not yet prepped to do!

"Bre, look up there! See if you hear something-turn down the T.V!"

"What? Oh no-is it a mouse?"

"Bre! Please, be quiet-I heard something!"

"Maybe it's a rat, I'm watchin 'Fear Factor!"

"Bre come on. Don't say that! You know I hate rats. Damn-why you gotta say that? You know I don't like you to say 'rat!' Thanks a lot-ruin my night-THEN go watch 'Fear Factor!"

There was another rumble coming from the ceiling!

"Oh God Breanna! There it goes again!"

Well will you look at that. If I thought I had summoned help I was sadly mistaken cuz before the noise could even stop my hard-rock do or die thug-life daughter had sprinted out the bedroom and slammed the door behind her! And you think you tough enough to make it in prison? Girl there's shit bigger than A RAT in prison!

"Bre! Come here!" The little chicken-shit was hiding behind the door! SCARED TO DEATH and peaking back at me!

"Ma, I heard it! I ain't comin back in there! CALL THE COPS!"

"Breanna, get a broom-and a chair. You gotta help me boo! Cuz I ain't sleepin in this house till we find out what it is!"

"But why's it buzzin like that?

"Oh my God-I don't know!"

"OH MY GOD!" We'd been invaded by a crazed rodent with magical powers able to harness the raw power of electricity into the palm of it's miniature 4 pronged claws!

"That's it-I'm movin out! TONIGHT!" But why was it nesting at MY crib? In MY BEDROOM CEILING? Breanna got the chair and the broom but I longed for something more sturdy. More radical! Like a cannon to launch this furry little cosmic invader into the outer realms of muskrat purgatory! I situated our makeshift artillery swearing that I would not be the fool to disturb the abode of an electronic racoon! But I had no problem sending my daughter up there to die!

"Bre, you go up there and get him out!"

"I'M not going-YOU GO! You're older!"

"Bre, you know mommy got a bad back? Please come on. YOU go up there-and bat it down to me! An I'll smash it's brain out an kill it!"

"I thought you told me 'Thou shalt not KILL," she said? YOU GO!"

Bre was a wus! A punk with delusions of grandeur. Willing to challenge Judges and Cops and Armies of killers and even me! But she had no heart for the 6 ounce burglar-impeding my evening nap! Now all of a sudden she thinks she's THE POPE! And I didn't want to go. I got 5G's! I'm too wealthy to die. THE RICH DON'T GO TO WAR-THEY SEND THE POOR TO DO IT! So we agreed to use the broom to dislodge the 4 legged God of Thunder!

"You sure you don't wanna call Canei? He's good at killing rats," said the adolescent coward! "He can kill ANYTHING!"

"Breanna, the only thing he's ever killed was your guppies!" I made sure to give HIM the credit for busting up the fish tank full of guppies. So what I did it! I wasn't ABOUT to tell my teary-eyed firstborn that her beloved guppies 'Bucky' and 'Mr. Peebles' were butchered by dear old me! ALL IS FAIR IN LOVE AND WAR! And to the victors go the spoils-and to the losers go the shackles, the gauze-pads-AND THE BLAME!

Bre finally agreed to boldy go where mommy wouldn't go! Deep into the cob-webbed wilds of my bedroom drop-ceiling! The forbidden lair of "BEN" the demonized rat! When she threw the ceiling tile to the side and stuck her unwary adolescent head into the midst of eminent danger I expected to see a Samurai Sword wielding gangster rodent-slicing off her enlarged dome-piece! I promised myself to retrieve the severed head from the floor and dial 911 before I ran screaming like a banshee. Maybe some Elmers glue and duct-tape could reanimate my tender prodigy who risked all for the eternal graces of mommy's evening nap. But the Paramedics would have to undertake that obligatory piece of First Aid! I'd be still beating my feet toward the Bronx increasing the amount of safe-space between the flailing corpse and my chicken-heart!

When she stuck her head and her hand in she came out with-SOMETHING! It was NOT a rat! There was no invincible creature from the upper Planetoid found in my ceiling!

"Ma what's THIS? It was some sort of Mission Impossible 'thingie'. Some high-tech electronics. When she handed it to me I almost flipped. Somebody had been bugging my apartment-and the fix was IN?

"Who put it there? Is somebody spying on us?" I didn't answer. I was TOO Damn mad to talk and had a good fucking idea who had done this! It couldn't have been Yago-that stinky motherfucker was nosy. Calculating-but absolutely incapable of something like this! No, it had to be someone else with more of a motive. Someone more close to my heart!

I picked up the Nextel and dialed. Dismissing the number for Crashdummy.

"Hello Floyd... I got the Cops here and they're coming over to your house now to lock your monkey ass up! Why you put a tape recorder in my house?

It appears that the signal from my cell-phone caused an electrostatic wave to emit humming noises from the planted tape-recorder. Therfore the buzzing sound that I heard was actually prompted each time my Nextel rang-or I made a call from it. (I KNEW it wasn't the weed) I had heard that slight buzzing before in the past but would dismiss it as nonsensical background noise. But this time I knew for sure the snake-like origin of that all too familiar buzzing noise. I was irate-and THIS shit would necessitate NOTHING less than a swift side-kick to his scandalous nuts the very next time I saw Floyd's face!

This was the last straw. I hung up the phone and put the bugging device in a shoe box in my closet! Evidence! I had discovered and dislodged the electric intruder reducing the indomitable air of Mighty Mouse to a 4 inch harmless surveillant device. I dispatched the 10 dollar reward money I'd promised her. (the bitch would do anything for money. Then again I hope not cuz as fucked up as I am-mommy don't sell no ass!) After cussing Floyd out in words he could not hear, I sent Bre to bed and slammed my room door shut!

My life, my personal conversations with mad niggers, my privacy-everyhing had been exposed! Open to that sneaky psychopath! I guess he found what he was looking for! Who knows how long he had that shit planted. And I didn't care! FUCK HIM! Hope he caught it all-and if he wants video highlights to go along with it I would deliver that too! A sneaky spy deserves to find what he looks for! To See what hurts him the most!

Well that slight throbbing impulse down there was telling me it was that time again! The weekend was coming and that 5 G's was singing tunes of 'Come Back To Jamaica' in the empty vindictive crevices of my mind! I would go meet Dexter Saint Jock! FUCK FLOYD! And I'd take porno-flix for his lonely ass to view for the rest of his surveillant voyeuristic days.

I redialed Kecia. "Take some time off! We goin to the Poconos!"

The creepy house-buggin faggot had messed up MY HIGH! You know some people could fuck up a wet dream-those are the kind you distance yourself from!

When you cage a free spirit like an eagle, it might COST you! Floyd had attempted to cage me. To stifle my limitless aspirations. And it was gonna cost him! The sexual Revolution was at hand! I couldn't help it! I wouldn't stop myself! That was the only way, besides knuckling up on somebody, that I knew to defend myself-my feelings! And I would ride it into unhinged ecstasy for the first day of the rest of my life! I'm not married! I was born free and their was nothing HIS sorry ass could do about it!

-22-

CRASHDUMMY

They say you can learn alot from a Dummy. This statement could not be more true. The abundance of wisdom and information I've learned from my dear friend could have taken a lifetime of pain and suffering to discover on my own. She taught it to me in 2 nights!

A crashdummy is the ghetto terminology that has a three-fold meaning. It is initially defined as the inanimate object used to test the degree of damage a human body might sustain during a motor vehicle accident. They are utilized as expendable replicas of normal people whose lives are at stake when examining both the exterior strength and durability of a car and the quality of it's safety features such as air-bags and seat-belts.

Actual human beings could never be used for such volatile testing because most applicants would not survive to make their pension! The Emergency rooms would be full of broken bones and shattered livelihoods. Medical insurance costs would sky-rocket, the mortuary business would careen out of control and those ruptured body parts would just keep oozing through plastic glad bags perpetually increasing the need for sturdy wooden coffins. The unsavory list goes on and on-hence the obligatory need for prosthetic average joes to man the unproven models in question and lower streaking mortality rates.

In my book a less conventional but more socially acceptable name has been given to describe this phenomena. A Crashdummy is also an individual who knowingly jeopardizes his or her own psychological welfare in a gallant quest for love. You're a crashdummy when you fuck a prostitute or an AIDS victim! Someone who might have AIDS! Who probably has AIDS or will soon catch AIDS! You're a Crashdummy when you know your mate cheats and you stay. Just because! When your spouse disrespects your relationship 24/7 and you stay. When you're involved with that married woman or that married man. If you are, you're a Crashdummy-AND YOU KNOW IT! You KNOW you're getting FUCKED but you stay cuz you don't have the strength to leave!

A Crashdummy knows that they have walked invariably into the Valley of the Shadow of Death! They have seen but could not interpret the handwriting on the wall-warning them not to partake of the forbidden fruit offered in dead-end relationships. In unholy bonds or intimate circumstances with those who cheat! They have seen the subtle signs as well as blaring alarms forecasting their chosen life of suffering and woe. Finally they've witnessed others fall by the wayside and heard the cries of penitent men and women who would give all to do it all over again differently.

Despite this incontrovertible proof of the abundant folly of their ways and lapse of judgement the Crashdummy choses to remain blind, deaf and dumb to the overwhelming evidence raging like an inferno before them. He knows about the other guy. She has seen the other bitch maybe even coming out of her house or riding alongside that worthless back-biter in her ride! Yet both she and he stays latched and bolted to the grimy tarpit of infidelity.

So although they know better, they chose to settle for a seat on the Express train enroute to the end of the road, the edge of the cliff and the bottom of the ocean. So much for discretion, discipline and sound judgement. Crashdummies are born to lose. To fail and to fall head-first and fast. They cannot resist their calling-their doomed occupation. They MUST be sacrificed, trampled, beaten and defeated in the game of life. They will never surrender. They will not be saved and they cannot win!

In life's Wheel of Fortune there are those born to achieve and there are those born to underachieve. And the only thing a Crashdummy could ever possibly successfully hope to accomplish is the preordained martyred destruction of self! The final phase of this definition to Crashdummyism can be accurately depicted and portrayed in just two common words-KECIA STAMFORD!

We went wild on the Tour Bus-you know black folks on Ski-Trips always spell trouble. We hate snow-can't ski worth a damn. But as soon as someone says Ski-Trip we're the first to sign up! Spendin our rent money and hitting the slopes. NO SKIING! Nah, fuck some skis! Oh yeah, we're still in our Lugz-hanging out. Drinking, partying-AND FUCKING!

It was Mikki, Hattie, Kecia, Marvin, Kim, Canei and myself. The ghetto Mod-Squad and we were living it up like it was New Years Eve. Everybody on the entire bus could hear the cussin, cackling, "Nigger pleasing," "bitch don't even go there" and carrying on! A middle of the bus section ensemble laden with project mentalities, illicit drugs and potential sexual rendezvous! Oh yeah-we was fuckin on THIS trip! That's what we paid the $450 apiece to do. To Hell with a snow mountain-there was another mountain we all sought to climb!

And there was no secret as to who was to be hittin who, who had already hit who before the trip and who would be abandoning the ship-wrecked vessel of mediocrity and 'bad ass' for more fascinating and satisfying stockades available on the peaceful shores of the 'Paris Ski-Lodge!'

Guess who the Hell we saw on the bus on the way? The gorilla.That bitch I smacked out that night I met Floyd at Honeys. The one who prayed to the gigantic sleeping Goddess named 'YOLANDA' while she was getting her ass kicked! Yolanda, the Supreme Mother of lost causes who leaves her followers to die! To succumb to the Henney and the Prada heel on Bingo Nights in Paradise! She could HAVE HIS ASS! I shoulda just backed off and let the gorilla have her way with the house-bugger. The psycho spy! Maybe they could've Ski-Tripped together toward a wonderful weekend of silent sinister zombie fuckin, right hook bar fight beat downs and the birth of multiple little eye-spy baby apes! What a life of Gerber products and secret hidden tapes and parental bliss!

I told my peeps the deal and we made up a fuckin song. right there for her monkey ass.

"Yolanda, YOLANDA!" We was trippin! Tearing past the sound barrier on the bus! And we rode that primate's skull all the way to the lodge! We didn't give a Damn about HER! The bitch couldn't fight anyway! So what was SHE gonna do! NOTHING! The bus driver was pissed but we paid our money so he had to swallow it too! Besides, the 'Comfy' and the 'Henney' were flowing and from the moment the first cork was popped there was no stopping us rowdy Negroes! So if he didn't like it he shoulda chosen a different profession. One offering more serenity-like an undertaker!

Hattie dissed him out loud-screaming out at the top of her lungs.

"I guess you shoulda went to College homey. To the University with the rest of the fuckin snobs! Then you wouldn't have to be susceptible to loud ass NIGGERS! SO LOOK AT CHOO NOW!"

And like I said: FUCK THE GORILLA AND FUCK HIM CUZ THAT'S HOW WE GOT DOWN!

I was glad to be away from Floyd! Now I could relax. I didn't have to watch my back like I did back in the City. Cuz knowing THAT creepy motherfucker he might be in ANY Club. Lurking! Peering through the darkness of the crowd unnoticed-while I'm out there humping up on Mr. Good-bar within my eternal scramble for Mr. Right!

There was a short dark-skinned female in the back sittin with her homegirl. Marvin and Kecia sat in front of me and Canei and for some reason that nigga Marvin couldn't stop turning around-lookin back!

"What you keep looking back here for Marv? Your woman is on your right. Turn yo ass around!"

"Yo, but there's a reason for that Monie-know what um sayin?"

Why do dumb niggers always ask that stupid ass question? I'll TELL YOU WHY! It's because they don't have a vocabulary extensive enough to articulate their thoughts! So when a man asks you: "Know what um sayin" he is crying out the abundant truth that he is literally too fucking dumb, TOO UNEDUCATED, to say what he feels. What he actually means to say by that question is: EXCUSE ME MA'AM BUT I HOPE THAT YOU CAN REMOTELY COMPREHEND WHAT THE FUCK I'M TRYING SO DESPERARELY TO ARTICULATE TO YOU! I AM A DUMB MONKEY WHO CHOSE A BATHROOM CRAP-GAME OVER MY LANGUAGE ARTS CLASS EVERY DAY UNTIL I DROPPED OUT OF SCHOOL! So if you would be so kind-PLEASE have patience with my illiterate ass and try to understand the limited communication methods that I have managed to obtain. I have the intellect of a caveman. So please say that you know what in the world I am ignorantly attempting to relay!

Now back to Marvin! The liar said: "I was just looking to see if somebody was in the bafroom! A nigga gotta walk his dog!"

'WORK!! OH MY GOD!' I told Kecia to watch that nigga cuz there's something back there that he wants! Why all of a sudden he gotta pee-pee so much! The nigger had perfect bowel control back home in Brooklyn!

I was Kecia's domestic Umpire. Self established and appointed to keep that piece of shit in check! I would not allow HIM to fuck her over! No time-no way! Not on THIS trip! I paid too much money to see the Crashdummy cry and spoil it for the rest of us! It was Kecia's Birthday-and she would have a GOOD weekend! And the only problem she might face would be over Marvin's dead body!

Then Canei jumped all in the business-callin himself standin up for his man!

"Yo Monie-you know we should let em do what they gotta do-they grown!"

Then I read HIS ASS!

"Shit-breathe-look at your ticket! Do you know how much it cost? NO YOU DON'T! You know why? Cuz you didn't PAY for the motherfucker! I spent MY MONEY! So SIT yo BROKE wannabe a drug-dealer ass down! You...DUMB NIGGA! Look atchoo! How you gonna sell drugs-AN YOU BROKE? Nigger PLEASE-DON'T GET ME STARTED! Just shut the fuck up an wipe that stupid LOOK off your face!"

He muttered some male coward's unspoken verse and situated his hands to block the dark clouds from emanating beyond his gullet but didn't open his fuckin ignorant mouth for the rest of the trip!

I couldn't understand Kecia! The bitch was so astute in writing. She'd won 13 Prizes and Awards for Literary Arts. She was a damn Shakespeare. Could probably write an entire novel in one day. All throughout High School she was tops in the field of linguistics, compositions and book reports. She did all MY papers for me in Junior High School and I repaid her in box-braids and gummy bears. Yet when it came to basic common sense and matters of the heart she couldn't bust a GRAPE!

Marvin was M.I.A. for the remainder of the trip and Kecia was crushed! HER MAN, HER DATE-VANISHING IN THIN AIR! ON HER BIRTHDAY! And you know what-I never saw shorty black with the burgundy braids and a perm in her hair again either. Imagine the odds! If you ask me they broke out together-found another Cottage far from where we was stayin. But kecia could not put 2 and 2 together! She wondered to her gullible self just what had happened to her trifling ass man! Maybe thought the Aliens took him. But the REST of us new. And for all intents and purposes Marvin and Shorty-wop were somewhere twisted like a fuckin pretzel in a 69 suckin one another's brains out! He was lickin the perm outta her hair-and she was blowin the snot outta his dog-like ass!

That's what Marvin liked but Kecia wouldn't give it to him. I didn't blame her. I wouldn't put my lips on his nasty dick either! In the past I'd kick some ghetto-pointers at her on the Fine Arts of Fellatio, hoping SOMEHOW-something might STICK!

"LOOK BITCH all you gotta do is smoke some weed AND SHOVE IT IN YOUR MOUTH while he eats your pussy! If he's lickin you right one of two things will happen.

Either you'll cum so hard that you'll forget Marvin's penis is jack-hammerin up an down your throat, OR the oral stimulation will make you wanna suck his dick HARDER-TILL HE BUSTS! Either way you'll come out smiling! SO GO FOR YOURS-BEFORE YOU LOSE YOUR MAN! It ain't so bad-DICK IS DICK! Kinda tastes like chicken!

Well there wouldn't be no 69's for Marvin! Not from Kecia! Now I PAID for this trip and wanted everything to go smooth. I bought BOTH their tickets to treat HER-for her Birthday! The trifling nigger was a C.O. at Rikers and COULDN'T afford to take his own woman somewhere nice for her Birthday. THAT'S why I did it! To see the Crashdummy smile! But if it was up to me she woulda brought along some other, MORE QUALIFIED, NIGGER AND FUCKED HIM! Put that 69 to good use!

Kecia was a very good looking 5 foot 9 dark brown-skinned woman-WITH A BIG ASS! A GA-DUNGA ASS! She had short curly hair, straight clean pearly-whites and a lovely girlish smile. Her Crashdummy parents put her together real well! They invested more time in her looks and anatomy than they did in the HOLLOW crevices of her mind! They shoulda KNOWN that no matter how beautiful a woman IS she still needs a functional amount of grey matter to navigate those comely assets safely through life! So unfortunately the compliments have to stop there-CEASEFIRE, because her self-pride and dignity were less than zero! She was the single mother of 4 kids-all by the same man and worked for the Telephone Company for 15 years. And to be perfectly honest-Kecia was the most beautiful 37 year old woman I had ever seen! But she didn't know it!

On Saturday night, Hattie, Kecia and myself went to the Player's Ball. Mikki didn't come-and Canei was nowhere to be found! And Marvin was still legally dead as far as I was concerned. We had a BALL! It was Apple Martini Night and everybody got SMASHED. On the way back we sang Happy Birthday and Kecia almost cried. We didn't know if it was the alcohol, tears of joy or tears for the sorry bastard who stranded her.

When we got back to the cabin Mik STILL wasn't there. She'd said she wasn't feeling well and would stay in. But the bitch was gone! So no Mikki and no Canei! Thank God-GOOD RIDDANCE! And like I said-Marvin was deceased!

Hattie and I stayed up till 4:00 A.M. and played cards. Kim had went back to some Shabba Ranks nigger's spot and told us not to wait up! She always did that! Whenever we hung out she would come in with us and then leave out with whatever she could FIND to get laid by!

Kim was a West Indian on a power trip! She thought she was better than ANY YANKEE ALIVE! And I often wondered if she had that kinda power back home-IN JAMAICA, WHERE SHE LIVED! She was the wife of a Real Estate Broker-HER MAN HAD PAPER! And she was a Corporate Attorney-so SHE had cheese. But their marriage had been dying a slow gradual 8 year death replete with one night stands and secret rendezvous. They musta took turns watchin the kids, ages 2, 5, 6 and 7 while the other went out and picked up as much dick or ass as possible! It's unbelievable how 2 cheaters could actually live together and be satisfied in a relationship of convenience. He won't tell if she don't tell.

"Hi honey, how was your day? Oh swell-a little fuckie-fuckie here and a little suckie-suckie THERE! I boned a Congressman. How about YOU dear? Oh I got my dick sucked by a teenaged runaway-oh, and I boned a Nun! Excellent dear-now let's wash up for breakfast! WHAT A FUCKING UNDERSTANDING!

He knew she cheated and she knew HE ran around! And like wayward matrimonial clockwork Kim was SOMEWHERE in the Paris Ski Resort TONIGHT dropping it like it's hot with some 'Jimbo' she met at the Player's Ball! And I wasn't mad at her. She kinda reminded me of ME. A relatively tall yet unattractive me-with 2 gigantic nipples, alot of money and a good piece of masculinity that night that she could call her own!

At 6:24 A.M. Canei dragged his drunken ass in asking me where I'd been. I asked him the same fucking question and he said he'd went over Mik's house looking for me but couldn't FIND me so he just hung out there and waited.

"Canei, YOU STUPID MAN, now I know your drunk cuz Mikki's house is in West Hempstead and WE'RE in Pennsylvania. So the only 'House' she got is right here with US! We're sharing the SAME cabin DUMB ASS! So what OTHER 'house' you went to last night looking for me!

A liar is NOTHING but a LIAR! A greasy cheatin low-life spawn somewhere in between scum-AND SHIT! I didn't WANT an answer! WHY WAS HE STILL LYING TO ME? Well fuck it-AND HIM! All I needed was some DICK-and some sleep! Within 5 minutes I climbed on top of his big black ugly ass, his deceitful ass, and closed my eyes. As I glided my starvation up and down his 'stoned' tranquilizer I pretended that he was somebody else. ANYBODY! Wesley Snipes, Denzel Washington, Taye Diggs, Shamar Moore, Busta Rhymes-ANYBODY BUT Canei Williams-the loser who periodically walked in and out of my miserable existence!

When I got back home to Carle Place I was so glad to see my daughter you'd have thought I'd been locked up! AGAIN! Mommies with criminal records spend a lot of time outta the house and miss their children terribly! I bought Breanna an R. Kelly shirt (her idol) but warned her not to get too attached. He might be going away for a long time. I was so happy to see her! We sat on the couch watching movies and eating popcorn until 3:00 in the morning.

I wondered what my biological mother was doing. What type of life, if ANY, did she live? Did she just snap and lose her mind-shattered at having abandoned her only child due to an addiction to drugs? Did she even miss or think of me at all? GOD KNOWS I THOUGHT OF HER and truly missed her every day although we had not seen one another since my wretched birth! Can a woman hurt for someone she has never seen? I did! But Heaven only knew if the feelings were mutual!

I had been accursed to a lifetime of sorrow and self-impugned misery. Rejection is a dagger to the soul of a child and implants itself and destroys its youth physiologically-

like an inherent cancer eroding the inclination to flourish and grow. That pain latches on-grafting itself to bone, tissue and flesh inevitably puncturing the grand design of nature to survive emotional dearth. Every 24 hours of my life I've endured unanswerable questions and although I attempted DESPERATELY to quell the burgeoning curiosities agitating my peace, that fucking little monkey perpetually reminded me of my self-abasement every step of the way. It is not a kind or friendly thing to LIVE through the misery of not knowing one's parents! There was an inexcusable emptiness, a lack of personal identity, which stared back mockingly each and every time I reluctantly beheld the emptiness of self sneering BACK despite my reflection in the mirror! And whenever I considered the person staring back at me, despite my outward beauty that EVERYONE raved about, all that I saw was the nobody who had NOT yet found the pleasure-OF MEETING HERSELF!

I thought about the Crashdummy-how Marv had told the bitch to stay right there IN THE HOTEL ROOM AND DON'T MOVE! How she would've waited TILL DOOMSDAY for the bastard to come back. Fuck work or food or the other priorities in her life and it deeply saddened me to think of a dear friend of mine so blatantly misguided. Of ANY woman foolish enough to obey, perpetuate and entertain that grave! She would do ANYTHING for Marv and believed in him more than she believed in herself. That's a problem we sisters must shed rather quickly. Before those Dogs we call men render our gender extinct due to misguided devotion and naivety. Word on the street has it the Spirit of Providence returned the favor to the philandering maggot. Says that same chocolate midget LEFT HIS ASS on the Highway enroute back to the City-with a rock-hard dick and no wallet! Somebody, probably a good Samaritan, picked him up on route 9 with alcohol on his breathe. He'd been robbed and stranded out in the boonies in a pair of red boxers and some K-Swiss on! GOD DON'T LIKE UGLY!

-23-

WHO STOLE THE 'KEYS' TO MY HEART?

Summer swam faster than anyone anticipated-summer always does. It was one week before Labor Day and our plan was to return from the trip before prime-time on Eastern Parkway. I never miss the Labor Day Parade! Too many naked men for a sister to stay home and ignore. And they be drunk TOO! I'd have that black stamina in and out of me before you could say 'SOBRIETY TEST' and they'd be too fucked up to remember who their molester was!

Hot steamy ghetto nights are a virtual catalyst for uninhibited carnal transactions. They just go together. You cozy up with feelings of intimacy and it just happens. How many lonely women are there in the hood on any given night? Probably one for every star in the sky-panting beneath her sheets at twilight longing for something nice to pass the time away!

You just grin and bear it cuz you KNOW that impulsive demon will come. Just like clock-work! Sure as the sun raises in the East then sets its tired ass down after a long hazy, hot and humid day of beaming down on motherfuckers and handing out heat-strokes! Just as sure as the gummy phenomena that oozes periodically between our legs every 28 days that some dummies call "My Friend!" What kinda friend makes you BLEED? You know-that constant variable-the impunctual shit that you PRAY will come (otherwise your ass is knocked-up) then when it gets here you're the most aggravated creature alive! It answers tearful prayers, blesses those it descends upon-then turns God's most sensuous creatures into breathing padded blood-clots!

Well that very same IMPULSIVE Demon, the one that swallows whole each and every predetermined ideal of discretion, chastity and restraint dear mommy instilled in curious adolescent vaginas had hit and instantly that thing breathing heavily behind my denim skirt got hotter than the sun!! Summer-time can ALSO find COUNTLESS sisters boiling, in the heat of their OWN flesh-dying for that red clad God-send to emerge from bright scarlet Fire Trucks with long THICK water-hoses who know how to EXPERTLY hit what they aim at! It's a fact that the female sex-organ has 10 times more sensory nerve endings than the male penis and therefore receives more heightened pleasure. This makes it doubly-MORE DIFFICULT to sit on her sexual cravings and display a will-power typically absent from the much less excitable male. And if I didn't know any better I'd have sworn that said Demon manifested itself within the lecherous embodiment of the one and only Canei Williams!

As I lay shivering in my bed from an invisible force which had ABSOLUTELY NOTHING to do with cold weather (it was fucking August) my minds eye scribbled a tragic soliloquy of the problems a sister must face and subdue through the many agonizing moments she spends WITHOUT her man. My pen jumped into the fray and so I wrote down just what my mental anguish had to say:

THE DON

There's gotta be more to it than THIS!
A marriage is supposed to bring with it a little more happiness
Do fairy-tale story-book Weddings ALL end up in Hell?
Like hidden deceptive tricks to drive a young black woman crazy
To drive my sex-drive haywire, hungry, laying here by myself
WITH MYSELF-trying not to finger-stick pent-up emotions into a sexual frenzy
Trying not to 'TOUCH' the zone that stirs beneath the sheets when you're alone

It's 3:27 A.M. on a hot and heavy Friday night Uptown
I'm on the West-side and my ride to sexual freedom
Won't be here for another 48 hours-he SAYS he's gotta work over-time
So what do I do in the mean-time?

'All My Children' are asleep but my body's heat
awakened with a shark-like appetite-and the only hope in sight
is the shiny black cordless phone on the dresser
Hmm…salvations Heaven is ONLY 7 pulse tone digits away
…but I CAN'T live like that anymore-I swore to myself before
that THIS time it would last
keep that runnin around shit as a thing of the past
and forget about Steve and Kendall's steel-thug blasts

The other day I found a woman's phone number
It was well hidden below the inner-soles of his Bill Blass Shoes
This CAN'T be, I thought at first-then a burst of rage took me
Sent me into the bedroom screaming like the 'Bitch from Hell!'

"What do you know about THIS shit Playa? Who the FUCK…is Sheila?"
"Sheila? Is this some kinda JOKE?" He spoke
like he didn't know what the HELL I was talking about!

I showed him the folded up sock stinky paper
And he asked me in astonishment "Where did you get THAT?"
The Devil told me to stab his ASS in the face with my hot-comb!
THAT'LL refresh a MOTHERFUCKERS memory

My Mother, who passed away from a heart attack 2 years ago
TIRED of all daddy's bullshit whispered to me a warning I was too irate to hear
Poppa LITERALLY worried her to death
But then God stepped in with some timely wisdom
And created within me a skillful ambiguous response
"I found it in your wallet! So WHO is Sheila?"
Not necessarily a LIE but I didn't wanna give up the TRUE stinky-shoe origin
Not just yet

He said "You couldn't have found that in my wallet-TRUST ME
And that's not even my handwriting!
Can't NOBODY catch me out there baby-I'M THE Motherfuckin DON!"

My brain suddenly calculated 17 domestic formulas simultaneously
and extracted one single thought
"You know its funny how the man you love-whose SUPPOSED to love you back
can swear he never wrote something on a tiny piece of paper he didn't even see!"
"Why don't you look at the fucking piece of paper before you swear up and down
you never WROTE it!"

His shifty-eyed masculinity betrayed within him
something his careless fragile esteem wished he could hide-I erupted
"Are you banging HER as bad and as quick as you CALL yourself banging ME?"
His frail throat tried to swallow his Adams Apple
And the feeling of his GUTS spilling out of the small torn hole in his pants
AS I CRUSHED HIS MENTAL NECK turned me on!
"I hope Sheila can use a roommate brother cuz YOU'RE IT!"
"And you cant take those lame-ass excuses, you BULLSHIT lies and-OH YEAH"
"That juvenile limp dick back over to HER place-GET THE FUCK OUT!"
I treated him like he NEEDED to be treated.
Because he didn't treat me the way I NEEDED him to-the way a real man would!

I was waiting for the stupid prick to say it wasn't IN his wallet
He knew that because he put it in his stinky shoe!
To admit knowledge of where it was would be an admission of possession
An admission of GUILT!
SO WHAT I searched his pockets and shoes! What ELSE could I do?
I was alone. And I KNEW his wavering penile focus was NOT on me.
He hadn't tried to jump in and hump me in 3 weeks! So who was he humping?
His horny little ass would NEVER go without 30 seconds of pleasure for that long!

WHO is getting MY 30 seconds? I NEED my 30 seconds!

How long must I endure being ignored by a male whore? An egotistical lover?
Hung like an impotent toddler
Talkng shit like 'He ain't got time!' an 'He's goin out with the boys!'
Well LITTLE BOYS STICK TOGETHER YOU MIDGET FUCK!
And what's that shit you said? "It's a MAN'S world?"
Then he came with one of those "Don't lock me up in Jail" speeches!
He reaches the deepest significant regions of my sanity
With ALL that Macho deceitful crookery. A CON MAN!
A little con man who promised to LOVE me for a lifetime-then comes home
LATE ONE NIGHT WITH sheila's PHONE NUMBER stuck in his funky shoe!
What IS it with these short men?
He jumped into my saced secret places-satisfied HIS fantasies-NOT MINE!
And broke out-leaving me home, alone in our happy home1

This shit ain't goin down like this-AND IT CAN'T BE REAL!
Cuz I swore to my momma on her death-bed then once MORE in her grave
That my once in a life-time thing would be saved! And it's NOT happeneing!
That was some time and five excuses ago-Yes,
I took his poor sorry-ass back-his WEAK back attack. A 5 foot 5
Male sex drive which is BARELY alive-because I loved him

Yesturday I detected the distinct scent of my cat
Perched on his mustache, dangled from his lips cuddled neatly in his goatee!
But the CAT wasn't mine! It didn't smell like mine!
This pungent NEW kitty purring in his nostrils was somebody ELSE'S pet.
Tabby must've gotten lost!
It just stood there-BOASTFULLY, shoulder high. Disgusting me-mocking me!

How could he kiss me good-night, sleep tight-strolling in tired at 2:00 A.M.
With another woman's kitten singing tunes of liberation on his breath.
The FUNK of fuck-me-not, eat-me-a lot following him all the way home!
It should have been obvious to me the type of pit-stop the little bastard made
Before routine dragged him back my way.
I retreated! My refuge the scattered depleted wreckage of denial
Too damn scared to face the truth!

It's 3:35 A.M. and I'm regretting the fact that I swore to stay for better or worst.
This is much worse than beter and I couldn't be more upsetter!

I promised to lick his mental wounds and fortify his shrunken male ego
If he could NOT satisfy me no more. I would forego pleasure
My OWN pleasure-the most vitally impassioned ambiance
of that secret passageway if I had to!
If he couldn't-since he couldn't kiss it-and put it to sleep at night!

I've imitated the Virgin Mary and played Mrs. I ain't getting none"
For a selfish bastard who don't deserve the treasures he's FALLEN from!
Ecstasy is a dangerous thing when its ignited-and left UNDONE!

This morning I called his job 2 times with Homicide on my mind!
Boss says he's out somewhere-best friend says he AIN'T BEEN THERE
But HE could be HERE in 30 minutes if I let him!
He said I'm waistin time with this jive-ass man of mine
And he would be more than HAPPY to bring me what I NEED!
Whatever I need-ALL I need till I don't need it no more!
A deed I've wrestled with since this fire began in my pelvic-brain.
Words can't explain and promises won't contain drastic impulses born of neglect!

Wedding Vows don't expect me to just lay here-100 degrees in the shade
And NOT pick up the phone-DO THEY?
If that little motherfucker is cheating on me I SWEAR I'll cut off his DICK!
O.K. girl-get a hold of yourself! (Pull yo SHIT together)
Better save 'Sorry' to glean the lean embattlements of a broken heart!

I'm gonna call the niggers job…see if this shits FOR REAL!
Wifeys gotta put her pride aside-before she calls someone else.
And if HE answers I'll bare this deep hunger tonight
His "I love you girl" will make things right!
But if I pick up the phone 7 pulse-tone digits to his job
And SOMEBODY tries to stimulate my intellectual insanity with a LIE…
Then he's said his LAST GOOD-BYE!
When I pick up the phone, if its NOT his voice
I'll just hang up the phone-and wait for the tone AND DIAL 911!

Just then my bell rang-GUESS WHO IT WAS? It was Canei! Speakin of the DEVIL! NO-WRITING ABOUT THE DEVIL! I'm expounding on the tricks assholes play and LOOK WHO jumps up like coincidental foreplay and stares me in the face-bloodshot eyes, drunken swagger and SOME NIGHT-TIME 'SEXCERCISE' on his mind! Just when a sister is trying to put the finishing touches on a MASTERPIECE disclosing the foul shit MOTHERFUCKERS like HIM do for a living!

I TOLD THAT THORN IN MY SIDE TO STAY THE HELL AWAY FROM ME-at least for awhile! What's WITH these bastards? MEN! Sometimes I wish they could detach those vital parts of themselves, namely their wallets and penises, and throw the rest away! What a wonderful night out on the town THAT would be! The perfect date! You get to spend his money and screw him anyway you please without the obnoxious side-effect of his ugly little head and worthless mind!

You can dump the Ego too-the ego that tries to kick down the doors of your privacy AFTER you've excused him and sent him on his way! But unfortunately life is NOT so simple and to date the wallet and penis without the rest of that stunted anatomy would be detrimental to both his physical health and YOUR image! So we accept the rest of his decayed body along for the ride in hopes to revive our unrealistic fantasies of 'the perfect man!' And we settle for the uninviting presence of a person who should've been dead a long time ago! Standing in the doorway at 11:45 P.M. uninvited and smelling like a brewery was THAT MAN! I put away my erotic note-pad to see what in Hell was on Satan's mind! I'd finish my Best-Seller later-but for NOW, Black Buffy had some Vampires that needed slaying!

Canei had some drugs stashed in the back of his car and his 'Trini' partner 'Vic' was assigned to transport them to an undisclosed location in Brooklyn. This was no unusual transaction for Vic cuz he had taken this trip over 100 times. It was a small time hustle netting them both about $2500 apiece per week! At least that's what Canei told me. But you know niggers! He could be lying and either ampin up his profits to make himself LOOK good or he could be knockin off a few bucks so a greedy bitch wouldn't ASK for much.

Well this trip had an unusual twist. Vic came back with a package that was a little light. Canei NEVER trusted Vic for some strange reason but couldn't quite put his finger on why. I told him to let the nigger go. Get somebody else to do the run or make it himself. But he always insisted he needed Vic, his road-dog to handle his business for him.

I never fully understood the concept of a cowardly criminal. A drug dealer with no balls-delegating the responsibility of dangerous moves to some peon who didn't know any better. But Canei was that manipulator-lettin the next man do something that he was too shook to do himself. And if justice and equality live in the same house then quiet as it's kept, Vic SHOULDA robbed him! I mean why would he risk life and limb for something while somebody else just sits back and collects from the fruit of your labor? That means Vic is getting 50% of the pot for doing 100% of the work! OH HELL NO! I swear from day one that if I were Vic, Canei woulda had to settle for 30%. Otherwise I'm cutting you loose! And if you fuck with me I'll sing like Whitney Houston at the arraignment!

Now the 2 Kilos belonged to a big time drug-lord! A REAL GANGSTER named 'Sammy!' Nobody ever met Sammy. Nobody talked to him. He had 200 hustlers peddling his shit but nobody could get close to him. When a dealer got shot down or knocked by 'Po-po' he'd either pay for the funeral arrangements or post bail respectively! But Sammy was a shrewd businessman (probably a white boy) who no one, NO PEON, had ever seen-but everybody feared!

I TOLD Canei "the nigger robbed you!" FINALLY! He had nothing to fear and nothing to lose! Now Canei is a 300 pound GRIZZLY-DIESEL nigger! But that won't keep a greedy bastard from stealin your shit! His life expectancy has to be threatened if you wanna keep him on the straight and narrow! You gotta roll up there in his crib or wherever you rendezvous like the fucking Terminator-like the Hit-squad in order to get his respect AND HIS ATTENTION!

"Canei, how you gonna get paid 5 G's a week for transportin-AND YOU DON'T TRANSPORT! You got some flunky doin all your perilous drug dealer work. In fact you don't do shit but set up the contact via a phone call from Sammy's associate. Then you call the road-dog. VIC and say 'FETCH!' Shit-you shoulda been robbed from day one!"

Well Canei got a problem. A real one and his name is Sammy! Cuz although he's not the runner he's bein paid to be, he IS responsible for the goods getting where they need to go. So now Sammy's got a vacancy in his Network. A hole. An empty slot and this synapse could cost Canei his good drug dealin health if he can't replace the 'Keys' or come up with 75 G's!

Vic told Canei the Cops took the car. Says he was stop-checked and the Boys in Blue said his vehicle's paperwork was not correct. So they gave him a choice. Have the car impounded-or HE would be impounded! Sent to jail! So Vic says he chose the lesser of 2 evils cuz if they woulda locked him they woulda still snatched the car and the drugs, anyway! So he chose his own freedom over Sammy's drugs. Yet somehow I don't think Sammy would have appraised Vic's freedom so highly-NOT MORE THAN THE 75 G'S WORTH OF COCAINE! And furthermore Vic had ignored the drug dealer's creed. 'Don't come back empty handed!' If you lose the weight, you gotta take the weight-or disappear!

So the Cops got the drugs stashed in a secret compartment in the trunk! And Vic is spillin his guts. Nervous, suspicious and grossly apologetic! He could sure use another long trip back home to Trinidad! And Canei's blood pressure and sense of well-being are out of control as he sits trembling in my apartment expecting an unscheduled visit from the Authorities or a much more fatal one from Sammy! He can't go to the Precinct to complain about the stolen shit cuz how you gonna march down to One Police Plaza and complain about losing 2 Kilos of Cocaine? That's some shit a drug dealer's gotta suck up! Contraband is Taboo! I can see it now.

"So you say your car was stolen? What were the contents?

Well Officer, there was my duffel bag, my work clothes and a ball-point pen! OH, YEAH, I almost forgot-AND 2 KILOS OF CRACK COCAINE!"

Canei said he wanted to either blaze Vic and bring Sammy his head in good faith to show him he was not responsible for the graft-or run! Now I know there is not a lost and found for illicit drugs and controlled substances so I reminded him of the utter gravity of the situation.

"Hold on a minute boo! Think about it. You won't find the Coke-it's gone! So you gotta pay Sammy back-AGREED? Good, now it's a bit late for this but I'm gonna tell it to you anyway. The NEXT time you wanna dispense drugs in your own Community stash a little money on the side. Just in case something like this happens. Maybe bank about half of your net every week-so if a motherfucker robs you or you gotta run, you'll have a fighting chance!"

"Secondly you just borrowed 200 beans from me last week. Said you'd hit me back up when you get it. What's the matter Playa, drug dealin business a little slow? Or you just out on sick leave? Anyway what I'm sayin is you can't pay Sammy back-but that's just half the problem! The real problem is you too broke to run! Where the Hell you gonna go on what-about a hundred bucks by now? Nigger you too poor to cross the fuckin STREET! Now Sammy got over 200 niggers out there watchin his back. You think one of those assholes won't spot you runnin for the hills? You can't even afford to leave the country-SO YOU FUCKED!"

"Serves you right tough Tony! You shoulda stayed in School. Don't shake your head at me BITCH-I'M TALKIN! You won't see no post-graduate nerds buried in Gangster's Cemetery for getting murdered for somebody else's drugs!" The belligerent monkey was about to open his mouth to say some fly shit but I raised my voice an continued! I was throwin water on a drowning victim-but he needed it! I had told him time and time again to stop sellin that shit! He wasn't smart enough to make money illegally! Some big black brutes just don't GET IT! I stopped with the buckets of water and decided to offer some 'soft-love!' I cared for him and didn't wanna see him go out like this. Perhaps I loved him-in my own degrading way. He was a kind person. I guess...all drug dealers are!

"LOOK, I sell DRUGS-plain and simple! You knew that when you met me...business is just a little fucked up right now!"

"BUSINESS? This nigga's bout to MURK YO ASS! AN I AIN'T GONNA BE CRYIN-FEELIN SORRY FOR YOU! You knew it was snowin 6 months outta the year but you still chose to sell ice cream-IN THE WINTER TIME! GET IT DUMB ASS? YOU HAD IT COMIN! So if the family fortune goes bankrupt an you starve to fuckin death-ITS ON YOU! And LOOK-every day you wake up not knowing WHERE you'll wind up! Either on easy Street-or in the God-Damned PENITENTIARY! You earn your daily bread fucking up other people's lives! You're a PARASITE-A LEECH livin offa other peoples tragedies! Look at it this way-if a crackhead straightens up and decides to get his life together-YOU GO HUNGRY! If they stop Crackin and fucking themselves up-YOU FUCKED HOMEY! Now what kinda life is that? Let an addict go to detox-you'll pitch a BITCH! Get PISSED off cause you KNOW that 5 dollar bag that USED to get you paid is now putting food in their baby's mouth. And they can finally get BACK all that you stole from them!"

"Bitch I ain't put a gun to a niggers head an tell em to GET HIGH! Who The FUCK you think you JUDGIN? Why you motherfuckers always blamin the little niggers! How about the BIG DOGS getting rich off this shit-WHAT ABOUT THEM? If you see a school of fish bitin the SHIT outta a bigger fish-and that fish is getting the SHIT chewed outta his ass. And then after the majority of the school breaks the fuck out cuz they satisfied and they got THEIRS then you see one last LITTLE tiny motherfucker who is a SMALL part of that Click although not a member in good standing-YOU'D BLAME him!

This POOR LITTLE HUNGRY BASTARD TRIES TO RIP TO SHREDS THE BLOODY CARCASS LEFT BY THE OTHER MORE VORACIOUS GIANT ONES! Your DUMB ASS WOULD PROBABLY BLAME THIS TINY NIGGER FOR ALL THE HARM DONE BY THE SINISTER NETWORK THAT GOT THAT ASS BEFORE HIM! And this tiny guppy motherfucker is just tryin to LIVE! He can't compete with the rest of the big school! They got big chunks-an he just got a tiny morsel! So who'se the real criminal Simone-the bigger legion or the little bastard? Don't say SHIT to me-PREACH THAT SHIT TO SOMEBODY ELSE!"

That's what his MOUTH said! But I could see that inside he new I was RIGHT! And I could see he thought he just said something profound! Hennessy drenched cannabis can do that to a BRAIN-DEAD HUSTLER! But I was NOT impressed!

"So what you gonna DO murder victim?"

"MONIE, what you think I should do?" The bastard was SO humble when his ASS was on fire!

"Boo, I think you should make Vic an offer he can't refuse. Have a heart to heart discussion-just you, him and your Glock 45 to his fuckin head! Tell him if the drugs don't turn up he won't live long enough to make 'de Par-tee at Carni-VAL time!' Make that nigger come clean! Also check out the word on the street. Find out who knows what and do what you gotta do accordingly! Finally Canei you gotta go to Sammy an come clean. Tell him you had delegates takin care of your business and they fucked up! They fucked you but you WON'T fuck him. Ask him to give you time-about a week to bring him either his 2 Keys, the money or Vic's nuts in order to prove your loyalty."

"And stop bein a punk motherfucker! Don't get other niggers to do your dirty work or next time you won't be alive to reap the benefits! And you oughta redeem yourself with Sammy. Put your ass on the line, well it's on the line already, but show him you're a man-with integrity. And when you've proven yourself add a stipulation to the agreement that the moment he's paid you're out of the game-FOR GOOD! Take up a hobby motherfucker-learn a trade! You know-like crocheting?" He didn't answer me-just stood there with his mouth hanging.

"Silence huh? I heard that one before." I kissed him gently. "Hey boo, do you know the Lord's prayer?"

The next day I threw Canei out!

-24-

JUDAS

It was Friday morning on the day after Thanksgiving and I had not heard a word from Canei since that night. One part of me missed him but another emerging ideal told me that he was better off dead. Floyd and I had reconciled, perhaps to fill the empty void left vacant by the worthless one but although some things changed, many things remained the same. And my existence teetered on a desolate path-the one tred by a lost and lonely fraternal twin seeking the comfort of his other half in the dark realms of what mystical pitfalls life brings to us.

I must say I felt happier, more at peace in the presence of Floyd and many of my vindictive aspirations no longer paraded themselves up and down the spine of his contentment. Yet the marauding intruder, the dubious memory of Canei, even now refused to die. Old wounds never heal-they just leave you alone for awhile. Mikki and I sat in my kitchen after a bitterly unfulfilled sisters Prayer Meeting of malevolence and disdain! Both of our lives were so disatisfyingly void that we garnered the necessity for one another's loathsome company. Our loving relatives had forsaken the ideals of our presence for a more imbibing time with others.

The 'Bitter Bitches Forum' went on! A Ghetto Summit of the 2 Stygian Witches for whom the rest of meaningful humanity had no need. Breanna had went away to her father's house and left me alone with my misery-AND Mikki Freedman!

After scrolling through some all too familiar numbers I looked at the speed dial and decided to leave well enough alone. Those digits had spelled tragedy numerous times. Perhaps a few hundred scenarios ago I might've weakened but a dog can only be kicked in the same place by the same 'MASTER' but so many times before it either YIELDS up another part of its anatomy that has not yet been so badly bruised or decides to BOUNCE! Besides-PAIN IS FOR THE BIRDS-AND HE KNOWS HE AIN'T NO BIRD! This oft beaten dog then resigns to another less agonizing canine's haven and nestles down to a NEW tranquility that he so richly deserves!

The Kiss F.M morning show was on. Sombody had just been 'CRANKED' and Talent was promotin a brand new comedy event he was hosting with Capone. As I put down the celly I listened in for the date and time. I could USE some comedy in my life!

"Come on girl, I see you grilling the Nextel. What's up-you gonna call the nigger or what," she inquired?

"Bitch, can I mind my own business while you're mindin YOURS? If I wanna look at my phone, I'll look at my phone! I ain't even thinking about HIM! Now finish your turkey! I raised you not to ask stupid questions with your mouth full!"

"So what about the 21 days?" I hadn't done nothing-WITH NOBODY, for 3 weeks and in my sexual starvation, my moment of weakness, I slipped and told HER nosy ass what I was goin through. Don't get me wrong-Mik was my girl. And I would do anything for her. She was like me in so many ways that often I found myself figuratively talking to another part of me, to my detached projected self when tuned into the wisdom ebbing from the sound of her voice.

In the middle of a conversation I or she would finish the thought invariably shared by the other. Like some telepathic Siamese communication spelled out and etched in stone in reverse. Too bad she was always right! I often felt as though she was one step ahead of me. You know how it is when you try to prove to someone that they don't have a single clue as to what the fuck you're about? Yet constantly with every conversation that person whom you'd like to consider ignorant has a psychic link to any and every dormant ideal in your head. She relayed to me my inevitable actions and inner thoughts as though she previously auto-biographed every aspect of my entire thought process.

I despised Mik for that! Stay outta my mind and don't offer me no 'I told you so' therapeutic advice on nothing that I could just as well fuck up for myself. ESPECIALLY IF YOU'RE RIGHT! Go have a thought sapping séance with somebody else's inner feelings. The two-way lines of communication are shutting down and I'm putting lock and key on my thoughts so stay the Hell outta my head.

Sometimes I felt obligated to put a steel plate on my head and wear it 24/7 for cranial protection because her curious ass was always into everything. Trying to analyze and mind-fuck my emotions. Calculate my reactions and a sturdy left hook was waitin for the bitch if she didn't knock off that Ms. Cleo shit! Fuck it! We could put friendship and sentiment aside for 12 rounds and duke it out! After the smoke cleared and the sirens stopped, the winner could go to the Precinct and the loser would go to the E.R! I knew I could take the 'yella-bone' bitch cuz she got beat the fuck up by that ghetto Puertp Rican bitch from the Bronx! And I had to save her!

Well I guess I shoulda taught my girl how to fight as well as she could psycho-analyze cuz THAT was the ass-whuppin of the Century! Mik's mind-fuck continued.

"Monie, CALL the nigger! You KNOW you want to! I can't just sit here and let you starve to death from pussy-malnutrition. Feed the CAT bitch! Look-your nipples is hard! Just pick up the phone an dial his number! Say ANYTHING-it don't matter! Tell him you ran outta radiation an you can't get the microwave to start working-ANYTHING! Just get the nigger here before I have to watch you commit suicide!"

"I'll KILL somebody ELSE before I take myself out-you know that! Besides, the last suicide I saw was when you let that little Chicano girl from the 'Boogie-down' beat you like you stole something!"

"Why you gotta go there? I was handling mine. Look whose talking. Them young boys whipped YO ASS! I ain't no man-handler like YOU! Psycho!"

Mik was acting strange-why was she so eager for me to call Canei? What did that have to do with HER? I dispatched the thought and kept runnin my mouth. I wanted to see just where the bitch was comin from!

"Uh-EXCUSE ME! Number one my ass was whipped by THREE young-gun Jail-baits. NOT one LITTLE bitch from Mexico! YOU got beat down by a Spanish-speaking Polly-pure-bread and she ain't have no company along with her! Just YO ASS-and Five-foot two, committin HOMICIDE on you!"

"I was handling my shit-you just couldn't wait!"

"You was fuckin up them pink knuckles with your forehead! The bitch Jap-slapped you and you just fell the fuck out! Who gets knocked out by a JAB? You went out like Mark Breland!"

"UH-you getting personal? Why you getting personal-what that got to do with...look you gonna call him or shall I?"

"Why? YOU wanna bone him-FUCK CANEI! I ain't sweatin that nigga! I GOT FLOYD!"

"Simone-you still mad about him bringing a dead white bitch to your crib an fuckin her and her partner in your bed?"

Mikki FUCKED UP!

"WHAT YOU SAY? BITCH! Who the Hell told you THAT?"

That voice-box went DEAD-She didn't say another word! IMMEDIATELY! Bitch got distraught over the hidden confession her babbling tongue had wrought. I had never told her about the other bitch! She had no knowledge of that cuz for some reason I chose not to tell nobody about that but Hattie. I told Hattie never to tell a soul. And I KNOW Hattie never would. And how did she find out the other bitch was in my bed? I never told the bitch THAT EITHER-unless Canei told her. But why would he? So she couldn't know-UNLESS THEY WAS TALKIN-OR SHE WERE THERE!

All of a sudden it all came back to me-everything became crystal clear. I KNEW there was a third person in my house cuz there were 2 glasses. One on the coffee table and one in the kitchen sink. It had dark lipstick on it and at the time I blew it off. Mikki is the ONLY female I know who wears dark lipstick like that but I didn't wanna think of the possibility of betrayal. I couldn't allow myself to conceive it. At first when I thought about it I believed there to be only one woman. But the other glass had red lipstick and I wondered "why would the bitch change her Maybeline mid-stroke? While creepin with another woman's man in their apartment." Now most affairs involve only one party, one ghetto bitch liftin her stinky legs up in the air for some nigger whose got a woman at home. So part of me was still unsure.

But MISS BITCH had just confirmed to me what should've been obvious! The other 'undead' bitch who tried but failed to wipe off the dark brown lipstick from the other glass and hightail it outta my apartment was my best female friend! SHE musta been in Canei's car with him when he drove off! It must've been HER! In fact it HAD to be!

The bitch had fucked my MAN! Who else knew those details cuz I never told her SHIT about where the body was. Was this some mena ge tois? Did Canei fuck her AND the dead bitch? What, did she just sit on the sidelines-AND WATCH? Or did the FUCKIN TRAITOR JUMP IN-AN PARTICIPATE? I looked at the wench who I THOUGHT was my friend-and confidant. And I pictured her-with Canei. Who knows-maybe she WAS fuckin the dead white bitch too! WHAT? WAS MY BEST FRIEND...A LESBIAN? ALL THESE YEARS? That bitch! That BONY LITTLE SLIGHTLY COCK-EYED TRAMP! ON TOP OF MY MAN! That TRAMP-with her knock-knees and PISS-COLORED SKIN and that FLAT ASS! The little ho WITH ONE OF THOSE ROVING BLOODSHOT EYES IN MY FUCKING FACE-PRETENDING TRUSTWORTHINESS, while the other 'GOOD EYE' was riveted unconscionably along the periphery of MY BOYFRIEND!

I never fully trusted those too together anyway because they always seemed to be scheming about some shit. Yet I DID trust them in many ways because I had to FORCE myself to! And whenever I caught those negative vibes-suspicions about my best friend and my man I dispelled them as the jealous folly entertained by the mind of someone reeling in insecurity. I dispelled them and attacked my OWN weakness-my projected feeling of disloyalty I wrongfully attached to the innocent persons very close to my heart. I thought they could be trusted-and so went out of my way to override any psychological warning that often presented itself and made me weary.

Eventually I made myself get used to seeing them together in a guiltless PLATONIC light-one composed of PURE innocence without the natural possibility of sexual undertones. Therefore Canei and Mik were of the SAME sex in my mind-TWO MEN just hanging out! And I'd no sooner expect them of doing the nasty anymore than I'd suspect any OTHER 2 of my male friends to rip off their clothes and go at it in an opposite sex romp in the sack. This is the type of moral justification a normal woman grants her mutual friends-but MY situation was far from normal. And in my desire for contentment, peace of mind and NORMALCY I'd lied to my own better judgement and forced myself into believing in and accepting their presumed innocence. Yet now I stand here looking that bitter truth in the eye as it laughs at me and shouts loudly with a toothy grin "I TOLD YOU SO!"

You know it seemed that sometimes talking to her was just like talking to him. Like they had spent so much quality time together in my absence that a sense of like-mindedness and personality kinship had been engendered-just like the semblances formed between Mikki and myself! Furthermore, only SHE knew I wasn't home that day cuz I had called HER from the jail and instructed her to notify Hattie, Kecia and Kim. And although they often argued, Canei spoke of her highly-as though he truly admired her. And what of all those cat-fights they would have? Were those just staged sound-effects to throw me off and make me think they hated each other-SO THEY COULD SLEEP TOGETHER right under my nose and under my roof? Who would suspect 2 assholes who can't stop dissing one another? Or were the arguments the typical cat and dog power struggles commonplace between 2 people who habitually suck and grind one another out?

How could I be so DUMB? Canei always drove Mik home last when we'd go out when I told his ass not to bother tryin to come over! And they slept together on my couch that night we played spades! OH MY FUCKIN GOD! And the time we fought an I smashed the guppies, the bastard had dark brown lipstick on his collar and scratches on his back. That was the night I told the Fuck to get outta my house an he took my ox-AND MY KEYS! He had gone to Mikki's house and THAT was why I was tryin to take his stupid fuckin head off! I smelled some ass on his goatie and I asked him whose pussy he had eaten! IT WAS HERS! And then, after the fight, I let him get on top of ME! THOSE TWO BITCHES! THOSE WORTHLESS BITCHES WERE BONIN EACH OTHER- FOR I DON'T KNOW HOW LONG!

I felt like a jackass! The donkey with 'dumb-dumb' painted all across my soul and she was the Judas pinning the tail on my gullible misspent trust and mocking me to scorn.

He fucked HER that night and I knew it! Knew it was SOME bitch but didn't know who! Who knows WHAT ELSE they did that night? And I let him drag his tired ass BACK in my apartment to give me sloppy seconds. All this time since I found the dead bitch I've been looking for the other bitch! The one who had the audacity to invade my privacy, disrespect my home and have sex with my man. And Mikki was that demon- that traitor who deserved to die.

I reminisced about the time in the Poconos. Canei had disappeared and said he was by HER house-the fuck slipped up. An SHE told me an Hattie she wasn't feelin up to goin to the Player's Ball. Instead she had ANOTHER pit-stop to make. To climb on top of MY man and take away something that was not rightfully hers to take. I BROKE!

"ANSWER ME BITCH an you BETTER talk fast! Where were you that night in the Poconos? Oh you better think FAST BITCH-BEFORE YOU DIE! You FUCKIN CANEI?"

She had NO time to respond!

"An I TRUSTED you!" I couldn't believe it-an I blessed it! I sanctioned it MAKIN THE NIGGER DRIVE THE BITCH HOME! An I accommodated the shit-lettin them both stay in my house together, when I wasn't home!

I grabbed that little piss-stain up in a choke hold and picked up the broken metal pot I had on the stove.

"Bitch, if you think Polly pure-bread beat your ass, remember-my jab is sharper. AND I WON'T STOP!"

"OH MY GOD! Now you know you don't think I had anything…"

"SHUT THE FUCK UP! SHUT THE FUCK UP! Or I swear I'll crack your fucking spine" I shouted! I had scathing in my voice and a fear littered my eyes that told me I must KILL this traitor, this JUDAS, and live to suffer the consequences! Betrayal is more dangerous than anything-I knew that cuz I had been bitten by that snake before.

At that moment the rainclouds of my mind began to drift. In the kitchen of my small one bedroom apartment my stunted perception began pulling the left-over turkey outta my ears! I came to my senses and suddenly it occurred to me: I had both deceived-and been deceived. I had cheated and been cheated on. NOW I knew what Floyd must have gone through-finding that the love of his life was a permanent fixture totally undedicated, lustful and dirty! But that was another battle-as for THIS thing-THIS ROTTEN PIECE OF SHIT COWERING BENEATH MY GRASP-there was another fate awaiting her. One without the compliment of clemency or a loving God to scoop that ass outta the guiltful fires of my revenge.

Canei was a bastard! A dog! Canine, promiscuous and stupid! And some kinda shit like this could be expected from a nigger of his Caliber! But my GIRL was supposed to be more faithful than that. More devoted to the bond females in various types of dilemma could identify with! That bitch sold me out for a piece of dick! MY DICK-or so I thought! And I would've NEVER did that shit to her!

I had told her all my secrets and there was nothing about me that was in anyway unknown to her. She appeared to be one step ahead of me as I said. And who knows, maybe each time Canei and I had fallen out she musta been right there to pick up the pieces. The 3 of us were inseperable. How many times did I leave them 2 alone? Anywhere from 5 minutes to 6 hours! I wanted to CRACK THE BITCHES RIBS and ram them through her heart. BUT SHE DIDN'T HAVE ONE!

Women often make the mistake of telling their girlfriends intimate things about their man. I had told Mikki about how good Canei was with his dick-game. Well I guess I convinced her and gave the green light for a greedy low-life ho to taste what doesn't belong to her. My fucking GOD! If I had ever come home and seen her skinny legs flying in the air with my man on top beast fuckin her, I'd burn the 2 bastards alive! NEVER TELL ANOTHER WOMAN TOO MUCH OF THE GOOD SHIT ABOUT YOUR MAN! She'll wanna fuck him for herself!

On the other hand never tell her about the problems. His and your failures. What he likes and doesn't like cuz she'll use that information as leverage to blow your man's mind in a way that he'll never forget! She will know exactly how to please him the way he NEEDS to be pleased! It'll also make her the perfect mate for him because she'll know NOT to do certain things that he does NOT LIKE! This will cause him to regard her as the perfect woman in his distorted conceptual world and she will be deified like a sex Goddess who came down from Heaven and saved his trapped soul from the mundane travesty OF YOU!

I wanted to throw Mikki out of the fucking window but the 4 foot drop would not suffice in sending her deceitful soul to HELL! I gave Judas 7 seconds to get the fuck outta my sight-and my life-OR DIE! Then I called Hattie. I must've woke her up cuz her voice sounded weak-and unattentive! I HAD to know for sure!

"Yo Hattie, tell me the truth-did you tell Mik about the other bitch? Or any of the shit I told you?"

"Girl you know I don't play that! Why you wanna…"

Catharsis got on the phone. "Uh, Simone-this you? Hattie can't talk to you right now! She'll call you back tomorrow!" "Click!"

-25-

BLIND BEGGING APOSTLE

I dindn't appreciate the way Catharsis Bogarted Hattie's phone like that-we was talking! The spaghetti-eatin criminal! I had some choice words for the Itralian bully the following day when I called back but Hattie pleaded with me not to make waves.

"Bitch don't start no shit-don't make waves-cuz I can't swim," she warned! Anyway we promised to meet-and talk that Friday night, December 7th at Honeys. Almighty asshole was listening to the conversation and musta gave her the O.K. so Hattie agreed to meet me there at around 11:30 P.M..

"Yo Hattie, what's up with that? That nigger ain't your father an he DAMN SURE AIN'T MINE! So what you askin him for? We goin out-fuck him AND the linguini squad!"

Christmas was comin but money was tight. And the 2 don't exactly go together. Jingle Bells-an poverty! That shit don't even SOUND right! All week long I had been waitin for the bullshit Child Support Check to come in the mail. I would use it to get Breanna's hair done in the 'Brook' if it ever came. Then we would survive for the rest of the week, till the 15th when MY punk check came in order to go food shopping!

I never went for the Christmas bullshit anyway. It's too commercial! Everybody goes broke and stock-holders and large franchises can count on the projected cash flow and BANK on the vast sales revenue to be collected. It's guaranteed! Like death and taxes! You can't get more sure than that. Customers spend! Department Stores business booms. International conglomerates earn 500% profits-while poor Ms. Maybeline Baker, the retired SSI recipient on a fixed income and a tight budget, has to scrape up pennies just to eat! She has over-spent-buying toys and gifts for all her 9 Grandbabies in keeping with the ghetto squalor prevalent during Holiday time. But now she tugs at the gross emaciation which used to be her stomach-vowing not to make the same DUMB mistake next year! So she whips up air-chops and wind-pies on her hot-plate to munch on for dinner till she can go out tomorrow and beg the Church on the corner for a hand-out until the first of next month.

But how do you explain that scenario to a 14 year old mind already corrupted by the diseased blanket of tradition and fallacy? So the mailman finally delivered our long-awaited $146. A bitch can't even wipe her ass fully with $146 every 2 weeks. An they call that Child Support? Whose child can that support? Surely not mine! Maybe a Premie! My daughter eats just as much as I and I gotta finance every ounce of junk-food that she pelts down her throat!

Now what am I supposed to do-tell her to eat up but only every other day? "Oh no! There's not enough food for DAILY consumption so we gotta figure out a schedule. Now on weekends and Holidays you can eat till your malnourished tummy bursts. But

238

remember, we must SKIP a day or so Breanna! Gotta be frugal you know-in good keeping with the dietary restrictions they have prescribed for us.

So Mondays, Wednesdays and Fridays are our fast days. No food Heipher! But on the OTHER days you can gorge yourself! This way by the end of the second week total starvation will not have yet set in! And you'll have enough life left in those long lanky limbs to reach for your favorite box of cereal in the Supermarket before you fall the fuck out! And Bre don't worry about mommy. I'll be on an even stricter diet. Living on a one meal a week basis due to the same budgetary guidelines stunting YOUR growth!

Then when Christmas comes we can have a real feast with bonafide lunch-meat, dried bread crumbs and all the trimmings! To Hell with a Perdue Oven Stuffer Roaster! You ever grilled fish sticks with Ramen Noodles? The noodles are 5 packs for a dollar and fish sticks take on that deep Holiday meaning when based in Duck Sauce. Gee, I can't wait! Finally after the tenement feast is over we can WALK on over to Prospect Park in Brooklyn and use the change to go shopping for a real live Christmas Tree.

Oh yes there was a famine in the land and I could already hear our conjoined stomachs barking out the Yuletide duet of the dead-AS VISIONS OF SUGAR-PLUMS DANCED IN OUR HEADS! So we sat on the train on the way to Brooklyn to get her hair done thinking about what we would eat after I gave the beautician $125 out of our allotted $146. I entertained the thoughts of Bre's juvenile interrogation. Questions like "Mommy how long can a person live off of a hamburger?" Or "if we bought 6 bags of Doritos and a gallon of Kool Aid would we survive till the next Child Support Check?" As we sat there cogitating our dismal fates a blind little man with a cane came stumbling through the train cars shouting about everything the Lord had done for HIM! I WAS SPEECHLESS!

What is this BLIND BEGGING APOSTLE doin looking for handouts on the '4' train? If he had a seat reserved in Heaven I'm sure the Powers that be could arrange adequate means of support or a decent JOB for God's elite righteous Ambassadors to thrive on Earth! It was like watching Moses or Mother Mary rummaging through the garbage cans trying to do for themselves what the Dear Heavenly Father forgot to do!

NOW YOU TELL ME-how could a spokesman for God be on the endangered species list? Sharing the plight of grave starvation with the destitute poverty stricken of East Africa? And what of his pungent odor? Did the Apostle Paul smell like this? Reeking of smoked salmon and soiled flesh throughout the Sacred Biblical Streets of Jerusalem? No wonder they stoned HIS ASS!

The middle-aged black man had a long thin brown cane and a raspy voice that just wouldn't do insofar as earning a decent living as a Gospel Chart-Topper was concerned!

The boisterous rotund spirited buccaneer walked to the center of the car in Stevie Wonder fashion, skillfully evading weary disgruntled straphanger feet like he could see into tomorrow ONLY that which he desired to see! Most of his reluctantly captive audience continued beaming into Daily Newspapers and Harlequin romance Novels as though the Pentecostal Revival had not yet come.

As I pondered on the rancid fate of God's nomadic elect, Breanna put her hand over her nose and said "Ew mom-HE STINKS!" I didn't have a prudent response for the outraged adolescent so I decided to leave well enough alone and place MY hands on my nose too! I gasped!

"MMFH! I know what HE needs for Christmas!"

His feet smelled like Cheetos-WITH EXTRA CHEESE! You know the kind in the red bag known Nationwide for its pungent zesty cheese odor and taste. The blind Apostle from the 'other' car then parked his stinky ass and his belongings and decided to begin a 10 minute long 'Sermon on the Mount' directly where we were standing. And I said to myself "OH DAMN! Now ain't THIS a bitch! Bre we gotta sit through a fiery Apostolic soliloquy from this homeless Holy man armed with a gut wrenching SMELL to punctuate the Divine uncompromising flavor of the Gospel of Jesus Christ!"

And we had Box seats! Them front-row shits that Elvis fans would die for just to get close enough to touch, to hear and to smell "THE KING!" Well the King was not quite stage-ready if you asked me and before he could launch his initial "It Is Written" or "Thus Saith The Lord" intro-I decided to send up a little 'Father forgive me-Lord have mercy' prayer of my own!

"DAMMIT, LORD! It's Christmas time! I'm fucking broke and we're TRYING to get my child's hair done! The ride is long and perilous filled with numerous pitfalls like 2 legged snakes, Gucci clad gorillas and stinky men trying to preach your Word! SHIT! They're all around us! The train car is FILLED with em and we're surrounded on all sides! So PLEASE JESUS (I sounded like the 'CHUCH-FOLK) save me an my child from YOUR child who probably MEANS well but just forgot to bathe this year! Instead he decided to wait until AFTER your Birthday-on December 25th to do it!"

Well I hoped God heard me-and I evoked the same plaintive supplication to Lord Buddha and Allah respectively. Just in case Jesus stepped out for lunch and left them in charge to take 911 calls and collect Divine Healing Fees!

For the next 10 minutes I was subjected to one of the most dynamic episodes of oratory failure and INCOMPETENCE ever attempted in history! Jesus must not have heard a single word cuz if he did I'M SURE he would've run down the stairs of Heaven single-handedly and hailed a taxi back to Earth JUST to stomp a mud-hole in this psychos ASS! And God the Father would've sent some Divine lightning bolts of his own-just to avenge the Gospel Campaign of his only begotten Son!

I'm sure the Heavenly Body Inter-Galactic Recruitment Center must have gotten a nasty letter TOO! A memo directly from the Throne of Glory as to the identity of the fool who hired this unlettered inept proselyte from the back alleys of Christian ghettodom to be a mouthpiece of the Greatest Story Ever Told! The Executive hiring process MUST be thoroughly revamped, audited, scrutinized and only then will a more rigorous screening for Evangelical applicants produce better qualified 'Train Missionaries!'

THIS Nigger fucked up the whole speech! Jumping from Moses to the Apostle Paul. From King David to Don King-then back to the Book of Daniel in a single bound! Now WHAT THE FUCK WAS DON KING DOIN IN THE OLD TESTAMENT? Sellin tickets to the Goliath fight? I COULD NOT UNDERSTAND what in Heaven's name he was talking about! It was not clear-the underlying theme of his corny-ass vagabond message! He was fucking up the game! Defeating a Divine purpose that did not deserve to be undermined or minimized!

My poor daughter shared in my confusion. I could see those perplexed adolescent earlobes STRAIN! Those chinky-eyes wince in the dumbfoundedness commonly born from the blaring sound of absolute bafoonery! Her unripened limited pre-teen capacities tried desperately to keep up with the blind begging Apostle-to separate the value of a disorganized speech from the noisome stench of the unqualified bastard spewing it carelessly throughout the Metropolitan Transit System!

You know its bad enough that you can't preach! O.K, so perhaps you missed your true calling. Maybe he would've been much more adept at a more conventional occupation-like the Butcher, the Baker or the Candlestick-Maker! And that's COOL! Cuz nobody's perfect and I won't tell if YOU don't tell! But homeboy actually thought he was THE SHIT! Like maybe he was THE MAN and HE taught Peter, Paul AND Jesus to preach!

It is obvious that the art of public speaking is not a common skill to be taken lightly. Most people can't talk properly! They can't articulate and unfortunately for the hundred some odd passengers on the train it appeared that earlier that morning the Devil himself had walked into the House of God and snatched the blind begging Apostle from its pews in order to cast this unordained stooge into a pulpit more worthy of his marginal abilities!

After the Sermon came the Altar-call and the blind begging Apostle began offering his lofty hand of healing to the teeming sinful masses.

"Is there ANYONE here who needs prayer? JESUS! My Lord...my Lord!" I thought he was getting the Holy Ghost or something cuz his right hand started to jerk and twitch. And I didn't wanna be too close to inhale the funky aftermath when he began his erratic Pentecostal Holy dance. You ever smell a Demon? DANCING?

No one seemed to find the need of his Spiritual assistance and continued on in their more secularly eventful lives. One passenger, a young white guy in Jeans and a Jersey with a Yankee Baseball cap (he looked like Eminem-AN UGLY VERSION) began yelling out crude obscenities shouting "Fuck YOU Jimbo! How you gonna pray for us-an heal us-when you can't even heal YOURSELF? You BLIND stupid!" Everybody laughed!

Bomani Shuru

The blind begging Apostle was mortified-then he became ENRAGED! Suddenly he abandoned his birth-defected sightless handicap and found the approximate area the vocal culprit was sitting via cane and strong prescription dark Ray Charles glasses! I KNEW this motherfucker wasn't blind! He wasn't handicapped! And the only thing he suffered from was a bad hustle and a lack of soap!

"How you know I was over here, Preach," asked the outspoken white boy? The Apostle drew close and I anticipated an old-fashioned 'fisticuff' was in the making.

"Mommy-they gonna fight?"

"Shhush," I warned! "No idle chatter before the first round!"

The 2 men erupted in an exchange of some of the most foul language I'd had the privilege of hearing all week! It was filled with "Yo Mamma" slurs and racial epithets. They both utilized 4 letter words and some shit I hadn't heard since Junior High! But the blind begging Apostle could not continue. He must've realized that he was rapidly losing Public Sentiment, valuable converts and essential funds! He could not maintain his position in this vulgar display of profanity because time was of the essence and his Transit Ministry jeopardized by this young defiant caucasian!

He then snatched his sharp profane tongue back into his Sanctified mouth-PISSED that he had lost temporary control on a budding white Demon.

"I'm sorry Ladies and Gentlemen! But the Devil is busy trying to upset the Lord's work! Can anyone spare some change...to help me continue...to spread the Gospel?"

"Fucking HYPOCRITE," shouted the Slim-Shady! Go beg Jesus for a REAL job and another hustle! YOU AIN'T BLIND!"

"KISS MY BLACK ASS!"

EW-MY GOD! I covered Bre's ears! Not wanting my innocent adolescent daughter to hear the brutal arguement between this belligerent Disciple of Christ and the loquatious white guy sent by the Prince of Darkness and his hoards to overthrow and usurp the Kingdom of Heaven!

The Apostle, sensing defeat-AND BANKRUPTCY, proceeded to walk through the car-tin cup in hand stretched outwardly to beg monetary redemption he knew would not come! Armageddon was here! He had stood toe-to-toe with Satan's emissary and succeeded only in casting doubt in the collective hearts of these, God's lost Children as to the efficacy and integrity of the 'GOOD NEWS' emanating from his lips!

He looked back at the Demon now sitting and ranting loud and boastfully over his alleged triumph over spiritual fraud! The Bible-toting soldier dug deep into the sanctified pit of himself and hurled the most lethal verbal onslaught he could produce at his snickering attacker. Horror's depiction of Eminem-The infidel who had cost him crucial monies and a good 10 minutes of roadwork! He puffed up his saggy chest-rearing his head back and expelled the most bitter tirade his lungs could hold-AND PRONOUNCE!

"GO TO HELL YOU FUCKING CRACKER! AND SUCK MY BIG BLACK DICK!"

242

TOO LATE-I WASN'T FAST ENOUGH! The sacrilegious venom had boiled and bolted from that blind begging Apostolic mouth at lightning speed and Bre, POOR BRE, had swallowed profane syllable!

With that Prophetic Proclamation of AMAZING GRACE, the outraged Apostle looked up to the vast Heavenlies (actually the grimy ceiling of the train) perhaps in a fervent belated plea for God's Eternal forgiveness-AND A MORE COOPERATIVE AUDIENCE IN THE NEXT CAR! He hoped not to find ANYMORE Caucasian devils awaiting him there! He had faced and held his own against the white rapper-M.C. ANTI-CHRIST! And NOW for the PROMISE LAND! Mount Zion! A land flowing with Milk and Honey, a less economically skeptical crowd and a few extra bucks for his hollow tin-cup! With another hardy "HALELUJAH" the disciple of Christ sauntered his stinky tattered frame onward and in seconds-HE WAS GONE!

-26-

The Book of 'REVELATIONS'

"Yo Hattie, what's wrong? You look like you JUST saw a ghost!"

"Mone, me an the bastard had it out again. He said he changed his mind and he didn't want me to come!"

If I was blessed with an enormous manly stature and a 45 or a thousand Do-or-die Brooklyn soldiers backing me up, I would have bolted outta the door RIGHT THEN and challenged that bitch AND his boys to a God-damned bloodbath!

"Oh, so a bitch can't go OUT now? What the fuck is he on Hattie? I swear you an me are goin to the Precinct TOMORROW to file a report on that ASS! YOU NEED TO LEAVE HIM GIRL!" I was getting loud. Somewhere in the twisted wreckage of these violent domestic circumstances I ventured to believe that at least ONE of Catharsis' boys was RIGHT THERE-IN THE CLUB SPYING ON US! Trying to gather intelligence on the supposition of Hattie's indiscretion cuz THAT'S WHAT INSECURE COWARDS DO! So I SPILLED it-hoping the GREEN EYED asshole would hear JUST what I had to say!

"Tomorrow we goin down to see a friend of mine-to get a hold of something you might need to protect yourself girl. He HIT you?"

Hattie was wringing her hands-looking around. She ALSO knew that we had been followed and didn't want anyone to hear the rebellious shit I was talking about. I looked at her awaiting an answer but her focus was on the 90 some odd patrons surrounding us and partying themselves into an alcoholic binge.

"Hey BITCH, I'm talking-pay attention! Did he HIT you?"

"Oh NO! Nothin like that-NOT THIS TIME," she said still peering through the dim red shadows of Honeys, the Den of Iniquity which we called our second home. "But I don't trust him girl! I'm scared...something might happen!"

"Yeah SOMETHIN'S GONNA HAPPEN ALRIGHT! That ass is goin either to Prison or to HELL!" Hattie didn't wanna talk about it any more. Not right then and my bladder was humming the pee-pee song. As I walked away this guy asked me to dance so I said what the Hell? I didn't come out tonight to waste my time worrying about that domineering Pasta-eatin homo-fucker OR what he thought I would stand by and LET him do to my girl! I have NEVER learned the Arts of fear and cowardice! I wasn't raised to be afraid of what a nigger MIGHT do to me because I AM MALCOLM X! Revived and exhumed and blessed with the indomitable accessory of womanhood! And like Malcolm, I DON'T GIVE A Damn about death! It doesn't scare ME! Its NOT an ominous eventuality one faces when confronted by adversity. Not in 'Da Hood!' Its the PREFERED ALTERNATIVE of the defiant soul when we are attacked by superior opposition! AND MY INVINCIBLE COMBATIVE SPIRIT WOULD NOT LET ME

LAY DOWN AND DIE-NOR SHED A TEAR-TILL MY OPPOSER'S BODY LAY DEAD ON THE BLOOD-SPATTERED SOIL BENEATH MY FEET! So Fuck him! He was a subject I refused to expend another minute on! If he FUCKED UP-CATHARSIS WOULD BE DEAD! And I don't discuss dead people! Especially not when I'm OUT trying to have a good time!

We both half-hazardly dropped the subject and proceeded to enjoy the remainder of the evening. But my mind was so far from being into it. We frolicked through the hollow moments spent by a condemned passion that offers a flicker of humor moments before it dies. The conversation was perfunctory. A problematic dialogue lacking the genuine stamina which once punctuated our closeness. Our words bearing the bleak demeanor of a firing-squad victim inhaling his final pleasurable smoke or the last words chosen by a felon attempting a good joke before facing the Electric Chair. For Hattie, I guess it was difficult to look into bright future prospects availing themselves to you on a Night for new lovers when yet ANOTHER sinister bastard had intentions on taking your life if you dared to be you!

Part of me just wanted to be alone-just to think about things. About my life. Why do lonely and confused women go to the Club for peace and quiet? And since MEN were my number one concern besides Hattie's well-being, why do we go out and surround ourselves with the same shit-heads that we needed time alone to figure out in the first place?

After a few R&B tunes I excused myself from the guy who looked like Kanye West and danced like James Brown to go to the ladies room. I passed Hattie dancing with some loser and whispered "Don't worry-I GOT YOU GIRL," in her ear as I passed by.

In the bathroom I smelled Cologne. Floyd's Cologne! I asked myself what type of woman would wear a man's Cologne-especially MY MAN'S Cologne! I heard some rumbling after the toilet flushed and noticed someone about to come out of the stall. It couldn't have been HIM cuz he was probably home asleep after working 16 hours! And what would a MAN be doin in the Ladies Room anyway? I never gave up the secret location of where we was goin tonight so HE COULD NOT BE HERE!

When the bathroom stall flew open I shitted on myself (well just slightly-a quarter of a tinkle) as I beheld a somewhat tall brown-skinned curvaceous woman with auburn streaked hair. SHE LOOKED LIKE ME! Damn-I LOOK GOOD! The chic was very very attractive! I mean she looked GOOD and I admired her and her style of dress. And I wondered, "What's a fine bitch like THAT doin in a place like THIS? In the bathroom smellin like MY man's Cologne?"

Well I dispatched the fleeting paranoia-TEMPORARILY! Now let me RE-EMPHASIZE, I'm not gay or anything! I'd risk MY LIFE for a hot 5 minutes alone with a GOOD MAN! But you know-if I WERE a lesbian, THIS is the kinda bitch I'd be attracted to! To do-WHATEVER THE FUCK FAG-BITCHES DO! She had it goin on and if I were a dyke I'd fuck her on SIGHT and marry her without hesitation! But I'm

NOT a fag-and I'd NEVER lick another woman's vagina! Besides, I can't stand the sight of my OWN so why the Hell would I want to eat somebody else's?

But I got a strange feelin in the core of myself that there was something about her that I wouldn't like. I stared unabashedly and she stared back. When she went for the mirror I forsook my excretal bowel movement. HEY! Some had already leaked out anyway and I was 'Mother Shit-stain!' Playin it off as though I HADN'T DEFECATED on myself! As though I was a 'NORMAL' party-goer with a whole lotta class and no bowel control impairment! (little did THEY know)

I struck up a trivial conversation with this chic seeking desperately to investigate the origin of her manly familiar scent. Now I KNOW that there must be much more than one bottle of 'REMEDY' Cologne in the Universe. Yet pardon my French but I FUCKIN HAD TO KNOW! And this bitch, THIS FINE BITCH, had BETTER not've come within 10 feet of MY MAN!

She said that she was glad to have finally gotten to see this place cuz her boyfriend had told her so much about it. Before I could ask another question she stated that she'd love to stay and chat but didn't wanna leave him alone out on the dance floor surrounded by all those low-lifes! DAMN! I wanted to demand of her the truth-SO I DID!

"So who's your man?" I couldn't help it! Cancer's are often blunt and a vague charade was not the order of the day!

"Oh, he's out there," she answered somewhat annoyed. As though she were the Secret Serviceman or Public Relations Manager trying to obscure a hidden affair from the wife of a philandering Congressman. I wanted to explode! I FELT something! But I couldn't define the badgering intuition-the eerie nature of what I was alluding to-of what I feared! So I FOLLOWED the bitch!

She almost lost me-and she was good! Plying through the crowd like a Terrorist who'd planted some shit he did NOT want to be captured for! Like he stole the Presidential condoms or procured the Judiciary toilet tissue on chili-night down at the Halls of Justice!

When she got to the R&B floor I was directly behind her. That sexy ho better NOT be with my man! Coincidence AIN'T NO JOKE! Yet frankly to ME it don't exist! There is a reason for EVERYTHING! And what fools often deem a 'coincidence' offtimes inevitably turns out to be the fruition of 'fate!' The moment I saw who she was walking up to, who she was hugging and caressing, a small but essential part of me died! If I remember correctly someone in the past once told me that that very tiny essence of the human self is known as 'THE HEART!'

When you FUCK people over and the shit comes back on you it's 10 fold! It's brutal! God makes it his business to allow the person you've 'shitted on' to be there to witness your eminent downfall. You curse and pray hollow supplications in a thousand directions simultaneously but no force in the Universe can stop the languishing pain. Or stop the gluttonous pig from bleeding out the agony and devotion he stole like a parasite from the somebody he said he loved.

A drunken binge cannot help you now because they haven't invented enough alcohol to quench THAT pain! Fifty pounds of Crack cocaine can't do it! Five thousand dicks and 10,000 balls shoved up your ass at lightning speed won't stop you till you have suffered just as much if not more than the murder victim of your OWN infidelity!! You try to slay the dragon of despair-but you can't kill a beast that you've created, nurtured and extoled! And you cannot atone for with self pity the foul shit that you once did-and bragged about!

I used to step on Floyd's ego like the proverbial placemat-designed to take the punishment of unsympathetic feet! He was my 'Vic!' My footstool! Yet somewhere God must have gotten sick of seeing his child perpetually devastated by the hateful rivalry of another sibling.

The woman led Floyd by the hand past the bar and into the Reggae room. I could see the way she smiled at him. You could feel the respect, the unconditional obeisance emitted from her eyes in a stare relative to the homage paid to a higher power by a fervent devotee. As she led 'GOD' by the hand into what could be deemed a seductive crawlspace between Heaven and Hell, the utter pinnacle of irony swiped me across the face prompting tears that would not stop.

THIS was the nigger I perpetually wiped my ASS with-being treated by another with respect. In her honor for him I could see the death of me-of what I represented to him in the past. Her caresses tortured my soundness of mind. Her gentle whispers bludgeoned the resonant calm I used to have. And when her eyes and gestures said I love you to the vile monster whose esteem I boasted of killing, I wanted to lay down in defeat to escape that mental Hell in the quietness of my grave.

THOSE WHO FUCK-GET FUCKED IN RETURN! Sometimes HARDER! I ran into the Reggae room-I don't know what the Hell for! Maybe I thought I could wrestle my hurtful eloping Prince back into the arms of the tragedy that destroyed him. Mental notes erupted in me-erasing themselves as I sought an answer to the dilemma these panic-ridden feet were leading me to. But I couldn't compete with this Cinderella bitch! This Fairy God-mother that was doing for Floyd what I should have done from the beginning! It had taken me almost a year in order to discover the true price of the scintillating diamond I had besmirched and smudged in the muddy waters of neglect. I WANTED MY FUCKING DIAMOND BACK! I wanted to pick it up, clean it off and cherish it to my heart from here to eternity! DON'T TAKE SHIT FOR GRANTED!

But the fairy God-mother had taken my JOB! By the time I got to them, arms flailing and mouth hanging, I tried to articulate in a blaring and hushed silence what it should not have taken me so long to say. "Hey Floyd, wait-IT'S ME! YOUR BOO! The one who rejected you and treated you as though you were LESS than a man! Don't you recognize me! Hey, come back and take some more of this highly pressurized domestic psychological violence! Why would you want to move on to the loving arms of THAT bitch when you could come back to all the shit I got lined up!

They saw me coming! I didn't know WHAT THE HELL I was doing but I HAD to try SOMETHING! Nobody looses all the gold in Fort Knox and sits idly by watching it happen! It would be wiser to defend your male Earthly treasure and offer some brutal resistance against that which seeks to casually take your life! One might justifiably offer up a strong argument, a hand-grenade, an expendable body part-ANYTHING to save that which is dearest from the more worthy clutches of another!

TOO LATE BITCH! Your man ain't the feeble useless rodent you made him out to be! Some OTHER woman with a higher social I.Q. and a keener look for male potential has taken over. One with an Eagle's eye view for finding and re-upholstering the shit that YOU errantly threw away into the junkyard! And THIS new woman is on a mission to UNDO and repair the psychological damage I had meted out against Floyd! CUZ HE LOOKED HAPPY-truly complacent! WITHOUT ME!

I shouted out his name in a voice GEORGE WASHINGTON probably heard and just stood there, like CARRIE, dazed and wide-eyed with pig's blood spattered all over her once immaculate Prom dress! You know its funny how some things can go from good to bad in the twinkling of an eye. Just 45 minutes ago I was the dainty frolicking bitch playing hop-scotch on my man's dreams while getting pipe for days in a winter-wonderland of selfish lust and debauchery. I had it made and thought I was the Motherfucking BOMB-a Societal Diva devouring hand-picked grapes from the Forbidden Tree of everlasting sexual satisfaction! I had LIVED that life and there was NOTHING ANYBODY could do about it! CERTAINLY NOT FLOYD!

But NOW, JUST LIKE THAT, I WAS CARRIE! The zombiefied crimson virgin! The Prom Queen from Hell! I was humiliated-and it was the blood of my own cruelty splattered all over my two-faced hypocrisy. All over the lily-white prison-fatigues of my sins against a man guilty of NOTHING-but loving me!

How could a woman expect a man to be more virtuous in a relationship than she's willing to be herself? And WHY in Hell would she crucify-denounce and condemn him for being more devoted to her welfare than she could ever be herself? THAT'S a profound irony that STILL haunts me to this day. And I could not look to him with remorse for finally crawling up out of the rock and choosing a life with someone who'd recognize the good in him? I could not DARE point the finger of Judgement labeling him a cheater because in escaping my treachery he had salvaged his life. And when one refuses to be violated again and again on a perpetual and daily basis that person may in NO WISE be labeled a cheater. It was I who sent him on a journey to that land! And it was I, me, who left him no CHOICE but to go!

Yeah, this was the ghetto re-run of the psycho-thriller 'CARRIE' Starring Sissy Spacek but Sissy sat this one out and I was playing the role BETTER than her! I could hear the jeers from the hysterical crowd shoving guilt and dehumanization down my lecherous throat! Siphoning my esteem! "They're All Gonna Laugh At You!" "THEY'RE ALL GONNA LAUGH AT YOU!"

My heart felt like gel and my vocals were latched chunks of flesh designed to articulate to Floyd, too late, the sincerest utterances of my imperfections! But I could not speak! I could not tell no more lies! The truth of my fanatic deception and unique love for him floated just below the icy waters of what was transpiring before me. (The loss of my Diamond) But the human voice-box cannot utter an audible sound when trapped beneath frosty solidified ice! I was drowning! 'Carrie' was in full ghetto effect taking her plasmic shower in the Hood and my gleeful shining diamond was floating away into the receptive grasp of a Fairy God-Mother with a hard-on for poetic justice and all the wonderful things my man could offer her!

After I shouted his name the 2 young lovers, astonished, looked back at me like a formerly dying Cancer patient glares back at the terminal disease from which he has now been cured! And the agonizing components of life which tortured and plagued him unmercifully during his perilous past. They stared at me with overt feelings of shock, abasement and jest! As though I was dressed as the Easter Bunny at a Christmas Party! I wished I WERE a rabbit so that I could hop off into the sunset, fresh carrot in hand and cut my own fucking throat enroute to a suicidal bunnies dismal after-life!

All my games, all my infidelity, all the lies and insatiable desires to have much more than just one had earned me THIS! A First-Class seat on the fool's freight train of lost love and squandered time. I could feel the donkey ears emanating from both sides of my forehead and I surmised that everybody in that dark huddled room noticed the Jackass-standing there like a fucking marauding Gorilla peering at the lovely new couple stunned and mortified by his unsavory appearance!

Floyd looked into the eyes of his new Bride, one hand around her waistline and another tenderly touching her cheek and he whispered something in her ear. She then looked back at me with a cold sarcastic smirk and turned back toward her dedicated Husband-the BEST FUCKING MAN IN THE WORLD! The ONLY one on the planet that mattered! The one I had carelessly offered her on a Silver Platter!

The 2 paramours began to walk away from me-who wants the repulsive company of a loud and bloody 'Carrie' ruining a wonderful night of heated romance? Fairy God-Mother peered back at my cadaver once more. Maybe she remembered me from the Ladies Room or perhaps it was her feminine way of saying 'thank you' for the once in a lifetime treasure that I blew.

Imagination is unkind! Memories can be brutal! And both imagination and memories commenced to beating my defeat into the ground! Stomping craters all over my senses with horrific detailed scenes of what Floyd would do to his newly appointed Queen later on that night! And just as savage were the thoughts of what the Fairy God-mother would give to 'Carrie's' ex-man in return. I didn't want to live anymore! To see, to feel, to remember the Heaven I lost that moment in the Reggae room!

In times past that room spelled the quenching of my lust-the answer to my prayers! There were numerous experiences I've had with strangers I had never SEEN before! I could have any man I wanted in there, except Floyd! He had BEGGED me to bring him to this unknown mystery Night Club where me an the girls spent countless grinding nights WITHOUT HIM! But "HELL NO" was the best response he could get out of me as I rushed my 'Make-up Masterpiece' time after time to get outta the house and AWAY from him!

Yet tonight he was summarily crowned 'King Of The Reggae Room!' And I was its Court Jester! Doing acrobatic emotional flips. Somersaulting and careening my bombastic way into THIS-fools Paradise! I have never since set foot back in that God-forsaken Room again! I would commit suicide at the very remote inkling of the pain I endured when I lost my man! Funny, almost every night of my life I went out whoring and groping for an ecstasy-a euphoria, a spouse that was already there. Providence had previously granted me what I had been running from-what I continued looking for!

Life has been snatched from right beneath my feet! This was December 9th-the day I died symbolically on a fucking dance floor! But my lungs were still going through the monotonous motions of inhaling and exhaling to prolong a demise that had already been established. I couldn't eat! I wanted to die! Everybody has an idea of how it feels when you KNOW that somebody else is 'WORKIN' your Gem! I'm not talking about a mere sexual thing because that word 'SEX' is an eyesore that is rapidly fading from my vocabulary. But when you know that someone has graciously gained from YOUR loss the pain is as intense as one might expect to be found in the agony felt from drawing too dangerously close to the SUN! It is a torment that is fierce, tormenting AND can be FATAL!

This tragedy was a wake-up call! An appeal to my higher senses of femininity. I wanted to change and become the woman I was MEANT to be-and no longer the deviant debutante that I was. I had given promiscuousness 10,000% of myself! Thus chastity would have a right to at least equal consideration! Everything slowly began to become crystal-clear. No, I was not thoroughly purged. Not totally cleansed from various moral lapses toward foolishness-BUT I WAS ON MY WAY! All that I needed was a little push toward the 'NEW TESTAMENT' of my being! And essentially my previous mistakes were gradually ebbing toward the void of non-existence!

You know it hurts! When a child is ill although he THINKS he knows what's best for him, his continuance depends on the parental intervention of the 2 people who created him. He just doesn't know any better although he thinks he does. It's hard-and somewhere between dilemma and much sought after peace he must chose to perpetuate his ignorance (an ignorance which could cost him his young life) or to embrace the bitter tonic of wisdom-the instruction offered by those same loving parents who seek his convalescence. He must TRY-OR SUFFER! There are no other ways about it! Well I was that child-staggered and suffering in the wake of my own misdeeds. And the loving parent represented a belated sense of intuitive instruction and self-discipline-the conjoined motivators which must be present in the minds of anyone brave enough to live beyond tragedy.

I could no longer survive THIS way-this old self-absorbed and self-defeating lifestyle which committed me to a livelihood of pain fostered by an irrepressible desire for stimulation. I WOULD NO LONGER LIVE LIKE THIS AND DID NOT FURTHER INTEND TO TRY! I was a Warrior! A SOLDIER-and Soldiers recover from their wounds or they will DIE from them! That's how I had come this far! And I refused to be laid to rest adjacent to the crucial part of me that had then surrendered to emotional manslaughter.

I looked back once more at the dreadful path which had led my weary soul into the blinding light of now. I saw a young innocent woman caught up in the treachery and indiscretion of her selfish ways. Then I saw a man desperately befuddled by a love for her. And beside his anguish was an inevitable situation which had turned circumstances against her in the hopes that she would run away from the whore-mongering that justified and served her waywardness. It nourished her sexual zeal to stave off broken-heartedness as she plunged toward a path of her own dignity's suicide.

I was always taught by my Christian father to seek forgiveness from those you've wronged. One can't be truly happy in life without first being exonerated from crimes against humanity. Moreover happiness cannot live in a house corrupted and tainted by self-abhorrence or transgressions against others. So I'm grabbing apology's broom and sweeping and cleaning out my house. And when this process is over I MIGHT be able to accommodate the seemingly eternally lost ideal of inner peace.

I picked up my cell phone and dialed Floyd's number-knowing that he had not yet reached home.

"Floyd, I'm sorry for all the hurt I've caused you. And I know tonight is not your fault! Baby, those 2 words 'I'm sorry' can never eliminate the pain you've faced from me in the past but I was always taught to seek forgiveness from those I've wronged. Perhaps its not enough and I won't blame you for never speaking to me again. If you do, I'll be here to ALWAYS love you and the biggest mistake I've ever made was not to become your bride. Take care love-you were,...you ARE, my happiness!"

I could not bare to hang up the phone, to end that painful chapter of my life. So I just put the cell phone down and let my tears hang up on what we had. From that day on I've never heard from my diamond again!

I tell myself "don't be ashamed to cry girl! JESUS DID IT-and it's as natural as breathing!" I asked Floyd from my heart to forgive me for being blind and I have asked God to forgive me for my undeniable foolishness. Intentional blindness and foolishness are not just crimes against humanity-THEY ARE CRIMES AGAINST SELF!

You know I used to point a convictive finger at Floyd for being DUMB enough to still be in love with me! To still want me and remain faithful after all the shit I put him

Bomani Shuru

through. I labeled him the lovesick ape not smart enough to spurn the proverbial banana daily causing a Cancer to decay his soul because he KNEW what went on-but loved me just the same. I remembered telling him how much dicks he sucked whenever he kissed me cuz some other nigger's semenal residue was cussing his gullible ass out! Screaming: "I HAD YOUR WOMAN LAST NIGHT!" But look at me NOW! Now I would STILL take him back-EVEN AFTER THIS! And I TOO am that ape! Still love-sick and sorry enough to be PRAYING that he'll change his mind, put away his new HEAVEN and come back to me!

The very next day I lay alone in my bed with the lights out. When I looked out the window at the rain I equated the steady downpour to the tears of the Creator. Tears for a disobedient and morally weak Mankind whom he had brought into existence. He looks at the way we smite and maltreat one another-with the same tortured perplexity that a parent would have when one of his children recklessly hurts and exploits another. "God can't be smiling," I thought! "Not while beholding the death of yet ANOTHER of his Earthly offspring!" I had been crucified on the cross of infidelity and forced to re-read the 'Cheaters Manual' which I bore in promiscuity yet forgot the hidden meaning of. THINGS HAPPEN! Evil and wrongdoing recur-they find you like a vindictive boomerang. The heartless bullshit you hurled callously at those you should have been loving can only return, shattering your heart from the blighted entranceway located in the crack of your ASS!

I've hurled a whole lotta shit my dear and devoted lover's way through the year but TODAY IS KARMA! The taboo that returns to a fool when it has nowhere else to go-no one else to destroy! Invariably it must travel the Earth's circumference to YIELD BACK to it's sender that hurt which we forced on those we found so unimportant! The World's cyclical axis rotates from point 'A' through the entire Alphabet and back to where it initially started. There is a highly pressurized velocity whose momentum both sends and receives; pulsates and ebbs; violates and is violated! It attacks AND IS ATTACKED! FAITHFULLY! And fate never falters! It cannot help but to retract after the constriction of circumstances and mankind's careless oversights are caught in the middle of a chain reactive Domino Effect of "WHAT GOES AROUND-COMES AROUND!"

Well it came! Right back at me and I got it WORSE than he did! The lanky portion of manure that I despised throughout our years eternity had been found by someone whose truly appraised his worth. Harlem-world's warty toad had found a home in the hand of a woman who loves him and his long sought after throne has been erected on my gravesite. Where the OLD SIMONE SINGLETON was laid to rest by a dejected 'Rags to Riches' variable that has cost her her life!

Can a person die more than once-cuz if not then will somebody tell God that he already took a sister's life so there's no need for those bastards in Heaven to prepare a table for the lost soul they've already got. Well my answer came swiftly. First there was the shit with Mik and Canei. And THAT pain is one that will take forever to heal. She

252

was my FRIEND-MY BEST FRIEND BESIDE HATTIE. An Canei was my man-or so I thought. Now I'd come to a focal stage in my life where the meaning of happiness and inner peace would never be the same because through my insatiable lust for sex, I had driven away my most faithful partner. I'd lost Floyd only to have rediscovered him in the loving arms of someone who had seen in him what I could not find!

I left the house at 9:00 P.M. noting that I had put my girl Hattie off. We were supposed to go to the Precinct to file a report and seek an Order of Protection against Catharsis. She swore to me the last time I saw her that she would dump him if I could garner the Order. Then we'd use it as leverage in case he tried something. You gotta have records of shit like domestic abuse but up till now Hattie insisted not to. But she seemed hopeful in this her new quest for freedom-and the removal of a bastard that put his hands on her whenever he got the chance.

That night at Honeys also spelled the first time either I or she had vocally made a threat to him or his constituents. I had raged and foamed at the mouth about how we would go to the Cops! We'd set out TOMORROW to tell somebody with a gun and a Badge and firm steel bars to incarcerate career felons just like HIM all, about his assaultive battery. Well 'TOMMOROW' was 'TODAY' and there was a Police Report that needed to be filed. EXPEDITIOUSLY! And me and Hattie were the 2 plaintiffs who were gonna set it off!

My mind fought back the tears-swallowing them in unrequited love's aftermath. And the swirling mental anguish was clearing-slowly ebbing back to normalcy from the psychological ramrod of what I'd learned about Floyd only yesterday. I was optimistic and looked forward to spending some quality time with my girl-the only friend I had left and helping her out with HER situation.

I went to Hattie's house after several attempts to reach her via cell phone. She didn't answer! She wasn't at work either cuz I called the Beauty Parlor and Cosmo, her boss, said he hadn't seen her-but if I saw her first "Tell the FAG he's fired!" Of course he wasn't serious but Hattie NEVER missed work without at least calling in! That wasn't like her. Earlier that day when she'd Text Messaged me she was telling me something about Catharsis but she had to interrupt the message cuz he was coming outta the shower-drunk and DICK HARD!

"Sorry Monie, I gotta go-talk to you later…" AND THAT WAS ALL!

There was a small white gold locket that Catharsis gave her and she loved it. She said it reminded her of something her mother had given her when she was 7. It was a pendant and inside was a photo of Hattie and her mother with the words inscribed on the back "You Are My Everything." This she cherished and wore every day for over 5 years. One day at school she looked in her locker to discover it missing. She had taken it off during swimming lessons but someone had over-estimated its sentimental value and stolen it.

Hattie ran home that day hysterical to inform her mother about what had happened to the pendant but by the time she got there she was too late. Tragedy had beaten the teary eyed 12 year old home-AND MOMMY, the only one in the world who loved her-was dead. Hattie did not take this bitter coincidence well and the loss of her pendant and the subsequent death of her mother sent her into depression. Also mysterious were the circumstances surrounding the trauma. On the day Hattie's mother had given her the pendant she said "Baby this is a gift from me to you. Its part of me-but I won't always be here with you. And when that day comes it will help you to get through the hard times." It was as though her mother had foreseen it-and given Hattie the pendant to remember her by. It was also then that Hattie began to lose herself.

She became confused and disillusioned. Feeling a guilt that told her she was somehow responsible for the death of her beloved. The one in whom Hattie trusted and wanted to be like-tall, slender and wonderful. Several months after the funeral Hattie's entire male psyche underwent a drastic traumatic change. Her heart, the guilt, the young boyish mass of confusion and low-esteem erupted into the 'Her' that she had now become. A fearful child having lost his female parent; his identity and his waning masculinity behind the tragic passing of his mother. What does a young boy do when he loses that special male part of himself and grows up realizing that he lacks what it takes to be a man? Easy! He transforms into a beautiful young woman-thus modifying his inefficiencies into a mold more adaptable and receptive to physical constraints and weaknesses. The male persona must be strong and self-motivating. Independent! Its female counterpart does not!

After that Hattie went to live with her uncle. But the man who moved in was not exactly the same 'person' who evolved and a few years later moved out! The locket from Catharsis contained a picture of Hattie and myself taken about 15 years ago. We were hugging one another at the ages of 17 and 18 during a Thanksgiving Day celebration at my parent's house. Hattie and her uncle, now her Foster Parent, had been invited over but as expected Uncle Jesse just drove up, dropped his effeminate outcast nephew on our doorstep and drove off. But the joys of the Holiday were salvaged by the genuine feeling of family-life she experienced in my home welcomed kindly by my adoring parents. This proved to be the best Thanksgiving she ever had she later confided to me; therefore, she preserved the locket in the same heightened manner of respect as she had done with the lost pendant she received from her mother.

When I got to the house the door was open and as I went in I saw what looked like an apartment that had been hit by a tornado. The entire place was trashed! Lamps broken, glass shattered-EVERYTHING! The 27 inch color T.V. was on the floor SMASHED! The wreckage resembled the final scene of a struggle. A violent desperate struggle! The type evoked when one is fighting for his or her life!

I could hear screams! Hattie's screams-taunting my head and ransacking the turbulent echoes of themselves. A frightened confused woman going through it all-alone and in love with the Devil's Son! He would punch her! The fury of his temper had peeked out from our worst fears retelling to us this significant story of what it might become. What life with Catharsis might entail.

As I stepped over the twisted garden of things once dear to her my mind blared out an ignorance we shared in fate. Four hundred bitches we had watched whose lives came to this spoke into my mind with deep pitiful lamentations. Like a Mass-Choir of the dead chanting Hymns of the perils that brought them there. Their destitute Psalms rose from blood-soaked walls testifying of how truly tragic existence could become living as a victim-beaten at the hands of a sadist who pummels his other half into a whelped-up heap of tears.

Why do men beat women? Perhaps I should ask the Devil that question when I see him. What type of answer might I expect from one disposed to domestic butchery and the scarring it presents. Perhaps he might tell me a story in a sit-down with words designed to justify and soothe the nightmare. The bad dream where predatory male boots stomp the life and profundity out of its helpless woman's esteem!

She cannot hide! For the system is merciless within it's vast network lacking Civil protection for the needy and after each brutal episode she comes closer to the reality that survival is at best minimal and must be meted out sparingly. Available only to the Chosen few! Some women will survive-and escape it! Yet even more WILL DIE! She will run every 24 hours of her battered life to Shelters, homes for domestic violence and Sanctuaries but all will fail inherently to salve the love-wounds. And for all the Bureaucratic structured prisons of proposed safety the vicious maurader with surveillant spyware finds it's way back to it's prey. The monster hones in-laying outside the tenement. By the door, under the stairwell, on the roof or in the School-yard. Just waiting! To catch up and avail himself of the 'Punching-bag' he missed out on when she ran for her life!

I don't think I wanted to continue prying through the wreckage of Hattie's tiny apartment-of her life. But friendship ordered persistence and guided unsteady feet onward into the bedroom to find out exactly what happened to the woman whose life I felt compelled to snatch out of harms way!

I could see blood-under the door! Waiting for me to let myself into what I knew had transpired. My hands were shaking and I began to mumble-sobbing aloud in words only the destitute could understand.

"M-mmm-mh...!"

I slowly opened the door-like a child rapt with Boogeyman stories afraid to go into the dark bathroom at night. A little girl-fearful to see mommy in the brutal aftermath of the war of words with a daddy who swore to kill her. The little girl knows of the fights and the noise common when terrified mommy is yelling at the unmerciful force that thwarts fruitless attempts to defend herself. She has recanted the scene of a drunken father kicking down at her mother and the sounds wrap an iron cord of defiance around her gaze-not letting her run from the sight that she's been primed for. It won't let her escape seeing it.

Momma said "I love you" last night in words that could not describe the fear of the moment. This was good-bye! Hattie said "I love you girl" last night in a telephone conversation that distances the presence of an eternal friend. Warning loved ones of what they fear will become of them. The words are soft and subtle but the reality is the same. There is a formidable behemoth that allows domestic violence victims no rest! And if you listen closely you can hear it. The teeming breath of that treacherous foaming beast! The one who torments and takes lives unfit for pain and death in the quiet wake of what we all saw yet never lifted an intrepid finger to prevent.

When the door of my mind was opened to me I could see pictures of what my blurred eyes chose not to stare at. Some blood, a broken wine bottle-and a limb hanging off the bed. My eyes, my REAL EYES, DID NOT SEE IT! But faith in the damned and constructive logic painted a vivid picture for my blighted intelligence to latch onto. And when I saw my girl laying there on the bed I carefully closed the door of my regrets-and reluctantly staggered back to the depleted catastrophe of the remainder of my life.

Anyone who has ever experienced the loss of a loved-one, I mean a truly LOVED-one who will be deeply missed, can understand the extreme pain it brings. This trauma is indescribable and brutal. Something NO HUMAN BEING is designed to withstand. That evening the world as I new it was bludgeoned by this all too familiar deviation from happiness and contentment yet SOMEHOW I sensed its looming presence. My unheeded intuitions had honed in on that unveiling omen, had seen its snarling head sitting atop and crushing the life of the conjoined dreams that myself and Hattie had dared to envision.

When one detects catastrophe leering in the hidden cracks of fulfillment there is a cold and terrible feeling of death that presents itself-stifling hopes light. When one is abducted by the Devil or casts his or her glare upon the filthy train, the wicked scaley haunches of the Chief Serpent ruling Hell, our mortality shudders. God never intended for his beloved mankind, for humanity's weakness to behold such raw powerful evil and live to tell.

Hattie had witnessed the beast. The unholy one composed of unadulterated venom! Its dark leathery diabolical wingspan riveted and raging girth hunched over the helpless mass of a doomed and desperate soul. And when she spat upon the Great Red Dragon, striving to rid herself of it before the sadistic end the creature had in store for her, Hattie's heart was ripped out of its breast and cast down into seething flames that will never die. I dwelled within that heart. My life lingering upon the furtherance of every drumbeat. And Hell became a more fiery grave as we breathed the final exhaled rhythm of what friendships seek to steer themselves from. The Eternal damnation…of separation.

She had been mutilated! Sodomized with a blunt protruding object impaled from her mouth. And her throat had been cut! The chain, the pendant that Catharsis had given her, was still lodged around her neck draped in blood-and the picture had been removed.

The Coroner had a hard time determining the true cause of death due to the amount of bludgeoning she had suffered before dying. YES! She suffered! At first it was suspected that she was beaten to death because her skin had been lacerated and bruised so badly that the Forensic Scientists speculated massive internal trauma.

There were 2 particularly severe blows that could have caused this. The one to the right side of the head. A deep gash in her temple perhaps caused by a heavy blunt object and the surgically precise slashing of the throat! It was a masterful job, the Autopsy Report noted. A wound that allowed its recipient to suffer the maximum amount of strangulation-of prolonged asphyxiation before dying! Who ever had done this had wanted her to suffer for awhile before succumbing to the blood slowly ebbing into her lungs. Meager pockets of air could be extricated in a futile quest for the furtherance of being. A few last moments of respite until the crimson deluge finally inundated her pulmonary cavity. And once this took place-those last few fleeting breathes would be replaced by a tidal-wave of plasma and stifling-and unconsciousness!

The gash to the temple was just as detrimental because its sheer momentum jarred the skull and sent bone fragments into the cerebrum. This violent shockwave caused a slow trickling edema which would result in acute pain in that region. It was designed also to render its victim intense agony, gradual brain-swelling and eventual death! Death would be eminent for the injured as the brain ultimately drowned in its own hemorrhaging and the aqueous humor cascading into the cerebral cavity would bring an end within just a matter of time.

The guy at the crime scene made a joke that he didn't know if the person responsible for this fatality deserved death by lethal injection or a Nobel Peace Prize!

"Is this guy a Serial Killer or a Master Surgeon? A brutal psychotic beast or an artistic genius imbibed in the misfortunate details of his slaughterous duties." That little white motherfucker found that funny! I wanted to grab the broken bottle at the crime scene and ram it up his stumpy cackling ass!

"Laugh NOW bitch! NO! Pull the glass shards from between your pockets first-THEN LAUGH!" I think I remember spitting at him and cussing him out. "Oh you think this shit is FUNNY? What kind of man are you? You little IGOR BASTARD! You think this shit is FUNNY?

The object sticking out of Hattie's mouth was the worst case of human mutilation I had ever seen! I was nauseas! There was a metal rod protruding out of her throat that had ruptured her windpipe! They said it had to have happened post mortem (I think that meant after she died) and I thanked God! No FUCKIN body deserved to die like that! I can't imagine the terror! The way the mouth and trachea had twisted and the angle of the body suggested that this vicious impaling had been done to an inanimate nonbreathing corpse. Like to add insult to injury!

I was stunned! I thought I had seen some shit in my day! As much as I had been through! But NOTHING…could have prepared me for the world that opened up to me behind that door!

You know a person can experience life to the fullest. See some shit like the dumb white bitch on T.V. about to die screaming screams and thinking thoughts and having ideas too late! Like "OH SHIT! THIS MOTHERFUCKER'S ACTUALLY TRYING TO KILL ME!" She realizes this 30 years AFTER the first ass-whippin! And so there she is- on her Anniversary of pain trying to pull the bloody hatchet out from the back of her head! Or a woman decides one day that she's had enough and marches downtown to the Precinct with a spear thrust through her back that has burst completely out of the other side of her body! NOW she decides to file a Complaint!

"Hey Officer! Cmere! Just LOOK what this motherfucker did to me! OH DAMN! And I had Choir rehearsal tonight! Now this is the 5th time this month! And honestly-the SHIT'S GETTING TIRED! You think its time for me to leave? Oh wait a minute-don't answer yet! First help me get this FUCKIN thing out of my chest!"

I mean we go through shit! Sometimes because we love him. Sometimes because we don't have nowhere else to turn-OR SO WE THINK! Sometimes because we want it to last forever although it has already died EONS ago!

"OH MY GOD! If I don't stay and let this lunatic KILL me I'm a DEAD BITCH for sure! Cuz he'll kill me ANYWAY-if I try and leave!"

Sometimes we just don't know WHAT the HELL to do! So we stay! Amidst a 24/7 threat of eminent danger. Its bad enough to SUPPOSE that on any given day, this nigga MIGHT whip your ASS! You know you got a 50-50 chance! He might stomp you out after lunch-or he MIGHT let you live till dinner time! So you can watch your favorite episode of Spongebob!

It's quite ANOTHER thing to know-THAT YOU KNOW, THAT YOU KNOW that every single solitary 24 hours of your existence, JUST LIKE CLOCKWORK, this BIG UGLY BLACK MOTHERFUCKER will wake up in the morning. Shit, shower and shave and LET you cook him breakfast. And after that LAST morsel of bacon and grits is stuffed down his psychotic throat, he will commence to WHIPPING YOUR NATURAL BORN ASS! Before the bacon is swallowed.

"WHAM, BANG, BONG, ZAP, BAM-ZOOM!" Pant-pant-Gasp-gasp! He's TIRED now-A BIT WINDED! Too many punches you know! So how about a little KICK? "BOW…BOW…STOMP, STOMP, STOMP!"

GET THE PICTURE? When you KNOW this shit is coming-THAT'S SOME SHIT TO KNOW! That's some preordained drama! Bitch! DON'T hang around for the bacon! Don't anticipate those spiked Combat-Boots being rammed upside your head! Run. RUN! I said RUN bitch! RUN! Do you LIKE you? RUN! Do you LOVE yourself? RUN! Did you see this shit COMING? Like YESTURDAY? RUN! Did you see what happened to the dumb WHITE bitch on T.V? RUN! Oh he's gonna beat my ASS? Sure as shit STINKS? You mean there's NO maybe? It's definite? GAURANTEED? INEVITABLE? FOREVER? NO! FUCK THAT! RUN, RUN, RUN, RUN-RUN! And the only time your dumb ass should even THINK to pick up a fryin pan at breakfast time for this BEAST is to SLAM it right and direct into his murderous FUCKIN SKULL! And I'll say it again! It is now the NEW BITCHES CREED! The new domestic violence abused bitches CREED! Survival tactic numeral ZERO and the First through 10th Commandments-annotated for YOUR DUMB SIMPLE ASS! R.U.N!

But we can't run! Unfortunately many of us made a choice long ago to love this man-or die trying! This impedes our freedom! We love him. WE THINK WE LOVE HIM! Usually we don't know the difference-AND WE STAY! AND WE DIE!

That's how Hattie went out! She did it for love! She told me that Catharsis was the only one that made her feel alive! And that the reason that she ran the streets and fucked everything in sight within a downward spiraling existence of self-guilt and shame was the longing to fulfill needs deeply internal and rooted in her rechanneled esteem.

It's hard to believe but Catharsis filled that void once vacant in Hattie. Did she feel worthy of the beatings-like she deserved to inherit grueling pain from him because of her supposed culpability for her mother's death? I don't know! But her killer satisfied that empty space that drives MANY women from their 'Happy Homes' into the streets to find that which they feel they cannot live without! Something they cannot properly DIE without!

From the first day they met somewhere in her heart she decided she didn't want the fast life anymore. I knew Hattie more than ANYBODY and I know for a fact that she was NOT fooling around behind his back! I know that! She just wanted to have FUN-you know, hanging out with the girls! Reliving her old self yet not succumbing to the sexual promiscuity that had once been her trademark. Sometimes a sister just wants to be a woman! To be herself and do fun things that women do. NOT philander or cheat-just enjoy the knowledge that we are STILL very special and attractive persons who should and must be respected by our oft-time unappreciative male spouses.

But Catharis could not see this! And he mistook innocent flirtation and hollow glances or trips to Ski Lodges and Ladies Nights at Honeys as the proof he needed to sign her Death Sentence and put an innocent woman in her grave.

We had a private joke! I always told Hattie that "THAT python would bite one day! Fuck around and that nigger might burst something! If he do, and your ass is hemorrhaging don't come runnin to me! I'll just buy a needle and thread and tell your hard-head to go back to work! You go for YOURS girl!"

Well the snakebite had occurred and its victim lay motionless on a debris-strewn floor-eyes open as though she had seen ahead of time what this dark day would bring. There is something to say of those who enthuse themselves with the harmless company of pet snakes. BABY SNAKES MUST GROW UP TO BECOME LARGER VENOMOUS ADULT SNAKES!

I was numb! I wanted to cry! I wanted to pick Hattie's body up out of that place and go bury her with dignity MYSELF! The Cops...THE FUCKING COPS made a homophobic parade of the entire ordeal! Taking bets on cause of death. Somebody drew 2 chalk-figures in a doggy-style position. One with a gun to the other's head saying: "QUIET FAG-OR I'LL STOP FUCKING YOU!"

They portrayed her as a joke-A CLOWN! A dead clown deservant of scorn and ridicule. And me as the living survivor of a friendship that they just could not understand!

"Hey Louis-you believe this? Joey, cmere! Louis, Joey-look! I think the fags tryin to tell us something!" IT WAS DISGUSTING! I grabbed my shit and left! If I didn't walk out there would be ANOTHER metallic object-this one down somebody else's tyhroat! And violent enraged me would be on the other end STILL shoving the device deeper and spewing out obscenities.

"Hey Lou, Joe-cmere! LOOK! I made another one. It's like a shish-kebob or something. Hey, and this ones smiling! Hah! Now the FAG wasn't smiling! BUT THIS ONE-HE LIKES IT! Go figure huh? Well uma go home now, maybe do the Misses and have a few beers! See ya around guys!"

" Hmh," I didn't think there was 'NUTHIN' funny ANYMORE!

-27-

N.Y.P.D. BLUE

I needed to get high! Just a few puffs to drag me away from what life was doin to me. But mortal wounds had no room for addiction! There was STILL some unfinished business that demanded my fullest attention.

I decided to go after Catharsis myself! It would probably take the N.Y.P.D. the next 5 millennia to even come up with a suspect-BUT I KNEW WHERE THE TRUE PERP LIVED! This Columbo looking Lieutenant at the crime scene told me that there were no fingerprints on the body or the murder weapon and although Catharsis' prints could be found throughout the house they couldn't prove in a Court of Law he actually did it. IT'S CIRCUMSTANTIAL! Well circumstantial in and of itself don't exist to me! You tell that circumstantial shit to HATTIE-the dead body you're investigating the murder of! Tell HER that!

"Ms...uh, I MEAN Mr. Hattie Wilson-SIR! We have no REAL proof of who murdered you! Uh-did you see his face while he was pummeling you? Maybe YOU could TESTIFY! There ARE latent prints yes but it's not solid enough to build a Case before the D.A! We're truly sorry-but there's nothing we can do! So all the best to you and your's-AND HAVE MERRY CHRISTMAS!"

FUCK THAT! Niggers-TRUE NIGGERS, don't need NO circumstances to beat a motherfucker in the head and slice his throat! To an intelligent person circumstances would embody those pertinent facts surrounding a scenario which would give any reasonable person probable cause to believe the validity of said scenario! In other words: if I add 1 plus-and I get 2! And if the trained-killer had a gun and a bitch in the bathtub got SHOT! Right after that SAME motherfucker with the gun SWORE up and down to shoot the SHIT out of her! Wait! Let me see now! DON'T WANNA IMPLICATE THE WRONG Damn suspect! But there was nobody else in the house...and she DID scream out his name moments before she died-old lady down the hall can testify to that! And this fool got her BLOOD on his Akademiks Jacket! GEE-this investigation stuff is so fucking HARD! I shoulda went to MEDICAL SCHOOL instead! Uh-er...an if it LOOKS like a duck...and QUACKS like a duck...! Ah well-no, no, no, no-NO! WE MUSTN'T JUMP TO CONCLUSIONS! Besides, everyone is innocent until proven guilty! So in my Professional analytical opinion the Verdict is "NOT GUILTY!"

THE HELL HE AIN'T!

The entire Long Island Police Department just sat around eatin Dunkin Donuts, sippin down piping-hot Espresso and reminiscing about the good old days of witch hunts and slavecatchers. They really weren't interested! They couldn't care less! They floundered and faltered and slept through the entire Investigation with clear consciences and their fingers up their noses! Who wants to dive whole-heartedly into the smudged puddle of shit one engages when investigating the death of a lowly transvestite! It's more of a laugher! "Oh yeah-sure we check it out! All the possible perps are screened-we're not STUPID you know! WE WILL FIND OUR MAN!" Then a week later they're sittin around joking about the whole charade and refusing to waste the manpower on something as trivial and nonconsequential as a fag who caught a bad one from one of his multiple gay lovers!

Well like I said I knew where Catharsis hung out! And if a single black woman had to do for Hattie what the entire Police Department was unable or unwilling to do then THAT'S just what would go down!

At 11:15 the next night I put on my Ninja attire and grabbed my Ox in my waist-line. Then I tied up my hair AND WENT HUNTIN! You don't do somebody harm where I come from and just stroll about caught up in your leisure life like nothing happened! When you're at WAR you don't walk around as though you're a CIVILIAN! If you do you'll be reminded about what you should NOT HAVE FORGOTTEN!

"Nigger-YOU ROBBED ME! YOU RAPED ME! YOU BEAT ME DOWN OR STOLE FROM MY MOTHER! Why you walkin around like nothing happened-with my BLOOD on your hands? You STUPID? Well O.K. STUPID! Since you think it's O.K. to walk around-hanging out and partying after you violated me let me show you EXACTLY how safe these streets are-now that you did that GRIMY shit? OH NO ASSHOLE-TELL YOUR MAMA GOOD-BYE! And tell JESUS you'll be right there-as soon as I finish stabbin you!"

So I grabbed a hammer and a pitch-fork from the junk draw and stuffed a Screw-driver in my high-heel Tim boot-TERMINATOR STYLE! Lets see if Catharsis is that kinda dumb-ass to go kill a bitch and have the audacity to go Clubbin the very next day-WHILE HER BLOOD IS STILL WARM!

I drained half-pint of Southern Comfort (bad move) and offered my supplication to a beneficent Creator who probably couldn't hear me through the alcoholism. That done, I ran up in the spot, 'The Cheetah' where he hung out and started shoutin out his name! I called him all KINDS of murderers and fag hit-men! While I was at it, howling like a disgruntled moose barred at the front entranceway unable to get in cuz of all the extra metallic hardware I brought in addition to my big fuckin mouth! Some of his boys was out there BOUNCIN-I remembered their faces. The patrons outside of the Club waitin on line didn't know what the Hell was goin on but had a GOOD idea that this irate ghetto black chic had SOME type of beef with the establishment! BUT THE BOUNCERS KNEW! Italian Hit-man hitmen know EXACTLY why a woman raises Hell after they've abetted in the death of her friend!

"YO CATHARSIS-WHERE YOU AT you FAG murdering MOTHERFUCKER! Why you kill my best friend? Hey-look, the owner of THIS Club killed my best friend! YOU HOMO FUCKIN GAY COCK-SUCKER! BE A MAN! WHERE YOU AT?"

Now THAT'S some negative publicity! I know how to get a nigger's ATTENTION! If he WASN'T there I knew his boys would get back to him! IMMEDIATELY! Cuz some trouble-maker was sreamin out his sacred name! Callin him a Mafia drug-dealin fag HITMAN! It was stirring up the customers-causin Mafia stock to fall-SHARPLY! And THAT was BAD FOR BUSINESS!

"HEY ANY OF YOU DOOFY MOTHERFUCKERS SEEN...."

"WOOOPS!" They snatched me straight outta my speech and dragged me into a large dim smoke-filled room in the back-behind God's back! We took an elevator-then descended some STEEP steps and went down a long winding passageway. And I thought: "What part of the Club is THIS? Ya'll takin me to the V.I.P. Section?" It was more like the P.O.W's quarters and I was beginning to get nervous-so I started some SHIT again!

"Yo let me GO!" I pulled away AFTER the behemoth had already let me go ANYWAY! A ghetto bitch gotta at least ACT tough-especially when she knows she's way outta her league!

"YO TELL THAT MOTHERFUCKER...TELL THAT FAGGOT I'M TELLIN! I'll TELL on that ass and he'll spend the rest of his gay life in JAIL! TELL THAT FUCK Simone IS LOOKIN FOR HIM!" What was I planning to do when I FOUND him-stab him to death with the fork before his 4 homeboys beat me to death? The extra-large stooge got nervous. Perhaps he was Catharsis' most faithful flunky and the one imparted with the wisdom and responsibility of managing the Club. He got on the cell phone. I don't know HOW he was able to talk amidst my screaming! He spoke in Italian, probably to Catharsis, then hung up!

And there I went again!

"Where's that FAGGOT at? Tell him to come out! I ain't scared of FAGGOTS! I look shook to you BITCH?" The gigantic flunky then beckoned to one of the other 3 assholes holdin me and whispered in his ear.

"Catharsis will let you live! Here, go spend some money! Here's 15 thousand-it's yours! But if you try to talk about this-YOU'D BETTER SPEND IT QUICKLY!"

"ASSHOLE! I DON'T WANT SHIT FROM YOU! GIVE IT TO YOUR FAT FORIEGN MAMA!" How the fuck did these Sons-of-bitches think I would accept a bribe? In repayment for the death of my best friend? They musta misconceived me as the desperate Slum-scum who would sell out their friends, THEIR FLESH AND BLOOD, just for a couple of bucks! I WAS NOT THAT BITCH! I would SHIT on that punk-ass 15 Grand! And I would shit on each and every one of THEM before I took that blood-money!

"ARE YOU STUPID? Eat MY ASS bitch-you think I want SHIT from you? You must be FUCKIN kiddin!" I spit in his face-tryin to provoke him! But he was just a stooge-a flunky! And I knew he could not lay a hand on me unless the mighty bastard gave the O.K! He looked at me as though I was the bully who had just KICKED THE SHIT outta his 3rd Grade son. Hey I KNOW that look!

Bomani Shuru

"This will help you forget about your friend. And you don't see him," he pointed at me! "In 2 days HE WILL COME SEE YOU!" He threw the money at me and the barbarians carried me out a back door screamin. Then they put me in a black Sedan and drove me home!

I kicked and I screamed and I bitched and I moaned all to no avail! The 5 men stopped in front of my house. Someone else drove MY car behind us and at 129 Hillcrest Road in Carl Place Long Island everybody got out of their respective vehicles. By now it had occurred to me that resistance was futile! I could not fight these bastards! There shit was too well financed and very well organized-to the fuckin letter! I was a small trickle of water-a slow-leak trying to defy a raging Tsunami! But I was never too clever when it came to picking a winner. I HATE to lose! And when I AM defeated I'm most often either unconscious or too Damn rebellious to notice!

The Mod-Squad opened my front door. THEY HAD THE KEYS! Who the Hell gave them my house keys? That meant to me that they could have murdered me LAST NIGHT if they wanted to! It ALSO meant that if I didn't act right TONIGHT-they could kill me TOMORROW! And how were they able to drive my car when the Jeep keys were still in my purse!? Oh shit-this nigger was GOOD! He already had everything about me at his disposal. In case he decided that I was too dangerous to be allowed to live. Only THEN would he send his Brute by Faberge wearing hulkish underlings to pop me in my sleep! And more importantly if I was in grave danger, what of my daughter-BREANNA? Someone might hurt her or even try to kidnap her from School or something. So I had to do the right thing-about this CATHARSIS BASTARD or not only would I lose my life (I didn't care about that) but I would jeopardize my daughter in the process-and that was something that I would NEVER do! OH FUCKING GREAT! Look what THIS shit now boiled down to. I might get 'WHACKED' but the fucking MOB! Only in America!

I was still hollering-begging for the bastards to let me fuckin go-to let me LIVE! I was hopin to attract some attention but for some strange reason no one could hear me! NOT EVEN YAGO! HIS horny Guyanese ass was always around! It was 12:15 A.M! Him and the nosy Misses should've been upstairs about their daily routine of 'LACK OF PURPOSE' AND 'PARENTAL NEGLECT!' So where the Hell were THEY? I can't even FART or cum too loud on a normal basis without them handing me a leaflet on the 10 tranquil rules of their mundane household! Now I'm screaming for my LIFE-WHERE THE FUCK IS MY LEAFLET NOW?

Oh boy! I done ran into the Crew from the Gates of HELL! The Satanic 'Click' that Whacked Yago, his stupid wife and...OH NO! DON'T tell me-they got my cat too cuz she's not standin on the steps for me to TRIP over!

"TALK TO ME PEPPER! DID THE NASTY ITALIAN MEN WHACK YOU TOO?"

The barbarians lifted me offa my feet like I weighed nothing! I ranted and I raved but it seemed as if they'd killed off the entire neighborhood! THIS NIGGER'S POWER

WAS FAR-REACHING! My feet dragged behind me like a Muppet and I felt like the violent Third-Grader, Nikki Farnsworth, who had beat me in the head with her handy-dandy crutch! Two dead feet draggin, reverberating wooden crutch and all!

"And NOW you will sleep-for a long time! WHEN YOU WAKE UP-YOU SEE CATHARSIS!"

Oh great-I get to see the Prince of Darkness when I get to the other side-after I walk into the light! I didn't know what the fuckers were up to so I started squirming-AND I TRIED TO SHOUT AND BITE THE SHIT OUTTA THE MUSCLE-BOUND ONE HOLDIN MY MOUTH! Somebody put something over my eyes an I felt somebody grab my breasts and hold me down into the couch. I couldn't breathe too well! Was I being RAPED-or strangled? I struggled hard as I could TO GET UP! Just needed some air but the strength of the brute pressing my face and my chest into the leather frame below me felt as though a baby elephant were crushing down on my upper body with the steel massiveness of its anatomy! I was being STRANGLED-then the force subsided-and I could once more feel the obligatory oxygen bless my constricted lungs.

I gagged uncontrollably-THEN THEY INJECTED MY RIGHT ARM WITH SOME WARM FLUID! Oh NO! NOW they gonna make me DRUG-related! A junkie! Fuck strangulation-STRING THE BITCH OUT! Make her do tricks for the MONKEY! The little MONKEY that 34 years ago sired me!

A helpless and over-powered feeling overcame me! I was out-gunned and all of my senses began to SPIN in a rapid vertigo rotation. Spiraling at lightning speed in a dozen directions simultaneously. I should have been dizzy-BUT IT FELT GOOD! Like God had me rested in his arms. I felt a HIGHLY STIMULATING SENSATION CLIMBING UP AND DOWN IN MY BODY! It coursed all the way from my throbbing pelvic-section (on fire with a familiar desire) to the intoxicated reality now stimulated from the climactic party jumping off in my brain. Was THIS what my mother felt-the joy and passion that she surrendered to and laid down with my absent father in search of? Was this Heaven-the other side a Junkie goes to after a bad-fix? Did I O.D. from what Catharsis put inside my virgin veins-or was this simply the peace that we all need and look forward to after life puts our restlessness to sleep? Whatever they did to me-IT FELT GOOD-AND I WANTED SOME MORE! That was all I remembered!

When I came to I saw a Merry-go-round of flying images streaking back and forth past the shaky narrow silver-screen of my senses. I could hear voices! Talking-laughing. My hands were tied because I could feel the heavy rope-burns all but permeating the radial arteries in my wrists. My legs were pried open and I thought-OH NO! NOT THIS!

My body had been restrained in some type of S&M contraption! A wood and leather freaks guillotine apparatus erected in a corner of a large spacious room. It had a sturdy oak frame with black vinyl straps and both my arms were tied in front of me. I was entombed within its grasp in doggie-style position semi bent over on my knees as the bulk of my thoracic cavity was being supported by what FELT like a solid wooden bench directly beneath and grinding against my abdomen.

What a FUCKIN PREDICAMENT! I felt like a corralled horse stuck and stifled to death within the narrow confines of a stable that was designed NOT ONLY to restrain him-but to cage his soul. My knees were bent-spread apart and the edifice had yet another cold beam of wood nestled between my legs to force them open. THIS SHIT spelled the death of a certain killer's homosexuality to me-at LEAST in MY mind. An unpleasant escape into the remembrances of the fine cuisine to be found in female bondage and helplessness.

The room was vacant except for a few old dusty crates and what appeared to be bundles of packaged merchandise-like shipping paraphenalia. On one of them I saw an emblem that read: 'The Castaway.' I filed that information away in my brain for a time I might be asked to describe the surroundings of where Catharsis had kidnapped me to.

Oh YES, this WAS a God-damned kidnapping! I had foolishly hunted down a known murderer. The one responsible for the death of someone close . But I knew THIS murderer was different, he was well-refined and calculating. Not merely a lunatic who could be caught. NO, THIS bastard had PERFECTED the art of taking peoples lives WITHOUT GETTING CAUGHT! God knows how many lives he had ended. And I had chosen to search and destroy this beast in the same manner that a militant rabbit, an over-zealous hare, packs up his military armaments (a bee-bee gun and a few dozen shit-pellets) and hunts down the 'Big Bad Wolf' or the 'King of the jungle!' And then very naively expects to live to celebrate the victory.

With THAT ominous and perplexing goal in mind, drugged or not, I realized the grave importance of taking mental notes as to just what I saw on my frolicking road to Hell! A victim shackled in a modified bear-trap SHOULD gather up vital evidence just in case she's still breathin by the time she's rolled outta harms way on a stretcher! And my mind absorbed EVERY single fuckin word in that DAMNED room to be used as a clue against the opposition for future references. JUST IN CASE I GOT LUCKY-AND SURVIVED!

I tried to turn my head but could not for the firm wooden board housing my hands and head in what reminded me 'The Chopping Block' must've looked and felt like!!

I had been BEATEN but I couldn't remember when and by whom. But my jaw certainly knew. It just COULD NOT communicate the terrors of what it had been through to the proper authorities in my brain. My entire anatomy writhed! As though someone were STILL stomping me. I could taste blood in my mouth. And I could SMELL myself-scantily clothed in a raggedy T-shirt drenched in the warm clotted fluid that separates itself from one's mortality after pain and injury! The bloody caked up unoxygenated nostrils vaguely detected sparsely perfumed sweatglands riding on the speculation of where I'd been-what I'd gone through for 12 rounds with Catharsis' baboon squad.

266

When you cock an ass up in the air-YOU'LL SMELL IT! No matter HOW clean it is! I felt humiliated at my predicament, at my nakedness! And I wanted to at least cover myself but there I was! The stinky black bitch sprawled out butt naked on the symbolic Pool Table of a butcher's Old-school heterosexual dreams. And I'd be DAMNED if I was goin out like THIS!

I recalled 6 very tall very well-built men dragging me across a vacant expanse-someone shouting at me! The bouncers! The savage fuckin gorilla's with musculatures like body-builders. The gorilla's who abandoned their lonely other-halves back home basting meatballs and boiling pasta-the sadistic baboons who caught cheap thrills ogling at every INCH of my over-exposed feminity! And my minds-eye can still feel the brutality and helplessness of when they held me down-FOR CATHARSIS!

The blue light filtering into the room was dim and I smelled the scent of Cigars. The odor was rich and I could tell by the flavorful tobacco ambiance of endless vaporous invisible fumes that The Assassin had to be nearby. That was all he smoked! The muffled overlapping voices gradually ebbed into the sound of 2 sharply accentuated Italian men engrossed in a long calm conversation. I recognized the voice! It was the voice of Hattie's death! And ultimately the mass of shape-shifting images settled down into what I later identified as 2 fashionably dressed men discussing some very important matters with an articulate stone-faced killer of best friends! IT WAS CATHARSIS!

"So sleeping beauty awakes!

"LET ME LOSE BITCH! YOU SICK FUCK! WHAT YOU ASSHOLES DOIN?"

What else you dumb bitch! You hog-tied an you bout to get trained-GANG-BANGED! You'se the Turkey an its 'GOBBLIN TIME' said my outspoken perception!

"You BITCHES…"

My id and my libido were doing flips against the left side of my consciousness-and the vibrations could be felt way down below. Countless gallons of testosterone, the war-drug, the violent hormone that talks a nigger into eating somebody's heart out seemed to run rampant! Coursing through my veins like a run-away train! I WANTED BLOOD! I NEEDED TO BE TOUCHED! And to feel the lightning sensations present in the combative throes of physical confrontation-BRUTAL PENETRATION, AND BATTLE!

I did not know that my bonds were mightier than I-that I would succumb to them. My sinews struggled only to be reminded of the unyielding durability of leather straps! They felt like Tungsten steel to my nullified senses!

Catharsis leered at me with his head tilted to the right-perhaps shocked at the vigorous efforts I exacted against my prison. He just stared, like a madman. Like a fuckin Norman Bates moron! A befuddled child enfatuated at his new pet hamster, and the way it ran for its life, in place, on the spinning wheel designed to keep unenlightened captive rodents devoted to life-saving crusades that are doomed to fail!

I continued.

"You been watchin TOO MANY MOVIES...SHITHEAD! Ooh BITCH-KEEP STANDIN THERE! WAIT TILL I GET...WHAT-CHOO LOOKIN AT? WHAT...YOU AN YOUR BOYS...THINK THIS IS A JOKE?

It was no use! The goon-squad was yuckin it up-at me, an I couldn't do ANYTHING about it! I hung my head and closed my eyes, dismissing the raging fruitless struggle and decided to attempt another approach. I would THINK my way out!

Catharsis clapped!

"BRAVO-STUPID! By now you must be very nauseas-AND a bit aroused! I added a little extra something that I knew would turn you on. Usually from the moment they wake up they wanna fuck the first thing in sight! I THOUGHT YOU'D APPRECIATE THAT SIDE-EFFECT. Oh but don't thank me NOW-plenty of time for that later! I have all day long TO FUCK WITH THOSE WHO FUCK WITH ME-WITH MY BUSINESS! Especially out-of-control black bitches!"

"Fuck YOU!" I was strung out! Felt like something was draggin my swollen genitals toward getting a hold of ANY piece of stimulation I could FIND! I wanted to be man-handled! EVERY woman has experienced that feeling! DAMN! What had this bastard done to me? Why was I so powerless? He had me bent over a barrel. But I would not relent so easily to being Satan's sex-slave! I didn't give a damn WHAT type of Serum he mixed up and stuck in my veins! There are so many forces in this Universe more powerful than that which takes a woman's desensitized will hostage by man-made sexual poison. And I swore to find that greater power before I allowed a wicked bastard DEMON like Catharsis to enter my body!

This was the moment I had anticipated-and shunned! I was face to face with the murderous scum who'd taken my life! And fear was not an option! I summoned every ounce of defiance flowing through my rebellion. He could kill me now if he wanted to but that reality didn't faze me. Because there are things far worse than death-submitting to Catharsis, the black Italian DOG, was one of them!

"You like to talk don't you! My friends told me all the things you said you'd talk about to the authorities. Well...they're not here-so talk to me! Tell me what's in that pretty little black head of yours!"

"Catharsis, I'm gonna tell them! YOU BETTER KILL ME NOW! You SICK FUCK, cuz if you let me go you'll wish your BAD ASS was never conceived! I HOPE YOU DIE IN JAIL!" He stared at me-like someone who had something ON somebody! LIKE A BLACKMAILER!

"How is your MOTHER Simone? I sent a couple of friends over to the house in Farmingdale to check on her and your dad! They followed her to the Supermarket over on...what's that? Parks Boulevard! Anyway they struck up a conversation-oh she's so friendly. Such a pleasant woman! And she spoke so HIGHLY of you. We assured her that her beloved daughter was PROUD to have a mother like her. And she bragged that you would NEVER let her down. How about that? Is the daughter from Heaven intending to let poor dear old mom down?"

"GO TO HELL CATHARSIS! DON'T TALK ABOUT MY MOTHER! She don't..."

"OH DON'T BE A FUCKING COMIC BOOK! We know you don't care about YOURSELF Simone! But PLEASE-think of mom!"

I wanted to stab that gay motherfucker in the chest! I was drugged-up, bloody, hog-tied and wondering about death! And he just stood there-threatening to do something to my family-MY PARENTS. I looked at CATHARSIS! Just standin there-with my life in his hands! And he stared back with just as much intensity-with an intensity I had seen before within the face of carnal desire! I ANALYZED MY ENEMY-This cool, calm and collect Son-of-a-bitch! The one who brought my life to a screeching halt-catapulted me into a sad reality. HE had done this! ALL THIS to me! And he just SAT there like a Choir boy-a FUCKING SUAVE LUNATIC! One with slick black shiny white-boy hair, light-brown skin, fine-designer suits. AND A PROPENSITY TO KILL!

He looked like a male-model! Like a Jet-set Playboy who'd gotten bored with pussy and elapsed into fag-forest never to be found by the ideals of heterosexuality again! And although one part of me wanted to curse this half nigger for even ATTEMPTING to threaten my life-the life of my family, another part of me latched onto the sumptuous notion of being TOUCHED before I died! Maybe it was the injection he pumped into my system. Maybe I felt what Hattiie felt-what kept her lingering on. I DON'T KNOW! But I DID know-and I COULD SWEAR THAT HATTIE'S KILLER HAD A THING FOR ME!

My God Knows I was willing to DIE for an opportunity to meet and murder him IN HELL! I don't know-call it my ego but sometimes a woman can TELL who craves for her! No matter HOW much he tries to hide it! That explained the look this bastard was kickin out at me-and why would an unwavering fag put some type of sex-stimulant inside a someone he refused to fuck? Who he DIDN'T want?

Catharsis looked like a hungry dog not wanting its master to see the desire within him for that delectable bone! He refuses to drool although he wants to. So instead his SOUL salivates! And his body articulated to me the strength of how much he truly wanted that which he'd taught himself to refrain from. In silent forbidden unspoken verse and subtle demands he unleashed the flames of himself. Seeking to be reinvited into the seductive cock-tail of a woman. THAT WAS HOW MY CAPTOR WAS LEERING AT ME! As though I was the juicy piece of meat that HE NEEDED TO TASTE! Despite the rampant idiocy of his reprobate self! Homo-and Heterosexual combined DON'T MIX! And it was time to distract his lusts from that objective!

"I have a tape! Oh you didn't KNOW THAT DID YOU? I thought you knew EVERYTHING BITCH! And if anything happens to me the footage goes PUBLIC! It's from HATTIE, you remember her asshole? WE TAPED YOU! On those nights when you beat her. We had your ass on TAPE! SMILE MOTHERFUCKER! And after the tape plays before the Grand Jury your ass will FRY! You gonna bribe 24 people BITCH? I DON'T THINK SO! And she tells it all-that if anything happens to her-YOU DID IT! Oh the PROOF-THE VIOLENCE IS RIGHT THERE! WITH YOU RUNNIN AROUND THE HOUSE WITH YOUR ROCK HARD DICK...AN YOUR FLABBY ASS-AND THAT BLACK-JACK YOU USED TO HIT HER WITH!"

He was seething-SO I CONTINUED. Cuz that's what a dumb BITCH does! That's what a BITCH from BROOKLYN does when she tastes somebody's NUTS being pulverized between her teeth!

"IF YOU EVER LEAVE ME BITCH I WILL KILL YOU! I WILL KILL YOU! WHAT'S MY NAME? WHAT'S MY NAME? WHOSE ASS IS THIS? CATHARSIS MANZONE-SAY IT BITCH-SAY IT!' That speech sound familiar-FAG-FUCKER? You goin down! YOU DON'T BELIEVE ME-it was 11 times ASSHOLE! You beat her 11 TIMES! Right Playboy!"

"I don't believe you," howled the frightened sadist! I think I was makin him nervous!

"I TOLD you we got proof! An we made over 50 copies bastard! You're a REAL porn-star! A cross between 'Long-dong Silver and The Creature from the Black Lagoon-swinging your DICK and your fists at some defenseless faggot at a Motel in Scarsdale-YOU REMEMBER THAT SPOT IN SCARSDALE? Hold up-don't answer that! The real question is do you think you can locate all 50 tapes-before your flabby ass goes sailin up the River?"

I spit at him and he got really mad! I was bluffin BUT HE DIDN'T KNOW IT! I wanted to die! My life had already gone on without me-with Hattie's passing and the only thing I craved more than death was to kill him!

Catharsis grabbed my neck and snarled!

"You think you smarter than me you black bitch? I fuck people like you for a living-then SPIT out their bodies on the doorsteps of their families!"

"It don't matter Luigie! YOU STILL GOIN UP STATE!"

"If you want to die then so be it. You like to talk-so I let you talk-THEN YOU DIE! But I'll FUCK you first! That's what you WANT isn't it-to be fucked? Right before I cut your throat?"

He pulled out the GUN of his notorious 12 inch dick and I spit at him again-cursing him in words I'm sure his Latin ancestors would not repeat! My Latin gets pretty THICK when a sociopathic mongrel ties me up in the dark, cocks open my legs and threatens me with the titanium spear of sodomy he PROMISES that I won't like!

"NOBODY WANTS YOUR HALF-PINK ASS Catharsis!" That's what my mouth said-but I knew better! My female intuition went into shuddering convulsions at the eminent reality of what might happen! Five-hundred Angels started huddling and talking shit behind my back plotting to turn my stupidity in to God's Court of Appeals. I had decided on DEATH-and they somehow had a problem with that! I had broken the pact-the silent contract to just shut up and try and save my daughter and myself. Now this beast wanted to rape me! I had given him no choice than to put me to sleep and give me what I reluctantly craved for. VIOLATION-and the peace of death that would follow!

I KNEW that ANYTIME that gay motherfucker had to give up some scum and bust a heterosexual nut a I would have to give up her life! The inner struggle tempting that him back to true manhood was a formidable foe-and bought with it an expensive lesson to be learned. He squeezed my neck some more and my Adam's Apple erupted in obscenities that my voice-box had lost the pleasure of uttering!

"Where are the TAPES? AND WHO HAS THEM? Tell me your secret BITCH!"

"Fuck you FAGGOT! I ain't telling you SHIT!" It was hard to get the words out! The grip of his fingers brought my senses to a panic and oxygen was an asset not to be wasted on too many hollow absurdities.

"OOAH! STOP! What...secret ? That you killed my girl?" This BASTARD was choking me-an all I could do was try and BREATH-AND PRAY THAT HE'D STOP! I thought of all the tricks I ever used to get SICK FUCKS like him offa me! But NONE of em applied to me being hog-tied to a steel crate in the darkest corner of Gangsta's Paradise!

Catharsis came in front of me-his pelvis by my head and I could see and feel the Roman monster against my cheeks. I wanted to PUKE!

"I'll have your mother high on heroine! She'll be the oldest trick in the hood! And Breanna will be selling Blow-jobs for a living before she's 15!"

"FUCK YOU! AND YOU'LL BE GANG-BANGED EVERY FUCKIN NIGHT FOR THE REST OF YOUR QUEER LIFE BY THE REAL NIGGERS ON LOCK-DOWN! What you coming...GET THAT SHIT OUTTA MY FACE SCUMBAG! Oh all of a sudden you want some HEAD? GET...YOUR BITCH-ASS BOY-FRIEND TO DO IT! KILL ME YOU SICK FUCK! BASTARD-why don't you KILL me?"

As I struggled to evade his advances the 4 stooges watching us just stood by waitin for him to sodomize and murder me-like he did Hattie. Like THEY musta helped him do to her! He stood in front of my fuckin face and I could SMELL him-and it made me sick! His hands and ass looked like dried prunes! All wrinkled and-and I swore I'd rather die than have that deformed mutant cum inside me! I did not know WHAT to think. I had mixed feelings about life and death. Part of me just wanted to go back to my old life but another side refused to endure another moment of that shattered façade! But if I let him kill me he might spare Breanna-and mommy and daddy. He could just shut ME up and my family would be safe! So MY PURPOSE was to provoke the Devil to possess me-to HAVE ME! So that MY personal sacrifice would guarantee the safety of the only ones I HAD LEFT to love! And if I was wrong? Then I'd DIE trying to save them!

"Catharsis! Uma TELL! YOU KNOW THAT SHIT-I AIN'T HATTIE! An I ain't telling you SHIT!"

OOPS-wrong speech bitch! He ran from MY PERIPHERAL VISION! So fast I could feel the breeze stirred up by his venom as he darted quickly back behind me! AND HE NEVER SAID A MUMBLING WORD!

"What the fuck you doin?"

I KNEW what the nigger was doin! His meat was out and I had pissed him off to the point where he REALIZED he would have to kill me cuz cooperation was too far away! So he'd might as well taste this rebel first-before he dusted me off! Catharsis YEARNED to dominate women. To punish them for his own deviant sexual preferences! And the ONLY thing that truly pleased him was to penalize their womanhood with the assaultive wave of his abundant anatomy. I could feel his throbbing pulse-the fiery battle-axe with which he tortured his victims. A maniac who fed upon damaging them as he sought psychologically to flee from the shame of his desire for a masculinity like his own! The Latin beast lustfully sprinted back around to the gaping tunnels. He clutched and fiddled at the erotic entranceway commonly offered up to him by my girl. The human sacrifice had been 'blessed' and was ready! Catharsis grasped onto the small of my back with his powerful trembling hands and leaned into me despite the noise of my defiance! It was high-time for that cruel fuck to unleash the full bounty of his malevolence-AND HE COULD NOT WAIT!

"ITS TIME FOR YOU TO RENDER UNTO CAESAR!"

"O.K, O.K, BASTARD! The secret-the secret to where the tapes are... I'll fuckin tell you but you gotta let me go!"

He didn't give a Damn!

"SLAP, SLAP!" OH SHIT! NO! The shit-hole slapped me on my ASS! THE PSYCHOTIC FUCKER STARTED GROANING AND BARKING OUT SOME ITALIAN STUFF-like he was performing the LAST Rites for the doomed flesh he was about to rip open! HE KEPT BEATIN ME-WITH BOTH HANDS! And I could feel the stings-from my butt-cheeks to my GOD-DAMNED CRANIUM!

"YOU WANNA TALK BITCH-THEN TALK ABOUT THIS!"

He grabbed my waist with both hands-then pulled me back to him! The bastard was STRONG! Like the Incredible Hulk-pissed off after being awakened from an emerald tranquil homosexual nap!

"O.K, CATHARSIS-DAMN!" HE WAS STILL WHIPPIN ME!

"AAIEH!" I COULDN'T HELP IT! IT HURT! I could see pictures flyin through my head! I remembered the way Hattie used to scream when he was drunk-sodomizing her! She cried and I could hear the pleas despite 2 pillows and 5 Long Island Iced Teas. I SWEAR more than a few times I wanted to barge in there and STOP IT! BREAK THAT SHIT UP! I remembered the blood-streaks she left on my bedsheets! How I had to throw them away and lie to Breanna that they were no longer any good! I recalled the day he ARROGANTLY strolled around the apartment waving that THICK black-pole around the room-after he impaled my best friend through the mattress with it! And I remembered just moments before THIS rage how he said he would FUCK me-then slice my throat!

My head was still spinnin! And that maniacal little monkey that possesses a woman's soul kept KICKIN! Bading me to give in-to give myself to him! This psychotic impulse would not relent! My head felt light and woozy and down below a tiny volcano mounted inside the erection of my unsated lust! My better Judgement-my sense of decency demanded me to STOP! "Don't let him HAVE you-don't WANT him to have you cuz the Devil don't deserve to have your soul!" But those toxins carried away my will-power back to a place to end ALL struggles!

Was this THE POISON that spellbound my mother long ago? Forcing her to submit sexually to every man she met for a fix? Was it heroine? The same toxin reaching down-plummeting into her battered womb to produce Simone Singleton. A crack-baby improvisario? I didn't know but I could feel the lifelessness coursing through my rebellion. Stifling it despite how truly rigorous I tried to wrestle and fight him off!

It might have been an aphrodisiac! A sex-stimulant, maybe Ecstasy! Nothing short of a drug with THAT MUCH POTENCY could have subdued the struggle I resolved to putting up against that naked Demon! If he had impregnated my womb with that rapacious semen that murdered Hattie I would become my mother-all over again. Drugged, raped and given a child born of toxicity to be reared in desperation-and addiction! I would be my mother and my unborn victimized child would be ME-in an endless succession of chemical dependency!

He hoisted himself behind me and up against my legs! I could feel his dilated appetite, sticking-poking at the lower corner of my rectum-begging to get in! Moving up against me! It felt like a baby mountain was trying to penetrate somewhere it did not belong! He wiggled his hips and I could smell the alcohol on his breathe as his sweaty forehead poured what felt like buckets of spent Italian energy on my neck and back. The gorilla couldn't get past the protective-pinch! I batted my anal-eye and winked it closed not wanting to go through what Hattie did. But then he must've changed his mind. He moved himself against me-bringing his erection upward into the direction of my vagina. Then he put his right hand on my clit, stroking it and kissing my neck while his other hand grabbed hold of my hair and forehead. And that euphoric injection steadily rode my desire and made me wet before the scrambling imp could even make it through the door. I WANTED TO DIE-TO FUCKING DIE WHEN HE TOUCHED IT. As I felt his power rubbing up and down the opening.

I almost vomited-my strapped-down body jerking vociferously forward and lunging for relief! Every semi-righteous precept told me that the Devil was molesting me-trying to make me as foul, Satanic and disgusting as he! My life of ethereal chastity began to end as he slowly rocked his pelvis into my shuddering and I could feel pure venomous Hell throbbing against my resistance as it widened to accommodate the pleasure and pain! I didn't know whether to beg him to fuck me-OR THROW UP! What could I do? My senses and my defenses drew back and went to sleep in a swirling gyration of the madness women often HATE to feel!

Have you EVER hated a man? Simply because you had reluctantly allowed yourself to desire him? And so you can't stand the motherfucker because as MUCH as you detest the very sight of him-HE TURNS YOU ON! Therefore you project an intense hatred for THAT son of a bitch which should be more accurately directed inwardly-AT YOURSELF! It's like "Nigger I can't stand you...cuz you make me wanna FUCK you! And I wish I did not want you like THAT! THAT'S why I wish you were dead-so I could stop wanting and being attracted to you!"

Countless members of my female gender have traveled this path-a sister fighting off her baby's daddy, her ex-boyfriend or a lover she promised never to let touch her or enter her again. But THEN the nigger goes DOWN! Licking her succulently-in the way he knows she wants-or needs. Now that he's gotten her attention he 'BLESSES' her with all the complicated foreplay that he never had time to distribute. Although her lips might STILL dare to form the words 'STOP!' or 'NO!' those objections have lost their innate defiance-their fortitude and now come forth as a more pleasant harmonious 'coo!' She wants to be made love to by the nigger she 5 minutes ago boasted of hating! His boo is now ready and would KILL him if he stopped the slow grinding motion of his penis inside her-and he penetrates! And does her the way he used to-giving her what she desperately needed when she shouted, repelled and fought him off!

Who wants to be raped by the Devil? He had murdered my girl-my best friend and confidant. The only person, male or female, who ever truly new me! He had taken away our dream and I hated his nastiness from that evil soul to the 12 inches that he was forcing inside me! THIS was the bastard who had beaten me like no man had ever hurt me before-the way I vowed I would never be treated! I remembered how he KICKED me in the face before they'd tied me up-while I was on the floor! And I remembered how every single lump and bruise assailed my body as he taunted and threatened to kill me when I screamed in a drugged stupor how I would tell the Police about him-or die trying! And his boys just stood there and WATCHED as the fucker beat me like he had beaten Hattie! For what seemed like HOURS before he ordered them to tie me up-so that he could MAKE A FOOL OF ANOTHER WOMAN THAT HE BATTERED!

But I don't know WHAT THE fuck was wrong with me! WHY was it that I was HOPING that he would penetrate-AND KILL ME?

I could feel my vagina rip! The faint odor of compacted flesh-and my uterine walls running for cover from the strength of his back as he pumped it INSIDE! By then I was grindin my hips-although at first I didn't want that murderer's friends to know how much he satisfied me-HOW MUCH I WANTED HIM! Suddenly I could see why Hattie was so confused! I could understand it ALL-the ASS-WHIPPINGS! The dominations and humiliations-she did it for the intangible ideal which we call 'Love!'

I WANTED IT! And I would have been outraged if ANYONE had burst through the door and tried to STOP this nigger from hammering me! That's when I realized that I truly had problems! Despite what Catharsis was giving me I felt ashamed! I was being RAPED! And while Catharsis was trying to FUCK ME-TO HURT ME, I was throwing MYSELF back violently AGAINST HIM-hungry for his length and trying desperately to make love to him! It was PATHETIC! I was ashamed-CERTAINLY Hattie would have been! WHAT RAPE VICTIM TRIES TO MAKE LOVE BACK TO THE SICK BEAST WHOSE VIOLATING HER-TRYING TO HURT HER?

I could feel several inches of him stroking and I opened my mouth to beg him NOT to stop! To say "YEAH" and "OH" and all that SICK twisted insatiable shit, that nymph monologue, that I had kicked back at motherfuckers who had HIT me right in the past!

My fingers found their way onto his pumping hips and were clutching them in a masochistic scenario! I begged my tongue, embedded at the roof of my mouth, for the noise that commonly frequented it! That blaring sound that will back a nigger off when he shoves past a creamy opened vagina and moves too dangerously close to a woman's heart!

Unable to articulate ANYTHING other than soothing elements of this illegal ecstasy, I asked the God of my mind to get this FILTHY SICK MOTHERFUCKER OFFA ME! But my conscience launched a surprise attack to the rationale that I musta been sicker than HIM not to want Satan to STOP! My verbal defenses were transfixed! Terrorized-eager to spit out the worst shit a bitch could tell a man! But my moaning organ hoisted a gender gun to my head telling me to "Just be calm! Don't say nothing - just let the nasty nigger MAKE YOU CUM-then maybe you can negotiate an agreement for your life! Maybe if he busts off RIGHT he might spare you!"

But my conscience wasn't havin it! I was shaking-Linda Blair STYLE from the 'EXORCIST' WHILE THS CATHARSIS WAS PILE-DRIVING! Drilling his penis THROUGH MY MID-SECTION and crushing the soft-tissues!

I squirmed. I SCREAMED! I TRIED TO PURGE MY WILL-my hurting, demeaned, and defiled true self! I gathered everything I was ever taught insofar as resisting temptation-straining my damnedest to extract that 12 inch intruder out of my foaming flesh!

And I came! AND I CAME! Harder than I've ever cum before! AND HE CAME! When he ejaculated I thought a whale had pissed inside me! THEN THE BASTARD CAME AGAIN-SOME MORE! Like an erotic TIDALWAVE-an echo! The second inundation felt larger than the first! When he stopped grinding against me I experienced the most agonizing pleasure this 34 year old body had ever felt!

Satan had dominated me and made my womanhood smile-despite and astride the memory of Hattie. And when I tabulated the moral ramifications of my fears, I felt like a fuckin traitor! A traitor to myself; a traitor to my girl for letting her killer get his SHIT OFF IN ME and worst of all I felt like a traitor to God!

LORD HELP ME! WHY DID I HAVE TO BE BORN A CREATURE WHO IS A SLAVE TO HER DESIRES? I HATED THE FUCKIN GROUND Catharsis slithered upon-the very air he breathed cuz of what he'd just done! And I hated MYSELF for having the AUDACITY to like it! To get caught in his web and allow myself to want him-SEXUALLY! Inside me after he had murdered my best friend! HOW COULD A WOMAN BE SO STUPID? And I called KECIA a Crashdummy! Well I must ADMIT, with all that BULLSHIT intelligence I credited myself for having, in my over-zealous LUST FOR DICK AND SEXUAL STIMULATION, I BECAME THE ULTIMATE MOTHER OF ALL RECKLESS FUCKING CRASHDUMMIES BOTH PAST AND PRESENT! It was at THAT moment my entire PSYCHE underwent a vigorous change and I saw how truly WORTHLESS and STUPID I had become!

There are times after sexual encounters when a woman feels unclean-defiled! So much more would that feeling apply to a rape-victim! THAT WAS THE EMOTIONAL TORMENT DEPRECATING MY BRAIN! And the attacker who'd forced himself on me was clinging onto my subdued frame gasping heavily.

THE STINK FAGGOT! THAT MUSTY ITALIAN PARASITE WAS DRIPPIN ON TOP AND INSIDE OF MY ABRUPT DEFIANCE TO LET HIM HAVE ME! The perverted FUCK decided to have a change of heart-a change in sexuality at MY FUCKIN EXPENSE!

"So I guess MY ass made you decide YOU didn't wanna fuck LITTLE BOYS on this freaks contraption no more YOU SORRY SHIT! What you gonna do NOW? WEAN YOURSELF FROM BEIN A FAGGOT-MAYBE SUCK 2 DICKS A WEEK TILL YOU STOP! OH LOOK-CATHARSIS IS GOIN INTO HOMO-DETOX! ONE LESS FAG IN THE WORLD AND ONLY 25 MILLION MORE TO GO-THANK GOD FOR EARLY RETIREMENT! GET THE FUCK...OFFA ME YOU DEVIL! GET YOUR...SLIMY DICK OUTTA MY..."

I couldn't STAND it anymore-HIS SICK FUCKING ASS THROBBING INSIDE ME! I wiggled-trying to PUKE, PISS, SHIT, FART-ANYTHING TO GET THAT DISEASED BLACK SNAKE AWAY FROM MY BODY! Enraged he pulled his long fat dick out in one lump sum without first assessing the damage he'd caused! And my perserverance exhaled! The pain was so intense! The image of Hattie abruptly invaded my thoughts and I felt like a woman who got busted fucking her girlfriend's man-LIKE MIKKI! But THAT bitter reminiscence was also suddenly trampled by the sour breath and post-intercourse brutality he felt obliged to hurl my way!

He SNATCHED up my head and smashed it ruggedly downward against the marble floor like you do to some OLD grimy paraphenalia you no longer NEED! After my temple hit rock-bottom I lay in a puddle of our, mostly my, own pleasures! After my body stopped twitching and the recurrent orgasm had faded, I closed my eyes-wondering if I was in love! I felt a penitent tear wander down my cheek-AND I PASSED OUT! Catharsis' voice chased me to that oblivion asking of me the all-pervasive question in my nebulous dreams:

"WHAT'S THE SECRET TO STAYING ALIVE?"

THE ANSWER... "DON'T SAY A God-damned WORD!!"

SOMETHING ABOUT A WOMAN

Well…what happened? What caused my life to plunge in 100 simultaneous directions and WHEN does tragedy truly end? Was it me who brought these untimely events upon myself in a fool's karma where reckless thoughtlessness yields various substantial dilemma to those who engage in it? Or was the sum of my destiny just the shit that happens (to any woman) despite her wisdom or lack of it? In these 12 months I have seen and tasted defeat in so many ways that the pleasures of a peaceful existence are no longer a palatable or accepted dream. Peace and destruction cannot co-exist. Not at the same time!

I have lost 3 people whom I'd certainly prefer to have around and their collective departure has rendered me the open wounds of 22 years of friendship up in smoke. Mikki chose to bite and devour the apple we as kids are instructed by carnal mothers and Heavenly Fathers not to partake of. And as the knife lay plunged and embedded in my back, blood draining of naivety and misplaced trust, she chose to lie and conceal the disgrace with which she betrayed me!

FLOYD IS GONE! Perhaps to the happier bliss prescribed for those few good men who scarcely walk the beat of decency. A breed nearly extinct and bordering societal annihilation-thanks to me and 'BITCHES' like myself! The death by him I had coming was my second departure. After that which I suffered at the hands of my closest female friend.

And that is what led me to the violence of today. My domestically congested better-half, Hattie Wilson, sought, found and was slaughtered at the hands of romances' Pied Piper who has tooted his bugle of unrest and codependency and sifted so many of our sister's lives into the Devil's Playpen. She yearned for a life more meaningful and abundant than the dire atrocities that nonfulfillment daily fed her through one-night stands and casual sex. Something was MISSING and she shared with me the fruits of her struggle.

I too sought the same thing! The sinister apparition that tells a woman to get out! Leave your nest of folly and dissatisfaction and find what you are looking for. Catharsis arrested those aspirations-that stir-crazy inherent feminine trait. He made her feel alive and satisfied her aborted lost soul. The one she had before she met him and after she fell in love she laid to rest that crooked deceptive monster that made her a whore. And Catharsis, after hearing her prayer and bringing to fruition her dreams, cast down the criminal overtures of himself. Of his brutal possessive insecurities and TOOK the life that he refused to be abandoned by.

But not only did he take her life, he took mine as well! Because it was impossible to murder just one! Death comes in two's or three's sometimes and fate would not make me an idle witness to my friendship's loss. I loved that woman, that human being, with a love that mothers often have for their children. That husband's feel for their wives and GODS hold for their precious Creations! Thus in THIS I had to respond and THAT is what propelled HELL'S fury MY way!

I have taken the bullets. I have sacrificed myself like a Saviour I have YET to meet and be acquainted with. Yet He saved me despite my lack of knowledge of him. And he granted me life although it cost me so much of my once tender self! The violated know the answers to pain and although wounded they fare far better and respond well to time's retrospective summaries as to who and what led them their.

There was something about Mikki which forced her greed to manifest itself at my deception's expense. There was something about Floyd that blew him off course from fool's path to chose BETTER for his worthy self. There was something about Hattie which inclined her naturally to seek better than what she had dug frantically in the same trash bin I've too often rummaged through myself. There was something about me obligating my conscience to rescue the esteem of a life-Hattie's life, that had already been lost. And there's something about a woman that directs her into domestic maladies, mistakes and carelessness in her quest to dig DEEPER beyond the multiple pockets of sanity as she seeks to find and know herself!

I would be remiss if I failed to take this time to go over a few important things we as women wrongfully do and must disassociate ourselves from. I am describing to you the mistakes but will leave the bulk of the solutions to you. To allow you to make most of your OWN mistakes. But NOT THE WORST ONES! These are just a few of the tools of survival. They are invaluable assets which will keep a sister on the right path, out of dead-end situations and allow her heart to steer clear of romances I.C.U. Many are they who encounter deceit at the hands of their overrated 'INSIGNIFICANT OTHER!' So let me take you through the infantile A.B.C's of domestic self-determination-step by step!

There is a DIFFERENCE between being in love-and getting FUCKED right! Just because a man fucks you right that don't mean you love him. It doesn't make him worthy of your love. And it SURE doesn't mean that he loves YOU. It IS what it IS! You've been FUCKED REAL GOOD! That's it! HALELUJAH! So put away the Wedding Dress! Savor the feeling but keep your guards up cuz you're NOT the first bitch the nigger's ever fucked. You DAMN sure as HELL won't be the last and there's no guarantee that he's not fucking Sheila from Uptown on the alternate days he's not beast-fuckin YOU! So keep your heart away from him!

If you give the wrong man EVERYTHING-heart, body and soul usually and eventually he will begin to take you for granted. He will shun you, no longer considering you a mental challenge worthy of the respect he had for you before he got the pussy! THIS IS A TRIFLING NEGRO!

Will a Player tell you he's a player? HELL NO! Your ignorance to deception is the most SEDUCTIVE essence of his attack! Will a liar tell you he's a liar? Would a vampire fess up an say "I'm a vampire?" No way! If he does he'll starve to death cuz NOBODY'S dumb enough to let someone LEECH off their entire life and suck them dry!

Just because a man ACTS friendly doesn't mean that he's nice! I'm sure Jeffrey Dahmer was nice to his victim's right up till the time he sliced them up and stuck that ASS between 2 slices of bread! Ted Bundy was nice-till he got them alone and the hammer began to fall.The Boston Strangler probably had a Kool-Aid smile TOO-and before his victims realized, it was too late and they'd walked into the light. And I guarantee a man will ALWAYS be nicer to you before he slides those panties down and the pump-fest gets underway!! Why am I saying this? Because we women have learned to be the most gullible and trusting creatures on the planet!

Thank God that a piece of pussy, some good head and a broken heart are the only things we've stood to lose where picking the RIGHT man is concerned-or NOT picking the wrong man! And why am I mentioning Serial Killer's and assholes who ate their dates for DINNER! Because many of those victims I've just mentioned had to make a conscious decision as to the trustworthiness and true intentions of those psychos who'd ultimately kill them. And if everyday domestic errors and misjudgments of character were based on life and death decisions FOR US the way they were for ALL those poor misfortunates A LOT OF YOU DUMB BITCHES WOULD'VE BEEN DEAD A LONG TIME AGO!

"Oh GIRL, I'm goin out today with Harry-OOPS! I PICKED UP AN AXE-MURDERER!"

A wolf acts friendly. But the wolf is ALWAYS the one that winds up with the lamb-chop on his plate! I REST MY CASE!

Speaking of wolves, men summarily believe that they know women. That they, in their infinite disillusioned wisdom, have somehow figured us out. Well a little bird tells me that the vast majority of them are 1000% wrong! They don't truly know us! Husbands don't really know their wives and this is why they are so ill-equipped to make us happy. This is why they have failed so miserably in reaching, satisfying and keeping their other-halves! I'm sure a lot of single broken-hearted men can identify with what I'm saying and there long spiraling downward plunge from that last relationship (the one they wanted to last forever) will undoubtedly confirm this.

How can you stimulate something which you know very little about? How can a person enthuse or entertain that which they have only a slight degree of knowledge about? And who on this Earth can satisfy a woman whom he has symbolically not yet met? You ask a lot of men what turns their women on and most of them don't have the foggiest idea! Not a fucking clue! So NEGRO if you don't know exactly what it is that makes me tick, then there's no way you can wind me up and get me to functioning properly. 'DUH!'

There is something about a woman that is gravely unique to her species that her male gender needs a thorough re-education on. Perhaps the equivalent of 10 years of intense 'BITCH BOOT-CAMP' or Medical School and then another agonizing 8-10 years in field training to garner the essential skills and knowledge of what makes a sister tick! Hands-on experience can be righteous! It can teach you shit you could NEVER acquire in the Academy.

Why you think brothers are so ill-prepared from the moment they plop off poppa's knee after the long mystical speech about "The bird and the bee?" Despite dad's own limited analysis and cognitive skills on why he and mom got together and what the Hell keeps them both here (besides you and your fucked up sister) in this SAD Creature-Feature called a marriage, there are still many elements of life that he is completely ignorant of!

He don't realize why 'Mom-dukes' spends so much time 'OUT WITH THE GIRLS!' His 'Ignant' ass can't construe why in 'Tarnations' his beloved wifey creeps in at 5:00A.M. 2 times a week and heads straight for the shower-then directly to sleep! And most of all he hasn't got a clue why the love making that used to make them both HOLLER, cum quick and wake the kids has now transformed into the dull blithe ceremony of uninspired grunts and barks that her soaring libido must avoid like genital herpes! Daddy is the PLAGUE! A walking talking boisterous 6 foot tall expanse that she must submit to periodically in order to explain the pretense of a loving relationship and a happy home!

So Don Juan daddy, the arrogant idiot savante whose lying to little junior about the irresistible charm that he holds mommy captive with, is basically NOT all that he's cracked up to be! He will boast and brag and stick out his chest. "Just follow me, my boy, and your new-found love-life will be as grossly fulfilling as mine!" Then he resumes his unenlightened spiel of 'The bird and the bee' as only 'FATHER KNOWS BEST!'

By the time Junior leaves the scene of THIS Fairy-tale crime-story, a criminal scenario decorated with fallacy and fabled conjecture, his mind is utterly and totally fucked up! Daddy, in his desperate quest to relay empowering fatherhood and spousal support to his firstborn seed, has disillusioned the impressionable Son-of-a-Fool into mis-educational bliss! The poor kid now embraces this Machismo rendition of what a man is supposed to be. He THINKS he is a MAN-capable of courting and enchanting any young Damsel in Distress stupid enough to give him the time of day. He carries this distorted view of life into adolescence and early adulthood and before you know it sisters, he's the one trying to buy you a drink and grind your denim jeans into nothingness at 'Da Club!'

It is not his fault! In fact HE IS THE VICTIM! Juniors' been mortally wounded figuratively speaking by the GUN OF IGNORANCE! Shot directly between the eyes with hollow-point bullets of misinformation regarding manhood! So how can he POSSIBLY treat you like a woman when he has not yet been properly taught to be a man! And this dummy grabbing you at the Bar who won't take "NO" for an answer has his prehistoric Pappy to thank for it! Such is the all pervasive Domino Effect of learned misconceptions as it infiltrates the very core of domestic relationships!

Can a monkey take a sister out and behave in a gentlemanly manner? HELL NO! He'll embarrass her in public-scratching his ASS. Picking scurrying parasites out of his fur and groping for and devouring bananas. DON'T GET MAD BITCH! You picked a monkey! HE IS A FUCKING MONKEY AND THAT'S ALL THAT HE IS! So why are you expecting him to behave like a man?

Can a CAVEMAN accompany you via Limousine to the Royal Palace Ball and be expected to exude elegance, refinery and grace? I DON'T FUCKING THINK SO! Now he might snatch your sophisticado virgin ass up and FUCK you for a few hours-thrusting his nasty little caveman dick inside your swollen genitals while ramming his thick unlettered tongue down your throat. This is what CAVEMEN do! Don't blame HIS ass! Who picked him out of the male prospect line-up and dressed him in a Tux? You even made him leave his Billy-Club at the house behind the sofa and tried to teach him to hold a Champagne glass and smile for the camera! DUMB BITCH! You have YOURSELF to blame! You should've known better! A caveman is NOTHING...but a caveman!

So there you have it! Your date is running around at the extravagant Gala-KNOCKING OVER Rembrandts! Galloping up and down the stairs! Consuming other peoples dinner trays-OH THIS MOTHERFUCKER IS OUT OF CONTROL! Taunting the guests. Pulling the hems of Baronesses dresses and ripping off their clothes cuz he has an erection that your bourgoise lips wouldn't satisfy back home at the crib! And you couldn't see this coming? Your caveman is far from being civilized-but you knew this before you invited the flea-bitten mongrel into your hard-up desperate life! So don't complain-LOOK AT YOU NOW! You're a dateless societal laughing-stock cuz you chose to embrace a caveman!

Where am I going with this? Ladies you must admit that THIS has been you! Have you ever gone out, ANYWHERE, and your man didn't know how to act? Check the scenario! He's that caveman and he's STARING at every derrier up in the spot except yours! He asks for a few minutes alone or dismisses you politely for that 5th trip to the Restroom within the last 10 minutes just to 'Go out and PLAY!' Well that must be what he's doing as you stand there crying tears of a CLOWN and holding your drink ALL BY YOURSELF! Or perhaps the bathroom is located down by the out-house 50 miles away and your loving other-half is just taking his sweet time sauntering on his merry way back to you-the woman he can't stand spending 2 minutes without! So you say "I'll just STAND HERE waiting for my caveman and holding my head up high as though I actually thought that there was nothing wrong!"

MEANWHILE MR. CAVEY IS ON THE OTHER SIDE OF THE DANCE FLOOR HUDDLED INCONSPICUOUSLY WITH DAT BIG-BUTT FREAK TRYING TO MAKE A BABY! Get it! This MOTHERFUCKER that you CHOOSE to call your man is uncivilized and unrestrainable! He cannot control his dicks mind to go out and fuck WHATEVER HE CAN! EVERYTHING! AND HE HAS NOT BEEN TAUGHT

TO RESPECT YOU! So If HE'S the caveman then PLAY YOUR POSITION as the jackass he's PLAYIN!

At times we are the exclusive victims of the unsavory choices we make in life! And it's foolish to blame others as we burn to death in a raging inferno of unsound judgement that WE started! Then you call your girlfriend and beg her to save you from loving and being dogged by this nigger who you'll be sleeping with AGAIN-BEFORE THE SUN GOES DOWN!

Now in this enlightened stage of my life I will no longer understand the sour enigma of self-defeatism. For example, we live our lives every day. We eat to nourish our bodies so we can stay alive. We sleep all fucking day for essential rest. We bathe for necessary cleanliness, good hygiene, etc. We eat properly for once again-healthful reasons. Why we even BREATH continually and involuntarily because our bodies know that oxygen is mandatory in our innate quest to preserve life. If no eat-WE DIE! If no breath-WE DIE! If heart stops-WE DIE! Such is the biological ecology of the most basic principle-self survival!

We flee danger and avoid detrimental shit cuz we like to live! We don't touch 'HOT' cuz we know 'HOT' will burn the SHIT out of us! We don't touch 'SHARP' cuz 'SHARP' cuts-and if we bleed TOO MUCH-WE DIE! So in our noble hopes NOT TO DIE, YET, we avoid certain shit!

Alright then-that being established, since we are creatures of habit and therefore naturally gravitate toward things that promote life, health, peace and fulfillment, then why is it that we are cursed with various urges to participate in some of the MOST precarious things that will invariably do us harm? We smoke, we drink, we get high, we fuck people who not even the DEVIL would touch! We risk our lives on a daily basis on some physical absurdities that would land ANY of God's creatures in an early grave. YET WE CALL OURSELVES CIVILIZED!

Relationships! We are the greatest and most knowledgable creations on the Planet Earth! MANKIND-bold, intrepid, wise, noble, and prudent! Yet we are the most FUCKED UP judges of character in the Universe! I think that we could learn alot from the OTHER, less learned, CREATURES-THE ANIMALS! You ever see a baboon in Divorce Court? Ever see a chicken on Jerry Springer-or a lizard on Maury Povich trying to figure out who her baby's daddy is? Or mother-turtle-does she allow herself to be stomped the Hell out-RIGHT IN FRONT OF JUNIOR, BY BIG BAD-ASS POPPA TORTIOSE? The HOSTILE Son-of-a-bitch she sleeps with on a daily basis? OH HELL NO!

I will fairly place MYSELF in this degrading category and afterwards include some of my budding female dummy counterparts! I have seen and paid for my mistakes and look to impart some obligatory wisdom in unsound minds to prevent them from deteriorating into the domestic ills which tragically afflicted MY life.

Now back to the animals! NO, NOT US-The 4 legged ones! I think that we ought to switch destinies with them. Put some of US in a zoo and let them feed us peanuts! Despite the gigantic sign "PLEASE DO NOT FEED THE HUMANS!" Or grab a cow or a hog or a chicken and let THEM run the country! I swear THEY'D BALANCE THE BUDGET BETTER THAN BUSH! And they wouldn't send our offspring over to the Mid-East to DIE for oil! HELLO?!? Let em drive the buses or serve drinks at Happy Hour while WE resign to spend the rest of our days living in the swamps, the oceans and the trees!

How about gathering all the cats and dogs and allowing them to preside over Grand Juries and try cases. While we are dispatched to Pet Land or petting zoos to be bought and sold like poodles and Persians! I think some of us might find our calling in life indulging in dog-fights while walking through the park leashed to some other beast, with 4 legs, who'se got more sense than us!

So stick the red and white Carousel-poles up OUR asses or in our backs so that horses and Jackasses could ride US up and down in Merry-go-round fashion! We have PROVEN to be creatures totally unaware of the true meaning or purpose in life and squander it carelessly! Like a dog chasing it's own tail-in an endless circle. Constantly spinning out of control yet unable to progress or go anywhere due to the revolving and self-ingratiating nature of our OWN STUPIDITY! I could more easily imagine, AND JUSTIFY, little monkeys riding OUR BACKS as we spin our lives back into the realms of destabilization, retrogression and uncivilization!

I'VE SEEN HOUSEHOLDS! Magnificent plush couches, 50 inch plasma color T.V's, and 4 car garages. I mean MANSION shit! A Tennis Court, heated-pool, a landscaper AND A BUTLER-all about their daily occupation of contributing to the splendor of the new couples HAPPY HOME! But wifey has 4 extra bedrooms to lay her head at for those nights when she don't exactly want her loving husbands limp dick sliding around in her genitals. And HUBBY-old fat jolly hubby, got 2 tricks on the side who stay in a secret quiet place just 10 feet from wifey so when that 'DOG-HOUSE' phraseology comes around his dead penis can take that Viagra nose-dive and FINALLY get hard again!

But they're building their castle in the sky-with no foundation. Mommy and daddy and sweet little baby Wilson have neglected the common denominator and most basic unit of peaceful co-existence. So the exercise in futility will fall without the mandatory component called 'LOVE,' 'TRUST,' 'LUST,' and 'DEVOTION' to maintain it's cohesiveness!

The Wilson Happy Home in the Hamptons, Flatbush Avenue or the backwoods of Hilbilly-ville will undoubtedly live to present itself to the Divorce Court-to rend asunder amicably its irreconcilable demise. Mr. Wilson will be sodomized into post-marital bankruptcy-losing ALL but an embittered heart! He gets to keep something alright-the bi-weekly Child Support and Alimony payments to appease Ms. Wilson's flight into independence! And Ms. Wilson will get to maintain the promise of a shattered life and distrust for MEN, MATRIMONY AND LASTING COMMITTED IDEALS! But thanks be to God she is allowed to shed from her life that ungrateful, basically obnoxious parasite who stole 10 years of her life! She's elated that he has gone to a better place where trifling bastards hang their hats and hopes he will pay for the next 10,000 years for her squandered happiness!

She will not re-marry cuz that would bring an end to her Alimony trick and shopping-spree money. No, she will hook up with the next best nigger to tempt her sexuality. But THIS new union, unlike the first, will be better-more carnal and less structured. And prudently 'off the books!' So in essence, for the rest of her days Ms. Wilson is symbolically Honeymooning in a distant Cottage in the Poconos with some new handsome and virile domestic candidate. AND MR. WILSON'S BROKE SORRY ASS IS PAYING FOR IT!

But Mr. Wilson is glad as well. "THANK GOD THE BITCH IS GONE," he utters to himself while calculating the inordinate amount of HIS life's proceeds that she selfishly took with her! And with the long-awaited relief one experiences after a 10 year long psychological and financial FLOGGING, he EXHALES, so DAMN GLAD the ass-whipping is finally over! It doesn't have to END like this!

We have to learn to separate past painful events from the present scenario because if we don't we will become bitter. At times we collectively drown TODAY in what we lost YESTURDAY and that dead weight becomes the extra-baggage to hinder our growth! DON'T DIE EVERYDAY! If you died yesterday then let yesterday REST IN PEACE-AND MOVE THE HELL ON!

If I go into a new relationship-a different situation with a man who is NOT the same lame motherfucker I HAD, I must go into that new scenario fresh-without prior paranoia's or preconceived notions that this next one will be JUST LIKE THE PREVIOUS ASSHOLE WHOM I FOOLISHLY GAVE MY HEART TO. Now, in this-MY NEW THING, if I decide I wanna be with you-I'll be with you! If I wanna give you a play and spend some time-I'll spend some time! If I wanna bend over and suck your dick-I'll bend over and SUCK YOUR DICK! If I wanna have your baby-I'll have your baby! If I wanna let you take me out to dinner I'll let you take me! If I decide to give you a special place my heart then you'll BE there! TILL I CHANGE MY MIND! And if I tell you 'Good-bye' or if YOU leave ME alone broken-hearted and crying on the floor-perhaps BOTH you and I can find some semblance of inner-peace to display to the rest of humanity for the remainder of our lives. And NOT chastise or mistreat THE NEXT PERSON WE MEET INAPPROPRIATELY! Peter must not pay for Paul nor Paul pay for ALL!

That being said I REFUSE TO BE THE WOMAN WHOSE LIFE WAS RUINED BY THE LAST NIGGER I MET-AND FELL IN LOVE WITH! That's where a lot of sisters lose their way because they're stuck on some horrific events a man did to them yesterday and cannot separate that trauma from the new unadulterated reality of NOW. So you've been hurt-well alotta women have been hurt! Some just as bad or even more than YOU!

One cave-woman lost her man sometime 2 million B.C. to some hungry Pteradactyl bitch who scooped up the Neanderthal-billy-club and all and carried him off to the nest for brunch to feed her howling babies. The entire carnivorous melee was over in a flash divided into 3 segments! "SWOOP!" "SCREAM" and the gnashing of teeth! Maybe one of the little prehistoric sucklings emitted a hardy belch, thankful for the belated scoop of stinky human meat, but that was that!

Then some eons later a lonely medieval damsel, while waiting in the enchanted castle for her man to come home, got the traumatic phone call via messenger (T-Mobile had not been born yet) that hubby won't be home for Christmas! Attila and the rest of those sadistic Huns were busy being their usual warlike selves and saw to it that little Bobby Finnegan of the Irish Celts would be a bastard before his 5th Birthday! He ASKED for the GI-Joe with the Kung-fu Grip-riding on a primitive belief of a fat white-boy, also from the West, who gave out MUCHO TOYS to all the good little girls and boys!

Well once more the Good Santa fucked up the order scribbled on his papyrus Holiday list and instead of the action figure he got wind that his noble POPPY is being Butt-fucked and pimped to the reprobate Huns (The ones that don't like pussy) in some God-forsaken brothel on the other side of town! Daddy dearest has been sold into slavery! Offering up his tight Irish Catholic ASS for a pound of silver and a keg of hops to sexually ambidextrious Mongolian Warlords who've forsaken their Asiatic virgins for the forbidden helplessness of Western male Prisoners of War!

Hah! So much for home for the Holidays! Daddy's been turned out! EMASCULATED! And from his precarious vantage-point there aint no mistletoe in the dark places he's bein kissed! Forced sodomy can be rather DISCOMFORTING without the benefit of a hug and a kiss to get one started and in the mood!

That brings us to the future of today! Somewhere, somehow there's a sister whose man is out there fuckin some trick named 'LOLITA!' This 'GOOD' woman knows that Lolita, the BAD bitch is hittin her BAD-ass husband named KEVIN real GOOD cuz she ain't seen KEVIN in a week! And she can't stop it! She's seen the signs plain as day but her niave desire for a brighter day and that blind unmerciful genetic trait that some call 'Stupidity' won't let her GOODY-GOODY sentiments leave Kevin the fuck ALONE!

She has tried everything but nothing works. All she's ever wanted is a good husband, some children and a righteous God to bless their union. Yet intead of marital bliss with Mr. Right she's received only disappointment from Mr. Wrong!

"What the Fuck is WRONG," she inquires of her aging mentality, but the answer to that question is as elusive as the peace she seeks living with the DEVIL! Sisters, I SAID THE DEVIL! Not just A Devil-but THE DEVIL! SATAN HIMSELF!

Not that I'm pointing convictive fingers at some women who are having a hard time but WHAT THE HELL MIGHT ONE EXPECT CAN BE FOUND WHEN ONE HAS CONSCIOUSLY DECIDED TO CO-EXIST WITH THE DEVIL! PURE HELL is ALL that he has to offer!!

You could be Mother Mary, Mother Teresa, Mother Goose and fucking Oprah Winfrey all mixed up in one but BITCH you can't change a leopards spots! ONLY GOD CAN! And since you AIN'T God then you need to leave well enough alone and throw the Prince of Darkness outta your house and outta your life!

Positives and negatives can't always make a connection suitable to form a true serene marital bond! FUCK 'OPPOSITES ATTRACT!' That's the kinda shit that messed up Adam and Eve! Sampson and Delilah! Sonny and Cher-did I mention Ike and Tina? Just because something ATTRACTS that don't mean they can mix well-in utter bliss and happiness! So I'm attracted to you-and your lying ass is also attracted to me! That don't mean that things will last FOREVER or even WORK boo! Think about it intelligently! A lot of people find in someone else certain characteristics that are unique and amicable. But that don't call for wedding bells and sacred vows. So you feelin this person-TRY IT OUT! But DON'T GIVE HIM THAT SACRED PART OF YOURSELF that you ain't prepared to let go or lose forever! And don't give up ANYTHING that you can't afford to miss or can't get back!

So Playboy says he loves you. He can't live without you or even eat or sleep 10 minutes absent from your requited love! THAT'S NICE! But sister-girl DON'T BE A CRASHDUMMY! Alotta men say some fly rosy shit but that don't mean you should slide down those thongs and give away the family FORTUNE! NO-NOT THE FAMILY JEWELS! Save em for a rainy day! And slow down-cuz it ain't rainin outside!

A great white shark might say he don't eat meat. But when you look at the bottom of the ocean and find a whole lotta broken gnawed-off skeleton bones you might doubt his sincerity! Shit-an alligator might tell you he's on a diet-a liquid diet! Open up the deceitful bastard's stomach! I bet you won't find much liquid! You might find the LAST dumb bitch that believed him-her severed head floatin around in his intestines. You might find a fish, a curling iron, a pork-chop or a fucking can of beer-ANYTHING but the liquid diet he swore he was on!

On the other hand you might find the rare brother who actually says and does as he says! Honesty is not EXTINCT-it's just scarce! Get my meaning? Put your guards up! Use them to defend the sanctity of yourself-but don't let them envelop you in a morbid world of bitterness and hostility towards life.

EPILOGUE

I GOT YOU GIRL!

A benevolent Police Officer disobeyed a direct order from his Supervisor and responded to something suspicious in one of the worse ghettos of Wyandance! It was the place where the NIGGERS ruled AND THE COPS DIDN'T GO! Catharsis had dumped my shallow breathing body in the snow and left me there for dead! My system had almost went into shock and the Doctors told my mother if I had been found minutes later my battered body would've been wheeled on a gurney to the Morgue-instead of to the Emergency Room! I had suffered alot-not so much from the beating but hypothermia had set in and I almost lost several fingers and toes. They say the extremeties are the most vulnerable parts of our body to the brutal cold.

I'd been found sprawled out in several inches of snow near an alleyway on the drug-infested side of town. I could've been killed easily because when they found me my pants and underwear were down by my ankles. So although Catharsis did not overtly decide to take my life, it's obvious that some of the locals could've finished the job for him.

So this Rookie Cop submitted to his instincts when he witnessed a dark colored mini-van abruptly speed off through a red light. As he drove to the area where the vehicle had been idling, he thought he'd heard a muffled sound-a whimper. He then radioed for assistance but was ordered by the Supervising Dispatcher to stand down and go on his Merry way. If he had listened-or hesitated minutes more-I WOULD HAVE BEEN DEAD! But he ACTED in total defiance to the instructions rendered by his disengaged Superior advising him to continue on within the guidelines of his Patrol and not to attempt to abort some ghetto fatalities that didn't need to be aborted! Common sense and human empathy invariably led him to the conclusion that SOME THINGS NEED TO BE LOOKED INTO-and as he drove up THERE I WAS! Laying there in the residue of my own downfall.

He was a Hero to me and I was able to behold my rescuer on the third and final day of my hospitalization. The Blue Knight came to me as I lay in bed still relatively weak and he hugged and kissed me. He was the kindest and most genuinely sincere Police Officer I had ever met-A YOUNG WHITE GUY! Right there in the Care Unit I cried on his shoulders and when I held him I could feel the pain he experienced for me right through his Navy Blue clad chest. As we embraced, for the first time in my life the terrified little girl inside me was allowed to show her TRUE timid face! To outwardly cry, to feel sorrow and mourn. Not having to fear the bitter consequences of her human frailties.

All throughout my bitter childhood I've known only PAIN! So I've become impervious to it! That has been the best defense mechanism I've known-complete apathy! I would fight it and fight it until my detachment prompted inner bliss-excusing the hurt till it went away. But I could not dismiss THIS feeling and the Blue Knight's earnest sympathy invited and dispelled my tears.

He was crying too and turned his head away from my double-vision not wanting me to see in him the humanity lost by countless of his law enforcement peers. Perhaps they taught him in the Academy not to feel for the victim's. He was embarrassed of his pity, his regret and I felt God alive in this good man reaching out to my helplessness despite the adaptive belligerent nature of his profession! It seemed a violation for an Officer of the Law to be anything other than callous and HE was NOT that man. He was my soul's rescuer-a Hero and a loving white Angel who had failed to accommodate the prerequisite criteria of the hostility it takes to don a blue uniform.

He introduced himself as 'Fred' and talked to me like I was his own daughter. WHY DO SOME BLACK PEOPLE HATE ALL WHITE FOLKS AND CALL THEM DEVILS? What in the world was Elijah Muhammed TALKING about? Surely he had never met THIS man cuz if he did he would have surely modified his social doctrines. The Blue Knight did not deserve to be condemned for his race and HE WAS NOT A DEVIL! Moreover; only a TRUE DEVIL would label this gentle man ANYTHING but an Angel! The Hell with the Nation Of Islam! What did they know? Too many helpings of bean pie and choking bow-tie stifle air flow and conceive errant hallucinations.

Catharsis had left a note in one of my pockets to let me know that although he didn't kill me-HE COULD.

It read: "If you talk-THEY won't live to see the Ball drop!" The threat was typed on a small light blue piece of stationary torn in half-and it had blood on it! Probably MINE! I hadn't told anyone there at the hospital about what I'd found-what in the world could THEY do about it! I closed my eyes and lay my head down to rest considering the warning as its resoundments carried me into a vigorous disquieted slumber.

I took care of everything at Hattie's Funeral! Like she always said: "I GOT YOU GIRL!" Due to the severe beating, the Funeral Director suggested a closed-casket ceremony but I said "NO! Leave it open!" I did not want her to be further humiliated by spending these last moments in a closed box-NO, let her friends and loved ones say 'Good-bye' to her as she WAS! And not have to view and wave at a pine-casket representative of her tragic ending.

"You dress her up! Hide the wounds as best you can," I insisted!

"But the job will be costly…," he started.

"SHUT UP! YOU PAYIN FOR THIS?" I was adamant. I was incensed! I was merciless! I WAS HER FRIEND!

I held it down-spent 11 G's on my GIRL to make her departure more pleasant and more palatable for her agrieved loved ones. Seventy-five guests were invited. Only 22 showed up! Her uncle was supposed to help with the funds. The cheap-fuck was RICH in my book-had 6 apartment buildings. That penny-pinching nigger OWNED 6 FUCKING

Bomani Shuru

BUILDINGS! Fuck it NIGGER-SELL A HOUSE! AND THEY CALL THE JEWS CHEAP-THEY AIN'T CHEAP! I bet they'd spend every nickel they could find in the Synagogue to bury their dead-and then receive donations from a tightly woven Hebraic Community to defray any OTHER costs to the mourning family. Therefore I surmised that 'CHEAP-AS-A-JEW harangue be re-evaluated to include the country-FUCK who abandoned Hattie in this-her time of NEED! He couldn't spend one DIME on the nephew he promised Hattie's mom he would 'look out for!' Just cuz he didn't agree with her homosexual lifestyle! Said she brought SHAME to the family's image and he would get outraged if Hattie attempted to bring ANY male company to her apartment-NOT IN HIS HOME!

SO FUCKING WHAT NIGGER YOUR NEPHEW IS GAY-NOW SHE'S DEAD! And the least thing you could do is show some human empathy-try and make up for the hostile upbringing you gave her after you became her God-father, swearing to your beloved sister to nurture and PROTECT her till death do you part! What kind of cheap shit is THAT? He was too ashamed of her to pitch in and help! And during the Service he didn't even stand when the Preacher asked that the family of the dearly departed file-in and come forward for one final viewing!

I wished that HE and ANYONE else like him were lying in that coffin and wished I could get away with putting him there! GOD DON'T LIKE UGLY! And I'm sure that when his time comes God will give him in death-that which he EARNED in life! And if the Lord could use a hired Assassin, a Mercenary to do his dirty work so as not to soil those great omnipotent fingers, I'd WHACK him MYSELF! For FREE! "Don't mention it Heavenly Father, this ones on ME!

My Credit Card took a ROYAL beat-down but I didn't care! Like I said-me and Hattie were tight! She was my all and all-and I would've GLADLY sold anything, ANYTHING, to accommodate the peaceful transition of her passing!

She had suffered enough! She had been humiliated moments before death, humiliated at the crime-scene and I would NOT let her go out as anything but a DIVA! A beautiful honorable DIVA! I dressed her body MYSELF-FORGET THE MORTICIAN! I told him to stay home! And I laced my girl in the FINEST most expensive Victoria Secret mini-skirt that the Store-Clerk could FIND! Accessorized with a Fendi hat and purse set spun in silk. THAT'S RIGHT! I'm PROUD of THIS! THIS WAS MY MOTHERFUCKING HEART! And if ANYBODY had anything NEGATIVE to say about it then there would be ANOTHER Funeral acomin-AND IT WOULDN'T BE MINE!

I was the first one present at the Procession and the burial and I was the LAST one to leave! Mikki DIDN'T COME! Kecia told me she said she had an emergency! Yeah RIGHT bitch-well good for YOU cuz if she woulda come THAT ASS would be playin a harp and exchanging beauty secrets on the OTHER SIDE with Hattie! I PERSONALLY would SEE to it! I didn't want no traitors present during my final moments with Hattie!

And Mik's attendance would've constituted A REAL EMERGENCY! It's funny but COINCIDENTLY, Canei was a no-show as well! I hoped THEY'D DIE TOGETHER-IF SAMMY DIDN'T BLAZE THE ENTIRE HOUSEHOLD FIRST! FUCK UM!

Demons from my past came back to haunt me and I could've passed out when I saw the Fairy God-mother who had accompanied Floyd in that first crucial day of the rest of his life without my knife in his back. She kept staring at me and my instincts immediately read to me the reason why. Floyd KNEW how much my girl had meant to me and this, I believe, was his way of offering me comfort-from a distance. Nevertheless I hung my head in the embarrassment of my pain and refused to return her glances.

I met Hattie's other family members-6 to be exact and a few of her close friends were there. Her God-nieces and nephews were also there and 2 of them said a prayer for her. It was wonderful and I cried! Happy to hear the appreciation of uncorrupted minds, who not tainted by the shame of their elders, were deeply sorry that their beloved was gone.

When Hattie's body was placed in the ground I LOST IT! I knew I would never hear her laugh, see her sly smiling face or commune with my fraternal twin. My other half who had to suddenly leave me alone in this friendless world! I couldn't fight the reality death posed. The permanency! My LOVE was gone-and I too slowly began to die! And my combative mind would not let me live it down because I every night I went to sleep knowing exactly who her killer was!

The Preacher told us at the wake that death is a time of Peace and Rest! Well-WHERE IS THE PEACE for the victim and his or her bereaved loved ones? How can Hattie REST IN PEACE? You don't rest at all when your life has been tragically ended by the scumbag you once loved! Love don't always love back! You won't rest until your killer is either brought to justice or murdered like you were! If he shares your fate and somebody takes him out then you'll be waiting on the other side-WITH ALCOHOL ON YOUR ETHERAL BREATH AND A 9 Millimeter in your hand!

THAT'S JUSTICE! That's payback. That's REST! And how can those of us you left behind LIVE in peace knowing that your murderer still walks among us ready and able to send US to that 'PLACE!' where the living can't go? I swear I will never rest until my conscience is appeased with the knowledge that THAT fag bastard is strewn helplessly in the gutter-bloodsoaked, immobile and deceased! NOW THAT'S REST!

What about peace? I have yet to experience the peace one finds in the abrupt realization that his throat has been cut! THAT AIN'T PEACE! So how in the world can Preacher-man climb outta the bed of hypocrisy and run up in the Pulpit swearing up and down that the collective dead are in a state of peace? How does HE know? WHAT BIBLE IS HE READING? Violence is violence! You think Christ was happy when they unloaded him off the cross after they just got through beatin the shit outta him? I don't think so!

They hung him on a tree by his wrists. Steel nails embedded in them! There were also nails in his feet! The nails in his wrists RIPPED right through the flesh from the weight of his body impaled and hanging by those wounds-from a tree! They stabbed him with a spear through his fucking stomach! HOW YOU THINK THAT FEEL? They stuck a razor-sharp crown of thorns on his head and you KNOW what brier thorns can do to a person's skin! I don't care if you're the Son of God or NOT-the shit HURTS! If you don't believe me-grab a needle and stick it in your flesh-TILL YOU BLEED! Feel it? Well multiply that pain times a hundred of those tiny piercing needles bursting through the capillaries in your bloody skillet!

Now he's hangin and bleedin and agonizing. All this-after about a hundred of Rome's finest, their roughest-toughest most brutal ruff-necks, had battered him savagely! You seen Mel Gibson's movie about 'The Passion of Christ!' That's how it went DOWN-TRUST ME! They used rocks! They used BATS, chains, Roman Brass-knuckles, titanium maces, wooden billy-clubs and scourges (whips) with flint and glass-shards at the ends of them! Picking up ANYTHING they could find to be used as an item of torture!

So he DIED! They beat him! They killed him and he died!You think during that torment he had anything good to say about his enemies? His attackers? And if he DID manage a brief pleasantry amidst the painful hysteria I don't think he really meant it! "FATHER FORGIVE THEM, FOR THEY KNOW NOT WHAT THEY DO!" BULLSHIT! Those APES knew EXACTLY what they was doin! Their intention, their sadistic purpose, was to beat the dog-shit outta this 'seditious lunatic' till he stopped breathing! And those KIND selfless words were just part of the Script! King James threw some SHIT in the game by having his translators inject that act of absurdity in his Bible.

Who would say some shit like that while they're being pummeled? Martin Luther King? Rodney King-NO I don't THINK so! The power structure removed all semblances of defiance and indepence of thought from the Bible because they considered things like freedom of speech and rebellion against authority as heresy. Anti-government! So they made up some lines for the bloody Christ to say to teach us to be humble when somebody's beatin OUR ASSES! To teach us to forgive somebody who is viciously mistreating us so that we wouldn't have the common sense to fight back! THEN you'll start believing that as long as the fractures and bruises riddle your body, you're ALRIGHT with GOD! And the moment you DEFEND yourself your violent non-compliant soul is goin into the Lake of Fire! LEARN from THIS because it's the TRUTH! But ask yourself what was REALLY goin through his mind. BLOW AFTER BONE-CRUSHING BLOW! I tell you he didn't LIKE IT! But let me not digress from my POINT!

Remember in the Garden of Gethsamene? Christ saw the ASS-WHIPPIN coming and it was NOT his preferred choice! So he started prayin-looking for a bit of Divine Clemency! He said: "Father, if at all possible-let this bitter Cup pass from me!" That was a moment of weakness-spiritual wavering! NO ONE WANTS TO BE BEAT TO DEATH! Not by PROFESSIONAL KILLERS! Those Romans were PROFESSIONAL KILLERS! That means they new how to KILL you-and make it STICK! Catharsis was a PROFESSIONAL KILLER! He ALSO beat and murdered people for a living!

O.K! So Jesus is defeated! And his Italian assassins pull his pulverized and bloody corpse down from Galgotha's tree! Do you think The Son of Man could rest in peace after what those sadists did to him? HELL NO! And I do mean HELL cuz THAT was what he went through. And I can PROVE he did not rest in peace! Cuz according to the same Biblical Story after 72 hours Jesus decided he couldn't TAKE it anymore! He jumped outta the grave having kicked the Devil's ass and went on a rampage! He had beef! Then he declared war on the MOTHERFUCKERS who had crucified him! Not in a carnal natural sense. His boxing gloves were of a more spiritual kind! But opposition is opposition and he opposed the HELL out of established evil!

Personally I would've chosen boxing gloves of a more fatal combative kind! Something toe-to-toe! From the minute I rose from the dead I would've ran through the Biblical streets of Galilee and chopped off the heads of all the Jews who wanted me to die! And every last Roman who carried it out! I would've even went for Barabbas too-the thief who they allowed to go free in their bloodlust to hang ME!

"Oh, excuse me sir, but don't I recognize you from the crucifixion? Oh yes, I thought so!" 'SWOOSH!' "Oh-and YOU were there too..." 'SWOOSH!' And motherfucker I KNOW I saw YOUR ugly ass. YOU AND your man!" 'SWOOSH-SWOOSH!' Got it? GOOD!

So eternal rest ain't happy unless you get to SHARE it with the animal who put you there! And Hattie could not rest in peace and neither could I until a minimal degree of Justice was sought after and rendered. "SWOOSH!"

I wanted to tell Preacher-man to sit his punk ass down-that he had no right to eulogize somebody he didn't even know based on circumstances he was NOT too familiar with! He fucked up the game-calling Hattie 'Henry Franklin Woodson' instead of 'Wilson!' It should be a sin to stand before a Congregation and talk about someone whom you'd never met! What you gonna do-make up things as you go along? I was raised in the mean streets of Brooklyn and where I come from improvisation is another word for lying! So the Good-Reverend was standing tall in the House of God-LYING HIS ASS OFF! And to this end the entire Sermon was transformed into a grueling perfunctory spiel that lacked the compliment of sincerity. A vacant wind-tunnel, attacking my better sense of judgement and spewing out of his mouth as my best friend lay underneath him inheriting the bitter droplets that lies tell!

I will never forget the look on Hattie's face as she lay there dead. A tiny brown smudge unskillfully laden with make-up to camouflage the area where he had cut. I thought about the Ski-Trip just a few months ago that we had spent together. Hattie had no money but it was on ME! I held her down in life as I did in death. I recalled our previous night out! She truly enjoyed herself after the initial apprehension that night because she'd eventually made up her mind to either live happy-or die trying. On the Friday that would prove to be her final weekend. It was good to see her smile-without HIM. But no one would have ever thought that returning home to that jealous Son-of-a-bitch would cost so much!

I told my girl "I love you" 2 days before she died. When she called me to get something off her chest she must've KNOWN. She must've expected it! That violent man would do ANTHING if he found her with another nigger! So in his possessive distorted mind her bein out with me that night at Honeys surrounded by other men had to mean she DID something. He demanded that she not go but in hopes of regaining her independence, and her life back, she defied him! That was a mistake! She KNEW it and I new it. And it was just a matter of time!

Women take chances often feeling that they SHOULD have nothing to fear from the animosities of their other halves! I new he was jealous. Highly volatile-but NEVER wanted it to come to this! I mean he'd slap her around but then we figured that was it! The 2 of us could not have been more sadly mistaken!

I'm done with having sex for sport! Its OVER! The relationship that strung out my girl and cost her her life has cured ME! My horizons are more widened and I have no delusions of immortality. What have I learned from the sum of my past? That a person will die if he or she is not careful and take time in making focal decisions in life. JUST ASK HATTIE!

Thanks to Catharsis today is my Wedding Day. Today I got married to the promise that I'm staying single till Mr. Right comes along. You see I had previously underestimated my self worth and overvalued the fleeting depreciative worth of an orgasm. I embellished in my lack of self-esteem every minute only to lose that even greater sense of dignity and higher-self! Don't get me wrong-I'm far from where I need to be! But I'm over that now and it's about time! And I won't give up on Celibacy till I KNOW-UNTIL I TRULY KNOW!

Imagine a person DYING because the 2 most vital organs in their body acted in concert to engage in some promiscuous dubious behavior that cost the rest of the anatomy EVERYTHING! Mr. ingenious brain told them it was O.K. to raw-fuck any and everything sexually desirable that moved! And old Mr. Happy invited his naive fallible self into that grave composition with the inept justification of emotional and carnal attachment. And so the story goes: "I know I shouldn't be doing this! But it's NOT like my feelings are not involved. SO WHAT THE HELL-GEERO-NIMOO!"

"Ooooh-there goes my shirt, up over my face...!" Intense psychological attachment is not the metaphysical scumbag that can save a hopeless romantic from multiple communicable diseases! And furthermore blind faith and unmerited devotion can't cure SHIT!

If I continued on this Road of Fire and Brimstone, with my luck I'd probably run into the most diseased nigger in the hood and go down in history as being the youngest dumbest woman to bite a chunk out of the raunchy ass of the MONSTER! Crisis, beef and dilemma all follow me-its magnetic. And I've been known to play a mean game of Russian Roulette-WITHOUT FIRST TAKING THE BULLETS OUT!

Well now I'm done-no more Ms. Horny-ho! Hoping that tragedy would somehow try to evade my fall as I career my destiny perpetually into it! Also gone is my intense desire for drugs. I had been fooling myself into minimizing the true extent of my habit. I've TOLD myself that I can quit if I want to. WELL NOW I WANT TO! And its about Damn TIME! How long must a person remain addicted to something that's causing the unraveling of their own morality? That was my mother's problem-and I'd be DAMNED if I won't learn from HER downfall! To prevent my own! I just thank God that it will not take inordinate funds to quell what I'd been doin to my body countless days per week- FOR YEARS! I could see myself now-the ghetto chic knockin on the doors of the Betty Ford Foundation trying to get them to desegregate their racial caste system in time to save my poor black ass! 'Belushi, Rob Downey Jr., Nolte, Bobby, Whitney, Michael, Elvis-people who have fought MY fight! Let me IN you guys-I GOT ISSUES TOO!'

Its 5:30 A.M. and I ain't had no sleep-but like daddy used to say: "Plenty of time for sleep in the grave!" As soon as I wipe my eyes I'm gonna shit, shower and shave. (in my case shit, shower and squeegie) I gotta catch the Cross-town Bus into the City and my first stop is to the Municipal building in Montrose to pick up an application to become a Librarian. I've always been quite partial to studying about history and research seems to be my forte! Moreover I don't intend to spend the rest of my life pan-handling for the State in a dead-end job!

After that I would like to go talk to someone about hiring a Private Investigator to assist me in finding out the whereabouts of my mother. I've spent my LAST day staring into the mirror and not knowing who I'm looking at! When a person hasn't a clue about their own origin, their own prodigy, they CAN'T have much confidence in fairly appraising exactly who and WHAT they are. Cuz they don't know WHAT they've come from! Finding my biological mother will eliminate a portion of that crisis! And on that day, if and when I find her, I will welcome her and let her know how much I've desperately missed her! I will let her KNOW THAT I FORGIVE HER for what she did to me during her drug-addiction! Although I attach very much of what I am, the good and the bad, to her tortured times I will no longer hold her responsible for the wayward and unrestrained path I've taken. Those mistakes were my choices to make-and I made them.

Perhaps with a different upbringing I could have resisted my vices-having a sound and well grounded maternal caretaker to see to my needs. Unlike my adoptive mother. But if that be the case then I will atone for that vicious cycle by eliminating all possible barriers between myself and my 2 children and SEE TO IT that they do not find

295

themselves serving the same prison sentence of the mind that I've been brought from. A woman should be there-to take care of her kids. I will forgive my own mother's delinquency by providing for mine-thus ending the cycle of the damned. I will be re-united with Mommy-and on THAT day, all told, I will find peace! Despite what our meeting would or would not mean to her!

Then it's back down to Planned Parenthood! Oh yes, didn't I tell you-I'm 5 months in and I can feel the baby kicking already! He's a WILD little man-trying to kick his way outta my womb 4 months early! Don't he know that the drop would KILL him? Well, I guess he's a dumb just like his mother was! I have no doubts in my mind who the father is. Catharis! Yes his goons were there but I know he would never let them touch me because despite his brutal attack, the rape and the assault, anyone could see that in Catharsis eyes I was sort of a prize. It remained apparent from that very first lustful look back in the Nightclub that he wanted me. And in my helplessness, I was his long-awaited escape route into the many missed pleasures men feel in touching a woman. He had been a sick fag FUCK! Molesting men dressed like women. But all in all many of those male hormonal ideals were left inside of his depraved mind. Enough in fact to make him actually desire and succumb to the smell of what he needed once more. I could detect the chemistry and I KNOW that despite his fears of my reprisal, to tell the truth of what he did, he wanted to keep me alive. Just in case-for himself.

I chose SILENCE! Deciding not to 'TALK' to the Police in order to save my lost self and the lives of my family. I had squandered mine but how could I risk their lives as well? It's been somewhat of a burden to me. The memory of the pleasure and pain I experienced at death's door. That's what Catharsis represents to me-DEATH. The death of my old self and so I must go on-start my new life in an effort to forget everything that he did to me!

I decided to keep the baby because I don't believe in murder. Abortion is murder! Although I am completely justified in the eyes of the world to get rid of that part of himself he put inside me I prefer to preserve life-no matter whose! It's not the infant's fault that he or she had a DEVIL for a daddy and it should not be murdered for that reason. To abort what's inside me would not be dissimilar to what my own mother did to me-to give me up due simply to unethical circumstances and I WILL NOT take THAT cowardly route!

My baby does not belong to its father and it is the living blood, sweat and tears of my travail. Another 'Mini-me,' having within it interwoven components of all the goodness of its mother. So what its daddy was a bastard, a pervert and a gangster! Mommy won't take that same murderous road in attempting to destroy the budding new life she has been blessed with! And I will see to it that all the mistakes I've made won't be repeated in this the vicarious mortality now forming despite what I've endured!

Kecia asked me "How COULD you have that MURDERER'S CHILD?"

Then I asked HER a question: "How could I NOT have my own baby?" The conversation was over!

BE CAREFUL WHAT YOU ASK FOR! On the day after the funeral I got the bad news about Canei. Sammy musta served him a deadly dose of drug-dealin dessert that his small intestines were not quite primed for. The allergic reaction found him wrapped around a telephone pole in his brand new gold colored Suburban with some extra credit attached to his forehead! Seems the crash did not kill him and the papers speculated that the cause of death might've had something to do with the 9 milimeter bullet lodged above his right eye. The bastard FINALLY made the news! He would have exclusive hoodlum braggin rights and a gangsters ticker-tape parade awaiting him on the other side. I didn't care!

Now I know that this was no mere accident. The free-falling over-sized guppy had waded into a sharkpool-so Sammy took him out! But if Sammy the Drug-Lord was a shark in the societal predators hierarchy, then Catharsis the Hitman was Leviathan! The most feared monster to grace the seven seas of what wrath and vindication are made of. And where little Sammy the shark swam gingerly in search of prey, Catharsis walked on water and ate motherfuckers alive! Devoured them in the bloody cataclysm preordained for niggers who should've known better!

I only regret that Sammy did not ferry Canei's traitorous bed-partner on that perilous leap into where flames never die! By now the doofy liar-the ill begotten moron would wander aimlessly through the famed streets of Valhalla with a spare air-pocket in his grill just now seeing more clearly (with his third eye) what I'd tried to show him all along!

Catharsis was never heard from again although I KNOW that he would just pop-up back into my life the moment the Cops got wind of WHO killed Hattie. So I kept my mouth SHUT! Sometimes a person must swallow things that seem IMPOSSIBLE to digest. Admission and acceptance of defeat became a paramount factor in life that I'd learned to deal with!

I saw a young girl on the bus arguing with her boyfriend and she reminded me of MYSELF! After the 2 had quarreled she distanced herself from him apparently fed-up with his tired ass! Her mouth was raw and she enunciated some vulgarity with the virtual cleverness of a Chief Prosecutor. These rare skills intrigued me-the teenie-bopper was better than I was at that age. Sister-girl musta been about 19. I came over and introduced myself then sat beside her and we talked for the balance of the ride while her boyfriend remained seated separately in the back crying blood cuz his 'Old Lady' had left him behind!

Her name was Vanessa and she explained to me all the hardships she'd faced during an upbringing of domestic violence and Foster Homes. After nearly beating mommy to death, daddy disappeared Christmas morning when she was 9. Her mother gave her up and adopted a crack-cocaine habit instead which brought her one day creeping through the right apartment window at the WRONG time. The occupants musta heard her coming up the fire-escape because as soon as mommy's feet landed inside the window 3 shots were fired.

One of them shattered the opened glass behind her-but the other 2 hit the target. Vanessa lived in and out of different men's homes for 3 or 4 years paying the rent in favors what she could not afford to render in cash! By the age of 15, after a lifestyle of hustling, boosting and larceny she eventually went to jail. There she met her present boyfriend and 2 years later when they got out the 2 young lovers had a Shot-gun wedding and went to stay at a 'Friends' house. Money was tight but drugs were in the abundance and as one thing led to another she got strung out!

Now 3 years after detox they're STILL together, he's driving her up the wall, if you hear HER tell it, and the future looks grim. This bus ride was supposed to be a second beginning-a desperate grasp at life having left the slums of the South Bronx for a fresh new start in a tiny room they shared in "Stong Island!"

THEN SHE CONFESSED! The only reason she was STILL with Marty (Oh God-the poor child! I would NEVER sleep with a 'MARTY!') was his devotion to her through thick and thin, a 16 week old baby on the way and he was sick like she was!

"What you MEAN," says immature me? You got your whole life ahead of you! People get sick-but you're YOUNG and wounds heal. And you have a baby to live for. But that life-that baby wasn't guaranteed to live long enough to see its parents when it grew up. And its PARENTS had no gaurantees that they'd be around to see bouncing baby as well. One of em might be gone because this precious 19 year old spit-fire-HAD THE MONSTER! She had contracted it and transferred it to poor Marty and the unborn baby! Doctor says because some internal bleeding from Vanessa had permeated the placenta, just as sure as SHIT, when the baby's born it would assuredly carry the H.I.V. virus!

I closed my mental eyes wide SHUT then opened them! THIS WAS ME! She had stumbled down the same path I had frolicked through with illicit-sex and mind-altering intoxicants! I had opened my legs for ANYTHING that reared its head sexy enough to pass through the flood-gates of my unlimited sexual criteria! I had literally RUN where she had walked but only one of us survived our feast of foolishness! And where God had spared ME, his errant daughter, this innocent well-meaning 19 year old had caught AIDS!

Why was I better than her? I wasn't! Why did I escape and she didn't or why her and not me? Despite my quiet internal bickering an answer was not ordained to me. Thus the truth would survive that she'd fallen to the consequences God protected me from. God is smiling on one even as he frowns on yet another! I had dodged a bullet! I deserved the death that was feeding on her youthful body but THIS poor child had inherited my shame and my devastation! Daddy taught me another thing.

"GOD'S GOT A SENSE OF HUMOR!" Why do the good sometimes suffer or the bad make it by? God's got a sense of humor! Yet despite this irony we must strive to enhance ourselves!

Well this is my time and it's been a very bad year. Turbulent, tragic perhaps the worst of my life. How many mistakes can a 34 year old woman make and live to tell? I guess Heaven only knows. Maybe I should write a book-an Auto-biography of my 12 month dilemma. And perhaps you should read it! So you will know NOT to make the same mistakes I made!

Perhaps I'm your loved one-or I might represent a mistake you've made that needs to be corrected. Then again maybe I exist and maybe I don't! Maybe I have my existence within the underlying overtones of your faults or someone else's imaginations. I've bled out my literary soul-the precious gem of self. And I've brought out what you NEED to know! Just a little SOMETHING...ABOUT A WOMAN...!

Bomani Shuru

REDEMPTION

I will not fold-when asked to by my superior male inferior
I fly high where fools flee for fear of falling
The essence of my female anatomy
Courage, intellect and fortitude-my organic trinity
So if he tells me to lay down and die
I will tell him no-for freedom is a slave to no man
My false pride don't fly that high-and my esteem won't flow so low

I will not fear what life can do to me
For cowardice lands flat on its back beside absurdity
And a woman shuddering in awe of what lies behind the door
Is the puppet beaten and born of what losers cry for

I will not settle-for settling thrives in the shadows of defeat
Wisdom bades me to await my soulmate's heartbeat
I will strive to stay alive through my willingness to try
But when I settle for less...my everlasting dreams die

Sisters...if your man comes from losers land
And squanders his lifetime all that he can
Exactly what makes him worthy of you?
Who said the trifling must stay with what the fruitful are latched to
If the milk is sour today-who said it would be better tomorrow?
What dog stopped being himself just because a beaufiful woman walked by
He'll still bark and wolf down that lovely image in his eyes
And if a fool is a fool and master of his art
Then why would Eve render to Adam that sacred part of her heart?
My God is my redemption-REDEMPTION be my deity
Allowing no man to point conviction amidst my imperfect decency
Oh my God don't let them condemn the sin in me-they CAN'T judge me
Let your precious arms of forgiveness find my soul standing proud...and free

Simone Singleton

Printed in the United States
By Bookmasters